VIRGINIA VIXEN

KAY McMAHON

D1092666

ZEBRA BOOKS
KENSINGTON PUBLISHING CORP.

ZEBRA BOOKS

are published by

Kensington Publishing Corp.
475 Park Avenue South
New York, NY 10016

First printing: May, 1989

Printed in the United States of America

Prologue

"Yo' gotta get word to her, yo' hear?" the young black girl's voice cried out.

"Hush!" her companion warned, his hand quickly coming up to cover her mouth. "Someone'll hear yo'." Wrapping his youthful, but muscular arm around his girl's narrow shoulders, he pulled her farther back into the shadows of the barn and closed the doors, his ebony face shining with perspiration, his dark eyes round and alert as he peeked back out through the slit. Once he was sure he hadn't been seen cutting across the yard to their meeting place, he turned to her and tenderly smoothed back the ruffled hair from her brow. "Now tell me again so's I knowd yo' heard right."

"Dey is plannin' ta kill her," she repeated, tears spilling down her dark face. "Ah heerd dem talkin' this mornin'. Dey didn't say how or when, but soon, ah reckon, 'cause it ain't long fo' her birthday. Yo' gotta find her and warn her. Yo' just gotta! She ain't never been nothin' but kind to us."

"Hush, sweet thing," he cooed, hugging her trembling body against him. "Ah, don't know how, but ah'll warn her. Ah gots a friend what lives near the docks. Maybe he can help me find her."

"Today?" she urged, deep brown eyes looking into his. "Can yo' do it today? Ah is scared for her."

He kissed her forehead and said, "Yes'm, today." His black brow furrowed with a thought. "Did dey say why dey plans ta kill her?"

5

"Why, for the money, ah s'pose. Dey ain't never been carin' about anythin' else their whole lives. Yo' know'd that. Ah done tol' ya she was lied to. That's what makes it all so awful. She ain't done nothin'. She doan know nothin', and dey is gonna kill her anyway." Her tears flowing faster now, she threw her arms around his lanky frame and buried her face in his neck, sobbing uncontrollably.

"Yo' ain't ta worry, sweet thing," he comforted. "Ah'll see she ain't harmed." Nervous, he glanced back at the closed barn doors. "Ah gots ta be goin' now. If'n ah is missed, ah'll be beat somethin' awful." Pulling her arms from around him, he kissed her cheek and said, "Maybe we oughta not see each other fo' a while. At least 'til everythin's all right again. Ah love yo', Cela, and ah'd die if'n somethin' happened to yo'. After this mess is fixed up, and missy knows the truth, we can get married. Ah promise yo' that. Now give me a big smile."

Choking back a sob, the young girl brushed the tears from her face with the back of her hand. "Ah can't. Ah's scared."

"Ah know," he soothed. "Ah is, too. But yo' gotta act like nothin' happened, like yo' never heard nothin'. Yo' understand?"

She nodded her dark head. "Yo' be careful?"

"Uh-huh." He grinned with a flash of white teeth. "Now yo' wait here 'til ah is gone. Then yo' go back to de house, and doan say nothin' to nobody. All right?"

Cela quickly made an X over her heart with one fingertip, then raised up on tiptoes and kissed his mouth. "Now go."

Lingering a moment longer, he tenderly stroked the smooth curve of her cheek then turned and quietly opened the barn doors far enough to squeeze through them. A second later he was gone, and Cela courageously straightened her back, squared her shoulders and turned around to make her exit out the side door. Her man would take care of everything. Missy would be safe, and they'd get married, just like he said. With a happy smile warming her eyes, she stepped through the aperture and out into the bright sunshine, coming to an abrupt halt in the next instant when a tall shadow crossed her path.

6

"Hello, Cela," the deep voice said, the greeting dripping with sarcasm and anger. "What are you doing out here? You're supposed to be helping your mistress bathe."

Cela lowered her eyes immediately. "Yes, massuh," she mumbled, a terrifying fear building up in her.

"So what are you doing out here?" His voice seemed to roar in her ears.

"Ah . . . ah . . ." she began, her mind racing. Suddenly, she was brutally seized by her hair and yanked off balance, her tiny body falling against the much larger one of her master. "Please, massuh, don't hurt me!" she pleaded.

"Then tell me the truth!" he bellowed, his fingers twisting in the dark locks of hair.

"Ah . . . ah . . ."

"You were here to meet *him!* Weren't you?" He gave her a bone-rattling shake, one that nearly snapped her neck. "I saw you! I saw how you were sneaking out of the house. You heard us talking, didn't you? You told him what we said."

"No, massuh! Ah doan tell him nothin'! Ah doan hear nothin'!" she vowed hysterically through her sobs.

"Don't lie to me!" he raged, raising a huge fist and smashing it against her cheek.

Blood spurted from the deep gash on Cela's face, but it didn't seem to matter to her. All she cared about was convincing the man that she hadn't eavesdropped. "Ah doan hear nothin'!"

"Bitch!" he stormed, throwing her to the ground. "You'll be sorry you lied to me. I'll sell you off so you'll *never* see that young buck again."

"No! No, massuh, please!" Cela wailed, grabbing his foot as he made to step by her.

"Damn you," he growled, shifting his weight. A black leather boot smashed against her temple and sprawled Cela unconscious to the ground. "I saw you," he hissed down at the unmoving form. "And I saw him." His green eyes shifted to the field where he could see the young black man racing through the knee-high rows of corn. "And I know where he's going."

7

Chapter One

Williamsburg, Virginia
Spring, 1774

Rebecca Wilde nervously paced the floor in her room, vaguely aware of the rhythmical ticking of the clock setting on the mantel or that she was keeping in step with its beat. Jon-Gregory had missed dinner and had yet to come home, and she was anxious to speak with him. The body of a seventeen-year-old black boy had been found near the docks where Jon-Gregory worked, and the conversation around the table at Miss Abigail's boardinghouse speculated on the probability that Jon-Gregory was the one who discovered it. Rumors were already flying throughout Williamsburg as to how the young man met his demise, and most agreed it was an accident; a runaway slave, in his desperation to be free, fell and hit his head. It wasn't the first time something of this sort had happened, and with the exception of the slave's owner, no one really cared. Rebecca did, however, for two reasons. First of all, the boy deserved to be returned to his family for burial. He was, after all, someone's son. But more than that, she sensed there was a story to be reported. Even though none of the other boarders agreed with her remark that maybe it wasn't an accident but murder, Rebecca planned to investigate the incident, put it down on paper and hand it over to Mrs. Rind at the *Virginia Gazette* where Rebecca worked.

9

For as long as she could remember, all Rebecca ever wanted to do was be a reporter. But because she was a woman, William Rind, owner of the *Gazette*, wouldn't hire her. "It's a man's job," he had said. Men were allowed places women couldn't go. How would she ever be able to report on the meetings of House of Burgesses if she couldn't get through the front door? It could get pretty rough for a reporter when the man being interviewed suddenly decided he didn't want to be quoted or that he preferred to keep his business matters out of the weekly newspaper. Rind, himself, had sported a few black eyes in his time when he printed something someone didn't want made public. Imagine what they'd do to a woman. No, as long as William Rind was alive, the only woman who would work at the *Virginia Gazette* was his wife, Clementina, and all she was allowed to do was set type.

Everything Mr. Rind had said was true—Rebecca knew that—but she wasn't the least bit discouraged. She wanted to be a reporter, and nothing would stand in her way. Then her luck changed. After William Rind took sick nearly six months ago and died, Clementina took over the editorship of the paper. She liked Rebecca's spirit and determination and offered her the kind of job Rebecca truly wanted instead of setting type or sweeping out the place—but under certain conditions. Every article she wrote would have to appear in the paper under a man's name. "For your own protection," Clementina had said. Rebecca wasn't too pleased with the idea—if she went to all that work, she should get the credit—but after a moment's thought, she had agreed. After all, writing was writing whether her name appeared on the by-line or not.

Rebecca had been working as a journalist now for nearly a month, and all that she had written about so far was how well the garden at the Governor's Palace was coming along for so early in the spring, an accident at Elkanah Deane's shop that left one of his men without a little finger when the knife he was using to cut leather for a saddle slipped, plus numerous advertisements for John Greenhow's General Store. Rebecca tried very hard to understand why Mrs. Rind

10

gave her such unexciting assignments and could only assume it was one of two things: Either Mrs. Rind didn't feel her young protege was ready for the kinds of stories Rebecca wanted to write about or Mrs. Rind had no interest in them. She prayed it wasn't the latter and decided that perhaps this story would be the one she could use to prove herself.

According to what anyone knew about the event, it was said that the unidentified boy's head had been bashed in. Now as far as Rebecca was concerned, that could only mean he had been murdered. A lump on his forehead would indicate an accident; but an injury of this severity couldn't be the result of a simple fall, and Rebecca was going to prove it . . . just as soon as she talked to Jon-Gregory.

The clock on the mantel struck nine, bringing Rebecca out of her thoughts rather abruptly, and she quit her pacing to stare angrily at it, as though she blamed the piece of metal for the late hour. The long shadows of night were already creeping into her room which meant the five mile trip to the wharf would have to be traveled in the dark, something she'd prefer not doing but that she knew couldn't be avoided. It also meant she'd have to sneak out past the watchful eye of Abigail Beecher, a feat that would take a bit of ingenuity to achieve.

Miss Beecher, the owner of the boardinghouse where Rebecca had been staying these past several months, was known as the town gossip, and Rebecca had often jokingly said that Williamsburg didn't really need a newspaper. If anyone wanted to know what was going on for miles around, all they had to do was ask Abigail. But the woman's loose tongue wasn't what really worried Rebecca right now. It was her strict rules regarding her boarders.

Breakfast was at seven o'clock sharp, dinner at six, and anyone arriving late went without eating. Since everyone living at Miss Abigail's worked during the day, no noon meal was offered unless they were sick, and then a bowl of soup was served to them in bed. Visitors were allowed only in the parlor and not in one's room, and in Rebecca's case, since she was the only female boarder, she could not entertain a guest unless she was chaperoned by Miss Abigail, herself.

The stiffest and most difficult rule to follow for many of the people living in the house was Miss Abigail's insistence that no one be allowed in or out after ten o'clock at night as she locked all the doors until six the next morning. Her reason had been that since she was getting on in years, she needed her sleep and refused to be disturbed by the sounds of people coming in at all hours of the night or rising before dawn. It was a condition she enforced quite easily, since she had the only set of keys and jimmying the lock was out of the question. Anyone caught breaking her rules would be asked to leave, and since hers was the cheapest place to stay in all of Williamsburg, Rebecca never wanted to do anything to anger the woman. Tonight, however, was a different matter. Rebecca's entire future could depend on her trip to the wharf.

Frowning thoughtfully, she went to the window and raised the sash to peer outside at the ground below. She had never had cause to leave the house after ten since first moving into Miss Abigail's, but with each passing minute, it became more apparent that that was something she'd have to consider. Luckily Rebecca had never been afraid of heights, so the two-story drop to the ground didn't worry her overmuch. Getting there, however, created a problem, since the only method offered her was climbing down the rose trellis, and with the yards of skirts fashion demanded she wear, she knew the task would be difficult. If only she had the breeches she used to wear when she was a young girl growing up on her father's plantation—

The thump of the front door closing spun Rebecca around. It had to be Jon-Gregory. All the other boarders had retired to their rooms after dinner . . . except for Miss Abigail. She always liked to sit in the parlor doing her needlepoint until it was time to lock up the house. Dashing across the room, Rebecca silently opened the door and leaned out into the hallway, listening for the sound of Jon-Gregory's voice as he made his excuses for missing dinner to Miss Abigail.

Only a few years older than Rebecca, Jon-Gregory Cole had taken an immediate liking to the young woman from

12

Richmond the moment Rebecca moved into Miss Abigail's for the simple fact that their pasts as well as their personalities were very similar. Jon-Gregory's mother had died some years ago, and because he could never seem to get along with his father, Jon-Gregory had moved away from home to make it on his own, settling in Williamsburg as an apprentice to Christopher Kurt, head carpenter at John Greenhow's General Store. Jon-Gregory had often remarked on how Rebecca reminded him of his younger sister, and Rebecca concluded that that was the reason he treated her the way he did, like a little sister. They were forever arguing over the simplest of things, and although Rebecca guessed there were times when he would have liked to club her alongside the head, he never raised anything more than his voice to her. Rebecca, however, wasn't as even tempered. She never thought twice about emphasizing her point of view with a jab to his ribs or an angry scowl accompanied by a few not-so-complimentary names, or even on occasion a sharp kick to his shins. Jon-Gregory, being a good head taller than she and several pounds heavier, took it in stride, but always with a promise that someday, God willing, he'd be there to witness her comeuppance. And maybe he would be, but Rebecca vowed that that would be a day in her very distant future as she had yet to meet a man smarter than she.

The creaking of the first tread on the staircase at the end of the hall told Rebecca that someone was on his way up. Praying it was Jon-Gregory and not Miss Abigail making her nightly rounds, she held her breath and waited until she could recognize the quickness of his step as he climbed the stairs. A second later his tall frame appeared from around the corner, and she darted into the hall to wave him down. Motioning for him to come into her room, she turned her back on him and missed seeing the way his shoulders drooped and how his mouth curled disgustedly.

"What, Rebecca?" he sighed impatiently. "What is it this time?"

Grabbing his arm, she pulled him farther into her room and quickly shut the door behind him, wrinkling up her face at him when he started to object. "I want to hear everything you know about the boy who was found murdered at the docks."

"Murdered?" he echoed, not caring who heard him. "Who said he'd been murdered? You? Is that overactive imagination of yours running wild again?"

Rebecca's chin came up as she narrowed her eyes and glared back at him. "No, my imagination isn't running wild. I heard the gossip, and simple deduction indicates that the boy was murdered. Tell me you don't agree."

"I don't agree," he replied, stepping toward the door.

Rebecca cut him off, barring the way with her tiny body. "Oh, yes, you do. I can see it in your eyes."

"About the only thing you can see in my eyes is my desire to get out of here before Miss Abigail finds us. I like living here even if you don't."

"Then you better talk fast because I'm not letting you leave until you tell me exactly what happened." To prove her point, she fell back against the door and spread out her arms.

His broad shoulders sagging, Jon-Gregory shook his head and asked, "Do you really think you could stop me if I wanted to walk out that door? I've carried sacks of flour that weigh more than you."

Rebecca stood her ground, never flinching and more determined than ever.

"All right," he surrendered, throwing up his hands and turning away. "I'll tell you what I know . . . which isn't much." Grabbing the chair at Rebecca's writing desk, he spun the piece of furniture around and straddled the seat. "Mr. Kurt sent me to the docks to pick up the wagon load of supplies we were expecting this morning. I got there before the ship docked and had to wait. I spent part of the time sleeping in the back of the wagon, the rest just walking around out of boredom. That's when I saw him."

"So it's true," she exclaimed, dropping her hands to her sides and coming toward him. "You really *were* the one who found the body."

"Yes, I stumbled across it. But it wasn't a very pleasant sight, and since I've had to retell it over and over again to every busybody in the whole of Williamsburg, I'd like to just forget it ever happened . . . if you don't mind." He pushed himself off the chair and headed for the door again.

"I do mind," she replied, stepping in his way. Laying her opened palms against his chest, she shoved him backward toward the chair. "I need to know where you found him exactly."

Jon-Gregory frowned. "Why? What difference does it make to you where I found him . . . exactly?" He sat down rather hard when Rebecca gave a healthy nudge.

"Never mind why I need to know, just tell me. And did it really look like it could have been an accident?"

"Rebecca." He scowled.

"Jon-Gregory," she hissed.

It had been a very long, trying day for the young man, and he knew that if he wanted any peace, he'd have to satisfy Rebecca's questions first . . . though he honestly didn't know why it would be of any interest to her. "He was laying about twenty feet north of the peer in some scrubs. From the looks of it, he stumbled and hit his head. Now, can I go?" He started to get up, but Rebecca quickly placed her hand on his shoulder and forced him down again.

"What did he hit his head on? A rock? What?"

"A rock, I suppose."

"You suppose? Didn't you see what he fell against?"

Jon-Gregory's tawny brows slanted downward. "Not really. The only thing I can remember seeing was all the blood." He shook his head. "He really must have fallen hard to crack his skull open like that."

The vision of that gruesome sight flashed before Rebecca's eyes, and she grimaced as she shook off the wave of nausea. Forcing herself to behave as any good journalist would, she asked, "So are you saying it wasn't an accident?"

"I'm not saying anything," Jon-Gregory barked as he bolted off the chair and knocked her aside when she thought to stop him. "A runaway slave turns up dead; I found him, notified the constable who is trying to send word to his owner, and you're making a squawk out of it all. Go to bed, Rebecca." He paused at the door and turned back, his hand on the knob. "Or better yet, do us all a favor and get married.

15

Let someone else stay up nights listening to you babble."

"Babble?" she shrieked. "Are you forgetting what I am?"

Jon-Gregory cocked a brow. "Guess so. What are you? Besides a pest, I mean?"

Rebecca gritted her teeth and snarled, "I'm a reporter. It's my job to investigate stories like these."

Jon-Gregory threw back his head. "Ha!" he exploded. "And I believe someday a man will sprout wings and fly to the moon." Angry with her, his pale brows came sharply together as he lowered his chin and added, "If you were really as smart as you think you are, you'd forget about being a reporter and learn how to sew and do needlepoint like Miss Abigail or cook. I hate to have to admit this, but you could be a very pretty young woman if you wanted to be. You could probably marry any man you wanted to marry, if you'd just stop trying to prove whatever it is you're trying to prove and learn to accept the fact that you're a woman. No man with any brains is going to look twice at you if you continue to treat them like they're some kind of animal."

Her blue eyes flashing, Rebecca defiantly tossed her head, sending the thick mane of raven-black hair shimmering down her back. "That's because they are," she snarled.

"And you're being unfair, Rebecca Wilde," Jon-Gregory rallied hotly. "Just because your stepmother's new husband—"

"You promised you'd never bring that up!" she shouted at him. "You promised!"

Jon-Gregory's shoulders dropped. "Yes, I did, and I'm sorry I broke that promise. But sometimes you make me so . . ." He gritted his teeth and exhaled a long sigh. "Please, Rebecca, forget about what happened at the wharf. If on the slim chance you're right about the boy being murdered, you could be placing yourself in a lot of danger. And if something happened to you because I didn't try to stop you, I'd never be able to forgive myself. Let the constable handle it. Let Gideon Blackstock decide what he wants done."

Rebecca's anger vanished instantly. "Gideon Blackstock? What has he to do with this? Was the slave his?"

16

Realizing he had said too much already, Jon-Gregory lifted the latch and pulled the door open. "Good-night, Rebecca. See you at breakfast in the morning."

Practically flying across the room, her hands outstretched, Rebecca hurled herself against the door to slam it shut again. "Was the slave his?" she demanded.

"Oh, for—" Jon-Gregory moaned resignedly, leaning his head forward to rest his brow against the cool oak panels. "Yes! The slave belonged to Gideon Blackstock, and his name was Eli." Caught up in his own feelings over the matter, he failed to see the horrified look that came over his companion's face. "And yes, it's questionable how the boy died. It's my opinion that he was hit over the head with something and was killed—accidentally or otherwise—because the ground was soft where I found him and there weren't any rocks anywhere near him. I believe he was clubbed to death with a stick or cane. I don't know why nor do I care. It isn't any of my business, and it shouldn't be any of yours." He turned an impatient, angry glare on her. "Now may I go to bed? I'm tired and I have to work tomorrow . . . providing I still have a job. Nobody wants trouble, Rebecca. You realize that, don't you? If you go around poking your nose into this, they'll figure out who told you, and they'll come down hard on me. Rebecca?" he questioned when she turned away from him and crossed to the window, a pained expression on her lovely face. "What's wrong?"

A long moment passed before she seemed aware that her friend was still in the room with her. Jerking to attention, she turned her head toward him but wouldn't look at him. "You said the boy's name was Eli. Are you sure?"

"Yes. Thomas Keenan, the man who runs the warehouse by the docks, recognized him. I guess that's part of the reason why I feel it wasn't an accident."

She spun around to face him, curious. "Why do you say that?"

Jon-Gregory shrugged a shoulder. "Because Keenan said Eli was a favorite of Blackstock's, and that Gideon never went anywhere without Eli by his side."

17

"So?"

"No one remembers seeing Gideon Blackstock in town today."

A chill embraced Rebecca, and she unwittingly hugged her arms to her as she dropped her gaze away from Jon-Gregory and looked outside again. "Meaning that Eli was here without his master's permission."

"Maybe," Jon-Gregory yielded. "But not necessarily. Blackstock could have sent Eli to Williamsburg on an errand."

"Then what was he doing at the docks?"

"Trying to run away," Jon-Gregory supplied. "It's what everybody is saying. They think he was waiting for the first ship sailing north."

"I don't."

"Obviously," Jon-Gregory agreed. "Otherwise we wouldn't be having this conversation." Sensing that she was trying to hide something, he moved closer. "Rebecca, I get the feeling you know more about this than anyone else involved, and you weren't even at the docks. Would you care to explain?"

She shook her head and continued to stare out the window. "I don't know any more than what you've told me. I'm just not as easily persuaded."

Jon-Gregory might not have known Rebecca for very long, but he knew her well enough to come to the conclusion that this discussion was at an end. "All right. I won't press. But just remember who's willing to listen if you feel like talking about it." He started to reach out and squeeze her shoulder, then changed his mind. Rebecca Wilde wasn't the kind of woman who appreciated having someone touch her. At least it appeared that way on the outside. "I'll see you in the morning."

Nodding, Rebecca turned her head slightly and listened to him cross the room, open the door and then make a quiet exit. She liked Jon-Gregory Cole more than she was willing to admit. He was a good friend . . . sort of the brother she always wished she could have had, but didn't. She trusted him . . . never to take advantage of her both spiritually and

18

physically, and she trusted him with her secrets. Blinking, a tear spilled over her dark lashes and raced for her chin, and she quickly wiped it away. But this was one secret she had to keep to herself. At least for now. She had to find out who killed Eli and why. She owed Eli that much.

Climbing down the rose trellis wasn't as big a problem as Rebecca had believed it would be. The difficulty had come in trying not to make any noise, since Miss Abigail's room was right below hers and the piece of latticework hung only a few inches from the woman's open window. Yet once she stood safely on the ground, a pleased smile on her mouth and a devilish look in her blue eyes, she suddenly realized her task was far from completed, and the smug expression on her face disappeared. After she visited the docks and gathered all the information she needed for her story, she'd have to climb back up again. Either that or spend the night with Penelope Dawson. She shook off that idea and darted across the yard for the shadows of a nearby oak. If she didn't come down for breakfast in the morning, Miss Abigail would come looking for her, and once the woman found Rebecca's room empty, she'd know one of her boarders had broken a rule.

"Maybe it would be better if I did move in with Penny," she muttered as she glanced over her shoulder one last time at the darkened house. "I'd certainly be able to come and go as I pleased." But the image of her auburn-haired young friend locked arm and arm with a man quickly dispelled that idea. Penny wouldn't appreciate the company. And Rebecca didn't like what Penny did after finishing up her work at The Red Lion.

The distant rumble of thunder brought a scowl to Rebecca's pretty face as she headed toward the center of town. It was bad enough that she had to walk all the way to the wharf without having to get soaked in the process. Glancing up at the sky, she noticed the faint flashes of lightning off to the west and how quickly the storm seemed to be approaching. She'd have to borrow a horse. With a stubborn set to her chin, she concentrated on the row of lights up ahead, focusing her attention on one set in particular . . . those belonging to The Red Lion. She'd stop by the inn and ask Penny if she could borrow Mr. Lewis's horse for an hour or so.

It didn't surprise Rebecca any to see the number of horses tied to the hitching rail outside The Red Lion. All the taverns in Williamsburg stayed open late when a huge frigate filled with supplies from the West Indies docked during the day. They did their best business when the captain and crew of the ship came into town . . . and so did Penny.

"Penny," Rebecca murmured with a shake of her head as she cut across the street to the sidewalk on the other side. "What would I have done without you all these years?"

Penelope Dawson, her childhood friend, had been there for her on the day Rebecca's mother died giving premature birth to Rebecca's baby brother. She had even been there by her side when Rebecca's father had to bury mother and son. It had been Penny's strength and optimistic nature that had helped pull the twelve-year-old Rebecca through those tough times, and she had tried her hardest to explain why Rebecca's father would remarry after only seven short years. She had always taken Rebecca's position whenever her stepmother tried to punish her—a difficult achievement considering the woman was only five years older than Rebecca. The worst nightmare she had had to endure, however, was the tragic carriage accident that took her father's life and maimed her stepmother. Without Penny, Rebecca never would have had the courage to go on. That will was tested again when her stepmother decided three months later to marry Robert Gilmore, an evil man who took a depraved view of his wife's stepdaughter. Rebecca managed to deal with the man's lecherous advances for nearly a year, excusing his twisted reasoning on the possibility that he had grown tired of his wife's deformity, the severely scarred face and twisted left ankle. But on the night he tried unsuccessfully to force himself on her, Rebecca decided it was time to leave.

Pausing outside the front door of The Red Lion, a crooked smile curled the corners of Rebecca's mouth as she thought about Penelope Dawson and the conversation they had had the day Rebecca announced her plans to leave

Richmond and move to Williamsburg.

"I figured it was only a matter of time before you did something," Penny had admitted. "And I must say I'm glad you chose this way out."

"What are you talking about?" Rebecca had snapped, irritated that her friend always seemed to enjoy prying into Rebecca's personal affairs. It was the girl's only trait that truly annoyed Rebecca.

"Are you serious?" Penny had rallied. "Do you think I don't know what's been going on in that house? I've seen the way Gilmore looks at you . . . undressing you with his eyes, always standing too close. If he was married to *my* stepmother, I'd throw them both out."

"How can I?" Rebecca moaned. "Papa left everything to her when he died. I don't own the plantation, so how can I tell them to leave?"

"Easy," Penny advised without the slightest hesitation. "Point a gun at them and ask nicely. I would."

"I'm sure you would." Rebecca laughed.

"So how do you plan to support yourself if you don't have any money? I'm sure ol' Lenore won't part with any of hers."

"I'll get a job, that's how," Rebecca answered confidently.

"Doing what? Being an apprentice to some stuffy ol' seamstress?"

Rebecca bobbed one shoulder. "I should, I suppose. I stand a better chance of being hired there than what I'd really like to do."

Knowing her lifelong friend preferred doing the things boys did rather than act like a lady, Penny chided, "And what's that? Join the militia?"

Rebecca's blue eyes narrowed, and her mouth pursed disgustedly. "No, Penny. I don't want to be a soldier. I want to be a journalist for the *Virginia Gazette*.

"What?" Penny shrieked. "You might as well try to join the militia. They'll never let a woman be a reporter."

A devilish smile lit up Rebecca's eyes. "Want to place a gold coin on it?"

"And where would I get a gold coin?"

"From your father," Rebecca retaliated. "He's got plenty

21

of them, and half of them are yours."

"Not until I'm married."

"So ask to have one early. You've a right."

A dark, auburn brow twitched when an idea came to mind. "I think I'll ask for the entire share," Penny had beamed. "I'm going to Williamsburg with you."

As Rebecca thought about it now, she realized that that day had been the first time she had really gotten to know Penny, for the nineteen-year-old girl had boldly admitted her plans to take her inheritance, move to Williamsburg with Rebecca and hire on at one of the local taverns as a barmaid, something she had always wanted to do. She loved people—or more specifically, she loved men—and this would be the best opportunity to meet plenty of them. Even now the idea of Penny's promiscuousness made Rebecca blush. She dearly loved the young redhead, but she could never quite understand how she could so guiltlessly give her favors to a total stranger. Granted the men were always very handsome or had a lot of money, but neither attribute justified Penny's reasoning as far as Rebecca was concerned. There had to be something more to it than that . . . something that always had Rebecca a little curious.

Mounting the half dozen steps to the opened front door, Rebecca paused at the threshold and quickly scoured the interior of the commons, looking for her friend's bright, auburn locks of hair among the crowd. Rebecca wouldn't go inside if Penny wasn't there. A man who had too much to drink wouldn't bother to ask if Rebecca was willing or not. He'd simply drag her to one of the rooms upstairs. A round of heartfelt laughter exploded in a far corner, drawing Rebecca's attention to the group seated around a table near the fireplace and to the young woman serving them. Obviously, Penny had said something the men found amusing, and Rebecca knew her friend was making her move on one of them. Penny wouldn't like being interrupted, but Rebecca had no choice. She wanted to get to the wharf before the evidence surrounding Eli's death was disturbed, or worse, washed away. Taking a deep breath to steel her courage to go inside, she squared her shoulders, set her gaze

22

on Penny and stepped into the room, wishing that her friend had already retired. It was much easier and safer for Rebecca to cut through the side yard between The Red Lion and the Ludwell-Paradise House, enter through a back door and take the second set of stairs to the upper level where Penny had a room, thus avoiding any customer who might think she was as willing as Penny. It would have been worth the risk of interrupting Penny should she happen not to be alone. At least that way, they could talk in the hall where Rebecca didn't have to worry about an overzealous customer making a grab for her.

"Rebecca!" the pretty redhead exclaimed once she looked up and saw her. "What are you doing here at this hour?" The expression on Penny's face changed instantly. There was only one reason why Rebecca was out after dark. She had a story that needed investigating. Excusing herself from her customers, she tucked the tray she was holding under one arm, took her friend's elbow and ushered them away from interested ears. "I suppose it's foolish to think you have Miss Abigail's permission to be out after ten."

Rebecca's upper lip curled disapprovingly. "Miss Abigail isn't my mother, Penny. I don't have to ask her permission for anything."

"You do if you want back in the house," Penny argued. "So what's so important you'd risk losing a place to stay?"

"I need a horse."

"A horse?" Penny repeated. "Where on earth are you going that you'd need a horse? And you know I don't have one."

"I have to go to the wharf. And I wasn't asking to borrow a horse you don't have. I was hoping you'd ask Mr. Lewis to loan me his."

Penny's brows came sharply together, and her chin dropped. "Are you insane?" she demanded in a harsh whisper, then glanced around to make sure no one was listening. "You can't go to the wharf at this time of night. Good God, it's bad enough for you to walk in here, let alone be on the road in the dark. There probably isn't a man for twenty miles in all directions who wouldn't think he'd been

23

blessed to find you all alone. Besides, you're out of luck. Mr. Lewis isn't here."

"Damn," Rebecca moaned, a faint line appearing between her dark brows. "Now what will I do?"

"You'll go home if you know what's good for you," Penny suggested, shoving her friend toward the door. "I've gone along with your silly notion of being a reporter because you've never put yourself in any danger until now. But if you continue with this ridiculous idea, I'll personally tell Mrs. Rind what you've been up to. Do you understand?"

"Penny!" Rebecca admonished. "I thought we were friends."

"We are. And that's precisely why I'll tell her."

Rebecca's temper flared, and she angrily jerked her arm out of Penny's grasp. "What's the matter with you? You've known about this for a long time. Why are you all of a sudden against my being a reporter?"

"Because I heard the gossip about someone getting killed. I also know it happened at the wharf. That's why you want to go there. You think there's a story in it, and that it will be the one to convince Mrs. Rind to let you write about something besides tea parties and flower gardens. The way I heard it, the boy's death was accidental . . . he fell and hit his head. But you don't think so, do you?"

Penny's attitude irritated Rebecca. "What if it wasn't an accident? What if he was murdered? Am I supposed to just forget about it because he was a black man? I'm sure his master won't. Eli was a valuable slave."

"Eli?" Penny echoed, her freckled face paling considerably. "*Your* Eli?"

Rebecca hadn't meant to reveal the fact that she knew the boy's identity or that his death meant more to her than just a story, but she had. "Yes, my Eli. It's the real reason I have to investigate how he died. He was a long way from home, and he was alone, which says to me that something peculiar went on down there at the wharf. If I don't look into it, who will?" She frowned angrily and added, "You can bet that gold coin you still owe me that had it been the governor found dead at the wharf, the entire British army would be checking out the place."

A sarcastic smirk wrinkled Penny's face. "Sorry, Rebecca, but I have to disagree. If someone killed ol' Murray, no one in Williamsburg would care enough to send for the British troops—except, maybe, his wife, and I even wonder about her."

Penny's mocking humor made Rebecca laugh. "Someday you're going to say something like that to the wrong person and wind up in gaol awaiting trial for treason."

"Maybe." Penny grinned with a quick shrug of one shoulder. "But I wouldn't be there for long. I've got too many influential friends who would miss me . . . if you know what I mean."

"I know what you mean," Rebecca assured her. "Just don't say it. I prefer remembering you the way you were."

"And I prefer you go home," Penny replied in all seriousness. "What you're thinking about doing is too dangerous. If you happen to be right about Eli and he really was murdered, whoever did it won't take kindly to your trying to prove it."

"It goes with the job," Rebecca answered drily. "And it's what makes my work so exciting."

"I'd rather have a man excite me." Penny scowled. "It's a lot safer. Go home, will you?"

Noticing that the men at the table were trying to get Penny's attention, Rebecca nodded their way. "I think you'd better get back to work. I'll talk to you tomorrow." She started to turn away when Penny caught her arm.

"I realize I might as well be talking to myself by trying to convince you that what you're planning to do is dangerous, but will you at least promise me that you'll be careful? You're the only real friend I have, and I'd hate to lose you."

Smiling warmly at Penny, Rebecca affectionately patted the girl's hand. "I'll be careful. I'm not in this because I have some sort of death wish. If I see trouble coming, I'll run like the wind."

Motioning for the men at the table to be patient, Penny turned back to her friend. "I want you to know, Rebecca, that if you ever do get in trouble, you're to come to me. I meant it when I said I had a lot of rich friends. All I'd have to do is ask their help."

"Even if they knew they were helping out a woman doing a man's job?" Rebecca teased.

"They wouldn't ask. I guarantee it." Someone in the crowd of men called out Penny's name, and she glanced back over her shoulder, saying, "Yeah, yeah, keep your wig on. I'm coming." She faced Rebecca again. "Look, I've got to get back to work. Promise me you'll give me all the details in the morning?"

"I promise." Rebecca smiled. "Better yet, maybe you'll read about it." Wiggling her eyebrows, Rebecca turned and hurried from the tavern, leaving her friend to stare worriedly after her.

Standing on the bow of the *Constance*, Alec Stone's dark brown eyes shifted their attention from the narrow expanse of water dividing the huge merchant ship from the wharf to the moonlit sky overhead, marred by the approaching storm. Black clouds obscured the western horizon, and flashes of white light danced among them, offering the chance of a soaking downpour before he reached Williamsburg. But the threat of being drenched wasn't what brought the dark scowl to his suntanned brow. His luck, of late, had turned sour, and although he prayed this trip would be successful, he had an odd feeling he was about to embark on a voyage that would change his life around. Thoughtful, he raised his left hand and stared at the signet ring he wore on his little finger. It was really too much to expect, and maybe it was because he was about to set foot on Virginia soil, but he was hoping that while he conducted his business in Williamsburg, he just might stumble across a clue to his father's identity.

The distant rumble of thunder lifted Alec's eyes to the black, rolling clouds and stirred up a flourish of painful memories. Nearly a year had passed since his mother's funeral, and the emptiness he felt now was still just as fresh and deep as it had been then. He blamed himself for all the grief Lora Stone had had to endure in her lifetime. After all, if she hadn't had a child out of wedlock, the people of London wouldn't have snubbed her and labeled her the cruel names they called her behind her back. If there hadn't been an Alec Stone, she never would have had to bear the shame the consequences of falling in love had brought her. She wouldn't have had to take in laundry or trade her skills with needle and thread for the flour to bake bread or for a pitcher of milk. Yet through it all, Lora Stone had remained a loving and strong mother to her bastard son, never once cursing the man who fathered her child or revealing his name to anyone. She had carried that secret to her grave. It had also alienated her from Alec.

Despite the warm, caring affection Alec received from his mother as a child, Alec grew into a very bitter young man, damning his father for abandoning his responsibilities and at times even cursing his mother for defending the blackguard. "He should be made to pay," Alec had often told her. "You've suffered; why shouldn't he?" It had been the cause of many arguments between mother and son and, finally, in the end drove Alec away. It never, however, diminished his love for her, and it wasn't until the day he received the letter advising him of her death that Alec understood why he had left and the root of his obsession to become quite wealthy. Riddled with guilt, he'd had to prove he was worth loving . . . to himself, his mother and the whole world. What he didn't realize was that he didn't have to prove anything . . . until it was too late. Being wealthy wouldn't change how his mother felt about him or gain the love and respect of a man who hadn't even bothered to get to know his son.

Absently toying with the ring on his hand, Alec heaved a long, weary sigh as he remembered back to the day it had been given to him. The letter he had gotten telling him that Lora Stone had died peacefully in her sleep after a bout with pneumonia had been written by Beth Anderson, a neighbor and childhood friend of Alec's. He hadn't seen Beth in more than two years, and even if she hadn't asked him to come home, he would have gone. He needed to visit his mother's grave, and he had needed to see Beth.

They had stood alone in the cemetery, a light, chilling mist dampening their cloaks, and Beth had been the first to break the awful silence that encased them when she turned to him, held out her closed hand and said, "Lora asked me to give this to you." Uncurling her fingers, she had presented him with the ring, and while he had studied the black opal setting with its carved figure of a bird in flight, Beth had gone on to explain. "She told me I wasn't to send it to you or to tell you about it unless you came home on your own. I don't know why really, only that she said it was important to her. I would guess she was thinking it would mean you had finally forgiven yourself for not being able to change the past. It belonged to your father, Alec, and before you ask, I'll tell you that that's all she wanted you to know."

Her refusal even on her deathbed to tell him who his father was had angered him, and he remembered uttering a low curse as he clenched the ring in his fist and turned away.

"Alec, I never understood why your mother wanted it that way," Beth went on, "and I can't say that I agreed with her decision. But I had to respect it. It was, after all, her business. I can only assume that she felt your knowing who your father was would do more harm than good. Now I think she was wrong, considering how things turned out. It wasn't fair of her not to allow you to make your own decisions concerning your father, and if I can help in any way, I will. I want to see you at peace . . . with yourself, your mother and most of all the man you've grown to hate."

"If she never revealed his name to you, Beth," Alec had replied, his expression the picture of hurt, anger and frustration, "how can you help?"

"I don't know that I can," she confessed, touching his arm, "But I can tell you what I saw."

Her statement had sparked hope in Alec, and he remembered thinking how blind he must have been all those years not to recognize the deep, unselfish friendship he received from Beth, a one-sided friendship, for he had never given back half of what Beth gave him.

"There was a man at the funeral, an older man with gray

hair and dark brown eyes. I noticed him for two reasons. First of all, he was terribly upset over your mother's death, so much so that he cried openly and he didn't care who saw him. And once I managed to forget about my own grief long enough to pay attention to what was going on around me, I suddenly remembered how many times I had seen him with your mother."

It had taken the two of them a great deal of discussion to come up with a name, but once they had, Alec remembered how many times Edwin Higgins had come to his mother's home to visit while Alec was growing up. Beth supplied the information that after Alec left home to find his wealth as a Jamaican planter, Higgins seemed to become Lora Stone's only close personal friend. It was Beth's thought that perhaps his mother had confided in Edwin Higgins, that perhaps they had even fallen in love, and she had, at last, felt comfortable in telling someone about her past, about the man who fathered her child. It was a slim hope, but one Alec felt compelled to explore. After meeting with Beth that day and promising to keep in touch, Alec had gone to the estate of Joseph Sanger where Higgins worked as a butler, only to learn that Higgins had quit his job and had sailed to the Colonies to visit friends in Boston. Although Alec hadn't really expected to learn anything new from Edwin Higgins, the denial of even having the chance to ask angered him. It left an opening, a hope that someone had the answer to a question that had long plagued Alec Stone.

"Sir?"

The sound of someone close by intruded upon Alec's thoughts and roughly brought him back to the present. Turning, he found Geoffrey Synder, the captain of the *Constance*, standing at his elbow.

"My apologies, sir, for disturbing you," Synder continued, "but we've dropped anchor, and the longboat's waiting to take you to shore."

"Thank you, Geoffrey." Alec nodded, pulling the strings of his cape tighter around his neck and readjusting its collar to ward off the cold night sea breeze. Shoving his tricorn down farther on his blond head, he reached for the curved-handled cane he had hooked over the railing and started to walk by the captain.

"Sir," Geoffrey said again, halting Alec before he had taken two steps. "I realize this is really none of my business, but I feel I must say something. I can't just let you go without expressing my concern."

Alec had known Geoffrey Synder for a good number of years, and although Alec counted few of his associates as friends, he considered Geoffrey to be one of those few. He was a trusted employee and a man who wasn't afraid to speak his mind even if it contradicted an order Alec had given him.

"What is it, Geoffrey?"

Shifting uneasily, Geoffrey looked out across the water at the shoreline, a frown drawing his brows together as he considered just how to explain his reluctance to allow Alec Stone off the ship. "You might think I've spent too much time in the sun, but the similarities between this and the last time I dropped someone off in Williamsburg have me worried."

"You're referring to Heller," Alec guessed.

"Yes, sir," Geoffrey admitted. "As you already know, we were sailing to Boston to deliver a cargo load of goods the same way we are tonight, and we dropped anchor long enough to put Heller on shore. It was dark, a storm was coming, he was alone . . . like you . . . and we never saw him again."

Alec appreciated the man's nervousness. The mystery surrounding Daniel Heller's disappearance was reason enough for caution, but not to the extent that Alec could just forget about it. Not only was there a man involved, but a man Alec had hired to do a job. It was Alec's responsibility to find out what had happened to him.

When Timothy Heller, Daniel's brother, became too ill to travel, Timothy had asked Alec's permission to send Daniel in his stead. Alec had never met the man, but trusted Timothy's judgment in hiring Daniel as his agent. His job was to go to America, Virginia precisely, and purchase land in Alec's name. The vast property Alec owned in Jamaica yielded a great number of resources for trade but lacked one important crop: cotton. Since Alec's business sense concluded there was a sizable profit to be made from owning land in the Colonies, he had entrusted a large amount of money with Daniel Heller. Other matters had called Alec away on the day his merchant ship, the *Constance*, captained by Geoffrey Synder, was ready to set sail and leave port, and he'd had to forward the money to Heller via a messenger. Thus Alec had never actually come face to face with the man and therefore had no idea what Heller looked like. He had a general description, however, given to him by Daniel's brother, and had Timothy's health not warranted a lengthy stay in bed, Alec would have taken him along. All in all, finding the missing agent promised to be a very perplexing feat.

"I'd feel better, sir, if you'd allow one of the crew to go with you," Geoffrey added once he realized his warning hadn't changed Alec's mind. "Williamsburg is a pretty good-sized town, and since you'll be a stranger in it, people will be reluctant to talk . . . especially if Heller is—" He paused and sighed heavily. He didn't like having to admit the possibility that the man might be dead—he'd left a wife and child behind in Jamaica—but it was the only logical reason why no one had heard from him in a very long while.

Geoffrey didn't have to say what he was thinking. Alec already knew, and he was in agreement. Daniel Heller had left Jamaica more than a year ago, and during the first few months, he had written regularly to inform Alec of his progress. The owner of a huge plantation had died leaving no heirs and a lot of debts. The property was up for auction, but the date was delayed due to some conflict between the merchants to whom the man had owed money. Daniel told Alec that the land, several hundred acres, was just what Alec was looking for, and since no other property was up for sale in the area right then, Heller said he would wait to make his bid . . . if Alec approved. Alec had, and more than a month passed before he received the deed to the property and a letter from Heller saying he would be coming home in a few weeks after everything was settled and he had hired a manager to run the place. Why Alec let another six months pass before deciding to look into the matter wasn't really something for which he could take full blame. His mind had been on other matters, such as the death of his mother and his subsequent trip home to England. Upon his return to Jamaica, a tropical storm hit the island and destroyed two of his warehouses, one of his smaller ships, several fields of new crops and even his own mansion. It had taken months to rebuild and a like amount of time before he was able to focus his full attention solely on his business affairs. But it had been a visit from Daniel Heller's wife stating her fear that something had happened to her husband that motivated Alec to personally look into the situation.

"I understand how you feel, Geoffrey," he replied, bending to pick up his satchel. "But you can't spare the crewman. I can take care of myself. I have been for a long time now. And it's important you get this cargo to Boston on schedule. That storm cost me a lot of money, and I can't afford to have the fruits spoil just because you're worried about me. Besides, I don't intend to let on why I'm really here."

"Why's that, sir?" Geoffrey asked, following Alec to the rope ladder at the side of the ship.

"If what we're both thinking is true," he went on to explain as he tossed first the satchel then his gold-tipped cane to the awaiting hands of Gerald Haugen in the longboat, "and Heller was killed for some reason, no one's going to want to talk about it freely. But if I can trick someone into telling me what happened to him, I will."

"And how will you manage that, sir?"

Tugging on the lace cuff of his shirtsleeve, Alec smiled softly. "I plan to run an advertisement in the Williamsburg newspaper, stating that I'm here in town looking to buy some property . . . a piece of land good for growing cotton."

A broad grin broke the serious line of Geoffrey's mouth. "Oh, I understand. That way if someone approaches you with an offer . . ."

"Exactly." Alec nodded. "And in the meantime, I'll pay the courthouse a visit." His tawny brows came sharply together as he silently cursed the hurricane that had destroyed a lot of his records, the most important being the deed Heller had sent him. "I may have a difficult time proving I own that land unless Heller saw fit to register it before sending me the deed," he murmured. "Damn. If this was some kind of scheme to rob Heller, I will have lost not only a large amount of money, but some good crop land as well, and all at the price of a man's life."

Geoffrey had seen that look in his companion's eyes before. Alec Stone didn't take kindly to being cheated out of what was his, and whoever was responsible would pay . . . and not with money, but more than likely his life. Bidding the man farewell and good fortune, Geoffrey stood silently watching Alec Stone climb down the ladder to the longboat, remembering the earlier days when Alec captained his own ship and Geoffrey was his first mate.

Geoffrey had been in Alec's employ for a little over five years now, and he wasn't any closer to knowing what went on inside the man's head than the first day he signed on as the captain's first mate. Alec was a quiet man, intense, with some dark secret he preferred keeping that way. Geoffrey liked Alec, and although the time had yet to come, Geoffrey felt reasonably certain he would stand shoulder to shoulder with the man should Alec ever need his help. What he *had* learned about him, however, was that Alec regretted his past days of running slaves from Africa to the Colonies. His guilt, Geoffrey guessed, was what forced him to sell his first ship and buy the *Constance*. He didn't want to hold on to anything that would remind him of how he had obtained his earlier wealth. The idea of men, women and children being sold into bondage sickened him, and Geoffrey assumed it had something to do with the argument he'd had with his mother. That tidbit of knowledge had been awarded to Geoffrey on the one and only occasion when Alec allowed himself to get drunk and had rambled on about how poor he and his mother had been and that now that he had enough money to change his mother's life-style, she refused his help. Lora Stone had told her son that she was ashamed of him, that what he did was wrong, and that if he didn't stop

33

running slaves, he would never be welcome in her house again. Alec had admitted to Geoffrey that that was all it took for him to decide on another way of life, but he had also told him that Lora hadn't approved of his blatant disregard for British rule, either.

"Disregard," he had raged to Geoffrey. "It isn't disregard. It's hatred! England owes her, and she's too stupid to see it."

Geoffrey had been sure Alec hadn't meant what he had said, and rather than allow him to continue and later regret everything he had declared, Geoffrey had helped his captain to bed, took away his bottle of rum and covered him with a blanket, then sat beside his bunk until Alec had fallen asleep. Whether Alec remembered any of what went on that night was something Geoffrey would never learn, for the next morning found Alec in his usual withdrawn and distant mood. Alec did, however, thank him—for what, Geoffrey wasn't sure and Alec never said.

Something else Geoffrey had noticed about Alec was his fondness for elegant clothes. Geoffrey, at first, thought it was foolish to spend every coin a man had on his appearance until he realized Alec had nothing else to do with his money. He paid his men well, had bought a small piece of land in the West Indies and never balked at the cost of repairs to his ship. He even at times loaned money to some of the crew. Of course, he always saw to it that he was paid back with a little extra for his generosity, but on the whole, Alec was a very astute businessman. Geoffrey never had been able to figure out what made Alec change his mind about smuggling goods into the Colonies unless it had been the simple fact that Alec had recognized his talents were being wasted sailing around the Atlantic. And no one liked running the risk of getting shot or worse imprisoned. Thus, he had settled in Jamaica and gained the respectable title of planter, and Geoffrey was offered the opportunity to work for him as the captain of the *Constance*. Although Geoffrey missed the adventure of outsmarting the British from time to time, he truly was happy with the way things turned out. And so was most of the crew.

"If you don't mind my sayin' so, sir," Gerald Higgins

spoke up as he rowed the longboat toward shore. "I think you're taking an awful chance going into Williamsburg alone. Don't you think one of us ought to go along?"

"Are you concerned about my health or your want to sleep in a feather bed?" Alec asked, his attention centered on the dark shapes of the buildings lining the shallow bank.

"I'd be lying if I said I wasn't looking forward to a mug of ale, a soft bed and a little female companionship. But my priorities are for my captain."

"*Former* captain," Alec corrected, his brow furrowed as he continued his perusal of the wharf.

"Yes, sir," Gerald mumbled. "Either way, I have you to thank for making my life worth living. Without you, I'd be too poor to afford anything more than a mound of hay in some farmer's field."

Alec's dark eyes shifted to look dubiously at the man. "Somehow I doubt that, Gerald. Of all my men, you seem to hoard money more than any of them. I would imagine you have quite a treasure chest hidden away somewhere."

"Oh, you're right about that. I don't spend it all on myself. I see that most of it goes home to my sister," he easily admitted, the muscles in his brawny frame flexing with each pull of the oars. "Our folks died some years back, and I'm the only boy in seven children. If I didn't take care of them, they'd be begging in the streets."

The young man's admission surprised Alec, and for the moment he forgot about scrutinizing the wharf for unwanted company. He couldn't remember exactly when Gerald Haugen signed on with the crew or even if he had hired the young man or Geoffrey had. The truth of the matter was that Alec had never bothered to get to know any of his men personally, and to hear that Gerald Haugen was supporting his orphaned family made Alec feel a little ashamed. Frowning, he studied the shoreline again.

"I'll be careful," he spoke quietly. "I always am. Unlike you, there's no one other than myself for me to take care of, and no one who'd give a damn if anything happened to me."

A moment of silence passed between the men before Gerald dared to contradict him. "You're wrong there, sir.

35

With the exception of one or two—maybe—the entire crew cares."

Alec couldn't name the sensation that came over him in that minute—surprise, perhaps, maybe even pride or honor. No one in his entire life had ever said anything like that to him, not even his mother. Oh, she cared. Lora never had to actually say it. He could sense it, feel it radiate from her. But no one had ever come right out and said it. What made him feel uncomfortable was that he didn't think he deserved such loyalty—from anyone. And now that Gerald had made the statement, Alec felt as if he had asked for the compliment. Averting his eyes, he glanced out at the shoreline again, a frown creasing his brow. What truly made him feel even worse was the thought of knowing someone depended on him. He had never been able to admit it—even to himself— but once his mother had been buried, he experienced a great sense of freedom; whatever he did from that point on was his choice alone to make, and he didn't have to answer to anyone. Learning that his crew thought so highly of him meant he owed it to them to make the right decisions, and that was something he didn't want to have heaped on his shoulders. He didn't want the responsibility. He wanted to be his own man with no strings attached.

The bow of the longboat glided into shallow waters, struck the muddy bottom and jerked to a halt, bringing Alec's attention back on the matter at hand. It was the first time in weeks that Alec had stood on solid ground, and while he stretched, he surveyed his surroundings before turning back to Gerald. Motioning for the young man to toss him the satchel, Alec caught it in one hand, tapped the gold-handled tip of his cane against the brim of his tricorn and silently prayed all would go well as he watched Gerald stab one of the oars into the water and shove off back toward the frigate, completely unaware of the cold, calculating green eyes watching his every move.

Bright silver moonlight lit the way as Alec turned for the small building adjacent to the warehouse. Next to it was a livery where he hoped he would be able to hire the use of a horse. He didn't relish the idea of walking all the way into town. He wanted to rent a room, have something to eat and perhaps a cool mug of ale or glass of wine, and then retire. Since it was nearing midnight, he knew he would have to wait until morning to conduct his business anyway. Remembering his comment to Geoffrey, Alec decided that maybe his first visit should be to the newspaper office, then the courthouse. While pretending to inquire about property for sale, he could examine the records to see if Heller had registered the purchase of the plantation he had bought in Alec's name. But first he'd get a good night's sleep before starting his covert investigation.

As he neared the door to the building where he guessed the manager of the warehouse would be at this hour, a soft breeze rustled the underbrush some twenty feet away and absently drew his attention to the spot. Realizing it wasn't cause for alarm and only the faint wind that disturbed the leaves, he glanced back in the direction he walked, only to come to a hesitant stop. Straightening his tall frame, he frowned, blinked, then cast another look to his right. He couldn't explain what it was that pricked his awareness, but there was something about the spot that acted like a magnet drawing him closer. Setting down his satchel, he crossed the distance to the line of trees and scrubs and slowly examined the ground before him. Silvery streams of moonlight filtered down through the leafy overhang and cast strange images upon the earth. With the tip of his cane, he pushed aside a spindly, low-hanging branch just far enough to allow a flood of light to bathe the area and noticed a dark stain in the soft soil. Stooping, he picked up some of the particles and rubbed them between his thumb and first two fingers to determine what had spilled there. Failing that, he let the dirt fall back to the ground and started to rise, wondering why such knowledge was of any importance to him, when a tiny, flashing dot of light caught his attention from out of the corner of his eye. There, a yard or so away from him, was a broken piece of glass that reflected the moonlight every time the leaves above it swayed in the breeze. But finding the small fragment of crystal wasn't what raised Alec's tawny brows. It was the bejeweled stickpin he saw laying on the

37

ground beside it that made him shift his weight and reach for the piece of jewelry. Holding it up to catch the moonlight, he easily concluded whoever owned it would be quite upset to discover its loss.

The snapping of a twig from farther into the underbrush instantly brought him out of his thoughts. Concentrating on the direction from which the sound came, he absently tucked the pin in the breast pocket of his waistcoat then guardedly secured the handle of his cane with his free hand. One swift pull would release the thin-bladed rapier from its wooden casing, and he'd be able to defend himself should the noise be a forewarning of danger. Several minutes of silence passed while he stood there listening, diligently scrutinizing the darkness of the woods until he was sure whatever or whomever it was had moved on. Relaxing a little, he let out his long-held breath and turned back toward the warehouse office. Upon reaching the door, he bent to retrieve his satchel, then straightened and glanced out across the water at the *Constance*. With sails unfurled, trapping the light breeze, the huge merchant ship glided slowly out to sea. Satisfied that Geoffrey would see its cargo delivered on time, he turned and soundly rapped the tip of his gold-handled cane against the door.

The closer Rebecca got to the wharf, the more she cursed the mare she'd had to borrow from the widow Potter. The animal was as stubborn as she was old and had fought Rebecca the entire way. Her arms ached from the constant tugging on the reins every time the horse decided to turn around and go back home, and Rebecca's patience was just as exhausted. If it wasn't for the long walk back into town combined with the promise of a good soaking along the way, Rebecca would have turned the mule-headed nag loose and traveled the rest of the distance on foot. But she also knew she couldn't spare the time. It wouldn't be long before it started to rain, and she had to get to the spot where Jon-Gregory had found Eli's body before the storm destroyed the evidence.

Pulling her cape tighter around her shoulders to shield her slender frame against the cool night air, she glanced up at the sky overhead and prayed Thomas Keenan would be sound asleep when she arrived. She couldn't risk his seeing her, and the light from the lantern she planned to take from the livery would certainly tell him someone was snooping around the docks. It was his duty to keep an eye on things, and the shiver that slithered down her back wasn't caused by the crisp night breeze but the realization that Mr. Keenan would shoot first and find out later who had been foolish enough to trespass after dark. She could wind up dead before she even had the opportunity to explain. Exhaling a quick sigh, she wrinkled up her nose and told herself it was a chance she had to take. Being a reporter had its risks, and she had known that before she had ever decided to ask Mrs. Rind for a job.

The road turned sharply to the right, and beyond the bend lay the docks, warehouse and other buildings. Deciding she'd get there faster if she walked the rest of the way rather than struggling with the mare, she guided the animal into the trees, slid out of the saddle and tied the reins to a branch. If everything went according to her plan, she'd write her story tonight then go to the office before Mrs. Rind, set the type, and have the article ready for print by the time Clementina had breakfast. Her first major story would be circulated around Williamsburg before she had washed the ink from her hands. And Eli's killer would be that much closer to being named.

Cutting through the line of trees surrounding the docks, she approached the buildings from the back and therefore didn't see the light shining in the window of the warehouse office as she darted across the opening to the stable and through its back door. Once inside, she fumbled around in the darkness in search of the lantern she was sure she'd find hanging on the peg near the entrance. Then, just as her hand struck it, a faint light from the front of the livery appeared and grew brighter, and Rebecca instinctively ducked down behind the huge wooden barrel next to her.

"I'm afraid she's the only horse I have available right now, sir," she heard Thomas Keenan apologize, and Rebecca squeezed her eyes tightly shut as if she thought the effort would make her disappear. "But I guess it's better than walking all the way into town, huh?"

The pot-bellied, little man laughed nervously at his own comment; but his companion remained quiet, and Rebecca's imaginative mind went to work. Keenan was obviously ill at ease about something. He seldom found anything humorous in his dull life and usually snapped at anyone who bothered him. And being awakened at this time of night would surely irritate him. It could only mean that whoever this man was, Thomas Keenan had reason to be frightened. Why? Rebecca mused. Had Keenan been threatened? And with what? Who was this stranger? Dropping down on her hands and knees, she decided to get a look for herself. After all, there just might be a story in it.

Peering out from behind the barrel, Rebecca's breath caught in her throat when she saw that the stranger stood only a few feet away from where she hid. Yet even so, there was no way for her to get a good look at him or even learn what he was wearing, as he stood with his back to her and the floor-length, gray cape he had draped over his shoulders hid everything except his black, shiny shoes. The charcoal gray tricorn on his head, however, was tipped forward enough that she could see the light color of his hair and that he had pulled it back on his neck and tied it fashionably with a black velvet ribbon. The only thing she could surmise from such a limited view was that his choice of clothes spoke of wealth. Only the Earl of Dunmore dressed more elegantly. The stranger moved then, and Rebecca ducked back out of sight, her heart pounding loudly in her ears as she huddled behind the barrel.

"Will you be staying in Williamsburg long, sir?" Keenan asked as he guided the mare from her stall and stood aside to allow his customer the freedom to tie his satchel to the saddle straps.

"Perhaps," the stranger answered noncommittally, and Rebecca's heart beat even faster. His deep voice had a smooth mellowness to it like none other she had ever heard,

40

and she decided, without getting a clear view of his face, that he was probably as equally handsome as his voice implied.

The light from Keenan's lantern faded as the two men left the stable, and Rebecca quickly scrambled to her feet to follow. At the doorway she paused, standing off to one side where she wouldn't be seen. Bathed in the last rays of bright, silver moonlight, the stranger flipped one corner of his cape up over his shoulder to clear his step, placed his foot in the stirrup and easily pulled himself up into the saddle. He sat tall and proud, and when the mare started to prance sideways, he skillfully brought her to rein. Then, with a slight nod of his head toward Keenan, he spun the horse around and cantered off down the road leading into town. It wasn't until then that Rebecca questioned his arrival. Leaning slightly to her right, she peered out at the shoreline. No boats or ships were anchored there, and the stranger's need to hire the use of a horse meant he had arrived on foot. But from where? And why had he chosen to come here at this time of night? Certain she had stumbled across something that needed to be looked into, she decided that in the morning she'd do a little research on him. She'd write her article about Eli, put it to press and then pay Mr. Keenan a visit under the pretense that she was told by Mrs. Rind to do a document on the success of the waterfront . . . or something. She shrugged, figuring to work out that part of it later, and turned her attention on the little man as Keenan headed back toward the office, lantern in hand. A few moments later, the light was extinguished, and Rebecca felt safe in leaving the stable.

Standing near the spot where Jon-Gregory had said Eli had been found, she realized she hadn't needed a lantern since the moon overhead still bathed the area with bright light. She could clearly see the dark blood stain in the soil, the broken twigs and damaged foliage where his body had lain, and the numerous shoe prints in the dirt. However, one set in particular caught her attention. Bending down to get a closer look, she noticed that the heel of one shoe had a nick in it. Realizing it could belong to any of the men who helped carry Eli away, she momentarily dismissed it but filed the bit of knowledge in the back of her mind. If this story developed the way she thought it would and Mrs. Rind gave her permission to investigate further, she would make a list of the men who had been here today, pay them each a visit and ask to see the shoes they wore this morning. By process of elimination, she just might stumble across a valuable piece of information.

She had just started to rise when she spotted another impression in the dirt, and something Jon-Gregory had said snapped in her memory. *Eli had been clubbed with a stick or cane.* There, next to the shoe print with the notch in it, was the distinct indentation of a small, round hole, the kind of mark the tip of a man's cane would make. A paralyzing fear came over her, one that nearly took her breath away, when she realized that she was standing on the very spot where Eli's killer had stood. Gulping down the wave of nausea that kinked her stomach into a hard knot, she awkwardly came to her feet and sucked in a long, cool breath of fresh air to calm her jittery nerves.

She had promised herself not to allow her personal feelings to interfere with her investigation; but as she turned away from the scene, a sadness tugged at her heart, and for a moment she nearly caved in to the grief building up inside her. She had known Eli her entire life, and up until Lenore decided out of spite to sell him off, he had lived and worked on the Wilde's plantation. They had been close friends while Rebecca was growing up, and it had been Eli who inspired her to follow her dream of being a writer. They would spend hours together after Eli's work was done, sitting under a huge oak tree where he listened while Rebecca read her poems to him. In turn she'd go fishing with him or climb trees and play the kind of games boys liked to play. On the day they buried Rebecca's father, Eli had cried just as hard and as long as Rebecca had, swearing to her that he'd take care of her now that her father was gone. A week later he disappeared, and she had learned from one of the black children that her stepmother had sold him to Gideon Blackstock. The only consolation she felt was that she knew

42

Mr. Blackstock was kind to his slaves and that Eli would have a good home. She never saw him after that, and now she was sorry she hadn't. She had missed him before; but now there was a permanent emptiness inside her, and it was all she could do to raise her chin bravely in the air and vow to make his killer pay. She owed it to Eli.

Chapter Two

Loud laughter rang in Alec's ears, and the aroma of ale and cigar smoke assailed his nostrils the second he opened the door to The Red Lion and stepped inside. He would have preferred a little peace and quiet, but since it had already started to rain and this had been the first tavern he had come to that was still open at this hour, he decided to make the best of the situation. He'd have something to eat then inquire about lodgings for the night.

A frown creased his brow as he approached the bar and saw that the keeper, an old man with white hair, was seated behind it on a tall stool with his arms crossed over his chest, his head down and his eyes closed. "Excuse me," Alec softly apologized as he set down his satchel on the floor. He truly didn't want to startle the gentleman, but when his summons went unheard and Alec's patience suddenly ran thin, he raised his cane and tapped the gold handle on the counter. The man snorted, jerked upright and opened his eyes. "Would it be possible to get something to eat and perhaps a glass of your finest wine?" he asked, taking his tricorn from his head and glancing over his right shoulder at the inhabitants of the room.

"A—a—yes, sir. I mean I got good wine, but the cook's gone to bed. I could scare up some bread and cheese if you'd like," the man offered as he slid off the stool. "I might even be able to find a couple of hard-boiled eggs."

A pert, little redhead laughing with the men at the far table caught Alec's eye. She was a delicate, young woman with a sparkling buoyancy about the way she moved and held herself erect, and Alec found himself envying her exuberance. He couldn't remember the last time he had laughed at something.

"Sir?"

Alec blinked and subtly cast his attention away from the girl, hoping the tavernkeeper hadn't noticed his attraction to her. "That would be fine. I'll take it over there." He nodded at a table far away from the other patrons, then picked up his bag and started toward it.

Settling himself down in the chair, his cape, tricorn and cane laid neatly in a pile on the one next to him, Alec stretched the tired muscles in his neck and shoulders and idly glanced out the front windows at the storm which had suddenly erupted. He never enjoyed the rain, really, since it seemed he always managed to get caught in the middle of it with no where to go for shelter, and he pitied anyone who found themselves in that same kind of situation tonight. This storm promised to last quite awhile.

Feeling the exhaustion of his trip, he relaxed back in the chair and folded his arms comfortably over his chest, his thoughts wandering back to the times he had spent sitting at the table with his mother, watching the lightning and listening to the thunder as he was doing right now. But perhaps it wasn't the storm that made him think of her. Being in the Colonies and knowing that somewhere on this vast stretch of land Edwin Higgins had taken up residence seemed to have sparked the memories of her. And until he found the man, Alec would go on remembering. There was still one question that had to be asked before Alec could put his life in order. He had to know if his father had loved the young Lora Stone on the day Alec was conceived. He wanted to be convinced his mother hadn't lied when she said she was happy the way she was, and that she never cursed the day he was born. If he could learn the answers to those questions, he was sure he could lay his bitterness toward his

45

father to rest. Unwittingly, he unfolded his arms and toyed with the ring on his finger, completely unaware that he was being watched.

Penny had never before experienced the kind of sensation that came over her the instant her gaze fell on the stranger sitting alone at the far table. He was probably *the* most handsome man she had ever seen, and she found herself wishing she'd had the chance to meet him under more respectable conditions. He didn't appear to be the type who'd be interested in a barmaid, but since there wasn't much she could do about it now, she mentally shrugged off the problem and sighed longingly, thinking that perhaps she could change his mind. Spotting Benjamin Lewis as he rounded the end of the bar with a glass of wine in his hand, Penny quickly and politely excused herself from her customers and hurried over to him.

"I'll take care of that, Ben," she grinned, reaching for the glass. "After all, it's my job."

Surprised by her sudden appearance, Ben stood there for a second or two without saying anything. Then remembering that their newest patron requested food as well, he nodded and said, "Yes, yes, please do. I have to see about finding him something to eat." Looking past Penny at the newcomer, he lowered his voice and added, "And he doesn't look like the sort who ever had to wait for anything."

An appreciative smile lifted the corner of Penny's mouth as she, too, studied the man. "He certainly doesn't," she agreed.

"Then, I guess I better hurry," Benjamin replied, starting to turn away. Then his business sense emerged, and he stopped and touched Penny's arm, whispering, "Keep his glass filled, Penny. And see if you can convince him to spend the night. We need more customers like him."

A devilish, shameless twinkle glowed in her eyes. "Oh, you can count on me, Ben. I'll do everything I can to get him to spend the night."

Her implication didn't register with Ben, and Penny knew it. The old man adored her and had often times intervened

46

when a customer got too friendly, unaware that Penny had deliberately provoked the attention. He would be appalled to learn of her favorite pastime, and chances were he'd more than likely force her to work in the kitchen away from the customers if he ever found out. Thus Penny kept her affairs as secret as possible . . . except for her best friend. Rebecca knew everything. And wait until she told Rebecca about tonight. She'd turn absolutely green with envy!

And then again, maybe she wouldn't, Penny thought as she approached the stranger's table. *Rebecca really isn't interested in men. What a shame. She doesn't know what she's missing.*

Lost in thought, Alec was hardly aware that someone had set a glass of wine on the table in front of him until he sensed the presence. Thinking it to be the old man, he didn't look up, but instead lifted the glass to his lips and took a drink. It was indeed a fine wine, no doubt smuggled into the Colonies by someone who enjoyed defying British rule.

"Is it to your liking, sir?" the definitely feminine voice beside him asked, and Alec turned his head to look at her.

The young barmaid was even prettier up close, and although she wasn't the first woman to pay him special attention, it had been a long time since he had shared the company of a lady. His dark brown eyes slowly traveled the length of her shapely form, taking special note of her rounded bosom and narrow waist, before settling on her face again with its intense brown eyes. Satisfied with what he saw, he smiled.

"Yes. The wine is excellent. Would you join me?"

Penny hoped her enthusiasm didn't show on her face. She didn't want to appear too willing lest it ruin everything. Men were strange that way. They liked to be the aggressive ones. If a woman came on too strong, they tended to shy away, and she didn't want to scare him off. Pretending to care about the other customers in the place, she glanced over at the table full of men who were playing cards, as if she worried about neglecting them.

"If they want another mug of ale, I'm sure they'll let you

know," he said, coming to his feet and pulling out a chair for her.

Who could resist a man who is so insistent? she thought, then said aloud, "I suppose. But only for a moment. I really do have a lot of work to do."

"It couldn't be that much." He smiled, waiting for her to sit down before taking his own chair again. "I would imagine the tavern will close soon."

"It depends," Penny replied, subtly complimented by the man's good manners. Most men who came to The Red Lion seldom treated her like a lady as he was doing. "We stay open as long as there's someone to serve. But that usually ends somewhere around midnight or one."

"And then you're allowed to go home?"

What a perfect opening! "Well, I guess you could say that."

"Guess?" Alec smiled. "I don't understand."

"I don't really *go* anywhere. I have a room upstairs." She purposely cast her attention away from him as if her admission was something they really shouldn't be talking about.

Alec wasn't sure, but it appeared their conversation had embarrassed the young woman. He decided to change the subject. "Would you like a glass of wine?"

Surprised that he didn't offer to walk her to her room later, Penny wondered if this was one man who was truly not interested in anything more than casual conversation. Maybe he needed to loosen up a bit. "That would be nice. Shall I bring a bottle?"

Spotting the innkeeper coming from a back room, Alec motioned for him to bring another glass then turned back to his companion. "My name is Alec . . . Diamond," he told her, fleetingly amused by the witticism. If he intended to unravel the mystery surrounding Heller's disappearance without giving himself away, he couldn't risk telling anyone who he really was. After all, Daniel Heller had been an agent for Alec Stone, and there was a good chance his killer would recognize the name. "Might I have the pleasure of knowing yours?"

A bright, excited smile lit up her face. "Penelope Dawson. But everyone calls me Penny."

"Have you lived all your life here in Williamsburg, Penny?"

"No, only the last few months. I'm from Boston." Now things were starting to move. Whenever she wanted sympathy, she repeated the story she had made up about her being orphaned at a young age and forced to fend for herself. She didn't have to worry about anyone finding out the truth about her because she told the same tale to everyone. Even Ben thought it was true. Rebecca was the only one who knew Penny had enough money to support herself and that she had very wealthy parents living in Richmond, people who would be horribly shocked to learn what their only daughter did with her spare time. But Penny also knew her friend would never give her away. They had an unspoken mutual pact about not telling each other's secrets, and as long as Rebecca wanted to be a journalist, Penny knew she was safe.

"You're an awfully long way from home," Alec observed as he watched Mr. Lewis place the tray of assorted cheeses, a small loaf of bread and bowl of eggs on the table before him. "Have you had the chance to go home for a visit?"

Penny nodded her thanks to Ben for the glass of wine he gave her and winked, her silent way of letting him know that this newcomer would be spending the night . . . more if she could work it out. "There's no need really," she said after taking a sip. "My family is all gone, and I've made new friends here. Besides, I couldn't afford it. I don't own a horse and carriage. I guess you could say I'm stuck here."

"Would you go back if you had the way to get there?" he asked, flipping out his napkin over one thigh, then reaching for the loaf of bread. Tearing off a piece, he wrapped it around a chunk of dark yellow cheese.

No one had ever posed the question to her before, and to give credit to her story, Penny decided she should act rather homesick. "Of course I would. My family might be gone, but there's still a lot of old friends . . . and a lot of memories."

49

She sighed forlornly for effect. "And I would dearly love to visit Mama's and Papa's graves."

While Alec finished chewing the tasty morsel of fresh bread and rich cheese, he reached for one of the eggs and began to peel off the shell. "I might be able to help, if you're really sincere about it," he offered after a moment.

"Of course I'm sincere," Penny returned emphatically and without much consideration to what he had actually proposed. Then it hit her. "Help?" she hesitantly asked, her voice low and eyes wide. "Help me go to Boston?" The only help she wanted was getting her clothes off and into bed.

Alec fought with the smile that tugged at the corners of his mouth. He had a feeling her story wasn't completely true—if at all. What he couldn't figure out was what she wanted from him. She didn't seem to be the type who used men for whatever she could get from them; but he'd had conversations like this before, and the women always wound up asking for money. He took another sip of wine, then leaned forward against the table with his hands cradling his glass.

"It can be arranged if that's what you really want. I've got a friend who owns a frigate, and I'm sure he'd have room for you if I asked." He cocked a sandy-colored brow at her and waited.

Penny wondered if her face was as pale as she suspected it was. Laughing weakly, she raised the goblet to her lips and prayed one of the other customers would need her right then. She wanted a moment to think. To her dismay, no one called her name, and she was forced to give him an answer.

"It's very kind of you to offer, Mr. Diamond, but it would be rather foolish right now."

"Foolish?" he repeated, certain now that he had been right about her. She was after money and that disappointed him. He was hoping she would be different.

Suddenly remembering all the talk she'd heard about the trouble in Boston, she gave a mental sigh at having been able to figure out a way to gracefully decline his proposal. "Haven't you heard? Some men dumped tea in the harbor last December, and the king sent armed troops to bring things back under control. I'd be silly to visit Boston right now. It wouldn't be safe." She smiled sweetly at him. "Especially for a woman all alone and with no money."

He was wondering how long it would take her to get around to her real reason for sitting down with him. Out of curiosity, he asked, "How much?"

Penny blinked and straightened in her chair. "How much what?"

"How much money would you need to feel safe?"

It took her a moment or more to realize this man was offering to hand over a large sum for what Penny guessed he assumed would be payment for a night spent in her bed, and it infuriated her. Her dark eyes snapping fire, she shoved her glass away and stood. She was out for a good time and nothing else. "More than you have, sir."

Her reaction surprised Alec. If she wasn't interested in his money, what was she after? "I apologize if I insulted you, Miss Dawson," he said, grabbing his napkin and slowly coming to his feet. "I assumed that was what you were after."

"Money?" Penny's voice changed to a higher pitch as she fought to control her anger. "I'm not the kind of woman who's after a man's money, Mr. Diamond. I have enough to take care of myself without anyone's help."

Alec's darkly tanned face wrinkled with his suppressed smile. "Enough to book passage on a ship bound for Boston?"

"To *England,* if I wanted," she rallied.

"Then why are you working in a place like this? I would think a lady with money would have people waiting on her, not the other way around."

Penny opened her mouth to tell him that she enjoyed working at The Red Lion and that what she did with her money was her business when she suddenly realized she had unwittingly told him everything about herself except that her home was actually in Richmond. Feeling a nervous perspiration begin to dot her brow, she gulped, looked away for a moment and licked her lips while she considered giving up her attempt to lure this man to her bed. It was too

51

dangerous having even one person know the truth about her without him being a total stranger.

"If you'll be honest with me, Miss Dawson, you'll have my word that your secret will go no farther than this room."

"What makes you think I'm keeping a secret?" she snapped, irritated with herself. She had never run across this problem before and couldn't help blaming herself for allowing it to happen. The men she dealt with usually weren't this astute. She turned her head to look at him. "And what is it you expect to hear?"

Smiling warmly, he held out a hand toward her chair, indicating that she should sit down again. Once she had—though reluctantly—he took his own chair and reached for the bottle of wine Mr. Lewis had placed on the table earlier. He refilled her glass, then his own, set the bottle aside, picked up his glass and leaned back in his chair to study her.

"You obviously and carelessly allowed me to guess that you're home isn't in Boston, that you have no need for a handout, but that you apparently want something from me. What is it, if it isn't money?"

A delighted smile slowly spread over Penny's mouth as she stared back into his handsome face. Now she knew why she had been attracted to him from the very first moment. He was no ordinary man. He was cunning, intelligent, perceptive, observant and *the* most desirable piece of male flesh she had ever seen. What surprised her was how long she had been able to keep her hands to herself and that she hadn't skipped the formalities of polite talk and dragged him upstairs to her room. Maybe he wouldn't live up to his word about keeping her secret, but it was a risk she was willing to take. Glancing toward the bar to make sure Ben had resumed his place on the stool and that he would soon be asleep if he wasn't already, she took a deep breath and looked into Alec's dark brown eyes.

"I've been telling everyone that I'm from Boston so my parents won't find out what I'm doing."

"You mean working here—in a tavern?"

Penny's eyes sparkled. "Well, sort of. You see, I enjoy

talking to people—"

"Men mostly," Alec cut in. She didn't really have to finish her story. He knew what she was getting at.

"Well, they are more fascinating. I mean, what do women do besides cook and clean and raise children? I don't want to sit around listening to women gossip. I want to hear what's going on in the world, and I won't be able to do that by going to tea parties. Maybe I haven't traveled any farther than this building, but I feel like I've been around the world."

"So all you want from me is to hear news," he baited, wondering if her words could be as brazen as her behavior.

A suggestive gleam lit up her eyes. "To begin with." She grinned, lifting her glass of wine to her lips and taking a sip while she studied him over the rim.

For the first time in years, Alec threw back his head and laughed in earnest. Maybe she wasn't a lady. Maybe she didn't act the way a young woman should, but he didn't care. She had done for him what he hoped she could. She had made him forget, and it felt good.

"Then drink up, Penny. You and I have a lot to talk about."

A loud crack of thunder overhead made Rebecca jump violently. The wind had picked up, and the damp, sweet smell in the air could only mean one thing: Within minutes she'd be soaked to the skin.

"I certainly hope you can get along without your mare, Mrs. Potter," she snarled as she half-ran, half-walked along the dark country road back toward town, "because I'm going to kill that worthless nag the minute I get my hands on her. How dare she run off and leave me behind!" Jerking her cloak around her, she lowered her head and quickened her pace.

As nearly as she could predict, it would take her another fifteen minutes to reach the outskirts of town. From there she'd have to walk all the way down Main Street to the capitol building, cut across the lawn to Nicholson Street until it intersected Waller then head north several blocks to the boardinghouse. In all it would be another hour unless she ran most of the way, and she was already winded from the short distance she had. Yet, the concern over getting wet wasn't what worried her. She feared the storm would awaken Miss Abigail and send the nosey old snoop running through the house checking everyone's room to make sure their windows were closed. And when Rebecca didn't answer her summons, Miss Abigail would know Rebecca wasn't where she was supposed to be.

Rebecca had realized long before she had ever accepted the job at the *Gazette* that not every aspect of it would be exciting. Some would be boring, some dangerous, others routine, but never had she expected something like this . . . to be stranded on a dark, deserted road with a storm approaching. And all because of Miss Abigail and her stupid rules.

"I hope the roof springs a leak and you drown in your sleep," she muttered angrily.

Cold, tiny droplets of rain started to pelt her, and she hugged her cape tighter around her and hurried her step again. She was a grown woman, for crying out loud. Why should she have to take orders from anyone? As the rain increased and quickly dampened her cape, she came to the conclusion that it was time she bought a horse. That way whenever she needed to go somewhere, she wouldn't have to borrow one. She'd take her own. And she'd find some place else to live, a boardinghouse without rules!

A sudden cloudburst hailed a torrent of cold, blinding raindrops upon the earth. Shrieking, Rebecca lifted her skirts and dashed off down the road, thinking to outrun it before she got too horribly wet. But her energy faded much quicker than she liked, and she stumbled to a breathless walk, her long, thick strands of hair plastered to her head. Runnels of cold, chilling water streamed down her face and in her eyes. Her outer clothes were soaked, and she knew it was only a matter of minutes before everything she had on would be saturated. If she hadn't been warned countless times not to stand under a tree when lightning flashed about the sky, she would have left the road for what little protection the leafy overhang provided. Her shoes were wet, and her stockings were damp all the way to her knees. She was just plain miserable, and with each hurried step she took, her temper shortened.

"This is all your fault, Abigail Beecher!" she shouted, but the sound of her voice was drowned out by the loud clap of thunder that exploded overhead. Its vibrating volley frightened her, and in a panic, she seized a handful of her heavy skirts and hurried off again as quickly as her feet would carry her.

By the time Rebecca had turned onto Main Street, her teeth were chattering so badly she had to clamp them shut just to hear herself think. Up ahead was The Red Lion, and she decided to wait out the rest of the storm in Penny's room, since it hadn't lessened any and her skirts were so heavy and caked with mud that it was difficult for her to walk. She was exhausted from all the extra weight she carried and longed for the moment she could strip off the soggy material and sit before a warm fire . . . and hopefully without a lecture from her friend. Penny was sure to tell her how stupid she was, and right now, Rebecca couldn't argue the point. She just didn't want to hear it. A frown creased her brow once the tavern came into view at the end of the block and she could see several horses still tied outside at the hitching post. One of the reasons Penny always slept until noon was because there were times when she worked quite late. She couldn't leave the commons until all of the customers had either gone to their rooms or returned home. And because of the rain, those who were left would surely stay there until the storm had passed. Only stupid people would get caught in the middle of it!

Once she came within one hundred yards of the place, Rebecca found a small reserve of energy and began to run again. At the corner she cut across to the back of the building, opened the gate in the red brick fence surrounding the structure and raced for the side door, praying the entrance wasn't locked. Much to her relief the knob turned easily in her hand, and she swung the door wide, hurried inside and staggered to a dripping, exhausted halt in the narrow corridor. Falling back against the wall behind her, Rebecca gasped for air as she took a moment to regain her strength and push the door shut again. The hallway was empty and dimly lit, something she appreciated since she didn't want anyone to see her. Fumbling with the strings that held her cape securely at her throat, she awkwardly loosened them and pushed the soggy garment from her shoulders, shivering when a chill shook her body. Pushing the wet, heavy strands of her black hair back off her brow with one hand, she started toward the stairs at the end of the hall, half-consciously listening to the muted laughter and buzzing of voices coming from the commons in another part of the building. As long as there were customers, Penny wouldn't be able to go to her room, and while Rebecca climbed the back steps to the second floor, she decided that perhaps it was a blessing in disguise. She would use her friend's place to warm herself by the fire for a few minutes and hopefully outlast the storm, help herself to some of Penny's dry clothes, then leave her a note and head for home without having to listen to Penny's sermon on how foolish she had been. She dearly loved Penelope Dawson, but at times she tried Rebecca's patience. And right now she had very little left.

At the landing, she paused and peeked around the corner to make sure no one was in the hallway. Finding it empty, she rolled up her cape into a ball, hugged it to her and hurriedly tiptoed down the corridor to Penny's room. Testing the knob to find the door locked, she reached up and took the spare key from the narrow ledge of the framework and slid it into the hole. The dull click when she twisted it freed the way, and she hurried inside.

The room was dark save for the pale light emanating from the glowing embers in the fireplace and the occasional flashes of lightning glaring in through the windows. Rebecca didn't bother to look around. The thought of being warm again was simply too overpowering. Locking the door behind her and tossing the spare key on a nearby table, she hurried across the room to the hearth and knelt on the braided rug as she dropped her cape on the floor beside her and pulled the blue ribbon from her hair. She could feel the warmth almost instantly when she held out her hands to the fire, but it wasn't enough to chase away the chill that shook her entire body. She had to remove her wet clothes if she ever wanted to be comfortable again. Rolling onto one hip, she slid off her shoes, peeled her stockings from her legs, and dumped the garments in a heap beside her cape before coming to her feet again. After working the buttons up the front of her dress loose, she wiggled out of the bodice, unhooked the fastening at the waist of her petticoats and dropped both pieces to the floor where she gleefully kicked them aside. Even her camisole was soaked, but rather than stand there completely nude, she decided to stoke up the fire a little first, find herself one of Penny's robes to wear and then shimmy out of the chemise. Dropping to her knees again, she took a couple of small logs from the brass woodbox sitting at the right of the hearth and laid them on the glowing embers, then reached for the poker hanging in its stand. Once the orange tongues of flame began to lick greedily around the dark pieces of wood, she returned the poker to its place, pushed herself up and crossed to the washstand where she grabbed a towel from the rack. Bending, she threw her head forward and let her damp hair hang down while she twisted it up in the white piece of linen to dry. She felt much better; but she still longed to be free of the clammy undergarment she wore, and as she turned for the armoire, she concentrated her attention on the lacy strings up the front of her camisole.

A loud rumble of thunder shook the timber and rattled the panes of glass in the window, momentarily drawing Rebecca's gaze to it. The storm didn't seem to be at all interested in dying down, and she curled her lip at the blinding flashes of light as if to mock its intense desire to frighten her. *Let it rain,* she thought triumphantly. *I'm warm and dry now, and if I have to, I'll wait until the last possible moment to return home. It certainly can't last that long.*

Struck by a cold shiver that tickled the hair across her arms, the flesh over her shoulders and down her spine, she looked away from the window and started toward the armoire again, only to come to an abrupt stop. For the first time since she had entered the room, she wasn't too preoccupied to study everything in it. Bathed in the pale light of the fire and the occasional flash of silver whenever the lightning shot across the sky and flooded the room with an ephemeral brilliance, she could see the dressing table and bench, armoire, tri-fold scene, free standing cheval mirror, a nightstand, paintings on the wall and the huge four-poster bed with its mounds of rumpled covers, the latter of which made her frown. Buried beneath the pink and white striped quilt was the distinct shape of someone lying there, and Rebecca took a hesitant step forward to get a better view in the muted light as she called out Penny's name in a loud whisper. Her friend neither moved nor responded, and Rebecca leaned in to give Penny a shake, then thought better of it. If Penny was in bed before all the customers had left the inn, it could only mean that she wasn't feeling well, and Rebecca wouldn't disturb her.

Quietly tiptoeing around the end of the bed, she moved to the armoire and opened it to pull out a white, eyelet-trimmed robe. Although she and Penny were nearly the same size, Rebecca had always envied her friend's well-defined curves and her outgoing personality. Whenever they were together, it was Penny who got the second looks from the gentlemen they encountered, and although Rebecca wasn't really interested in men, the attention her friend always received made her wonder at times if she shouldn't find out what it was that made Penny so attracted to them. As far as Rebecca was concerned, men were arrogant bullies who thought women should do women's work and leave the rest to the men. That thought irritated Rebecca, and after slipping out of her camisole, she yanked the sash of the robe securely around her waist and returned to the hearth to drape her wet

58

clothes over the rocker to dry. Why couldn't women do other things besides caring for their children or cleaning the house? Men weren't any smarter than women.

A half smile lifted one corner of her mouth as she knelt on the braided rug and unwound the towel from her dark hair. She'd soon prove all of them wrong. She planned to unravel the mystery surrounding Eli's death, and once she had she'd show them who was smarter. After all, hadn't the *men* concluded it was an accident without even bothering to ask a few questions? No, of course they hadn't asked. There was no need. They were right, so why question their first assumption?

While Rebecca rubbed the dampness from her hair, she began to feel the exhaustion seep through every muscle in her body. The warmth of the fire made her tired. Fluffing up her hair, she shook her head and pushed the heavy strands back off her face. It was uncomfortable sitting on the hard floor, but if she moved to a chair, she'd start shivering again. Glancing over her shoulder at the bed, she considered lying under the covers for a while until she was completely warm again. A loud crack of thunder made her jump and seemed to answer her unspoken question. The storm was in its fullest with no immediate promise of easing up, and since she had no choice but to remain in Penny's room awhile longer, she might as well make the best of it. But she'd have to sit up with the blanket drawn around her neck. She couldn't risk falling asleep! If Miss Abigail discovered that one of her boarders hadn't been in his or her room all night, Rebecca would be looking for a new place to stay in the morning.

So you simply won't fall asleep, that's all, she silently told herself as she left her place by the hearth and crossed the room to stand beside the bed.

Studying Penny's unmoving shape snuggled deep beneath the covers for a moment, Rebecca wondered how the girl could breathe with the quilt drawn up over her head like that. But then, there were a lot of things about Penelope Dawson that made Rebecca wonder. Hoping she wouldn't awaken her friend as she climbed in beside her, Rebecca gingerly lifted the edges of the sheets and coverlet in one hand and dropped down on the soft mattress, giving an inner sigh of gratification at being awarded the warmth and comfort this little piece of heaven afforded. Carefully propping herself up against the headboard, cushioned by a thickly feathered pillow, she closed her eyes and gently pulled the blankets up under her chin. The only thing that would make her any happier, Rebecca decided, was if she were in her own bed and about to go to sleep. Next time she had a story to investigate, she'd make sure it was done in the middle of a bright, warm afternoon.

That's what you say now, she smiled to herself, *but you know better. If there was news to be uncovered in the middle of a blizzard in January, you'd go. That's why you're a better reporter than any man could ever hope to be. You're dedicated.* A yawn caught her off-guard, and before she realized what she had done, she laid her head back against the pillow and relaxed while she mentally went over everything she had learned from her trip to the docks. It wasn't enough to write a column about quite yet, but after she paid Blackstock a visit, she was sure she'd have enough information to raise a few questioning brows. And tomorrow she'd start asking around about a stranger who walked with the aid of a cane. Shifting a little more comfortably on the bed, she glanced over at Penny to find she hadn't moved, and closed her eyes again. Just as soon as it stopped raining . . .

A volley of thunder penetrated Rebecca's sleep-filled mind and she stirred. The covers had slipped off her arms, and as she languidly stretched out a hand for them, she lazily opened one eye to see that the fire had died to glowing embers. She also noticed that the storm hadn't calmed down in the least, which meant she didn't have to get out of her warm bed for a while longer. Drawing in a long, relaxing breath, she inched down farther under the covers and rolled over onto her side so that she could watch the muted light coming from the hearth and the occasional tiny flame that would flare up now and then. But only a moment passed before she drifted off to sleep again, completely unaware that she had.

Rebecca seldom remembered her dreams, if indeed she dreamed at all. But this one seemed so real . . . and pleasurable. She was lying in a huge brass bed with a thick down mattress and silk sheets. Moonlight trickled in through the opened window and carried with it the soft fragrance of wild flowers. She had just taken a leisurely bath in rose water and dared to slip beneath the covers in her bed completely naked. The slick fabric felt cool and invigorating against her flesh and brought a smile to her lips. Rolling, she turned over on her stomach and buried her face in the pillow, reveling in the sweet smell of freshly washed linens. Then, suddenly, mystically, a warm hand touched the back of her thigh and slowly trailed a burning path up her leg to her buttocks. She moaned deliriously but didn't resist. The caress became bolder as it moved along her spine, across her shoulders and down her side again, then over the small of her back to her hip. There was a strength and firmness in the touch as if her phantom lover had practiced many times before. But no matter. He had come to *her* this night, and though it be in her dreams, she would explore the full extent of his lovemaking and learn what it was that sparked such wanton desires deep within her.

The blankets were pushed aside, and that same hand came up to brush away the thick strands of her hair falling wildly over her shoulders. She murmured incoherently when warm, moist lips kissed the back of her neck, and something inside her stirred when he pressed his body full against her side, molding those strong, rock-hard muscles along the curve of her delicate, much smaller frame. The masculine scent of him filled her nostrils, and as his lips moved softly along the smooth flesh of her throat to her ear, she shivered delightedly at the blissful sensation it aroused. Never having experienced the pleasurable thrill of a man's embrace and totally ignorant of what it could evoke, Rebecca willingly

61

and eagerly twisted around to welcome his kiss. The heat of his sinewy body, pressed against hers as he slid his arms beneath her and pulled her to him, left her breathless. But when his lips met hers, a fire erupted in the pit of her belly and spread rapidly through her. Yet, once he raised above her, braced on his elbows, and gently nudged her legs apart, her beautiful, radiant vision of rapture exploded into full-fledged reality. *This was no dream!*

In that same instant, when the shock of what was truly happening hit her, the powerful stranger pinned her beneath him and began to kiss her fervently. And once he forced her lips apart with his probing tongue, Rebecca's eyes flew open. Dear God, how did he get into Penny's room? Or *was* this Penny's room?

A flash of bright light seared the dark space for only a split second, but it was long enough for her to recognize the furnishings and bring to mind the events of the night. Yes, this was Penny's room, and he obviously thought *she* was Penny. Oh, God! She had to make him stop! She had to make him realize the horrible mistake he was making. Squirming beneath him, she tried to work her arms in between them and break his hold. But it seemed only to impassion him further when his mouth moved hungrily over hers and his hands began to explore her silkened curves. His touch burned her flesh. His kiss added fuel to the already raging fire that shot through every inch of her. And while her mind cried out for him to stop, her body begged him to continue.

A muffled scream tore at her throat when she felt his manly boldness intrude upon the intimacy of her soft woman's flesh, and she quit wiggling beneath him. In all her imaginings she had never dreamed it would be like this. It was frightening! How could Penny possibly enjoy— Her thought was never finished, for in that moment he pressed the fullness deep within her, and Rebecca stiffened beneath him when a burning pain exploded in her loins. Tears stung the back of her lids, and she kept her eyes tightly closed, fearing he would mock her if he knew. Surely that was a part of it. He wanted to hurt her, know that he had, then laugh when she begged him to stop. Well, she wouldn't. She'd be strong. She'd endure all that he could give her, then flee this place before he discovered his mistake. She'd show him. She'd educate this barbarian. At least *one* man would know that not all women longed for their touch, their love-making—if it could be deemed love.

Suddenly Rebecca was aware that he had raised above her and was staring down into her face. She opened her eyes. Lost in the darkness of the room, she could only make out the light color of his hair, the firm set of his jaw and possibly a frown marring his brow—but she wasn't sure. Then he cocked his head to one side as if in doubt, and she knew she had won. She hadn't cried out. She didn't beg him to cease his lustful advances. She wasn't behaving at all the way he expected. Unknowingly, a triumphant smile parted her lips, and the joy of victory gleamed in her bright, blue eyes. However, the pleasure was short-lived, for it seemed he took her bravery as a challenge. Lowering his wide-shouldered frame once more, his opened mouth descended upon hers again.

Rebecca's first impulse was to turn her head and push him away. But she realized that would be a mistake. He'd know that she preferred he leave her alone, and that would undo all she had achieved so far. Stealing herself against the pain she was sure would follow, she tried to relax. To her surprise, it never came, and her own brow furrowed in uncertainty, failing to understand how his forceful intrusion could hurt one moment and be almost pleasurable the next. And when he began to move, slowly, gently at first, a new sensation attacked her. It started with a warmth from deep inside her and spread through every limb. Her heart beat a little faster. Her flesh tingled. Her breathing quickened. His strides were long and sleek and titillating, and the fullness pressed deep within her rekindled the burning fire that coursed through her veins with every thump of her pulse. Without knowing it, she encircled her arms around his neck and returned his branding kisses with all the energy she could muster. Her womanly instincts took over then, and she arched her hips against each thrust of his. Her nails clawed his back. His heart thundered wildly against her naked breasts, and together they soared toward their heavenly release on wings of fiery splendor until their passion reached its glorious peak and exploded in a blaze of unequaled ecstasy. Gradually, blissfully, they floated earthward, too exhausted and fulfilled to comprehend their mortal world or to utter anything more than a contented sigh.

A long while passed before the stranger raised his head and tenderly kissed Rebecca's parted lips once more. And it wasn't until that moment that the full weight of what had happened came crashing down around her. She stealed herself against the growing need to cry and pound her fists against his broad back, and silently prayed their masquerade would continue. She didn't want to know his name, and she certainly didn't want him to discover that the woman he'd made love to wasn't who he thought she was. All she longed for right now was that he'd fall asleep before that damning piece of evidence became quite clear.

He rolled from her then to lay at her side, his eyes closed, his body gleaming with a thin veil of perspiration, and Rebecca dared to study his long, muscular physique from out of the corner of her eye when a flash of lightning lit up the room. He looked like a bronzed god lying there. Every aspect of his sinewy frame was perfectly proportioned and well-defined—and tempting to touch. She closed her eyes, willing the sensation to go away. It made her feel cheap. Despite her efforts, she shivered.

"Are you cold?" his deep voice asked.

Rebecca was afraid to move, lest she stir his passion again—the way hers threatened to do.

Pushing himself up on one elbow, he reached for the blankets that were crumpled at the foot of the bed and drew them up over them both without waiting for her to reply. Then, leaning in, he lightly kissed the tip of her nose and fell to her side again.

"Thank you," he whispered after a long, relaxing sigh. "I

can't remember ever having such pleasure from a woman."

In the darkness he searched for her hand and covered it with his own much larger one. Fingers entwined, he laid their hands against his side, and Rebecca could feel the strength of his thickly muscled ribs and the slight movement of his chest each time he took a breath. If she hadn't been so frightened of what he might do should he learn it wasn't Penny lying beside him, she might have enjoyed his tenderness. As it was, she worried he wasn't through with her as yet. Biting her lower lip, she kept her eyes tightly closed, praying he would think she had drifted off to sleep.

What seemed like an eternity passed before his steady breathing told Rebecca that he had fallen asleep again. Carefully, she slid her hand from his, then waited to make sure the slight movement hadn't awakened him. He stirred, then rolled to his side away from her, and she gave a breathless sigh of relief. Now all she had to do was get dressed and go home. A tightness gripped her heart when she realized how easy that was to say, while in reality it wasn't that simple at all. Yes, she could leave this bed, don her clothes and return to the boardinghouse, to her own bed. She could pick up her life again as if nothing had happened. But she would never . . . *never* be the same again. A strange feeling came over her then, and she struggled with it while she slipped from beneath the covers. Fighting desperately to ignore it, she hurriedly tiptoed to the hearth and tugged on her damp clothes. Maybe Penny thought lying with a man— or in her case, a variety of men—was something to do with her spare time, something she could forget about when the sun came up. But Rebecca knew differently . . . now. She would never forget what happened here. She would never forget the night a man made love to her. She would never forget *him*. Lifting her heavy cape off the chair, she turned with it clutched tightly against her chest. It wouldn't take much to learn his name. All she'd have to do is ask Penny . . . subtly, of course. She didn't want Penny to get suspicious. This was one secret she'd keep to herself. She didn't want *anyone* to know she enjoyed— She flinched at the thought and moved toward the bed, drawn by some mystical force.

The storm had grown less violent, but lightning still illuminated the sky occasionally and flooded the dark room with a searing light. Maybe it was best she never know his name, she thought, but she deserved to know what he looked like. Hesitant, she started to circle the bed, realized that without the aid of a candle she wouldn't see much more than she already had and turned back for the fireplace and the taper sitting on the mantel. Laying aside her cape, she touched a flame to the wick, shielded the flickering light with her hand cupped around it and walked back across the room. The moment the soft glow from her candle fell upon his sleeping face, Rebecca's breath seemed to leave her. He was the most exquisite looking man she had ever seen. His dark blond hair was streaked with golden strands, his jaw was strong and square, his lips full and sensuous, his nose straight and thin, and sinfully thick, black lashes lay against the copper complexion of his face. He had wide, high-set cheekbones that added strength to his rugged brow, and even while he slept, a slight frown deepened the faint lines at the corners of his eyes. He was stretched out on his side, and the coverlet lay enticingly over his hip, leaving his upper torso bare and gleaming in the warm glow of candlelight. It took every ounce of self-control she had not to reach down and trace her fingertips along the smooth contour of his wide shoulder and thickly muscled arm, or the sinewy ripples of his chest and lean, hard belly. Even the distinctly rigid cord in his throat looked tempting, and she longed to press her lips against it. Flooded with a burning desire to set aside her candle, draw up a chair on which to sit and quietly treat herself to this magnificent view awhile longer, Rebecca sucked in a long breath and firmly reminded herself of the consequences if she did and he awoke to find her there. He would never believe she had been the one who came to his bed. He would think she was here now to rob him. That idea made her hand tremble, and when a distant boom of thunder reminded her that Penny would be coming to her room shortly, Rebecca forced herself to look away. All that she had now were memories. Experiencing the stinging bite of emptiness, she frowned at having felt such an emotion and retraced her steps to the hearth. Blowing out the flame and returning the candle to its place, she picked up her cape and headed toward the door. She paused a moment, fought the urge to look at him again, then took the key from the table and unlocked the door. Maybe she would never see him again, but the vision of his handsomeness and the beautiful moment they had shared would live forever in her heart. Twisting the knob, she quietly opened the door and made a silent exit.

Chapter Three

The sweet, fresh smell of early morning after a cleansing rain, the fragrance of magnolia blossoms and the soft, pale light of dawn filled the bedchamber and roused Alec from a peaceful slumber. Rolling onto his back, he stretched, yawned and lazily opened his eyes to look at the bright sunshine spilling into the room. It took him a moment to realize the window had been raised to let in the cool morning breeze, and once he had, he pushed himself up against the headboard, the cotton sheets pooled around his hips and a frown wrinkling his brow. As he recalled, the storm had been raging its fullest when he left the commons, and although he'd had a little too much to drink, he doubted he would have opened the window. It had been raining too hard. Another yawn caught him unawares, and he raised a fist to his mouth, suddenly remembering where he was and to whom this room belonged. A smile warmed his dark brown eyes as he thought of the little redhead he had met last night and the pleasurable moments they had shared right here in this bed. Obviously Penny had opened the window before she left the room this morning.

Crossing his wrists and placing them behind his head, he casually studied the interior of the bedchamber bathed in the pastels of early dawn. It definitely had a woman's touch. Pink curtains trimmed in white lace fluttered in the gentle breeze. The spread, which was crumpled at the foot of the bed, was of the same material and color. The walls were done in a pink and white patterned wallpaper and subtly complemented the red brick fireplace. The towel rack, woodbox, chamber pot, candleholders and numerous picture frames were all made of brass. White lacy cloths covered the table next to the door and the top of the dresser. Even the folding screen standing in the far corner had been artfully painted white with pink cloth inserts. Although it was a pleasant looking room, Alec knew he would tire of all its frills rather quickly if he were forced to live here. He preferred something a little more masculine. But then, he didn't plan on staying at The Red Lion Inn for very long . . . and certainly not here with Penny.

He drew in a long, relaxing sigh and stretched the muscles in his neck as he dropped his arms to his sides. He would have liked to spend another night with the young lady. She had made him laugh, something he hadn't done in quite a while. But he had learned long ago that sharing the company of a woman for more than one night could prove disastrous. They tended to think he cared more about them than just a passing fancy. And he neither had the time nor the inclination right now to get involved in any kind of relationship.

A vague smile wrinkled his cheek and revealed the faint dimple in the corner of his mouth as the memories of last night clouded his mind. Even now his blood warmed as he recalled the gentle thrust of hips in response to his lovemaking, and the passionate kisses in answer to his. He never suspected Penny could pleasure him so fully. Yes, it was tempting to stay one more night. It would be worth the risk just to taste those sweet lips, feel her nails claw his back in unbridled lust, and experience the release of *the* most delicious, wanton sensation he had ever enjoyed. His dark eyes sparkled with the vision he conjured up: pale, silky skin, thick, luscious hair, firm round breasts, delicate features, and those eager kisses that made his pulse quicken even at the thought of them.

Closing his eyes and resting his head back against the pillow propped up behind him, he recalled how very nearly he had cheated himself out of such a gratifying evening.

When he suggested that the two of them resume their conversation somewhere more private, Penny had told him that she wouldn't be able to leave the commons until the last customer had gone. It was part of her job, and if she disappeared early, Mr. Lewis would get suspicious. And *that* could mean the end of her employment. Not wanting to be the cause of Penny's having to find new work, he relented. But when it became apparent that the men sitting around the far table had no intention of leaving for some time to come, and the wine he had drunk and the exhaustion of his trip made his eyelids heavy, he had asked if he might wait for her in her room. Penny had been quite willing, he remembered, and he could only assume it was because he had finally committed himself. However, once he had stood, his liberal consumption of wine made his head spin, and he'd had to lean heavily against the table to steady his balance. Laughing, Penny had slipped her arms around him and guided him up the stairs, down the hall and into her bedchamber. He wasn't sure if she helped him disrobe or not, but he could remember being alone in the room when he fell into bed. The cool sheets against his naked flesh felt good, and he had buried his face in the pillow to wait. Obviously, he had fallen asleep within minutes, for the next thing he remembered was the smooth skin beneath his hand when he rolled to his side and stretched out his arm. He wondered now if maybe Penny had changed her mind when she didn't awaken him or simply didn't want to disturb him. Whatever the reason, he was glad he hadn't had *that* much to drink not to come fully aware of the tempting treasure lying beside him in bed.

Long, lean fingers absently rubbed the smooth flesh over his wide, muscular chest as he pleasantly recalled the feel of her naked breasts pressed against him. A smile graced his lips. A long, happy sigh escaped him. Then, suddenly, his eyes flew open, and he sat up in bed. Staring down at the mattress where they had shared an exquisite night of passion, he bolted, came up on his knees and yanked the covers off the bed, sending them sailing to the floor.

"Sweet God in heaven!" he growled, his brow knotted in a

fierce, angry frown.

The blood stains on the fresh, white sheets confirmed what he had vaguely suspected last night. He had felt her stiffen beneath him at the first thrust of his hips against her. He had drawn back. He had searched the darkness for the look on her face that verified what he had done. He had waited for her tears, her cry of anguish. He expected a sign—something, *anything*—that would have told him he had bedded a virgin. But she hadn't moved or uttered a sound. In truth, he thought he had seen her smile.

"What have I done?" he moaned, falling on one hip, his knee bent and his elbow braced on it while he combed his fingers through his light brown hair. "Why didn't she tell me?"

The glorious memories destroyed, he twisted and swung his bare feet to the floor. Leaning with his hands braced on the edge of the mattress, he let his head fall forward, his eyes closed and a sick feeling tightening the muscles in his stomach. He never would have guessed in a million years that Penny was a virgin! She was too at ease. She said all the right words. She knew how to entice him. She hadn't been coy or shy. She hadn't blushed or been reluctant. *She* had been the one to suggest they spend the night together. Or had he imagined it all? Had he had *that* much to drink that he envisioned her saying it while in reality she had actually avoided the subject? Was that why she came to bed later without waking him up? Filled with remorse, he violently shoved himself off the bed and went to the washstand, there to pour the basin full. Bending, he splashed the cold water over his face and neck, praying it would erase the cobwebs from his head. He must remember . . . every word, every look she gave him. Failing that, he straightened and absently allowed the cool rivulets to trickle down his chest and stomach. Chilled, a wide hand stopped their descent when he unconsciously rubbed away the moisture from his belly and then up over his chest while his gaze wandered to the window and the bright morning light sparkling on the panes. Long ago he had vowed that the only virgin he would ever take to his bed would be his wife. He wouldn't do to a woman what

71

his father had done to Lora. 'Twas his pledge. But in his heart he knew he would never marry, and that was the reason he avoided having affairs with women of a respectable moral standing. Penny, in no way, could be classified a whore—at least he didn't look at her with such ideas in his head—but he certainly didn't expect—

Angered, he whirled away from the washstand and crossed to the corner where he had shed his clothes the night before. Why had she done it? Why had she given herself to him when she hardly even knew him? Yes, they had talked and laughed for nearly an hour, but that hardly justified anything. And she had told him—or at least had given him the impression—that he was not the first! Was it a ploy? Was that what she *wanted* him to think? Why? What was her reason? Yanking on his breeches and stockings, he grabbed his shirt from the chair and shoved his arms into the sleeves. Surely she didn't assume he'd marry her just because she had tricked him. Having hooked the last button, he stuffed the shirttail in his breeches and reached for his ascot. He didn't believe that. Penny was too smart. He had realized that shortly after she sat down at his table. And she wasn't after money. Then what? Totally frustrated, and not being able to tie a satisfactory knot, he crossed to the mirror hanging above the dresser to watch as he tried again. Maybe he should just pretend he wasn't aware of what he'd done and let her be the one to bring it up—if she ever did.

Having come to a decision—vague as it was—he returned to the chair where he had laid his satchel and searched through it for his brush. If she really wanted something out of all this, she'd let him know. A half smile wrinkled his mouth as he stared at his reflection in the mirror again. Penny hadn't been at a loss for words last night. And he doubted there was anything that could change that aspect of her personality. Brushing the thick strands of his dark blond hair into place and wishing he had taken the time to shave, he crossed back to his satchel, tossed the brush inside and gathered his things. He'd have breakfast in the commons where he was sure he'd find Penny, then visit the newspaper office. Walking to the door, he twisted the knob and pulled the portal wide. But before he moved to step into the hall, he paused long enough to glance over at the bed. A mixture of pleasure and regret knotted itself around his heart, and with a heavy sigh, he lowered his gaze, shook his head and strode from the room.

Penny wasn't sure exactly when she had come to the decision to make an exception with Alec Diamond, but she had. It might have been from the moment she saw him and realized that he wasn't the usual sort she took to her room for the night, or perhaps once it became apparent that he'd had too much to drink. She preferred her male company to know exactly what they were doing. Alec Diamond obviously hadn't. She knew that when he stood up and had trouble balancing himself. It wasn't that she didn't like making love to a man who'd had a little too much wine, but it was more gratifying for her to think that he wanted her solely for herself and not because he'd had to bolster his courage. Whether she had already made up her mind or not, however, the moment she found him sleeping soundly in her bed, she had elected not to disturb him. What confused her was why. The chances of her ever seeing him again after tonight were slim, and even if she did, there was no guarantee he would be interested a second time. So why deny herself the opportunity of spending one blissful night locked in his embrace? Wasn't he everything she had longed for in a man? He was gorgeous, *extremely* well-built, had money and dressed better than any man she had met. His manners were superb. He had a sense of humor and was keen witted, and not once did he talk down to her or raise an accusing eyebrow. He laughed at her jokes and made her feel good about herself. He was a gentleman, and Penny could think of no other reason for not crawling into bed with him except perhaps that she feared doing so would change his attitude toward her. And why that bit of knowledge made any difference, she'd never understand. They could have spent a very hot, passionate night together.

When morning came and she had awakened alone and in a

strange bed, she wondered if she had done the right thing. Seeing him now as he descended the stairs in the full light of day with his satchel and cape in one hand, his cane and tricorn in the other, made her curse her momentary need to feel righteous. All she could hope for now was that he understood. She'd simply *die* if he laughed at her. Grabbing a pot of hot water and the cup in which she had sprinkled tea leaves, she headed toward the table where he had elected to sit, doubting that he'd ever laugh at her. After all, hadn't she concluded he was a gentleman?

Alec spotted Penelope Dawson the moment he had a clear view of the commons, and he mentally braced himself for what was to come. In the short amount of time they had talked, he had come to like her very much. But it certainly wasn't enough to force him into marrying her if that had been her plan. And supposing it had been her reason for luring him to her room, he couldn't understand why she had chosen him. She didn't know anything about him. A sudden, chilling thought struck him, and his steps faltered as he left the last tread on the staircase and headed toward one of the empty tables in the back of the room. Maybe that wasn't true. Maybe she *did* know something about him. Maybe *she* was the one he was looking for.

Setting his satchel on the floor, his tricorn on the chair seat, his cape draped over the back and his cane propped up against the edge, he pulled out a second chair on which to sit and settled into it, his tawny brows drawn together in thought. Alec, like Geoffrey Synder, had assumed the worst about Daniel Heller, that the reason they had not heard from him in close to a year was because he was dead. Cold logic explained his demise as a simple form of robbery. After all, Daniel Heller had been a stranger in town, and he had brought a lot of money with him. Granted it didn't make sense that whoever killed him had waited until *after* Heller had spent his money, but perhaps that had been a part of the plan. Maybe there wasn't such a plantation up for sale as he had been led to believe. Maybe it had been a trick, and Heller found out about it after it was too late; and they had killed him when he tried to reclaim the money. A movement to his left caught his attention, and he looked up to see Penny walking toward his table. Perhaps her job was to select a man ripe for the picking, a man alone with money to spend and new to the area. It was possible, he supposed, but something about it didn't ring true.

"Good morning, Alec." She smiled sweetly as she set down the cup and poured hot water into it. "Did you sleep well?"

His suspicions about her faded with the reminder of how pleasantly his rest had been interrupted. Without realizing it, he smiled. "Never better."

Pulling her skirts to one side, Penny slid into the chair beside him, set the pot on the table and quickly glanced around the room to make sure no one was sitting too close. "Before you say anything, I want to apologize," she told him, her voice low and hardly more than a whisper.

"Apologize?" he questioned, genuinely surprised. Was this a part of her ploy? Frowning, he reached for the sugar bowl and spoon. If it was, he'd let her play it out. "For what do you feel the need to apologize?"

Penny wasn't sure just how to begin or what choice of words was best. She didn't want to come right out and tell him that she hoped their friendship could grow into something deeper. If he didn't feel the same way about her, that confession could send him running. And not into her arms! Chewing on her lower lip, she watched him add a teaspoon of sugar to his cup.

"For not coming to your room last night." Her heart fluttered when he set those delicious brown eyes on her. His soft laughter made her pulse quicken.

Alec couldn't believe she was that embarrassed about what they had shared that she'd go to the extent of pretending it hadn't happened. But then again why wouldn't she be? She'd been a virgin until last night. Maybe this was her subtle way of letting him know she hoped he'd keep it a secret. The smile disappeared from his lips as he studied the pretty face staring back at him. Was it possible this young girl had been all talk up until she met him and had suddenly decided to find out what it was really like to lay with a man, then regretted her decision once she had? It certainly explained a lot of things. It also made him feel quite guilty—and stupid for not having figured it out before it was too late. Tenderly, he reached over and covered her hand with his.

"I understand." He smiled softly.

Penny straightened in her chair. "You do?"

Alec nodded and raised his cup to his lips. Wincing when the hot tea burned his tongue, he set the cup back down and leaned forward against the table, his arms folded in front of him. "A woman's first time should be special."

Penny's brown eyes widened, and laughter danced in their ebony depths. Her lower lip trembled, and the muscles in her throat constricted. Unable to contain her mirth, she quickly raised a hand to her mouth and nearly strangled on her glee. "Oh, I agree," she giggled, tears glistening in her eyes. "But it's been so long ago that I just wish I could remember if it was."

Alec couldn't explain the sensation that came over him then. He was both hot and cold, relieved and appalled, positive and confused. Unable to reply, much less draw a breath to speak, he just sat there staring at her.

Mistaking his silence to mean she'd insulted him, Penny swallowed her laughter and quickly touched his arm. "I don't mean to laugh. Your concern and thinking I've never—well, it's *very* gallant. I'm flattered. And a little surprised you couldn't tell right off—" Trying to explain made her uncomfortable for some strange reason, something she seldom experienced. She, too, suddenly found herself unable to speak. Several times she opened her mouth and started to reply only to snap it shut again when the right words wouldn't come. Frowning in frustration, she fell back in her chair and glanced off to her left, wondering if she shouldn't just admit to the truth . . . from the very beginning. But her companion denied her the opportunity to let him know what she was considering.

"I've always enjoyed a good laugh, Penny," he began, a bitter tone in his voice, "but not when it's directed at me. Perhaps you should start at the beginning. I'm curious to know what you and your friend hoped to prove?"

"Prove?" she echoed, turning to look directly at him. "I

wasn't trying to prove anything. And I wasn't laughing at your expense but my own." The anger that glowed in his dark eyes told her he wasn't at all convinced. Then something else he said hit her. "My friend?" she asked slowly.

One tawny brow raised dubiously. "Well, you certainly didn't act alone."

Penny didn't understand what he meant. "I didn't?"

His patience running thin, Alec heaved an irritable sigh and said, "What is it you want from me?"

Penny was tempted to tell him that all she wanted was what she had foolishly passed up, but from the look on his face, she knew he was in no mood to hear it. She also wondered if it was worth all this. Her gaze slipped from his handsome face to the wide expanse of his chest and shoulders and the perfect fit of his richly tailored clothes, and she knew the answer. Yes. It was more than worth it. She started to rise and was jerked off her feet when Alec grabbed her arm and shoved her back down in the chair.

"I just thought I'd bring your breakfast, and I could explain while you ate."

"I've lost my appetite," he snarled. "Just talk."

Penny really couldn't comprehend his anger. It wasn't as if she had stolen anything from him. She had simply changed her mind about sleeping with him. Had he been any other man she propositioned, she would have told him to go to hell and stormed off. But he wasn't. She liked Alec Diamond. A lot!

"I moved here from Richmond a few months back," she began, "to get away from my parents. I love them dearly; but they're such stuffy sorts, and I knew they'd never approve of the kind of work I wanted to do." She thought of Rebecca and her friend's similar attitude and smiled. "I'll be the first to admit, openly and willingly, that I enjoy a man's company—in and out of bed. They lead such adventurous lives and add a little zeal to my own. Then you came along." She hoped what she was about to admit wouldn't send him on his way. "I knew right off you were different. Your smile was sincere, your laughter honest and you treated me like a lady, even if you thought otherwise." She grinned at him, but when he merely stared back at her without so much as blinking, she cleared her throat and continued. "I'm probably insane for telling you this, and I'll more than likely regret it for as long as I live; but the reason I changed my mind about coming to your bed is because—" she gulped, took a deep breath and blurted out—"I didn't want you to think I was a whore. I was hoping there might be a chance for us."

Alec had sat by silently listening to every word, wondering just how much of it was true. But when she said she hoped he didn't think she was a whore, it struck a painful chord in his past. His mother had been undeservingly labeled with such a title.

"I never consider a woman a whore simply because she chooses to lie with a man without the benefit of wedlock, Penny," he said quietly, solemnly, his gaze drifting away from her. "And that includes you." Whether she responded to his generosity or not, Alec wasn't aware of it. His thoughts had wandered back to the luscious curves, silken flesh and sweet fragrance of the woman he had held in his arms, and he frowned when the full weight of what transpired twisted his insides. *If she wasn't Penny, then who was she?*

"Do you have a roommate?" he asked suddenly, his eyes still averted.

"A roommate?" Penny frowned.

Praying he was right, he looked at her. "Do you share your room with anyone?"

"Not on a return basis." She grinned wickedly. "My 'roommates' only spend one night and never two in a row."

"I mean a woman," he corrected.

"God, no!" Penny shrieked. "I thought I made myself perfectly clear. I like men!"

Alec started to amend her misinterpretation and decided against it. *This* woman had been a virgin, and until he found out who she was and what she was doing in Penny's room, he'd keep their interlude a secret.

"Oh, I get it," she mocked disgustedly as she came to her feet. "You're telling me that I missed my chance and you're

78

no longer interested. Well, even if I had a roommate, I wouldn't tell you about her. And I wouldn't tell *her* about *you*. She can find her own man." Realizing that she was talking about someone who didn't exist, she shook her head and started to walk away. "I knew I'd be sorry."

"Penny," Alec called, stopping her before she had gone very far, "that isn't what I meant."

"Oh?" Dark brows slanted downward. "And what did you mean?"

"That I was disappointed you had changed your mind." He smiled. "I truly was looking forward to a pleasant night spent with you." Rising, he held out a hand to the chair she had vacated. "Please, sit awhile with me."

Penny's face glowed. "Really? You're really sorry?"

"I'd have to be a fool not to be." His grin widened, and he laughed at the way Penny fanned her fingers beneath her chin as if the room had suddenly grown hot and she was about to faint.

"All right. But I'll get your breakfast first. Then maybe I can convince you to spend another night here at The Red Lion—at least until you've concluded your business."

"You won't have to talk too hard, Penny," he admitted. "I was already thinking I'd do just that." What he didn't tell her was why. If he could fix it so that his room was next to hers, he'd be able to watch for any guests of the female gender coming to pay Penny a visit. If she knew nothing about the young woman he had gotten to know quite intimately, he guessed he'd have to figure out who she was on his own. He settled back into his chair and absently watched the bubbly, little redhead walk away toward the kitchen while he mentally went over everything he knew about his mysterious lover—which wasn't very much.

He vaguely remembered hearing the door to Penny's room open sometime in the middle of the night, after he had fallen asleep. He also remembered Penny telling him to lock the door behind her when she left and that she'd use the spare key hidden on top of the door frame to let herself back in. He was almost certain he had, and that meant whoever his visitor was knew about the second key and where it was kept.

Thus, the lady had to be a friend of Penny's. One sandy-colored brow lifted skeptically. That bit of knowledge might not be as valuable as one would think. Penny was a very likeable sort and probably had numerous friends—both men and women. But at least it was a start.

Reaching for his cup of tea, he took a drink while he idly cursed the shadows that had kept her identity a secret. He wasn't absolutely positive about the color of her hair, only that she wasn't a blonde. He'd have noticed the pale locks of hair whenever the lightning flashed. Since redheads weren't that common, he deduced his lady was a brunette. He didn't even bother speculating on the color of her eyes. She was delicately boned—he knew that firsthand—and he guessed her to be nearly the same height as Penny. She wasn't as well endowed— A devilish smile flashed across his face and disappeared as he imagined himself staring at the bosom of every woman he came across and how often he would get his face slapped. And yet there was a strong chance the woman he was looking for wouldn't react that way. She'd more than likely blush and turn away and hurriedly excuse herself from his presence. That thought brought a frown to his brow. If he didn't know what she looked like, then how could he assume she'd be able to recognize him?

This could be more difficult than I first thought, he mused, drinking the rest of his tea and setting the cup aside. *And I truly don't have the time to waste right now.* A disappointed look came over his handsome face when he decided finding the little lady would have to wait. It was more important right now for him to investigate Heller's disappearance. Glancing up at the clock which hung on the wall behind the bar, Alec guessed he had about a half hour to eat his breakfast before the newspaper office next door opened up for business. If he had to, he'd pay extra to see that his advertisement ran in this afternoon's paper. Otherwise, it would have to wait a week, and he didn't have that kind of time.

Standing in the doorway of her office, Clementina Rind

silently watched her young employee blowing her nose for what seemed the hundredth time this morning. And Rebecca had only been at work for an hour. "Darlin'," Mrs. Rind called to her, "are you sure you shouldn't go home and climb back into bed? You sound awful, and it could get worse."

"It's only the sniffles," Rebecca swore, rubbing her sore nose and then stuffing the handkerchief back in the pocket of her apron. "I'll be fine. And if I went home, who'd help set type?" She nodded at the tray of tiny letters she was artfully arranging into words.

"I could ask the Henderson boy. He loves to help."

"I mean no disrespect, Mrs. Rind, but if Tommy did it for you, you'd spend half the afternoon correcting his mistakes. I'll be all right," she promised with a smile. "Besides, you have an appointment that will probably keep you busy all morning, and I want to finish my article. If you approve, I'd like to see it get in today's paper."

Taking her shawl from the coat rack just outside the office door, Mrs. Rind draped it over her shoulders and said, "I might possibly save you a lot of time if you'd tell me beforehand what the article's about. You know the newspaper has restrictions on the kind of news we print."

Rebecca understood what Mrs. Rind was really saying. She didn't want to print a story that might cause trouble—for the *Gazette*, herself or her young protege. Rebecca couldn't do anything about the first two, but she knew she could take care of herself. After all, if the article had a male by-line, who'd know she wrote it? And if Rebecca told Mrs. Rind ahead of time, Mrs. Rind would say no before Rebecca could prove how exciting the story was. Maybe Rebecca was truly writing it to satisfy her own needs, but she planned to point out to Mrs. Rind that a story like this would sell a lot of newspapers. And that meant more money, something the *Gazette* could use.

"I'd prefer you read it the way it should be told rather than hearing me say it. Besides, I can use the practice."

Mrs. Rind knew she didn't have to read it to know it wasn't the sort of story that should appear in the *Gazette*. She knew Rebecca too well to think otherwise. The lovely young lady had already written a great number of articles Mrs. Rind had had to turn down. And it wasn't because Rebecca didn't pen an exceptional piece of work, but because of its topic and content. If William were alive and Rebecca were a man, her stories probably would have been printed. As it was, taking such a chance was too dangerous. Rebecca knew that, since Mrs. Rind had told her often enough. Yet, despite their differences on the kinds of articles that should appear in the *Gazette*, Mrs. Rind had to respect the young woman's courage and determination.

"Very well," she replied, heading for the front door. "Just don't let it interfere with your work."

"I won't," Rebecca guaranteed, excited now that Mrs. Rind had at least given her permission to write her story. It was a beginning. Now all she had to do was present it in such a way that Mrs. Rind couldn't possibly say no. Biting her lip to keep from shouting out loud, she watched Clementina Rind open the door and step out into the hall, the tiny bell hanging over the archway tinkling loudly.

"I'll probably be gone for most of the morning," she advised, her hand resting on the knob. "Now, should you change your mind about going home to bed, find Tommy and tell him I said he was to finish up. All right?"

"Yes, ma'am." Rebecca nodded. "But—"

"But you won't," Clementina finished with a chuckle. "I know." Smiling warmly at her young friend, she pulled the door shut behind her and missed the restrained but exuberant squeal of delight coming from the one she left behind.

For the next half hour, Rebecca worked frantically to finish up setting the type with only a minimum of interruptions. Andy Burns delivered the paper Mrs. Rind had ordered from the mill, she had to pause a moment to blow her nose, Carl Shrump came in to pay his bill and Tommy stopped by to see if there was anything he could do to help. Rebecca had been tempted to say yes, that he could set type if he'd do it for nothing. It would give her a little extra time to finish her story. But she also realized that what she had told Mrs. Rind about Tommy's numerous mistakes was true, and she'd wind up with more work than what she started with if she allowed him to help. Therefore, she had to tell him that there wasn't anything for him to do right then, but that maybe he could check back later, in case something came up. Glancing up at the clock, she was surprised to learn how much she had accomplished in such a short time, and since she was more than halfway done, she decided to sit down at her desk behind the counter and start working on her story.

On her way to the office this morning, she had gone over most of what she wanted to say in her head and in what order it should be written. Thus, the first three lines came easily. She wanted the people of Williamsburg to know that there were some unanswered questions about the death of a young, black slave named Eli and that it was the opinion of this writer that his demise wasn't the result of an accident. She wasn't sure if she should add the part about the possibility that the murderer walked with the use of a cane or that footprints near the scene showed a distinct impression in one of the heels, a mark that would be easy to identify. Falling back in her chair, she absently ran the feather tip of her quill under her chin, deep in thought. If only she had the time to visit Blackstock . . . if only she had the time to find the man with a cane and a nick in the heel of his shoe . . . if . . . if . . . if—

A sudden, unexpected sneeze tickled her nose, and Rebecca barely had time to retrieve her handkerchief. She'd suffered with this kind of ailment before and knew she would again. But it was the manner in which she had taken ill in the first place that made her resent being sick. Suddenly her entire experience from the night before flashed to mind, and the most devastating part—the part she had, up until now, forced herself not to think about—brought a hot blush to her cheeks. Fighting desperately not to give in to the vision, she abruptly left her chair and crossed to one of the side windows to stare outside at the bright morning sunshine.

The Ludwell-Paradise House was located next door to The Red Lion. The structure, the largest townhouse in the city, was originally built to accommodate the Ludwell family. But space meant money, and after a short time, the family moved out and the rooms were rented to various businesses. William Rind had chosen one of the more spacious rooms on the first floor to house his printing press, files and desks as well as the supplies it took to run a newspaper, while his family lived upstairs. Only a distance of thirty feet separated the Ludwell-Paradise House from The Red Lion, and once Rebecca stood before the window looking out, her efforts to put last night behind her crumbled when her gaze darted across the narrow lawn and fell upon the building where it had all taken place.

Her first reaction was to close her eyes and turn away, but only a second passed before she was staring at the two-story, brick structure again. Although sunlight gleamed golden against its red wall, in her mind darkness surrounded its stalwart presence and lightning flashed about the sky. A lithe form raced across the yard and disappeared inside. Laughter filtered out from the commons. Candlelight glowed in every window. But it was the shuttered aperture on the second floor that drew Rebecca's gaze. Inside the room, a warm fire burned brightly in the hearth, and beside it stood a man draped in white, silkened sheets. His bare, suntanned chest gleamed coppery in the flickering light, and his dark blond hair caught the pale shafts radiating from the fireplace. His eyes were shadowed by his puzzled frown as if surprised and confused by Rebecca's presence. Then he raised a hand and stretched out long, lean fingers, silently luring her closer. Rebecca could feel her pulse quicken, and even though she knew it was wrong, she started toward him. A faint smile parted his lips to reveal sparkling white teeth. Even now Rebecca's heart began to thump loudly in her chest, and the same titillation she felt last night tingled every nerve in her body. She truly didn't want to admit it—not to herself and most assuredly not to Penny—but she understood why her friend chose not to spend her nights alone, that being, of course, if they all were spent in such a manner.

Hugging her arms to her, she closed her eyes and let herself be swept along on the glorious waves of her imagined bliss. No harm would come from daydreaming. Then, just as their fingers touched and he was about to draw her into his embrace, his parted lips descending upon hers, the intrusive tinkling of a bell shattered the illusion. Startled by the sound, she jumped and opened her eyes, failing to understand the importance of it. There had been no bell, no untimely interruption. What did it mean? Suddenly embarrassed by the fact that she had allowed her good intentions to slip, she touched cool fingertips to her burning cheeks and turned around.

"Hello, Rebecca," Robert Gilmore leered as he stood with his arms folded over his chest and one shoulder pressed against the door frame. "I've missed you." His gaze boldly swept the length of her, lingered on her bosom then settled in a cold, devouring stare on her face again. "It's been a long time."

"Not long enough," she seethed, fighting down the revulsion that twisted her stomach into a knot and shattered the sweet memories of the night past. In their place came the sickening vision of the last time Rebecca had been alone with this man. She gritted her teeth and snarled, "What are you doing here?"

Smiling, he pushed himself away from the door and casually strolled closer to the counter separating them. "I had business to conduct here in Williamsburg, and since your stepmother and I haven't heard from you these last months, I decided to check up on you." He grinned suggestively and leaned his folded arms on the countertop, his eyes raking her slender form a second time. "But I can see you're perfectly all right."

"I was until two seconds ago," she hissed, raising a hand and pointing toward the door. "Get out!"

"Tsk, tsk," he mocked. "Is that any way to treat a customer . . . especially when he's married to your stepmother?"

"Lenore ceased being my stepmother on the day my father died," she raged. "I consider the two of you nothing more than leeches, and if I had the means, I'd see both of you thrown off my father's land."

An evil smile kinked the corner of his mouth. "Ah, but it's

no longer your father's land, Rebecca. It belongs to Lenore."
He straightened and moved toward the end of the counter.
"Or it did. Actually, it belongs to me now. Lenore gave it to
me as a wedding gift." He laughed venomously and rounded
the corner toward Rebecca. "The ugly bitch was so grateful
when I said I'd marry her, that she didn't care what the
conditions were. But you never knew that, did you?" He
paused in front of the desk when Rebecca darted behind it.
"It could be yours again, you know. I'm willing to forget
everything that's happened between us."

"What are you saying?" she howled. "That you'd get rid of
Lenore for me? You bastard."

The humor faded from Gilmore's eyes, and the muscle in
his cheek flexed repeatedly as he gritted his teeth, a sight that
made Rebecca tremble. She had seen that look one other
time. It had been the night he caught her alone in the stable,
the night he tried to force himself on her.

"I thought I had made myself perfectly clear the day I left
Twin Oaks. If giving up my father's land is the price I must
pay to be free of you, then I'll gladly pay it. You disgust me,
you lecherous viper, and if I didn't hate Lenore so much, I'd
tell her what you've said." She pointed at the door again.
"Now get out!"

Enraged, Gilmore made a grab for her outstretched hand,
catching her wrist in a cruel, bone-bruising hold as he
rounded the desk and yanked her forward into his arms.
Rebecca, caught off-guard, wasn't able to scream before his
wet mouth covered hers, but the instant she felt his hand
roughly grab her breast, she unleashed all the strength she
could find, provoked by her immense hatred of him and her
desire to see him dead. Slamming her forearm against his
wrist, she managed to knock his hand away while at the same
moment she tore her lips from his and spit in his face.
Shocked by her assault, Gilmore stiffened and let go of her.
But only a second passed before his rage boiled up tenfold
and his desire to have her turned to cold, hard fury. Fist
clenched, he raised it high, ready to strike when something
caught his arm and spun him around.

"I believe I heard the lady ask you to leave," the stranger

snarled, unhooking the handle of his cane from Gilmore's wrist, then jabbing it in his breastbone. "And I suggest you do so now."

There was something ominous behind the threat, and it glowed in the dark brown eyes glaring back at him, snapping Gilmore to his senses. Shifting his gaze from the intruder to Rebecca and back again, he slowly stepped away as he wiped the spittal from his cheek. He had no desire to test this man, but there would come a time when he would. He was sure of it. Rounding the end of the counter, he headed for the door, pausing when he reached it to snarl, "You'll be sorry you interfered." His hateful gaze fell on Rebecca, and in his thoughts he promised, *And you'll be sorry he did.* Whirling, Gilmore marched out and disappeared down the hall.

Trembling violently Rebecca fell back against the desk, her eyes affixed to the empty doorway while she rubbed the back of her left hand across her mouth, hoping to erase the sickening sensation of Gilmore's lips on hers. She despised that man with every ounce of her being, and she was sure all he felt for her was lust, a damning combination that promised to have a fatal end. If only there was some way to get him out of her life, she would.

The movement of the stranger crossing back to the door and looking out brought Rebecca out of her trance. But the second she recognized the man who had stepped between her and Gilmore, a flood of confused thoughts raced through her head, and she staggered back a step. What was he doing here? How had he found her? She turned her head in the direction of The Red Lion. Surely Penny hadn't told him. They were friends. Penny wouldn't tell on her best friend. She mentally shook off that possibility when she realized Penny had no idea what went on in her room last night. Then how . . . ? She shifted her gaze back on the man who stood silently watching her.

"Are you all right, Mrs. Rind?" he asked. "He didn't hurt you, did he?"

The deep resonance of his voice fell softly on her ears and made her heart flutter as she forced herself to shake her head. If Penny hadn't told him, then how could he have figured out who his late night visitor had been? And what did he hope to achieve by confronting her? Was he after an encore in exchange for her silence? Well, he wouldn't have it. She'd deny everything . . . about being at The Red Lion or even leaving her room at the boardinghouse. Miss Abigail could attest to that, since she hadn't the faintest inkling that Rebecca had climbed down the trellis. Rebecca would even deny knowing Penny. But first she'd have to meet secretively with her friend and tell her that they'd have to pretend they didn't know each other. If they weren't even mild acquaintances, how could he possibly think— Suddenly, the title he had used registered in her brain.

"Excuse me?" she questioned a little shakily.

"I asked if you were all right."

Rebecca's brow furrowed. "No. I mean, what did you call me?"

"Mrs. Rind," he replied, a bit puzzled. He thought that was the name he had been given. "You are Clementina Rind, owner of the *Gazette*, aren't you?"

Rebecca had to bite her lip to keep from laughing out loud. He didn't know! The arrogant fool hadn't recognized her! She was safe . . . for now anyway. But she'd still have to talk to Penny, if she wanted to keep it that way. Dropping her gaze away from him, she admitted, "No, I'm not Mrs. Rind. I only work here."

Alec felt a little foolish once he realized his mistake. This young beauty couldn't be much more than twenty, and he'd been told Mrs. Rind had five children. Unwittingly, his eyes dipped to her flat belly. She hardly looked like a woman who could have had that many offspring. She was simply too slender. "My apologies, miss. I guess I just assumed any woman I found working here in the office would be Mrs. Rind," he admitted, remembering his manners as he took his tricorn from his head and stepped closer. "And I know it's none of my business, but don't you think you should report what happened here just now?" He glanced briefly over his shoulder at the door. "Next time you might not be so lucky."

"I'll be all right," Rebecca told him as she gathered up pen, ink and paper and came to the counter. "I think you gave him enough of a scare that he'll head for home without trying something like that again." She could feel her cheeks pinken as she added, "And thank you for helping out. I don't—"

"You're welcome," he cut in with a smile. He would have liked knowing a little more about the man since he had openly threatened Alec, but since the whole episode seemed to distress the young woman, he decided against asking. Yet who could really blame a fellow for wanting to steal a kiss from her. She was probably the most alluring woman Alec had seen in a long while. Her thick, raven-black hair accentuated the pale blueness of her eyes and her creamy white skin. Her delicate features and pink lips would tempt any man to overstep his restraints on the chance she might be willing. Obviously in this case, she hadn't been, and Alec cooled his thoughts about her. She'd probably spit in his face, too, if he tried. She was definitely all woman, but there was a certain spunkiness about the manner in which she had dealt with the situation that warned him she could take care of herself.

He smiled warmly at her when she looked up to ask him something, then straightened with a frown when she wrinkled her nose, grabbed something from the pocket of her apron and spun away from him to sneeze. "God bless you," he remarked lightheartedly as his gaze quickly took in the long length of her slender back, her narrow waist and well-rounded hips. The vision of another flashed to mind, though he didn't know why, and he frowned again.

"Thank you," Rebecca replied, turning back to look at him as she dabbed at her red nose. "It's the price one pays for not coming in out of the rain." The smile she had managed to present him vanished instantly once she realized what she had said. The only thunderstorm that had hit the area in the past two weeks was last night. Admitting she had been out in the rain was nearly the same as telling him she had been at The Red Lion . . . in his bed! Her face flaming, she grabbed the quill and stabbed it in the ink bottle. He wasn't here to discuss her health, and the sooner they concluded their business, the sooner he'd leave! "I assume you're here to place an advertisement in this afternoon's paper," she said rather crisply, eyes averted.

Alec had been too busy enjoying her beauty to pay much attention to what she said. Now he wished he had. She seemed angry with him, though he couldn't imagine why. Or perhaps he had embarrassed her somehow. She certainly was blushing.

"Yes. I am," he answered, remembering that he truly had more important things to do than flirt. "I'm interested in buying some good cropland, four or five hundred acres, and I thought I'd advertise it in the *Gazette* to save time." He tilted his head to one side trying to see her face when she continued to stare down at the paper in front of her. "Unless you know of a place that's for sale."

"Sorry." Rebecca's tone was a little sharper than she had meant it to be, but she honestly didn't feel like being sociable any longer. Her head was pounding, she felt as if every ounce of her strength had drained from her, and she was tired of trying to pretend his presence didn't bother her. Then, suddenly, she realized what buying property meant, and her head came up. "You're planning to move here?" she asked, her eyes wide and chin sagging.

"Not necessarily," he laughed. "I already own a plantation, but I'm looking to expand. Why? Would that upset you if I did?"

Rebecca could feel her cheeks pinken all the more. "Of course not. I . . . I . . .". She frowned and lowered her head again as she concentrated on the message she scribbled down on the paper. "Will that be all?" she asked a moment later as she dropped the quill back in the bottle of ink.

"For now" came the quiet reply.

Rebecca's heart pounded in her chest, but she managed to appear as if she hadn't read more into his comment than what was on the surface. "And where will someone contact you if they're interested in your proposal? We really should include that."

"Yes, I suppose you're right. Just say they're to ask for Alec Diamond, and that I'm staying next door—at The Red Lion."

In Penny's room? she thought acidly, then wondered why

she had. "Yes, sir." She nodded as she picked up the pen and added the extra line. "That will be two shillings."

Alec dug in his waistcoat pocket for the required sum and instead withdrew the stickpin he had found near the dock when he arrived. He'd forgotten all about it until now, but seeing it again suddenly triggered all the events of the last twelve hours: being drawn to the spot where he had found the pin, thinking he had been watched, his ride into town, meeting Penelope Dawson, and finally and most vividly those pleasurable moments in bed. But with that thought came the memory of his discovery that he had made love to a virgin, a fact that rekindled his anger all over again. If he had only known beforehand, he never would have touched her.

Cursing beneath his breath, he shoved the pin back into his pocket in exchange for the correct amount of money he needed to pay his bill, unaware of how his sudden change in mood had brought a frown to the young woman's brow. He further failed to notice the shocked look that came over her face after he had laid the coins on the counter and stepped back to shift his cape to his other arm once he had donned his tricorn. Nor in his haste to make an exit was he conscious of the way her pale blue eyes widened as they dipped from his broad back and well-tailored clothes to the gold-handled cane he carried.

Chapter Four

"Ben," Penny called from the foot of the stairs, "since it's not very busy and I didn't get much sleep last night, would it be all right if I went to my room and took a nap?"

"Of course, Penny," the old man smiled. "To tell you the truth, I was surprised to see you up so early this morning anyway. You usually sleep in when you've had a late night."

Penny hoped the blush she felt warming her cheeks didn't show. "Couldn't sleep for some reason. It was almost as if I was lying in a strange bed. But I'll be all right after I've rested. Send someone up to get me in about an hour or so, would you?"

"Sure thing," he said, waving a hand before turning to the sole customer in the place.

An impish smile darkened Penny's brown eyes as she mounted the stairs, feeling a little guilty about lying to Ben. The bed she had slept in last night hadn't been her own, but the one in the room next to hers. In fact, she hadn't even gone to her room until the following morning and only then to check on Alec and change her clothes. When she found him still sleeping, she had gone to the armoire for fresh things, stayed long enough to don them and open the window a crack, then pause a moment at the foot of the bed to enjoy the view. His dark-blond tousled hair glowed in the morning sunshine, and his wide, muscular shoulders and bare chest gleamed a golden hue. He would never know how much willpower it took for her not to shed her clothes and climb in with him. He had *the* most magnificent body she had ever seen, and if she hadn't already made up her mind to court him into something a little more permanent, she would have torn the buttons off her dress in her haste to have him. But then he would have been like all the rest she had bedded, and she truly wanted their relationship to be different.

Upon reaching the top of the stairs, Penny stopped, sucked in a short breath and exhaled quickly while she straightened her spine and forcibly stilled her growing passion. If she ever did give in to her lust, Alec wouldn't get out of her bed for a week! The poor thing, she giggled to herself. He'd waste away to nothing. But think of his epitaph! Amused by her wanton thoughts, she chuckled out loud and headed toward her room as she searched the pocket in her skirt for the key he had returned to her this morning. Their talk had been encouraging, though at first she feared she had ruined everything. He promised he'd spend another night at The Red Lion, and that they'd dine together once he finished up his business at the newspaper office, visited the courthouse and talked with John Greenhow. He had confided in her that aside from his desire to purchase some land in the area, he was hoping to do some import business with the town's largest merchant. As she thought about it now, she realized Alec had never once named the place he called home, and although she found that curious, she excused her failure to ask on being tired. She'd correct that discrepancy at dinner.

Having unlocked the door, she flung it wide and went inside, nudging it shut again with the heel of her shoe. It felt marvelous to be alive, and if everything went as planned, each day that passed in her life would be even better. In all her twenty-one years, she had never been so attracted to a man as she was to Alec, and for all the wrong reasons! Was this what it felt like to be in love? Popping the buttons up the front of her dress free, she strolled to the window and raised the sash all the way open, her gaze drifting across the narrow plot of grass to the building opposite The Red Lion.

"Oh, Rebecca," she murmured, resting her brow against the cool windowpane, "wait 'til I tell you what's happened to me. You just won't believe it." Straightening, she squinted in the bright sunlight to see into the room where her friend worked, hoping to spot her as she walked past the window. There had been countless times before when she had, and she seriously considered hollering over at her if she did today. After several minutes passed and Rebecca never appeared, she realized this was something better left said in the privacy of her room anyway. Just as soon as she got a break in her work downstairs, she'd go to the newspaper office and—

"My God!" she exclaimed, remembering that Alec had said the *Gazette* would be his first stop this morning. "You've already met him." A warm smile lit up her face. "So what did you think, dear friend? Isn't he perfect? Doesn't he have great shoulders?" She sighed dreamily. "I'll bet he's magnificent in bed. How could he *not* be?" Shivering when a delicious chill ran down her spine, she hugged her arms to her and turned away from the window. "And how will I ever keep my hands off him?"

A splash of blue on the rug before the hearth caught her eye, and she turned her attention on it. Blue had never been and still wasn't a color she liked simply because she didn't look good in it. She didn't even like having blue satin trim on her petticoats or a piece of jewelry with a blue stone. Whatever it was, she knew it didn't belong to her. But might it be something of Alec's? Smiling enthusiastically, she started toward it, thinking to have something of his as a souvenir. But that thought vanished once she got close enough to see that it was nothing more than a blue ribbon. The image of her friend flashed to mind, and Penny remembered that Rebecca was wearing a blue ribbon in her hair when they talked last night in the commons. *But how did it get here?* she wondered. Had Rebecca come to visit her? When? Thinking to figure that out later, she yawned, laid the piece of satin on the mantel and turned for the bed. She'd take a nap, see if Ben could get along without her for a while longer and then go to the newspaper office and talk with Rebecca. She wanted to tell her friend about Alec anyway. Grinning deliriously, she paused beside the bed as she wiggled out of her dress and let it fall to the floor.

The color in her cheeks and the smile on her lips faded instantly once her gaze fell upon the bed, its rumpled covers, and more shockingly, the blood stains on the sheets. Confused, she couldn't imagine how they had gotten there. She had put fresh things on the bed just yesterday. If she didn't know any better, she'd swear Alec had company last night—Penny's tiny frame stiffened. Twirling, she stared, open-mouthed, at the blue ribbon while the conversation she and Alec had had this morning exploded in her brain.

What did you and your friend hope to prove? You couldn't have acted alone. Your friend! Rebecca! Blue ribbon. The blood stains. A virgin. Rebecca was a virgin!

"She *was* a virgin," Penny raged, "until she sneaked in here. *How could she?*" Furious, Penny whirled back to the bed, curled her fingers in the covers and ripped the sheets from the mattress. "He was mine! I saw him first! You don't even like men. You told me so. You said they were arrogant and that they used women for their own benefit. You said you'd *never* marry, that all you wanted to do was be a writer!" Tears burned her throat, and she choked back a sob. "Why did you have to lie to me, Alec? Why didn't you just tell me the truth, that you *do* think I'm a whore, that you prefer women who are virgins?"

Feeling as if her whole world had just crumbled down on her shoulders, Penny sank to her knees and buried her face in her hands to weep. Hadn't Rebecca tried to warn her? Hadn't she told her that someday she'd regret being so free with her affections? That one day a man would come along who would steal her heart and that he'd turn away once he learned about her past? Hadn't she agreed with Rebecca, but swore it wouldn't bother her? Hadn't she told her friend that she'd just laugh it off and look for someone else? Well, she wasn't laughing now. She was dying inside. Sobbing hysterically, she suddenly wished she had never left home. Maybe her mother and father were snobs, but they loved her. And right now she felt as if no one else did. Even her best friend had stabbed her in the back! How could she have been so cruel? Why? What had Penny ever done to her to deserve such betrayal? And right here in her own room! Her own bed! Dragging herself to her feet, she staggered to the wash basin and filled it with water. How they must have laughed at her. Poor, stupid Penny. She honestly thought someone like Alec Diamond would actually be interested in her! Bending forward, she splashed cold water on her face and washed away her tears. Well, she'd fool them. She'd never let on that she knew. She'd pretend—

A puzzled frown chased away her guilt, and she straightened as she mentally recited the words Alec had said and recalled how angry he had seemed to be. At first, after she apologized for not coming to his bed, he had told her that he understood, that a woman's first time should be special. Turning, she looked over at the mantel and the thin piece of ribbon. He had thought Penny was a virgin because the woman he had made love to last night had been a virgin. When she laughed and told him that she thought he knew she wasn't, he had grown very angry and accused her and a friend of tricking him. The color drained from her face. Dear God, could it be . . . ? Weak, she went to the bed and sat down to think.

Rebecca had stopped by the inn to borrow a horse so that she could investigate the site of Eli's death. An hour or so later, Alec arrived on horseback, and Penny hadn't wasted a moment drawing him into conversation. Granted, Alec and Rebecca could have met on the road along the way, but Penny doubted it. Rebecca wouldn't have put herself in that kind of a situation. And it certainly wouldn't have been enough time for Rebecca to change her mind about men! After Alec had eaten and they had shared a few drinks, she walked him to her room and left the key with him. She had been reasonably sure he'd fall asleep within minutes. What happened after that Penny could only speculate. Calculating the amount of time it would take for Rebecca to walk to the dock and back again placed her somewhere on the road when it started to rain. By the time she reached town, she would have been drenched and probably very cold. Thinking to wait out the storm, she would have come here . . . to Penny's room . . . a place where she could dry her clothes . . . a friend's place, a friend who knew all about her midnight activities.

Suddenly, Penny hated herself for thinking what she had about her best and only friend. And she was beginning to doubt her first impression concerning Alec. She knew Rebecca too well to think that she had freely given herself to him. She would have more than likely clubbed him over the head with something for even trying. And she certainly would have screamed!

Massaging her temples with her fingertips, she tried to envision what might have happened. Rebecca obviously let herself in with the spare key. Alec was probably asleep in bed, and Rebecca might not have noticed. Putting herself in Rebecca's place, she mentally acted out the part. Seeing the fire in the hearth, she would have hurried over to it and shed her clothes. That's why the ribbon was lying on the rug. Wondering if she was right so far, Penny left the bed and crossed the room, there to kneel on the rug and touch the thick braided cords. They were damp, and Penny's heart sank, thinking that the only way those stains could have gotten on the sheets was if Alec . . . had raped . . . Rebecca.

"Oh, Rebecca," she moaned. "This is all my fault. If I hadn't invited him here . . . if I'd have stopped you from going to the wharf, you wouldn't have gotten caught in the rain . . . if I had just left work early or told the other customers they had to leave . . ." Sighing heavily, she closed her eyes. And what happens now? If Alec didn't know who was in his bed, he'd surely like to find out. But then what? If he knew, what would he do?

"Well, it's something we'll never find out, dear friend," she announced aloud, pushing herself to her feet. "Until he's concluded his business here and left for home, you and I will pretend we don't even know each other."

Now all she had to do was find a way of talking to her without Alec seeing them. An idea came to mind, and she decided her nap would have to wait. If he saw her going into the newspaper office, he wouldn't think a thing of it. After all, hadn't he done just that as well? She cringed when she imagined how horrified Rebecca must have been to see him standing there in the full light of day. Another thought struck her. If Alec thought Rebecca was her, it had to mean it was too dark in the room to see her face. And if Alec couldn't see her, then maybe Rebecca didn't know what he looked like. It was all too much to try and figure out! And what if she was completely wrong about the whole thing? She shook her head and crossed back to the bed and the dress she had dropped on the floor. There was only one woman who knew about the spare key, and there was no other way into the room. She had heard Alec lock the door behind him. It *had* to be Rebecca.

A sadness came over her then, realizing the subject she and her friend were about to discuss was very delicate. She'd have to use a great deal of finesse in bringing it up. And if Rebecca didn't want to talk about it, then . . .

Every time Rebecca started to rewrite her story concerning the murder at the wharf, her hand would shake so badly that she'd make a mess of the paper and have to start over. And every time someone came into the office, the staccato sounds of the bell seemed to explode in her ears. She'd jump and glance up wide-eyed and half expecting to find the man who had made her so nervous standing in the doorway with his pistol drawn and aimed at her head. Robert Gilmore was a vile, lowlife; but he was nothing compared to Alec Diamond, the cur who had killed Eli, and as far as she was concerned, the fact that he had saved her from Gilmore's brutality made no difference. It sickened her to think that she had lain in the arms of a murderer, that she had actually *enjoyed* what happened. Glancing up at the window that overlooked the yard dividing the Ludwell-Paradise House from The Red Lion, her tiny chin dropped once she recognized the possible danger Penny was in. She should be warned. She should be told about Rebecca's suspicions and that she should stay away from Alec Diamond. Turning her attention on the printing press and the type which was still left to arrange, she dropped her quill in the bottle of ink and stood. She had to talk to Penny right away, and it would take another hour to finish her work here.

"Tommy Henderson," she muttered, rounding the counter toward the door. She'd lock up the office, find the Henderson boy and give him the key with instructions to finish up here while she ran an errand. Pausing at the threshold, she glanced back at her desk, wishing she had been able to finish her story. It really should go in today's paper. The people of Williamsburg should be warned. A hopeful gleam brightened her eyes. And who said there couldn't be a special edition? Hurrying into the hall, she pulled the door shut behind her, locked it and raced for the stairs. Tommy Henderson lived one block over and a few doors down. She'd take the back way out of the building and cut through the yard. Then she'd go to The Red Lion and talk with Penny.

An irritable frown creased Rebecca's brow a few minutes later as she hurried down Nicholson Street on her way to Palace. From there she'd head south a block to John Greenhow's General Store. Mrs. Henderson had sent her son there to pick up the bolt of cloth she needed to make new curtains for the parlor. Tommy had been told not to dally since his mother wanted to get a good start on her project before it was time to fix supper, but Rebecca knew that telling Tommy to hurry was like racing a tortoise against a snail. Any distraction that came his way would send him off in another direction. All she could hope for was to find him before that happened.

Glouchester Street, as always, was crowded with people and horses and carriages since this part of town, known as Market Square, was the busiest almost any time of the day. Rebecca had mixed feelings about the throng she encountered. It meant Tommy would have to wait his turn to buy the merchandise his mother sent him for, but it also meant Rebecca would have trouble spotting him in the mass of bodies milling in and around the general store. Nodding politely at the woman who bumped into her, Rebecca quickened her pace toward the front entrance.

"Good morning, Rebecca," someone called, and she looked in that direction to find Jon-Gregory exiting a side door of the wood-framed building. He was obviously on his way to the lumber house a few yards farther on where they stored items too big to display in the main building, since the muscles in his brawny physique flexed with the weight of the rocker he carried. "You aren't looking for me, by chance, are you?"

Rebecca quickly changed her destination and lifted the latch on the gate to step through it. "Only if you can tell me where to find Tommy Henderson."

Jon-Gregory stopped, set down the rocker and pulled a red bandana from his pocket to wipe his brow. "I saw him earlier this morning. But that was about an hour ago. Is he supposed to be here?"

"Yes. His mother sent him to buy some cloth. I need him to set type." As she spoke, she peered inside the doorway, craning her neck to look over the heads of the people in the way.

"Well, if you'll give me a minute to put this away, I'll help you look." He grunted as he lifted the rocker onto one hip. "But you know Tommy. His mind wanders. And so does his body."

Rebecca's cheek wrinkled. "Yes, I know. And it's extremely important that I find him right away."

A faint dimple showed with his smile. "Got a story that needs investigating, huh?" It was more of a statement than a question, and he didn't wait for her answer. "Somebody plant more flowers?" he called as he went inside the lumber house.

"I don't think learning about marigolds is any more important than you do, Jon-Gregory," she shouted back at the darkened entryway. "But it's a start. If I prove myself to Mrs. Rind—" A sneeze surprised her, and she grabbed her handkerchief to cover her nose and mouth.

"So, did you find out if they open and close at night?"

Rebecca finished blowing her nose while she frowned back at the black cavity where her friend had gone. "What are you talking about?"

A moment passed before Jon-Gregory's tall, blond-headed frame appeared in the doorway again. A smile graced his fair features as he stood with his arms folded in front of him and a shoulder braced against the doorjamb. "I assume that's why you sneaked out of the house last night—to see if marigold blossoms close when it's dark."

Rebecca felt as if she'd been hit in the chest with a rock. She couldn't draw a breath or collect the right words to respond. She just stood there, mouth agape, eyes wide and the color draining from her face.

Seeing her shocked reaction made Jon-Gregory chuckle. Straightening, he stepped down off the stoop and approached. "You'll never learn, will you, Rebecca?" he teased, drawing up close and reaching out to place a fingertip beneath her chin and lift it upward. "One of these days you'll pay for your foolishness."

I already have, she mused bitterly as she cast her attention away from him. "Does Miss Abigail suspect?"

"If she did, you'd be busy looking for a new place to stay," he guaranteed her. "Next time—and I'm sure there will be—come and get me. I don't want my witless friend roaming about the streets at night unchaperoned." He draped a long, muscular arm over her delicate shoulders and turned with her toward the store. "So did you learn anything?"

Rebecca had never been able to hide much from Jon-Gregory, but she was hoping he didn't have the slightest inkling as to what sent her off in the middle of the night. Keeping her eyes averted since they always seemed to give her away, she shrugged one tiny shoulder and said, "That marigolds always stay open."

"Rebecca," he warned, quickly grabbing a fistful of thick, black hair at the nape of her neck and giving her a shake. "This is Jon-Gregory you're talking to. I'm not stupid, you know. You went to the docks last night."

"Who says?" Rebecca snapped, angrily removing his grip on her hair and giving him a shove away from her.

"I do! I saw you climbing back up the trellis in the middle of the night, and since the last thing we talked about was Eli, I'd have to be a fool not to know where you had been. If I had suspected you'd go off chasing your fantasies about being a journalist, I would have tied you to the headboard for the night!" His lighthearted mood changed to one of vexation.

"Fantasies!" she rallied hotly. "I have no fantasies about being a journalist. *I am a journalist!* And the truth about Eli's death should be told. People have the right to know."

"To know what? That he died accidentally?" Jon-Gregory's suntanned face wrinkled with his angry frown.

"You don't think so!"

"That's one opinion!"

They were shouting at each other by now, but it didn't seem to matter. Nor did they care that people were beginning to stare at them from beyond the fence at the sidewalk and from within the general store.

"Two!" she screamed.

Jon-Gregory suddenly became aware of the eyes watching them, and rather than air their discussion publicly, he roughly took Rebecca by the wrist and dragged her toward the back of the building, unaware that his employer and a stranger were standing only a few yards away.

"Jon-Gregory Cole, let go of me!" she raged, yanking at the strong fingers wrapped around her arm. There might have been a time when Rebecca could win a wrestling match with her friend. But that would have been a few years ago when he was a half-grown willowy youth. He was a man now, with the strength, temperament and convictions of one. This was one match she wouldn't win no matter how hard she struggled. "You're hurting me!"

"Well, somebody ought to!" he stormed when she tried to kick him in the shin. "For your own good." He gave her a shove as he let go which nearly tumbled her to the ground, but he didn't care. And the icy-blue glare he received for his actions didn't affect him. He'd seen it before, and nothing really came of it except a few not-so-ladylike adjectives in reference to his character and parentage. He lowered his voice and grated out, "Let's just suppose the two of us are right about Eli. Let's assume it was murder—whether intentional or accidental. Right now his killer thinks he got away with it, which means you and I and everyone involved, unknowingly or otherwise, are perfectly safe. Then along comes this mule-headed troublemaker who insists on telling the whole world that she *thinks* Eli was murdered."

"I have proof!" she exploded.

Her announcement stopped him cold. He may have seen her running back across the yard early this morning and suspected she had been at the docks snooping around, but he had also deduced she wouldn't have found anything. Eli's body had been carried away quite some time earlier, and there was nothing left to see.

"What kind of proof?" he asked quietly, his blond eyebrows drawn together in a dubious yet interested frown.

Rebecca's anger disappeared instantly once she realized that at least one person was skeptical enough about the situation to listen to what she had to say. However, she didn't feel like sharing her information until *after* it appeared in print.

"You'll have to wait and read about it," she answered with a cocky toss of her thick, black mane.

"Rebecca," he growled through clenched teeth. She certainly could be hardheaded when she wanted, only *this* time it wasn't over something as unimportant as who should have the last piece of pie. *If* she was right about Eli, she could get herself killed, and he'd never be able to live with it knowing he could have done something to prevent it. "I suggest you tell me everything you think you've learned *before* it appears in the newspaper. There's a slight chance, you know, that you could be wrong, and printing a story that accuses someone of murder could have some very permanent effects."

"And it could also bring the murderer out of hiding," she countered sarcastically.

"Oh, yeah, I agree," he snarled. "Right out of hiding and chasing after you! Give your evidence to the constable. Let him handle it."

"He already has," she snapped. "He's decided it was an accident."

"Then maybe it was!" Jon-Gregory roared.

A movement from in back of Rebecca gained his attention, and he shifted uneasily, cleared his throat as a warning to her that they were no longer alone, and nodded respectfully at his employer and the man who had stepped with Greenhow from around the corner of the building.

"Jon-Gregory?" Greenhow's expression told him that the man had already heard too much. "Is there something I can do to help?"

"Thank you, but no." Jon-Gregory smiled lamely. "Just a friendly squabble, sir."

"It sounded a bit more than that to me," Greenhow frowned. "Miss Wilde?"

Rebecca had chosen not to look at the man, hoping he would decide their discussion was none of his business and leave them alone to finish settling their differences in private. But having heard him address her, she realized it would be horribly rude not to acknowledge him. And since Jon-Gregory worked for the man, she didn't want to do anything that would jeopardize his job. Giving Jon-Gregory her meanest look, she masked her displeasure with a smile and turned around.

John Greenhow could have been standing there naked for all Rebecca knew, for once she had made up her mind to respond to his inquiry and had turned to look at him, her eyes instantly settled on the one who accompanied him. The color in her cheeks faded to an ashen hue, her mouth went suddenly dry and it felt as if someone was standing on her chest. Of all the people in Williamsburg, why did John Greenhow have to be talking to *him?* A pang of fear stabbed at her heart. Or had he followed her here? Did he somehow know she had figured out that he was the killer? Her gaze lowered from the man's golden hair and deep brown eyes to the cane he carried in his left hand.

"Miss Wilde, are you all right?"

Greenhow's voice as well as the pinch her companion gave her on the back of her arm startled her out of her stupor, and she blinked, then nodded.

"You'll have to excuse her, sir," Jon-Gregory quickly cut in. "Rebecca didn't get much sleep last night. Ouch!" The last was wrenched from him when Rebecca stomped the heel of her shoe on his toe. "Well, you didn't!" he snarled. "The storm kept a lot of people awake. That's all I meant." Tears of pain glistened in his blue eyes, and he was sorely tempted to return a hurt for a hurt. Up until the day Rebecca came to live at the boardinghouse, Jon-Gregory had been missing his little sister. Rebecca had been a substitute. But it was times like these he regretted ever wanting to change his quiet, uneventful lifestyle. Grabbing her arm, he jerked her back toward the side door of the general store, saying, "We're sorry to have bothered you, Mr. Greenhow. Next time Rebecca wants to talk to me, it will have to wait until we get home." He glared down at her. "Isn't that right?"

Rebecca didn't like the humiliating manner in which she was being led away, but since it had been her want to leave, she begrudgingly allowed Jon-Gregory's rough treatment of her. "Yes," she sneered, then shot Mr. Greenhow a halfhearted smile, glanced briefly at the handsome man standing next to him and hurried on ahead of Jon-Gregory.

None of the conversation Alec had overheard made any sense to him other than it was rather obvious the young man and his beautiful, fiery companion were in disagreement over her choice of a newspaper article. Something he did learn, however, was her name. Rebecca Wilde. He chuckled to himself, thinking that it suited her. She was definitely wild. And he was glad she was Jon-Gregory's problem. He wouldn't have the time to fend her off the way the young man had. One tawny brow lifted with the thought. Of course the distraction might be enjoyable since she had a lot of curves to make the contest interesting. Shrugging it off, since he had other matters to attend to right now, he turned his full attention back on John Greenhow and their discussion on the possibility of becoming business partners.

"Damn it, Rebecca," Jon-Gregory fumed as he led her through the crowded room toward a not-so-populated corner. "Why did you try to break my toe?"

"Because, you knothead, that man out there is the one who killed Eli, and you so much as told him I knew!"

Jon-Gregory straightened his lanky frame and peered over the heads of the customers toward the side door.

"John Greenhow?"

Rebecca's shoulders fell in exasperation. "No, not Mr. Greenhow," she moaned irritably. "Are you really that addle-brained? The man with him."

The lines around Jon-Gregory's eyes and mouth deepened. "You mean Alec Diamond?"

"Yes, Mr. Diamond," she sneered. "And how do you know him?"

"I don't, really," Jon-Gregory frowned. "But I do know enough to know you're wrong."

There it was again. Just because she was a woman, she was wrong. "Oh, yeah?" she jeered. "Well, you'll be crawling to me on your knees, begging my forgiveness once I've given my proof to the constable."

Jon-Gregory let out a long, disgusted sigh. "Why don't you just stick to things you know, like marigolds and what the governor had for dinner?"

Her tiny frame stiffened. "And why don't you concentrate on what *you* do best—carrying furniture! You don't have to *think* to do that." With an indignant toss of her silky hair, she spun on her heels and left the store through the front door.

Angry, green eyes watched Rebecca's departure from within the safety of the crowd milling about outside Greenhow's store, then shifted to the two men about to enter the side door.

"That's him over there," he said quietly to his companion. "The one with Greenhow."

A moment of silence followed while the second man observed the one pointed out to him. "I've never seen him before. Do you know who he is?"

"It doesn't matter," the first snarled. "What does is that he has the stickpin."

"And you want me to get it back."

"Of course, you fool," his cohort growled. "If she ever sees it and learns where it was found, you and I will be finished."

"And what about him? Do I kill him?"

"Only if he gets in your way. We don't want any attention drawn to him in case he's already shown that pin to someone. I don't need to tell you the consequences."

"So what do you want me to do?"

The first glared hatefully at the empty doorway. "Wait here until he comes out, then follow him. I don't know where he's staying, but I would guess you'll find the pin in his room somewhere."

"Then what?"

"After you've stolen it back, meet me at Raleigh Tavern."

The second man glanced in the direction Rebecca had gone. "And what about her? Something has to be done about her and soon."

"I know!" his companion barked. "But *I'll* be the one to decide what and when, not you. She's my problem. Remember that. And without me, you have nothing. You got that?"

His companion lowered his gaze. "Yes, sir. I understand. I just—"

"Well, don't! I'm not paying you to think or to talk . . . just to do as I tell you." He glared at the general store again, his green eyes glowing with contempt. "And if you mess this up, I'll find someone else who won't. You get my meaning?"

"Yes, sir," the other mumbled.

"Good," the first replied, his upper lip curled. Jamming his tricorn down farther on his brow, he turned and strode away.

Chapter Five

The warm, early afternoon sunshine poked through the sprinkling of clouds overhead and flooded the streets with a bright, golden light, quickly drying up what water puddles were left in the wake of last night's downpour. The melody of song birds filled the air, and the sweet smell of flower blossoms floated along on a gentle breeze. In all, it promised to be a pleasant day, and for the first time since his arrival, Alec was able to get a good look at Williamsburg. Although there were no palm trees, ferns or sandy, white beaches, the bustling activity on the streets reminded him of home. The capitol building at the far end of the main avenue seemed to be the center of everything, and Alec paused outside the courthouse long enough to study the three-story, brick structure before stepping off the sidewalk on his way to Shield's Stable and the horse Keenan had loaned him. Politics never interested him; but England's quarrel with her rebellious sons had opened up a perfect opportunity for him, and he decided to take further advantage of it.

He had changed his mind about visiting the courthouse first when his walk took him past John Greenhow's general store. He had been considering the prospect of expanding his trade with other merchants in the Colonies, and since Williamsburg sat so close to the bay, he wondered why he hadn't chosen it sooner. The disagreements between the Colonies and England had grown quite tense, and everyone seemed to be certain war was inevitable. If that happened,

Boston would be one of the first cities under siege, and the consequences would be devastating to his trade business. It was already becoming more difficult for his ships to sail into Boston harbor under a neutral flag, and since he had no desire to fight with or for either country, he'd be forced to withdraw his trade. Williamsburg, however, was far enough south and had enough of a population to warrant the risk, and John Greenhow had offered him an alternative.

Thinking of his conversation with the man brought a vague smile to Alec's lips as it also reminded him of the young lady he had met at the newspaper office this morning and again outside Greenhow's store. He'd never come across someone like her, and once he thought it over, he hoped he never would again. Her beauty and innocence were as alluring as water to a thirsty man. But her spitfire nature could be dangerous for one who hadn't the time to deal with it. Or the patience. Alec had neither. As much as he would have liked to get to know her better, he wisely chose to steer clear of her. She seemed the type to scream loud and long should she not have her way, and drawing attention to himself was something he couldn't afford. And he'd already done that by coming to her defense.

Pulling his gold watch from the pocket of his waistcoat, Alec checked the time. The courthouse, much to his displeasure, didn't open until noon, and since Greenhow had suggested he look over the warehouse at the docks and talk with Thomas Keenan concerning the manner in which a shipload of merchandise was dealt with once it arrived, he decided to use the time beneficially. Since the majority of Alec's goods—bananas, citrus fruits and other perishables— had to be handled quickly, it was essential that the warehouse and crew be large enough to accommodate the shipment, and this was something that had to be cleared before any kind of a deal was made.

Slipping the watch back in his pocket, Alec secured his hat over his brow and stepped off the sidewalk, carefully looking both directions lest he be trampled upon by one of the numerous rigs traveling the street. The stable was only one block over, but rather than follow the practical route to it, he decided to save time and energy by cutting between King's Arms Tavern and Coke's Office, through their side yards and on to the small, unpainted building in back. His return trip, hopefully, would be by carriage. He much preferred the softer ride of rich leathered cushions than the hardness of a saddle. He smiled crookedly as he hurried across the street and onto the sidewalk on the other side, thinking how much of a snob he had become. He never used to dislike horses. As a young boy living with his mother in their humble abode, he would have given just about anything to own a mare or even a swayback mule. It made travel a lot more bearable . . . and quicker.

Alec came to an abrupt halt once he had opened the gate dividing the two establishments and was met by a pair of youths playing tag. The first obviously thought to escape his friend in the same manner in which Alec meant to save time, and since the stranger didn't seem in any real hurry, the boy shoved Alec aside as he raced through the gate and off down the street, his partner close on his heels and laughing loudly. The image of a young blond-haired boy playing much the same game with a little girl back in London came to mind, and Alec smiled as he turned to watch the pair scamper off into the crowd moving along the sidewalk. Beth was pretty quick on her feet, but she could never manage to outrun Alec.

Beth, he thought, his smile fading. If he had stayed in England, he probably would have married her.

With a shake of his head, he absently glanced across the street and noticed a very slender, bedraggled young man staring at him. But once the youth realized Alec had spotted him, he quickly turned his head away, the floppy, wide brim of the straw hat he wore hiding his face from any further scrutiny on Alec's part. It didn't, however, stop Alec from appraising the young man's attire. The jacket hung from narrow shoulders, and its sleeves had been rolled up to free the use of the boy's hands. His breeches were baggy, his stockings torn and his shoes appeared to be too large for his feet. In all, he was a pitiful sight, and Alec decided to watch over his shoulder until he was well on his way to the docks.

This youth was obviously put upon by hard times and would probably go to any extent to have a man's purse . . . including Alec's. Drawing the gate shut behind him, Alec looked back at the boy one last time to find him studying something in the store window next to him, though Alec doubted it really held much interest for him. Cocking a brow, he turned and headed for the stable.

Bright blue eyes dared to steal a peek at the man across the street, then widened worriedly to find him gone. Making a grab for the hat that threatened to tumble from his head in the breeze, the unkempt youth hurriedly stepped into the street, then darted around the freight wagon in his way and raced for the gate where he had last seen his victim.

His dirt-smudged brow wrinkled irritably once he came within view of the man again, for it was painfully obvious he intended to go for a ride when he went inside Shield's Stable. It would be difficult to keep up with him unless the boy had his own form of transportation. His worry and the urgency of the moment increased when the man appeared again reining his horse onto Francis Street and heading west. It was a good guess he was going to the docks, and it was too far for the youth to run all the way. And he certainly couldn't afford to hire a rig or even the use of a horse. Frustrated, he moved out of the protective cover of the stable and stood, droop-shouldered, as he watched the well-dressed man ride away.

The heavily traveled Jamestown Road surprised Alec at first, and he could only assume a merchant ship had docked when he passed several carts and wagons covered with tarpaulins. He wished it was one of *his* ships they were unloading and that his business here was finished, that he had found Daniel Heller alive and well, and they were both back home in Jamaica. But it wasn't one of his ships, and he still hadn't a clue as to where Heller had gone.

As he neared the warehouse and the scores of men busily working in and around it, he pulled out his watch and took note of the time. Ten-thirty. He had an hour and a half to kill before the courthouse opened, enough time to talk with Keenan, observe how efficiently merchandise was unloaded, and return to town by noon. Edging the mare through the string of workers loading wagons, he only briefly glanced out at the huge merchant ship anchored at the end of the pier before focusing his attention on finding Thomas Keenan, the owner of the mare Alec had come to tire of. If he must ride, he'd like one with a little spirit. A devilish smile kinked his mouth as he thought that particular description could well fit his attitude about women. He liked them to have a little spirit, but he also preferred they come to rein the instant he demanded it. He thought of Rebecca Wilde and shook his head.

"Good morning, sir," Thomas Keenan called once he spotted Alec riding toward him. "Beautiful day, ain't it?"

Why do people always resort to discussing the weather when nothing else comes to mind? he wondered, nodding in halfhearted agreement. Reining up beside the man, Alec dismounted and handed over the leather straps.

"I'm here at John Greenhow's suggestion that I inspect how you run things when a shipload of supplies arrives," Alec confessed, his gaze averted to the procession of men carrying boxes and crates down the wooden walkway from the ship.

"Oh?" Keenan asked nervously. "He got a complaint?"

Alec turned a puzzled look on the little man.

"I do my best. If he's dissatisfied—"

"No, it's nothing like that," Alec interrupted once he realized Keenan had drawn the wrong conclusion. "Your job's not in question. I'm thinking about working up a deal with Greenhow as one of his suppliers, and I need to be assured you and your men can handle the goods I'd be shipping here, the kind that spoil if they're left in the sun too long." He glanced at the warehouse. "Or locked up somewhere."

"Fruits and the like?" Keenan guessed.

"Yes. But that wouldn't be all. From time to time I'd be shipping rosewood and mahogany and other kinds of lumber."

"I see no problem, sir," Keenan proudly guaranteed him. "I've been running the docks now for near to ten years, and ain't never had a complaint. But you're welcome to look around and see for yourself."

Alec glanced briefly at the man then out at the ship again. "Exactly what I had in mind."

For the next hour Alec wandered about the docks, watching and listening to the score of men working there. The merchant ship anchored at the wharf had just sailed in from Philadelphia carrying earthenware, flour, bread, chocolate, saddletrees, soap and a few pieces of furniture. Though Alec's cargo would have some of the same products, it was the silks, spices and tea that interested men like John Greenhow, not to mention the rare treasure Alec had offered him for a special price, an item which lifted the man's eyebrow appreciatively. While visiting in the Bahamas last month, Alec had met a man who was down on his luck and had been forced to sell some of his more cherished belongings, one of them being a Rembrandt. How the man came to own it, Alec didn't ask. But he planned to sell it for a lot more than he paid, and if Greenhow refused to meet his price, he'd keep the painting and find someone who would.

The sun high overhead and reflecting off the water turned the cool morning air into a hot, sultry day. Alec had long before shed his cape, and when Keenan offered him a cool glass of fresh cider to drink, Alec eagerly accepted it and moved into the shade. Fanning out his cape in the tall grasses near where he had found the stickpin the night before, he sat down, tossing his tricorn and cane beside him on his makeshift blanket. He always enjoyed moments like these— the solitude they offered— and for some odd reason, the image of Rebecca Wilde came to mind. He raised a curious brow as he fell back on one elbow, his long legs stretched out in front of him, ankles crossed, and the glass held in one hand. Instinct warned him to stay away from her, for no other woman in his life had ever attracted him the way she had. What puzzled him was why. They'd only spoken to each other for a few minutes. Granted, she was very beautiful, but there was something about her that made her different from all the other women he had known. Perhaps it was the way she had handled herself when that bloody reptile tried to force himself on her. Or maybe it was because Alec had found her working at a newspaper office. That was men's work. Someone like Miss Wilde should be married and chasing after a half-dozen children, not getting ink all over her hands. A vague smile lifted one corner of his mouth when he recalled the cute way she sneezed. It was a dainty kind of sneeze, one that embarrassed her.

The price one pays for not coming in out of the rain, he recalled her saying.

Absently, he studied a couple of workers struggling with the heavy chest they were trying to load on the back of a wagon, remembering how many times he had paid the same price for his foolishness as Miss Wilde had. And how much sleep he had lost because he had spent most of the night coughing, sneezing and blowing his nose—the way Miss Wilde's friend had said she had done. A frown flitted across his brow and disappeared. But was that really what her friend had meant? He had gotten the impression that Miss Wilde couldn't sleep because of the storm, not because she had been up all night sneezing. The frown returned. If that was all there was to it, why did she kick Jon-Gregory for stating simple fact? It was a question he wasn't meant to explore, for in that moment his attention was drawn to the man walking toward him.

"So, what do you think? Can we do the job?" Thomas Keenan asked, shoving his pudgy hands deep into his pockets and glancing out into the bay.

"I believe so," Alec remarked with a nod of his blond head.

A moment of silence followed in which Alec got the distinct impression Thomas Keenan wanted to say more. But before Alec could ask if something was bothering him, the little man exhaled a quickly drawn breath and smiled down at him. It was then Alec realized the warehouse manager simply liked to talk and that he was probably looking for Alec to start the conversation.

"Say," Keenan exclaimed, dropping his thick frame down in the grass near Alec, "did you hear what happened here yesterday morning?"

No, but I'm sure you're going to tell me, Alec mused,

114

hiding his grin. He shook his head rather than voicing his thoughts.

"One of Gideon Blackstock's slaves died practically right here where you're sitting."

Alec glanced briefly at the foliage surrounding the spot where he lay, then looked back at Keenan. "Oh? What happened?" He might as well ask. Keenan was sure to give him the full account anyway, and he should do the man a favor by acting interested.

"Nobody's real sure. One of Greenhow's men found him. He was already dead, but there was blood everywhere."

"Blood?" Now Alec truly was interested. He remembered the dark stain in the soil he had tried to identify before finding the stickpin. "Had he been shot?"

Keenan shook his head. "It looked like he had fallen and cracked open his skull.

Alec sat up and studied the area. "On what?"

Seeing that he had the man's full attention, Thomas was eager to tell his version. "That's just it. Me and Jon-Gregory—he works for Mr. Greenhow—"

"Yes, I know," Alec cut in. He had also learned from Greenhow that the young man seemed to be the only one who could control Rebecca Wilde.

"Well, anyways. He was the one who found him." Keenan scrambled to his feet and moved to the place where the young, black boy's body had lain, a distance of only a few yards from Alec. "Jon-Gregory said the boy was laying face down, but the wound was on the back of his head. And there weren't no rocks or anything here hard enough to do that kind of damage." Keenan glanced over his shoulder to make sure no one was close by. "You know what me and Jon-Gregory think? We think he was kilt—murdered."

"A runaway," Alec concluded.

"Naw," Keenan quickly disagreed. "Blackstock is good to his slaves. His have it better'n most." He pointed at the ground, indicating the one who died there. "This one was Blackstock's manservant. And the ol' man really liked him. Treated him like a son, some say. I don't know the man personally, but Jon-Gregory does. Everywhere Blackstock went, he'd take the boy." Keenan's eyes widened as he hurried back to sit down near Alec again. "Odd part is, Blackstock ain't been seen around town in months. So how come the boy was here? He weren't no runaway. Jon-Gregory's sure of that."

"Has anyone asked this Mr. Blackstock?"

"Nope, 'cause me and Jon-Gregory's the only ones what think the boy was murdered. Even the constable says it was an accident."

"So what is Jon-Gregory doing about it?"

"Nothin'." Keenan shrugged. "What can he do? Everybody's too scared to find out what really happened."

"Scared? Of what?"

"Losin' their jobs, for one. Nobody likes troublemakers. But more than that, they're afraid whoever kilt the boy will come looking for them if they start pokin' their noses in where they don't belong." Keenan drew up his knees and wrapped his arms around them. "'Sides, he was just a slave."

Keenan's final statement hit a raw nerve. That was the same kind of attitude Lora Stone's neighbors had about her death. She wasn't important enough for them to even bother attending her funeral. Just bury her and forget she ever existed. For a moment, Alec felt like smashing his fist into Keenan's nose without telling him why. The black boy was a human being, just like Lora Stone. They both deserved more. Suddenly Alec's past flared up to haunt him, and he felt like a hypocrite. There was a slight chance the young boy had been brought to America on Alec's slave ship. Sickened by the thought, he grabbed his tricorn and cane, quickly came to his feet, handed his glass to Keenan and then bent to swoop up his cape.

"I'll be going now. If you'd kindly fetch the mare . . ."

Alec's sudden decision to leave surprised Keenan. Awkwardly pushing himself up, he muttered something about it taking only a few minutes for him to get the horse, and hurried off.

Alec's deep brown eyes darkened with his anger as he watched the little man's clumsy gait. How long would this nightmare last? Would he ever find peace? The muscle in his

116

cheek flexed as he gritted his teeth and cast his gaze out toward the wharf. It seemed to him that every time he got close to forgetting about his illegitimacy, something flared up to remind him. Jamming his tricorn on his head, he tucked his cane under one arm and began to fold up his cape. It was too warm to wear it now, and Alec knew that the heat he felt had little to do with the temperature of the air.

When he thought about it later, he couldn't explain why his attention had been drawn away from what he was doing, but it had. And it had settled on the slender shape of the young man he had seen on the street in town. Surprised at first, then angered, he concluded the little ragamuffin had followed him! Well, it wouldn't do him any good. Alec was leaving, and if the urchin wanted to keep up with him, he'd have to race his horse full gallop—that was, of course, if he had one. Irritated when it seemed no one would leave him alone, he stormed off toward the stable and the man who awaited him there. A few minutes later he swung himself up into the saddle, and with a hard jerk on the reins, he spun the animal around and raced off away from the docks toward town, leaving Keenan and the young boy behind to stare in wide-eyed confusion.

The speed of the mare surprised Alec. Her stride was long and sure, and she soon put a good distance between them and the waterfront. The pace also soothed a little of Alec's dissension, and once the mare's breathing grew labored, he pulled back on the reins and set them at a slow, easy gait. Twisting in the saddle, he glanced back over his shoulder as if expecting to see the little beggar hightailing it down the road behind him as fast as he could run, and the vision it created made Alec laugh out loud.

"That will make you think twice about following me," he declared with a chuckle. And if he had time, he'd rein the mare off the road and wait for the boy. He deserved a good scare. The smile on Alec's lips faded into a devilish twinkle in his dark brown eyes. So why not? It was still a half hour before the courthouse opened, and it had been a long time since he had enjoyed this kind of sport. Besides, he just might be doing this scalawag a favor by teaching him a lesson

117

before he picked on someone who didn't take kindly to being followed—for any reason. Choosing a spot where the trees grew the densest and the foliage offered a place to hide the mare, he guided the animal off the road and dismounted.

Nearly twenty minutes passed while Alec stood behind the widest-based tree he could find, his cape draped over one arm and ready to be thrown the instant he saw the bedraggled youth pass before him. The traffic on the road had thinned to only an occasional cart or wagon now and then, which Alec greatly appreciated. To an innocent eye, it would appear the youngster had been attacked by a madman, and Alec didn't feel like wasting time trying to explain. After all, the child hadn't honestly done any-thing . . . yet.

Thinking to steal a glance that might give him a clue to the boy's whereabouts, Alec removed his tricorn and tossed it on the ground beside his cane. Then, with his back pressed against the tree trunk, he leaned to his left and slowly peered out to give himself a clear view of the road. To his delight, he immediately spotted the young man coming toward the place where Alec stood, his head down, the wide brim of his straw hat shadowing his face and the rest of the road devoid of witnesses. Grinning victoriously, Alec straightened and ducked back behind the tree to concentrate on the sounds of the boy's footsteps as he walked along the hardpacked earth. Only a few minutes passed before the urchin came into view, and Alec waited a second longer to allow himself the opportunity to attack from the rear. When it came, he spread out his cape and advanced.

The earsplitting scream emanating from the youth seemed to ricochet throughout the entire woodland once his vision was obscured and strong arms locked around his delicate frame to lift him off his feet. Certain he was about to be murdered in much the same manner as Eli, the young man lashed out with all that was left him—his feet.

The heel of his oversized shoe caught Alec just below the knee. The pain was excruciating, but rather than let go of his quarry, Alec gritted his teeth, twisted and hurled them both to the soft bed of dried leaves at the side of the road. They rolled several times until Alec managed to trap the boy beneath him. Pushing himself up, his legs straddling the youth, he grabbed the corner of his cape and yanked it off. A flood of long, black hair spilled from beneath the straw hat that had been knocked off the youngster's head during the scuffle, and for a second, Alec was too shocked to say anything. Then bright, blue eyes found his, and he quickly jumped to his feet.

"What the hell is going on?" he demanded.

Rebecca wasted very little time getting up off the ground, positive that her only chance for staying alive would be if she could outrun him. She had cursed her luck earlier when she followed Alec Diamond to the stable and had to stand by helplessly watching him ride off. She had been sure he was on his way back to the scene of the crime and wanted to be there to witness everything. With no other alternative but to walk, she had begrudgingly set off toward the Jamestown Road and was fortunate enough to hop a ride in the back of an empty wagon driven by an old man who was either dimwitted or deaf or both not to know he had a passenger. Once they neared the docks, she had jumped off unseen and hidden herself among the crowd of men working there. It had taken her quite a while to spot Alec Diamond, but once she had, she wondered why she hadn't looked there first. The wily bastard was practically sitting on the very spot where Eli died! Seeing that he was alone, she took up a position opposite him where he wouldn't notice her and had to be content merely to watch. Then Keenan joined him, and she damned her inability to get closer where she could listen in on what they said. Whatever it was, however, she guessed it had made Alec Diamond angry. He had irritably come to his feet, sent Keenan after the mare and raced off back toward town. And somewhere along the way, he had seen her. Otherwise he wouldn't have been waiting here in the woods!

"I asked you a question, Miss Wilde!"

The violence in his tone of voice made her tremble, and she wished there were some way for her to easily slip out of the oversized shoes. She could run much faster without them. "Nothing's going on," she managed to reply.

119

"Oh, really?" he jeered, cocking his head to one side, his dark brown eyes blazing. "Are you telling me you always dress in boys' clothes and follow people around?"

Rebecca decided the best defense was denial. "I—I wasn't following you."

He opened his mouth to respond but instead exhaled an angry sigh and looked away. Getting the truth out of this young woman wasn't going to be easy, if at all possible. Reaching up, he raked his fingers through his hair, then irritably dusted off his clothes while he decided on the best way to go about it. He certainly couldn't just let her walk off thinking she had gotten away with something. She not only didn't have the right to snoop into his personal life, but her methods were damn stupid . . . and dangerous! If he hadn't mistaken her for a boy but rather a man, he might have just run her through with his rapier and *then* elected to ask why. His temper grew even shorter. And he honestly didn't have the time for any of this.

"All right," he relented, bending to retrieve his cape, "we'll pretend I believe you. So explain the need to dress the way you are."

It wasn't difficult for Rebecca to realize how angry this man was. She could read it in his eyes, the way he moved and by the sharp edge to his words. Yet, she couldn't and wouldn't tell him the truth. It would mean her death. "What I do, Mr. Diamond, is none of your business."

"It is when I'm involved," he barked. "I saw you watching me back there in town, and I know you followed me to Shield's Stable. Then all of a sudden—out of the blue—you just happen to be at the docks. Are you going to deny that?"

"It was a coincidence. I was on my way to the docks, too, and off at Shield's to hire the use of a horse." Pleased with her quick response, a smile curled her mouth as if silently daring him to challenge the validity of her statement.

Alec raised a doubtful brow and glanced all around them as if looking for something. "And where is it?" He quickly raised a hand to stop her from answering. "No, let me guess. Either Mr. Shield didn't have one you could use or you were thrown off. Which is it?"

He knew she was lying. That was obvious. But she couldn't back down now. "You wouldn't believe me no matter what I said."

Lowering his chin, he offered, "Try me."

Since Alec had been inside the stable and knew whether or not there were horses to be hired, she decided it was best she not claim to have even talked with Mr. Shield. "I didn't have the necessary coin."

"Good answer," he smirked. "Now, suppose you tell me why you're dressed as you are. And before you restate that it's none of my business, let me tell you what I'll do if you continue to lie." The fearful look in her blue eyes told him that she believed every word he had said and that she was convinced he would carry through with whatever threat he promised. "I'll throw you on that horse over there—" he jerked his thumb in the direction of the mare—"and take you, dressed the way you are, to see your friend. I believe his name is Jon-Gregory? And as I recall hearing, he wasn't too pleased with you the last time you two talked. I can imagine what he'll think seeing you like this."

He was right in assuming Jon-Gregory would be angry with her. The truth was, he'd be furious! Yet, if that was all she had to deal with, she'd take it. It certainly looked more promising than being clubbed over the head. Having made up her mind, she squared her shoulders and stared silently back at him.

Alec seriously considered wringing her pretty, little neck in retaliation for her show of defiance. In all his years, he had never come across anyone as stubborn and foolhardy as this one! His mood softened a little. Or as beautiful. Dropping his gaze as he shook his head, he silently repeated his pledge to stay away from her. She was trouble. He could see that already.

"All right," he concurred, taking a step toward her, "we'll go and talk to Jon-Gregory. Maybe he can get you to tell me why you've suddenly become a thorn in my side."

Rebecca jerked away before he could grab her arm. She thought he meant he would deposit her in Jon-Gregory's care, not wait around to hear her explanation! "Just wait one minute," she rallied, twisting out of reach when he tried a second time to seize her wrist. "What he and I talk about is no concern of yours. And I'm sure he'll agree."

"Then the two of you are working on this together?"

"No," she exclaimed. "He doesn't even know."

"That you intended to follow me here?"

"That's right," she stormed. "He—" Rebecca felt as if she had drawn her last breath. Her heart thundered in her ears, the blood in her veins turned to ice and every muscle in her body became paralyzed. Until this moment she hadn't admitted to anything, but in the course of one careless slip of the tongue, she had confirmed what he suspected. Her blue eyes round circles of fear, she willed her feet to move and spun around.

Unfortunately for Rebecca the noon hour was the reason there were no carts or wagons on the road. Everyone had taken a break from their work. Thus, she was on her own, and her only salvation was if she could run faster, harder and longer than Alec Diamond. Her mistake was in forgetting the man had a horse, until she heard the sound of thundering hooves bearing down on her. Before she had the chance to glance back over her shoulder and see how much of a head start she had or decide that cutting into the trees would make it difficult, if not impossible, for him to follow on horseback, strong fingers seized the collar of her jacket and jerked her up and off her feet. She let out a bloodcurdling scream when he unceremoniously dumped her belly down across the mare in front of him. But the outraged cry that followed came when a stinging slap hit her across the buttocks.

"You . . . you *bastard!*" she wailed, flinging her arms and legs and fighting desperately to connect a blow to his thigh and win her freedom. If anything his attention would be drawn to the jittery horse while she made good her escape.

Alec realized in that moment that they both were about to be thrown. The mare, unaccustomed to such treatment, snorted, pranced nervously, sidestepped in a fit of high-strung defiance, then bolted and reared up on her hind legs. Instinctively, Alec slipped his feet out of the stirrups and half jumped, half fell from the saddle, thinking to easily land on the ground unharmed. To his dismay, however, he had momentarily forgotten about the extra passenger and the direction she would fall until he had very nearly done as he intended and was thrust off balance by the screaming banshee who was hurled against him. Unwillingly, he took the brunt of the fall when Rebecca landed on top of him. Although the contact was not totally unpleasant—the soft curves beneath his hands when he thought to set her from him were minor compensation for the pain he endured at her expense—the discovery that both of them would have to walk back to town once he saw the mare galloping off down the road enraged him. Giving her a none-too-gentle shove, he slid out from under her and stood to dust off his clothes and present her with a murderous glower.

"Well, don't look at me like you think it's *my* fault," she snapped, struggling to get up.

"And who shall I blame?" he growled. "Your mother for not teaching you how to behave like a lady?"

Her pain became secondary now. "Why not blame yours for not teaching you how to behave like a gentleman?"

Alec's nostrils flared. "And what man would when he's confronted by a little tart dressed in baggy clothes with ink on the end of her nose? It's rather difficult to figure out that you are a woman."

A tiny hand came up to rub the mentioned spot before she understood the implication behind his words and that there truly was no ink on her nose. "What's that supposed to mean? That just because I'm a woman, I can't do a job that's usually done by a man?" She took an angry step closer to him. "Well, I'll have you know I'm the best reporter Williamsburg has ever had!" She straightened her spine indignantly. "And even if you *could* recognize a lady, you wouldn't know how to act!"

Alec's brown eyes darkened a bit, and his brow furrowed in unspoken rage. Then, without warning, a hand shot out, seized her arm high above the elbow and yanked her into his embrace. Two iron-thewed limbs encircled her tiny frame, trapping her within his grasp while his mouth swooped down to capture hers. Had either of them been given the chance to contemplate what the affecting result of that kiss would be, neither would have even come close. For Alec, the feel of supple curves pressed against him, the narrowness of her waist, her slender back, the soft, sweet fragrance of her hair, and the warmth of her lips touching his nearly set his mind whirling. But more than that, it sparked a flame of passion that quickly flared up and threatened to shatter his steel-willed reserve.

Rebecca's discovery was much the same. Only for her, the embrace awakened the delicious memories of the moment's they shared the night before. Without realizing it, she responded, slanting her mouth across his and sliding her arms up over his chest to encircle his neck and pull him closer. In her wildest dreams, she never imagined a simple kiss could thrill her so. But when he parted her lips with his tongue and pushed inside, cold, hard, terrifying reality exploded in her brain. This man—the one who ignited strange fires deep within her—was a murderer. Instinctively, she unlocked her arms, tore her lips from his and shoved away with all her might.

Alec had felt her yield to his advances, sensing she too experienced the excitement of the kiss. But now, confused by her sudden change, his passion cooled and his temper flared again. The little tease! She knew all the right words, the certain look, the beguiling moves it took to lure a man. Had it been a game with her? Had she meant to find his weakness? Well, never again! And before they parted, he'd know the truth.

"Since we seem to be at a crossroads in determining whether or not you're a lady—or for that matter if you even slightly resemble one—then how I treat you isn't of any real importance. Therefore, I suggest you tell me why you were following me." His nostrils flared as he dipped his head forward a degree. "Or could it be you yourself have trouble figuring out if you're even a woman and thought to use me to find out?"

Rebecca's chin dropped. In a rage and highly insulted, she brought back her opened hand and struck him across the face. The force behind it jerked Alec's head to one side, and while the impression of her fingers darkened on his cheek, Rebecca suddenly came to her senses. This man was capable of murder! He had already killed one person. It wouldn't bother him to do so again. Terror widened her bright blue eyes, and while she was frantically deciding which direction to run—back to the docks and Mr. Keenan or all the way to Williamsburg screaming at the top of her lungs—Alec was considering turning her across his knee. If she wished to behave like a child, he'd treat her like one. But the horror he saw shining in her blue eyes cooled the desire. It was not his practice to abuse women—though in this case he was truly tempted. Heaving an exasperated sigh, he turned to absently glance back down the road, wishing he'd had the sense to just return to town rather than mess with this little wildcat. He laughed inwardly at the use of the word, reaffirming his earlier conviction that her name suited her. Wanting now more than anything to simply be done with her, he drew in a tired breath and looked at her again.

In that instant, Rebecca made her decision. Catching him off guard, she shot out both hands and rammed them hard against his chest to knock him backward. While he tried to regain his balance, she sprinted off down the road—toward town. She didn't know how far ahead the last wagon would be, but it had to be close enough for someone to hear her scream. However, her plan went horribly awry when she felt the painful entrapment of her hair in his hand just before he yanked her off her feet.

"I've had enough!" he raged, locking strong arms around her tiny frame and half-carrying, half-dragging her to the side of the road. It didn't matter to him anymore that he shouldn't be rough with her. He wanted some answers, and he wanted them now! Giving her a healthy shove, he sent her sprawling on her backside in a bed of leaves.

"Don't . . . even . . . think about it!" he snarled, a finger thrust toward her nose when she started to scramble to her feet. "You're going to stay right there for as long as it takes, so help me God!"

Rebecca wasn't sure which part of her body hurt the worst. But none of it seemed important right now. He wanted an explanation, and he obviously wasn't going to allow her to leave until he had it. Her only hope would be if she could convince him that she didn't suspect he had killed Eli. Gulping down the knot of fear, she chewed on her lower lip for a moment while she collected her thoughts and put some sort of order to the story she would tell.

"Well?"

His demand made her jump. "I—I'm a reporter," she began, but the skeptical lift of his brow in response to her declaration angered her. It always did when someone gave her that look. "I am!" she exploded. "Maybe I'm not as well known as some, but I'm just as good. Probably better!"

"And what has that to do with me?" He stood with his weight on one foot, the other knee bent slightly and his arms crossed in front of him. His dark eyes were shadowed by an impatient frown, and the muscle in his cheek twitched in anger.

Now came the tricky part. She'd have to be careful how she worded it. "Being a newspaper reporter means I have an inquisitive mind."

Alec was quick to correct her statement. "You like to snoop into other people's lives."

"If they're hiding something, yes!" she rallied with little forethought and then wished she hadn't.

"So you think I'm hiding something."

Rebecca's journalistic cleverness surfaced. "I don't know. Are you?"

"If I was, I wouldn't tell you about it." His anger had faded somewhat. He always enjoyed matching wits with someone and despite her methods, he'd enjoy testing hers.

Now she was getting somewhere. The fool didn't realize he was about to be tricked into telling everything. "Why not? Are they too horrible to share?"

"It depends on who's hearing it." He'd give her just enough to spark her imagination. "Now a woman, for instance, would be appalled. A man would applaud me."

What man in his right mind would applaud another for taking a life? No matter what the reason? she wondered disdainfully, casting her eyes away from his lest he read her thoughts by the look on her face. "And what might that be?" she asked, slowly coming to her feet.

Alec masked his smile. "That I spank young women who get too nosy."

Every muscle in Rebecca's delicate frame rebelled. He was laughing at her, and she hated him for it. Well, let him have his fun. He wouldn't be laughing after her story was printed.

"What really brings you to Williamsburg, Mr. Diamond? Besides your interest in buying property?"

Her questions finally convinced him she was telling the truth, that all she wanted was something to write about. He also decided she was harmless. Smiling at her brashness, he started back toward the place where he had left his cane, hat and cape.

Suspecting that he was deliberately avoiding her questions, Rebecca hurried to catch up. "Or is that just what you want everyone to think? Perhaps you're here for some other reason."

Her query struck too close to the truth. "Such as?" he baited, feigning disinterest while he scanned the underbrush for the spot where he'd left his things.

"Suppose you tell me?" she coaxed excitedly, quickening her pace to keep up with him.

"Tell you what?" he proposed, coming to an abrupt halt and turning to face her. "That I was sent here by King George to spy? Is that what you'd like to hear?"

"All I want, Mr. Diamond, is to report the truth," she declared, unafraid. His vagueness had to mean she was on the right track.

Alec raised a sun-lightened eyebrow at her. "All right. Then I'll tell you. The truth is . . . it's none of your business."

His dismissal of her when he turned his back to gather up his tricorn and cane angered Rebecca. "Fine. If that's the way you want it, that's how it will be. I'll find out some other way. I'll ask John Greenhow why you paid him a visit. *He* doesn't have any property to sell."

Alec couldn't help but laugh. "Be my guest. But I should probably warn you that he isn't going to tell you anything more than you already know."

"Is that a fact?" she mocked, turning and heading back to the road. "Then maybe I should talk to someone who knows everything about everybody."

"Oh? And who might that be?" he called, smiling openly as he watched her slender figure draped in boys' clothing walk away.

"A friend—someone who makes it her business to know what's going on for miles around," she tossed back over her shoulder. "I'll ask Penny Dawson."

The smile on Alec's face disappeared.

Chapter Six

Every time the front door to The Red Lion opened up, Penny's attention was quickly drawn to the person standing at the threshold, and each time she was disappointed not to see either Alec or Rebecca. The sun was beginning to go down, and with each minute that ticked away, she grew more worried for her friend's safety. If what Tommy Henderson told her was true, there was a good chance that Rebecca had gotten herself into more trouble than she could handle.

Once Penny had come to the deduction that Rebecca was the friend Alec had mentioned this morning, Penny had left The Red Lion through the side door, hurried down the sidewalk to the Ludwell-Paradise House and raced up the steps to the door to the newspaper office only to discover it was locked. Frantic and determined to find Rebecca before Alec figured out the identity of his late night companion, she had proceeded to the second floor and the last door in the hallway and knocked loudly. The youngest Rind child answered the summons, and after a few minutes of questions and answers, Penny learned the child's mother had gone to lunch with the governor's wife and that Miss Wilde should be working at the office. The only conclusion to be drawn since the child hadn't actually seen Rebecca this morning was that Rebecca had stayed home today. It was her practice never to leave the office until the end of the day or unless Mrs. Rind was there to take care of customers. But even so, *someone* should have been there. The paper was due out this afternoon. This bit of knowledge worried Penny. For some reason she sensed trouble.

She was on her way back to The Red Lion when she decided to talk to Jon-Gregory. He always seemed to know what Rebecca was up to. It had been a good idea but one that didn't award her anything other than the knowledge that not only had Jon-Gregory talked with Rebecca, but they'd had an argument and she had stormed off from the general store in search of Tommy Henderson. When asked what he and Rebecca had disagreed on, Jon-Gregory merely gave Penny a two-word answer—"something stupid"—then excused himself and went back to work.

Penny's next mission was to find Tommy Henderson, and everyone knew how difficult that could be. The young man never seemed to be where he was supposed to be, except when it came to working at the newspaper office. It was his one true interest, and if Penny hadn't just come from there, it would have been the first place she looked. As it was, she wandered the streets for the next half hour asking everyone who knew him if they had seen the young man or perhaps Rebecca Wilde. The response had always been the same, and out of desperation, she had returned to the *Gazette*.

This time her luck changed. She had hoped to learn that her friend had given up trying to locate Tommy Henderson and had returned to the office to finish her assignment, but instead she found Tommy busily at work running off this afternoon's edition of the paper. She considered herself blessed after all the trouble she had been through until Tommy informed her of Rebecca's newest adventure. The young man couldn't supply all the details since Rebecca refused to give him any, but what he did know nearly frightened Penny out of her undergarments. It seemed her friend was on to something concerning the death of Gideon Blackstock's slave, and the only way she would be allowed the freedom to investigate her leads would be if she were in disguise.

"And you helped her?" Penny had raged. "How could you? The damn fool could get herself killed!"

"I don't see how," Tommy had argued. "I gave her some of

130

my old clothes to wear. If anyone sees her, they'll think she's a boy."

"Oh, that's just great, you lardhead," Penny had shot back. "If they knew she was a woman, they might not shoot her. This way they'll probably just throw a rope over her and drag her down the road until she breaks every bone in her body. Good God in heaven, boy, don't you ever think?" She had tossed up her hands in unwilling surrender and turned for the door. "Of course not. You and Rebecca are exactly alike—too stupid to know better!" With one hand on the doorknob, she had paused to ask, "And I don't suppose you know where she went?"

Tommy didn't like being blamed for something he honestly couldn't have prevented. Rebecca would have gone with or without his help. Frowning, he had muttered something about Rebecca saying she'd start her surveillance at John Greenhow's, and went back to work. Next time Rebecca asked him to do something for her, he'd say no. That way he wouldn't have to put up with Penny Dawson's smart mouth.

Penny knew it would be a waste of time trying to tail her friend. According to Tommy, Rebecca had left over an hour ago. But Penny had to try. Since Tommy didn't know who Rebecca intended to follow, finding either of them was impossible for the simple fact that if Rebecca didn't want to be seen by anyone, then she wouldn't be. Returning to the general store, she had asked several of the customers coming out of the place if they had noticed a rather scruffy lad hanging around outside, and when no one admitted they had, Penny decided it was time she went back to work. All she could do now was pray that nothing happened to her foolish friend.

The noon crowd came and went, and now that it was well into mid-afternoon, Penny's nerves were on edge. Not only hadn't Tommy come to tell her Rebecca had returned as he had promised he would, but Alec hadn't shown up to dine with her. Maybe it was just her overwrought imagination at work, but she feared the two were somehow connected.

"Penny," Ben softly cooed when he noticed how often she

studied the customers coming into the place, "is something wrong? You look worried."

"I am," she admitted, setting the tray of empty glasses down on the bar. "A friend of mine might be in trouble."

Ben's brow wrinkled. "Serious trouble?"

"Probably. She doesn't know any other kind."

"She? Are you talking about Rebecca Wilde?"

Penny nodded. "See there. You knew who I meant without asking. Everybody knows she's always getting in trouble. Everybody but her."

"Well, maybe you should go and talk to Jon-Gregory," Ben suggested, his words etched with concern.

"I would if I thought it would do any good. But if I don't know where she is, how can he be of any help?" she pointed out.

"Well, at least there'd be two of you looking for her."

Penny's brown eyes widened with her surprise. "You mean it, Ben? You'd let me leave work to see if I can find her?"

"And what good are ya to me when all ya do is stare at the front door? 'Sides, it's not that busy." He leaned in and patted her hand once she had removed her apron and laid it on the bar near him. "But you must promise me this, that if Rebecca is in any danger, you won't do anything foolish. You're to find the constable and let him take care of it. Understood?"

"Yes, Ben, I promise," she grinned, resting both her hands on the bar and leaning forward enough to place a kiss on the tip of his nose. "And I'll promise you something else. Once we find her, I'll bring her back here and let *you* be the first to holler at her."

"It's a deal," he laughed. "Now be careful. And take my horse. You'll save time."

"Thanks Ben. You're a sweetheart."

Penny had high expectations of tracking down her wayward friend within a short amount of time, talking some sense into her as well as threatening to tell Mrs. Rind if she didn't agree to stop acting like a fool. Then she would have a heart-to-heart discussion on what happened between her and Alec. It was her plan. But as she neared the front door

132

and reached for the knob, it was suddenly thrust open before her, and the sight of Alec standing haloed in the framework made her gasp. Certain that if she glimpsed past him, she would find Rebecca bound and draped over his horse at the hitching rail, she just stood there, too afraid to look or say a word.

"Before you say anything"—Alec grinned warmly—"let me apologize."

Penny's dark eyes reflected her puzzlement. "Apologize? For what?"

"For being late," he went on, moving aside to let the door swing shut behind him. Politely removing his tricorn, he held out his arm for her. "I promised to dine with you, didn't I?"

Penny didn't know whether to excuse herself from his company claiming business elsewhere or thank God his presence meant Rebecca was safe. Or was she? Glancing nervously at the sealed door then over at Ben who watched questioningly, she decided to find out the easy way. She'd cunningly ask where he had been and what had delayed their evening plans. She smiled—though it hardly reached her eyes—and slipped her hand into the crook of his arm.

"It depends," she said, walking with him to a vacant table set apart from the other customers.

"On what?" he asked, pulling out a chair for her.

While he turned his attention away from her to place his hat, cape and cane on a second chair before taking his own next to her, Penny glanced back at Ben with a silent plea for understanding. He mustn't approach the table and ask why Penny had changed her mind about looking for Rebecca. When the little man shrugged in response, she smiled her thanks and turned back to Alec.

"It depends on whether or not I was stood up for another woman," she artfully baited. If he had indeed been with Rebecca, Penny's question would still seem innocent enough. After all, he wasn't aware they knew each other.

The vision of a poorly dressed, ill-tempered youth came to mind, and Alec laughed at the image as well as the memory of the argument he and Rebecca had had on the subject.

"No, Penny," he smiled, waving at Ben to bring them

some wine and two glasses. "I'm late because I ran into a little trouble at the docks."

Penny again thought of her friend. She always did when someone mentioned the word trouble. "Oh? What kind?"

The worst kind, Alec mused with a mixture of irritation and humor. Rebecca Wilde was a nosy, high-spirited, foolish female who, if she wasn't knocked down a peg or two, could cause him serious grief. Her parting comment earlier about talking with her friend, Penny Dawson, had given Alec all the pieces he needed to put the puzzle together. Now all he had to do was trick Penny into verifying his suspicions, although he didn't really think he had to hear it. Rebecca had pretty much done that already.

After their spill from the mare, Rebecca had walked on ahead of him at a fast clip until she had apparently realized her mistake in announcing her association with Penny. Her steps had faltered, and Alec was sure she was about to turn around with some sort of revised declaration that would hopefully lead him down a different path. But she had obviously decided no comment was better than a feeble one when she straightened her shoulders and continued on. He would have liked to hear her trying to undo her mistake but had to be satisfied with knowing that before long he'd confront her with the whole truth and be awarded the pleasure of listening to her attempt to explain.

They had traveled down the deserted road for more than a half hour in silence, Rebecca walking some thirty feet ahead of him and not once looking back to see if he still followed. In a way he wished she had. The distraction would have taken his mind off the thoughts racing through his head. He was so bent on learning the facts about last night—what she was doing in Penny's room, why she didn't stop him before things went too far, was the whole affair planned beforehand and what was to be gained by it—that he hadn't given much consideration to what he'd do afterward. Nor had he considered, until he was appreciatively aware of the stubborn way she held her head and walked with an air that said she would take on the whole world and win, that this beautiful, tenacious, young woman had been a virgin until

134

she met him. He had bedded his share of the ladies, but never a virgin, and his pledge to make sure the only woman who fell in that category would be his wife brought a pained expression to his brow. He certainly didn't want to marry Rebecca Wilde! And he didn't think he was too far wrong in assuming she wanted nothing further to do with him. But what if their little interlude produced— He cringed at the idea of the little vixen carrying his child. He most certainly would be honor bound to stand before the altar with her at his side.

That thought had barely crossed his mind when he began to consider the positive side of such a union. Not a day would go by without some sort of excitement. He already knew how pleasing she was in bed, and he'd be the envy of many to have such a beautiful wife. The memory of her soft, luscious curves filled his head, and he took a deep breath to cool his rising desires, failing to understand why she affected him so. All the other ladies he had been with had stirred his passion at the moment but never lingered on his thoughts the next morning the way Rebecca had. It bode ill. He knew that. He sensed that after he had concluded his business in Williamsburg and boarded the *Constance* and set a course for home, he'd never be able to put her from his mind. She was like a fever that had infected his very soul, and no amount of doctoring would cure him. His only explanation was the guilt he felt for what happened.

A short ways farther, they came across the mare at the side of the road, lazily munching on the sweet grasses at its feet. Alec hadn't truly expected to see the animal again, but he wasn't about to question his good fortune. He never enjoyed a long walk since he always seemed to be in a hurry. And his reason today was an important one. A frown had furrowed his brow when Rebecca walked right on by the horse as if she hadn't seen it or cared if the animal was there. He, however, felt differently. Cooing softly to the mare as he gathered the reins, he tied his cape to the saddle, secured his tricorn down over his brow and stepped up into the stirrups.

"It's still a long walk back to town, Miss Wilde," he had said once he had reined the horse in alongside her. "Suppose

135

we call a truce."

Rebecca's chin had raised a notch at his suggestion, but she in no other way acted as if she had heard him. She had kept her eyes trained on the road ahead of her and never slowed her pace.

Alec had tried again. "A young woman shouldn't be walking the road alone. It's—"

"Thank you, Mr. Diamond," she had acidly replied, her gaze still averted, "but I've done this countless times before. And the way I see it, I'm safer on foot than riding with you."

Alec had opened his mouth to argue the point and tell her of the story Keenan had just recited to him a short while earlier but changed his mind. Her response would more than likely be that she could take care of herself which would then lead to a lengthy debate on the subject. Irritated by her stubbornness, he was tempted to ride on ahead and leave her to fend for herself. But whether he cared to admit it or not, he was, in a small way, responsible for her well-being. If he hadn't come to the docks, she wouldn't have followed and put herself in this situation. Gritting his teeth, he inhaled a deep breath and hauled back on the reins. If she wanted to walk, let her. He'd merely ride along behind her.

Once they had neared the edge of town, Rebecca had paused long enough to twist her thick, black hair into a knot and stuff it beneath the straw hat she had carried. Then, once she had pulled the collar of her jacket up around her neck and stiffened her spine, she had marched off down the avenue leading through the center of town as proudly as if she were Joan of Arc returning from battle. The sight of her both amused and annoyed Alec. She had nothing to be proud of. She had made a complete fool of herself. But he had to admit that through it all she never backed down or melted in a flood of tears. It would be interesting to see how she handled herself once he confronted her with what he knew.

Alec had guessed right when he figured she'd head straight for home rather than stopping off at The Red Lion to see Penny. What he wasn't sure about was whether or not she'd try to contact her friend later tonight. A soft smile had reflected itself in his eyes once he had reined in at the hitching post of the inn to watch her young figure hurry along the sidewalk, quickly lose herself among the crowd and disappear from view. Or perhaps Penny would go to her. Either way, he realized he would be losing sleep again this night, for he planned to keep an eye on Penny's room.

"Alec?"

The sound of his name on his companion's lips brought him out of his musings rather abruptly. He blinked and focused his attention on her. "I'm sorry. What did you say?"

"I asked what kind of trouble you found at the docks."

"Nothing I couldn't handle." He grinned, remembering his shock when he unveiled the young woman trapped between his knees.

Penny considered the possibility that her imagination was reading things into his words, but the grass stain she noticed on the elbow of his jacket and the way he had drifted off a moment ago hinted otherwise. And if Rebecca was missing the same length of time as Alec and she was off somewhere investigating Eli's death—which more than likely placed her at the docks—it was simply too coincidental not to be connected in some way. Running her tongue over her dry lips, she silently prayed she was wrong and that if she wasn't, her next question wouldn't give her away.

"Well, if you're not going to tell me about it, I'll have to assume you're hiding something from me." She smiled, though she truly didn't feel like it.

Alec cocked a brow. "Strange you should word it that way," he said, wondering if the little redhead was as nervous as she seemed.

"Why?" she asked, forcing a laugh.

"Because someone else said nearly the same thing to me." Penny could feel it coming. "Oh? Who?"

"She said she was a friend of yours."

A tiny whimper knotted her throat, but she gulped it back down. "Oh, really? What's her name?" She asked but she didn't know why she had bothered. She knew who it was. Folding her hands in her lap under the table, she squeezed them so hard her knuckles whitened.

"Well, she didn't actually say. But I've seen her before. I was hoping you could tell me." Alec had to fight down the laughter that burned his throat. The expression on Penny's face told it all.

"I—I hope you realize I know a lot of people, Alec. It might not be that easy." *God, what a lie!* she mused, feeling sick inside. "Describe her."

"Oh, I can do better than that."

I'll bet you can, Penny thought, suddenly worried that he was the sort to openly discuss his affairs. *You can give me every intimate detail about last night, you rogue. You unprincipled—*

"She's a reporter for the *Gazette*. I met her there this morning and again at the docks. She had followed me there, claiming she wanted to do a story on me. When I told her there was nothing worth the cost of her ink, she said I was hiding something."

Penny's eyes had moved from his face to the grass stain and back repeatedly while he spoke. "So what did you do? Beat her up for asking?" She nodded at his sleeve when Alec straightened in his chair and gave her a puzzled look.

"Oh, that." He chuckled, once he had examined the damage. "No, I didn't beat her up as you so delicately put it. We fell off my horse."

Ben appeared then with the wine Alec had ordered. He poured two glasses full, set them down in front of Alec and Penny, and walked away, but not before frowning at the young woman. He had apparently heard at least a part of their conversation.

Alec was quick to notice the older man's disapproval and could only assume he too knew what was going on. Penny's nervousness told him that things hadn't developed as arranged. And Rebecca's failure to follow him without being seen rather confirmed Alec's prior notion that this entire episode had been preplanned. What he couldn't figure out was why. Was it their mistake in thinking he was a wealthy, *married* businessman who would willingly pay to keep his transgressions a secret? But why, for God's sake, would they use a virgin? Or wasn't it supposed to have gone that far? Just

138

when he thought he had the whole mess figured out, other possibilities arose to confuse him. Lifting his glass, he took a long drink to soothe his growing ire.

"So who is she, Penny?" he asked after a moment, leaning forward with his arms braced on the table and staring her straight in the eye. "And why does she think there's something about me worth reporting?"

Penny's courage dissolved the instant he set that cold, hard look upon her. But he talked as if he hadn't a clue to whom his late night visitor was. And if that was the case, she wasn't going to say anything to change it. "If you're talking about the pretty brunette who works next door, her name is Rebecca Wilde. As for our being friends . . . I don't think so. She and I have nothing in common." *Except you,* she silently added.

Except me, he thought, his patience running dangerously thin. If this group wanted to blackmail him, why hadn't one of them said something by now? What were they waiting for?

"Listen, Alec," Penny smiled as brightly as possible. She didn't want him to think she was upset over learning he and Rebecca had met—under any circumstance. But she also wanted to be excused from his presence for a while. She had to talk to her friend and right now. "I was just on my way out when you arrived. I can feel one of these awful headaches of mine coming on, and I wanted to get to McKenzie's Apothecary Shoppe before it closes. Since I've already eaten, why don't you have your dinner while I'm gone, and we can talk after I get back? It won't take me long."

Alec started to object. He contemplated grabbing Penny's arm and squeezing until he had forced the truth from her. But a similar tactic hadn't worked with Rebecca Wilde, and since the two of them were friends, he concluded such a method wouldn't succeed with this one. He wasn't really sure who had the more obstinate disposition, but he guessed Penny would be just as difficult to break. Besides, he'd just wait until after she left, then he'd follow her.

"All right," he concurred. "I'll have something to eat and wait for you here." He smiled, but it came only as a form of courtesy, not how he truly felt.

For effect, Penny pressed the fingertips of one hand to her temple as she rose. "I'm sorry to spoil everything. I really was looking forward to a quiet moment with you."

So was I, he mused. But it wasn't the first time his plans had gone awry. Only this time things would work out in his favor for a change. Coming to his feet, he nodded politely at her, then remained where he was until after she had left the inn and closed the door behind her.

Once Penny stood on the sidewalk in front of The Red Lion, she could feel how badly her knees were shaking. Her confrontation with Alec had frightened her, though she honestly didn't know why. Maybe it was just something she sensed about him—or perhaps more what she sensed about Rebecca. No one ever used Rebecca without paying the price, whether she lashed out at her foe with fist or tongue. Whatever her method, Rebecca got even, and Penny worried that this time her friend wasn't aware of the kind of man she had taken on. She had to be warned and *before* Rebecca had set the wheels of revenge into action.

Turning, Penny glanced up at the windows belonging to the newspaper office, concluding that Rebecca hadn't returned there after her encounter with Alec, since Tommy hadn't stopped by to tell her that she had. Her accidental meeting with Alec had probably sent Rebecca running for her room where she could hide and plot out her reprisal, and it was in this direction that Penny hurriedly walked.

Once she neared the capitol building, Penny cut across the yard and started to run, not noticing the man on horseback who deftly maneuvered his animal around the carriages in the road or the way his choice of direction matched hers. She was simply too busy trying to decide just how to broach the subject of Rebecca's late night escapade.

By the time she reached the narrow, stone pathway leading to the front of the house, Penny had remembered Tommy saying that Rebecca hadn't been feeling well and that Mrs. Rind had assumed Tommy was finishing up her work because Rebecca had gone home to bed. Penny was wishing that had been true. She was wishing Rebecca had gotten sick two days ago and hadn't been able to leave the house. None of this would have happened then. Walking across the cobblestones to the porch, Penny reevaluated her last thought and concluded that Rebecca's health had very little to do with keeping her out of touchy situations. If it hadn't been Alec, it would have been someone else. A vague, halfhearted smile parted her lips. At least he hadn't been an ugly, old man with a wart on the end of his nose.

Penny was both pleased and surprised when she met up with Jon-Gregory coming from around the corner of the house. It made things easier for her. If Miss Abigail had answered the door, she would have had to explain why she wanted to talk to Rebecca. Jon-Gregory wouldn't pry. "Is Rebecca here?" she asked, keeping her voice low in case the town gossip happened to be sitting close to an opened window.

"I'm assuming she is," he frowned. "She's the reason I'm home in the middle of the afternoon. I need to talk to her, and the Henderson boy said he hadn't seen her since this morning when she asked him to set type for her." His blue eyes flashed sparks of rage as he reached and opened the front door. "Damn fool woman," he muttered, slapping the newspaper he held against his thigh. He took a step sideways to allow Penny to enter ahead of him. "You here for the same reason?"

"I doubt it," Penny sighed, ducking past him as she moved into the hall and waited for him to close the door behind them.

Jon-Gregory was one of the few men Penny desired but never bedded. Out of respect for Rebecca, she had told herself. But the truth of the matter was that she didn't think he'd be interested. He was friendly enough and always went out of his way to talk to her whenever he could. He often ate his noon meal at The Red Lion just so they could sit and exchange gossip and have a few laughs. But the topic of continuing their discussion upstairs in Penny's room was never mentioned, and Penny never pushed it. She just didn't think it was right to have an affair with Rebecca's best and only male friend. It didn't, however, cool her want to see him standing before her without a stitch of clothing on. His broad-shouldered, lanky frame intrigued her. The obscure vision of another tall, well-muscled, blond-haired man came to mind, and she curled her upper lip. She'd never see Alec that way either, and she felt cheated. The good ones always seemed to get away.

"It's been a while since we've talked," she smiled. "How are you?" He didn't really have to answer. He was delectable . . . and beyond her reach.

"To tell you the truth, Penny," he admitted in hardly more than a whisper, "I'm worried."

"Worried?" She had assumed he was upset with Rebecca over something that concerned the *Gazette*. Was it possible he knew about Alec? "About who-er-what?"

"You were right the first time," he frowned, touching her arm and pulling her back away from the parlor door. He didn't want Miss Abigail to hear, and she usually spent the afternoon doing her needlepoint in the front room. "I'm worried about Rebecca. She's gone too far this time."

Penny could feel the blood draining from her face. "Have you ever known her to do what's expected of her?" she asked with a nervous laugh. How could he have possibly found out?

Jon-Gregory shook his head. "Nope. But what worries me is how lucky she's been so far. It's bound to change, and I'm afraid it'll be something neither of us can correct . . . if it isn't too late already."

It's too late, Penny mused.

"Is that why you're here? To tell her how stupid she's been?" Jon-Gregory asked.

"Among other things," she admitted. "And if you don't mind, I think it's something she should hear from me."

Jon-Gregory's tall frame straightened, and the frown that kinked his brow told Penny that she'd have to explain her need for privacy.

"We need to talk woman to woman. It isn't the kind of thing a *man* and a woman discuss. Do you understand what I mean?"

But before he could reply, the hinges squeaked on the kitchen door at the end of the hall, and their conversation came to an abrupt end when they turned to find Rebecca staring confusedly back at them, a cup of tea held in her hands.

"Penny?" she asked hesitantly. "I thought I heard your voice. What are you doing here?"

Deciding the best approach was a direct one, Penny gave Jon-Gregory a nudge toward the stairs and turned back to face her friend. "I'm here to play mother. Now, shall we talk in your room, or would you prefer we go for a stroll where we're sure not to be overheard?" She jerked a crimson-curled head Jon-Gregory's way.

Rebecca understood her meaning. "Let's go outside. We can sit in the grass under the oak tree," she replied, setting her cup on a nearby table. "You'll excuse us, won't you, Jon-Gregory?"

The young man gave both women a disapproving scowl but knew better than to argue. If they wanted him to know anything, they'd tell him. If they didn't, he never would. Shaking his head disgustedly, he turned and went into the parlor to keep Miss Abigail company and out of the girls' conversation. He'd take his turn with Rebecca once Penny was finished.

Penny was bursting with hundreds of questions for her friend and had to practically bite her lip to keep from rattling them off one on top of the other until they were out of the house and standing beneath the oak a safe distance away. Yet once they had the privacy both women felt they needed, neither knew what to say or where to begin. This revelation surprised Penny. She had never been at a loss for words in her life, but then the topic of conversation had never been as delicate a one as that which they were about to discuss. Finally, out of desperation, she said the first thing that came to mind.

"I want to know what happened last night."

Rebecca felt a sneeze coming on, quickly grabbed her handkerchief and turned her back. "Last night?" she asked, blowing her nose and choosing not to look at Penny. She had the sinking feeling that she knew exactly what Penny was getting at.

143

"Yes, last night," Penny snapped. "And today, this afternoon. I've got a pretty good idea, but I'd rather hear it from you. And before you say I don't know what I'm talking about, I'll tell you I do. His name is Alec Diamond. He's the man you found in my bed last night."

Rebecca felt as if every ounce of strength had left her. How could Penny possibly know that? But rather than confess, she forced herself to stiffen her spine and turn back around with a shocked expression on her face.

"Penny, I don't know what you mean. I'm not in the habit of looking in your bed."

"You weren't *looking* in it. You were *in* it. And you weren't alone."

Rebecca was thankful that she had to sneeze again, and that Penny wouldn't think too much of it when she spun away from her again. Otherwise Penny was sure to see how red her face was getting. Maybe Penny was her best friend, and there had never been a secret they didn't share; but this was one time Rebecca wanted to make an exception. "You're crazy," she frowned, blowing her nose.

"Am I? Then explain the blue ribbon I found near the fireplace, the damp spot on the rug where someone knelt wringing wet, and the blood stains on the sheets."

Rebecca felt sick inside. And something she seldom experienced started to happen; tears were gathering in her eyes. Choking back the sensation, she swallowed hard and said, "I'm not the only woman who owns a blue ribbon, you know."

"But you're the only woman who knows where I keep the spare key to my room." Penny wasn't aware that her friend thought she was angry with her, even though her tone implied it. And Rebecca was right to some degree. Penny *was* angry, but at Alec, not her friend. In a fit of temper and frustration, she reached for Rebecca's arm and spun her around to look directly at her. She'd know if Rebecca was lying by the expression on her face. "Did he force himself on you? Because if he did, I'll tell Jon-Gregory. I might even tell the constable."

"No-o-o, Penny," Rebecca pleaded. "Please don't tell

144

anyone . . . ever!" There was no use in denying it. Penny had all the evidence she needed to be fully convinced, and right now Rebecca needed a confidante. Her tears started anew, only this time she couldn't hold them back. "If I tell you everything, will you promise not to repeat a word of it to anyone? There's more to it than what appears on the surface."

Penny made a quick examination of Rebecca's face for any sign of abuse. Seeing no obvious marks that would indicate she had been beaten, she asked, "More to what? I don't understand."

Angrily brushing away the moisture from her cheeks with the back of one hand, Rebecca glanced past Penny toward the house to make sure Jon-Gregory hadn't changed his mind about leaving them alone, then took Penny's hand and drew her even farther away. "What happened last night was an accident. He thought I was you, and I—" She dropped her gaze, too ashamed to go into detail. "The point is, Penny, that he doesn't have any idea *who* was there, and I don't want him to ever find out. Now promise me it will be our secret."

It was difficult for Penny to agree. It didn't really matter what actually went on in that room last night, only what the result had been. In all the years they'd known each other, Penny had never seen Rebecca cry until this very moment, and she was torn between doing as her friend asked and turning Alec in to the authorities. The former would guarantee she and Rebecca would remain good friends—something that meant the world to her—while seeing that Alec Diamond was punished for what he did would only bring shame and humiliation down on Rebecca. Well, maybe Alec wouldn't pay publicly, but if it were at all possible, Penny would see to it that he paid in some other way.

"I promise," she quietly said. "But I wish you would at least tell me how you managed to put yourself in such a predicament. Maybe then I'll stop thinking I should find a pistol and blow his brains out."

Penny's support made Rebecca smile. She could always count on her friend when things weren't going her way. "You won't have to, Penny. Once I report what I know about him to the authorities, *they'll* see he's punished."

The freckles on Penny's face seemed to stand out more clearly against her creamy, white complexion as she stared wide-eyed and mouth agape. "What do you mean? What has he done that the authorities would be interested in?"

"I believe he's the one who killed Eli."

The announcement couldn't have stunned Penny any more than if Rebecca had declared she had lost interest in being a journalist. Nor was it any more believable. "Oh, I don't know . . ." she began, shaking her head. Maybe Alec was a rogue and a scoundrel, but Penny refused to accept the idea that he was a murderer. "What proof do you have?"

"Enough to raise a few eyebrows." She took Penny's hand and pulled her down to sit on the grass beside her. "After I left you last night, I walked to the docks. I wanted—"

"I was sure you had," Penny interrupted. "You never have used the full capacity of your brain for as long as I've known you."

Rebecca's lip curled into a snarl. "Can we just get on with this? Or would you rather not hear it?" She waited until her friend reluctantly consented before continuing. "I went there to examine the spot where they found Eli's body, and you'll never guess what I saw."

"Alec Diamond standing there wringing his hands with glee." Penny's tone was sarcastic.

"No, I didn't see him there," Rebecca hissed through clenched teeth. "But what I did see told me he had been there." She smiled mockingly at Penny's sudden, genuine interest. "I found the impression of his cane in the soil. And the heel print of his shoe. It had a nick in it."

"*His* cane. *His* shoe print. How do you know they were his?" Penny proposed, obviously not as convinced as her companion. "And supposing they are. When were they put there? Before Eli died, while he was dying or several hours afterward? If that's all the proof you have—"

"It's enough to make the authorities want to talk to him!"

"Oh, really? And what do you suppose their first question will be? Excuse me, Mr. Diamond, but you're not from around here. When did you arrive in Williamsburg?" Penny's dark brows lowered over her eyes. "And you know what his answer will be? He'll tell them that he only just arrived—by ship—late last night and long *after* Eli died. Hrumph," she snorted, turning her head away to glare angrily off into the distance. "And you call yourself a reporter. You have a lot to learn, Rebecca Wilde."

Insulted and her temper flaring, Rebecca asked, "Then why wouldn't he answer my questions? It's because he's hiding something, that's why. I just know it." Suddenly realizing that her friend chose to defend Alec Diamond rather than listen with an open mind, she reached over and heartlessly tugged on a bright red curl falling over Penny's shoulder. "Why don't you believe me? Why are you on his side? Don't you care that Eli's murderer is walking around free?"

"Of course I care!" Penny retorted as she rubbed the tender spot on her scalp, certain Rebecca had yanked out several strands of her hair. "But I also care about you! Making accusations like that without any real proof to back them up could and *will* get you in a lot of hot water."

"With Alec Diamond?"

"With anyone you wrongly accuse of murder!" Penny shouted. "Can't you see that?"

Rebecca shrugged a delicate shoulder and stood up to smooth the wrinkles from her skirt. "Maybe. But there's another side to it, you know."

"Oh?" Penny jeered. "And what's that?"

"If, say, an article appears in the newspaper without naming names but has just a hint of whom the story's about, and that person suddenly becomes very angry and confronts the person who wrote it, wouldn't that mean that person is worried about someone else finding out the truth?"

A confused frown drew Penny's brows together. She had heard what her friend had said, but didn't understand any of it. Then, suddenly, it became very clear, and she scrambled to her feet and grabbed Rebecca's arm. "You didn't. You mustn't. Oh, Rebecca, say it isn't already too late. God, tell me you didn't print such an article about Alec Diamond!"

Irritated by her friend's rough treatment of her, Rebecca

jerked her arm free. "Well, sort of. It just hasn't been printed yet. But once I tell Mrs. Rind what I've found out, she'll gladly print it."

"And you weren't listening to me a minute ago. I said Alec Diamond wasn't in Williamsburg at the time Eli was murdered!"

Now it was Rebecca's turn to do the questioning. "How do you know that? Did he tell you that? Did he suddenly appear at The Red Lion late last night pretending to have just stepped off a ship?" When Penny's mouth opened and closed several times but without a denial, Rebecca scoffed, "See there. You can't prove he *isn't* the murderer. All you have is his word for it, and he certainly wouldn't tell you the truth . . . not if he's guilty."

Penny wasn't about to give up. "Then tell me why he's hanging around. If the man killed someone, he'd be stupid not to hightail it out of here." She answered her own question. "I'll tell you why. It's because he came here to Williamsburg on business, and since he isn't guilty of anything other than being careless enough to run into you, he has no reason to leave."

Rebecca's mouth twitched with rage. "So now *I'm* the one who's a threat? Is that it? Just because you were itching to get him in bed and got cheated out of being first, you're taking his side." She leaned in, her nose only inches from Penny. "So tell me something, Penelope Dawson, if I were a man, would that make a difference?"

The resounding crack of Penny's opened palm against Rebecca's cheek filtered through the trees and brought tears to Rebecca's eyes. But they were not tears of pain, rather full-blown, unbridled rage. Over the years they'd had many arguments on varying subjects, but never to the extent that their disagreements led to blows. Dangerously close to curling up her fist and smacking it against Penny's jaw, Rebecca changed her mind when she caught sight of the tall figure on the porch over Penny's shoulder. Jon-Gregory would hound her for an eternity to learn what had brought on such a display.

"I think this discussion has come to an end," she hissed,

and before Penny could apologize or tell her that she had it coming, Rebecca brushed past her and stormed across the yard in silent dismissal.

"Mind telling me what that was all about?" Jon-Gregory demanded as Rebecca came to the porch.

"I do," she barked, racing up the steps and hurrying for the front door.

"Well, it certainly isn't my idea of women talk." He glanced back at Penny in time to see her spin on her heels and march toward town in much the same manner as Rebecca was entering the house. He'd been aware of their fights long before now, but he had never assumed they got this violent. What worried him was the thought that perhaps this might be the end of their friendship. He liked Penny and didn't want to see the relationship dissolve . . . no matter what or who was the source of their disagreement. Deciding to voice his opinion, he turned back with that thought in mind, only to find himself alone on the porch. The slamming of a door from some distant part of the house reminded him of why he had intruded on the women in the first place, and his irritation rekindled all over again as he stared down at the newspaper he held in one hand. It wouldn't surprise him any to learn that what made him angry with Rebecca was the same reason Penny had stormed off. Rebecca had an uncanny way of getting under a person's skin. Leaving the porch, he went upstairs to confront Rebecca.

"Rebecca," he called once he stood before her closed and locked bedroom door, "open up. You and I have something to discuss."

"I've done all the talking I care to do for one evening, thank you" came the curt reply. "Go away."

"I will not. You have some explaining to do, and if you won't talk to me, I'm sure Mrs. Rind would like to hear it." He took a step back to wait, certain such a threat was all that it would take, and grinned victoriously when he heard the key turn in the lock. "Shall we go outside or talk here in the hallway?" he asked, trying not to stare at the bright, red mark on her cheek once she had opened the door and stood there glaring back at him.

"Here" was all she would say.

"All right," he relented, then thrust the newspaper at her. "I want you to explain the article at the bottom of the page."

The briefest of frowns wrinkled her brow as she took the proffered item and searched the numerous columns for the one he indicated. As she read, her anger waned and her face paled considerably. There in bold, black and white print was the article she had written about Alec Diamond this morning, the one she hadn't completely finished and the one she hadn't had time to show to Mrs. Rind.

"I know you're the one who wrote it, Rebecca," Jon-Gregory was saying, "so don't try to deny it. And I know who you're implying is Eli's killer." He took a step closer to her, lowered his chin and glared into her eyes. "Well, let me tell you something, Miss Know-It-All. You're wrong about Mr. Diamond. He couldn't possibly be the man you're after. Eli was already dead when I found him, and that was yesterday morning. Mr. Diamond's ship didn't dock until late last night. And if you don't want to believe me, ask Thomas Keenan. But . . . just in case you're still too mule-headed to accept his word, take a look at this." Bracing one hand against the door frame beside her, Jon-Gregory lifted his left foot and presented her with a clear view of the heel of his shoe, the one with the nick in it.

Chapter Seven

Morning dawned with such a vivid, blinding brilliance that Rebecca angrily rolled over on her stomach and buried her head beneath the pillow to block out the light. But even that failed to give her any comfort, for the agony she felt had little to do with the sunshine streaming into her room. She had skipped supper last night simply because she couldn't bear looking at Jon-Gregory from across the table, and now that another day had presented itself, she regretted having to face him at breakfast . . . or ever again. She dreaded even more having to account to Mrs. Rind—that was, of course, if she still had a job . . . which she doubted. The woman had a right to fire her. Rebecca had made a joke of the *Gazette* even though it wasn't all her fault. That nitwit Tommy Henderson should accept part of the blame. If it hadn't been for him—

"And who are you trying to convince?" she growled, flinging the pillow off her head and onto the floor as she practically threw herself out of bed. "You can't blame anyone but yourself. *You're* the idiot! Jon-Gregory said so. Penny said so." The angry flush to her face disappeared with the mention of her redheaded friend, and she sank back down on the mattress with a moan.

She had no right to talk to Penny the way she had. Penny had only wanted to warn her, and she had hurt her. And she had done it coldbloodedly. There was no excuse for her actions, and if Penny told her to go straight to hell without looking back, she wouldn't blame her. How could she have been so cruel? And how could she have been so stupid?

Bouncing off the bed again, she marched across the room to the dresser, intent on making herself presentable as quickly as possible and then finding Penny. She'd deserve it if Penny never forgave her—she had said a pretty mean thing to her—but at least she'd try. An impish smile wrinkled her cheek as she bent, caught the hem of her nightgown and pulled the garment up over her head. Maybe she could convince Penny that she had gone temporarily insane like some of the patients at the Public Hospital. It was known to happen. Slipping into the fresh camisole she had taken from the dresser drawer, she foolishly wondered if she could use that excuse with Mrs. Rind. It just might save her job. A frown returned and she shook her head. And then again it just might get her free room and board at the institution. Who'd argue with her? Jon-Gregory wouldn't. He'd often times told her she was crazy. Mrs. Rind would probably agree just to clear the *Gazette* of any wrongdoing. And as for Alec Diamond . . .

The mere mention of his name sent a chill through her. He was sure to read the newspaper. After all, he had placed an advertisement in it. What would he think when he read the article? Would he know it was written about him? Numb, she reached for her petticoats and stepped into them. Maybe not. The story was about a stranger in town who claimed he was here to buy some property, a man who said he didn't plan to move here, only expand his business—a rather vague excuse as far as the writer was concerned. She cringed. That pretty well marked Alec Diamond. But the part about the cane and the nick in the heel of the shoe print found at the scene might mislead him. The shoe belonged to Jon-Gregory. And several men in the area walked with the use of a cane.

"And he'd have to be addle-brained not to figure out I meant him," she mumbled, reaching into the armoire and grabbing a pastel green dress with emerald ribbons woven in at the waist. "I think, Rebecca Wilde, that you'd better go into hiding for a while." Fumbling with the last button up the

152

front of her bodice, she returned to the dresser and picked up her hairbursh to smooth the tangled mess of long, black locks, then pull the heavy strands back off her face with a ribbon in a similar hue to her dress. She'd sneak into The Red Lion through the back entrance, wait for Penny in her room, and apologize for being such a hardheaded fool. Then, after stopping off at the newspaper office to explain to Mrs. Rind, she'd return to the boardinghouse to hide. Alec Diamond was only here on business, which meant he didn't plan on staying in Williamsburg for long. Rebecca crossed her fingers, glanced heavenward and mouthed the words, *Please, God,* then settled herself on the edge of the bed to pull on her shoes.

Once Penny had unknowingly shown Alec where the little hellcat lived and had verified his suspicions that the two of them were friends, he had decided to do a little investigating of his own. Penny had pretty much told him about her background—providing they weren't lies—but he knew very little about Rebecca Wilde except that she lived in a boardinghouse, and aside from Miss Dawson, Jon-Gregory seemed to be Rebecca's only close friend. In order to understand what it was the two of them were after, he'd have to find out more about Miss Wilde.

Donning a clean shirt once he had shaved and rinsed the soap from his face, he picked up his brush and halfheartedly ran it through his dark, blond hair while unconsciously wandering to the window.

In order to make sure neither Penny nor Rebecca would see him while he witnessed their secretive meeting, he had reined his horse in near a cluster of trees several yards away. Not long afterward he saw the two women cross the porch and walk to the huge oak in the middle of the yard. He couldn't hear a single word they said, but from the agitated way they moved in response to something the other would say, Alec was reasonably sure they were arguing. And he was convinced *his* name was the topic of their conversation. However, when he saw Penny slap Rebecca, he was totally confused, and serious doubt began to creep into his thoughts.

He had hurriedly turned the mare around when Penny stomped off toward town and seemed to be heading in his direction. Her rage probably would have blinded her to the fact he was there, but he wanted to make sure he was already at The Red Lion when she returned. There had been a marked difference in the young woman's attitude once she had sat down at his table, and within minutes, she had excused herself from his presence and gone to her room, claiming her headache had worsened. Deducing that that was the last he'd see of either of them for the day, he had decided to put aside figuring out what to do about the pair and had gone to the courthouse to check up on the deed he prayed Heller had registered there. What he found surprised him even more than learning he had bedded a virgin. And it had made him even angrier.

Heller had seen fit to register the deed, but the property Alec *thought* he owned far exceeded what he had actually purchased. It was painfully obvious at that point that Daniel Heller had been hoodwinked. *Alec* had been hoodwinked. And right after breakfast, he planned to take a ride out to the property to see for himself. He rather doubted it, but he was hoping he might find something there that would tell him what had happened to his agent and who was responsible.

The first image that came to mind when he awoke a few minutes ago had been of the two women standing beneath the oak tree and how Penny had slapped her companion. Rebecca had unwittingly admitted that the two of them were friends, and he had decided that whatever Rebecca had said to Penny must have been pretty bad for a friend to lash out physically the way Penny had. Tossing down his brush, he grabbed his jacket off the chair and headed for the door. He knew he'd be the last person Penny would confide in about the fight, but if he worded it right, maybe she'd at least give him a hint. He'd have breakfast with her, lure her into a conversation about various kinds of friendship and what was expected of them, then visit his property.

The commons was unusually busy this morning, and it

154

surprised Alec not to find Penny in the midst of the activity, smiling and laughing with the customers as she normally did. Deciding that perhaps she was just late in coming down, he crossed the room and took a seat at the only available table.

"Good morning, Mr. Diamond." Ben smiled as he approached with a cup of steaming tea. "Sleep well?"

"Yes, thank you." Alec nodded. "It's rather busy this morning. Is something going on that I should know about?"

"Oh, it only seems that way because I'm all alone to wait tables this morning. Service is a little slow."

"Is Miss Dawson ill?"

Ben raised his eyebrows and sighed. "Yes. And it's always like this when I don't have her help. I don't know what I'll do if she ever decides to quit her job."

"Is she thinking about it?" Alec's darkly tanned brow wrinkled with his frown. Had the argument between Penny and her friend been so devastating that Penny was considering a change of scenery?

"Oh, no. Wasn't what I meant," Ben quickly amended. "But the thought always crosses my mind whenever she's sick and can't work." Handing Alec the newspaper Ben had tucked under his arm, he added, "Here. This will give you something to do while I fix your breakfast. Anything special ya want?"

Alec shook his head. "Whatever's quick and easy for you. I've business to take care of this morning."

"I'll make it as fast as I can," Ben guaranteed before turning around and heading back to the kitchen.

Until Ben produced a copy of the *Gazette* for him to read, Alec had nearly forgotten about the advertisement he had paid for, and as he started to unfold the newspaper, he realized what—or rather who—had distracted him. A soft, amused smile curled his lips as he envisioned the long, luscious strands of rich, black hair, the pale, creamy skin, full, tempting curves, the gentle thrust of her hips in response to his lovemaking— The image vanished and the smile disappeared. He would never be able to think about that night without remembering the price Rebecca had paid. He jerked the newspaper open and settled his attention on the

155

first page. And if he had to sit on her to get her to hold still long enough to tell him why she had given herself to him, that's exactly what he'd do. One tawny brow slanted upward as he stared blankly at the paper he held. *And then what will you do?* he asked himself. *Ask her to marry you? Ha! You'd have to tell her. And if you don't want to marry her, she certainly wouldn't want to marry you!* Exhaling a quick, angry sigh, he frowned and forced his eyes to focus on the print. A second later his thoughts were on Rebecca again. She didn't need a husband. She needed a keeper. *And* she needed to be taught a lesson. She was too impudent for her own good. Spotting the cup of tea Ben had left him, Alec laid aside the newspaper and took a swallow, wincing when it burned his throat. Rebecca Wilde was like a summer rain storm: exciting, sweet smelling, violent, full of energy, unpredictable and something over which Alec had no control. He couldn't ignore her any more than he could ignore the thunder, lightning and rain. He couldn't stop a downpour, and he couldn't stop the thoughts of her from creeping into his mind.

Oh? he silently announced. Well, he'd certainly give it one helluva try!

Grabbing the newspaper again, he opened it up and scanned the many words and columns, looking for the advertisement he hoped would unravel the mystery around Daniel Heller. A moment later, his brown eyes darkened all the more, for there at the bottom of the page was an article that at first had only sparked his curiosity until the subject and the man mentioned in the story struck a chilling resemblance to himself and his situation.

"Two days ago, Gideon Blackstock's manservant, Eli, was found dead near the docks on the James River," it read. "His skull had been crushed by some*thing* or some*one*. It is the collective opinion of the men in Williamsburg that the young Negro boy died accidentally. If that is true, then why was his body lying in a place where there was only soft soil, sand, grass and leaves? Where was the rock he supposedly hit his head on? It is the belief of this writer that he was murdered. Why? One would have to ask the man responsible. And who is this man? Is he tall, blond, handsome, well-dressed, walks with a cane and has a nick in the heel of his left shoe? Does he claim to be in our fair city on business? What kind of business? Where did he come from? How did he get here? What was his reason for murdering young Eli? Could it be that Eli knew something this man wanted kept a secret?"

In Alec's estimation the story wasn't finished as if the writer had other thoughts *she* wanted to add but had run out of time. As he slowly and deliberately crumpled up the newspaper, his temper rapidly rising, he suddenly understood why she had followed him. And he understood the price he was going to pay for bedding the saucy wench. They weren't planning to blackmail him. He doubted, now, that Ben even knew about that night. Penny obviously did. And she obviously knew what retaliation Rebecca had planned for him. *That* was the reason the two women had fought. Well, he'd put an end to this before it went too far. Furious, he pushed himself up, tossed the newspaper on the table beside his half-finished cup of tea and headed for the front door. He'd talk to Rebecca Wilde right now, and he didn't care who overheard him.

The door to The Red Lion resounded with a loud crack when he slammed it shut behind him. People on the sidewalk and in the street stopped to stare in mild curiosity, but Alec paid them no mind nor did he honestly notice them. His attention was centered on the main entrance to the building some thirty feet farther on, and if anyone had the misfortune of stepping in the way, he'd more than likely knock them aside in his haste to get at the little vamp who had caused him so much trouble of late. Bounding up the front steps, he seized the knob and swung the door open, silently arguing with himself not to get too violent with her. *Maybe I'll just wring her neck,* he mused, his mouth set in a hard line. *Or maybe I ought to simply take a horsewhip to her. God knows she has it coming!*

His rage lessened a bit once he stepped into the newspaper office and was met by a tall, lanky woman in her early thirties, who introduced herself as Mrs. Rind and asked if there was something she could do for him. He felt like shouting at the top of his lungs and demanding to know where the arrogant, troublesome, little vixen was at the moment, the one who called herself a reporter, but realized he shouldn't take his anger out on this innocent woman. During his somewhat limited encounters with Rebecca Wilde, he had drawn the conclusion that the little imp did whatever she liked without answering to anyone. Well, *that* was about to change.

"I'm here to speak to Miss Wilde," he told Clementina, somehow managing to keep his mounting ire under control. But once she informed him that Rebecca had yet to come to work and that Mrs. Rind assumed it was because Rebecca was too ill, Alec had to fight the desire to laugh out loud. *She's not sick. She's hiding!* Without the courtesy of thanking Mrs. Rind for her help, he turned and quickly left the office. Now that he knew where she lived, he'd simply go there and have it out with her!

Once he stood on the sidewalk outside the Ludwell-Paradise House, Alec paused in thought. He'd waste time going after his horse; but the long walk to Rebecca's would probably cool his temper, and he'd rather that not happen. He didn't want to back down in the slightest. She should see his rage in its fullest. She should see firsthand the results of her careless reporting, her prying into other people's affairs. How dare she accuse him of murdering anyone! Well, maybe that would change. He certainly felt like strangling *her!*

His indecision was a godsend, for in that moment of consideration, a young boy on the sidewalk ahead of him caught Alec's attention when he raised a hand to wave at someone he saw cutting through the side yard dividing The Red Lion from the Ludwell-Paradise House and out of Alec's view. Alec would have brushed it off since he didn't know the youth, and would have turned to his left and started off toward the boardinghouse had the young man not called out the name of the very woman he was looking for. Alec's head came up, his ears tuned for her response, and before the boy could get away, Alec hurried toward him and roughly caught Tommy Henderson's arm while he scanned the empty yard off to his right.

"Hey!" the boy exclaimed, his pale green eyes widening in a mixture of surprise, irritation, then fear.

"Where is she?" Alec ground out.

Tommy tried to wrench his arm free. "Where's who?"

"Rebecca Wilde!"

Tommy quit struggling. He could tell by the look on the stranger's face that he didn't want to acquire the knowledge of Rebecca's whereabouts to express his concern for her health. Tommy also sensed he was about to be the brunt of Rebecca's problems again, and since he had already made up his mind earlier that he was not going to take the blame for anything she did, he raised a trembling hand toward The Red Lion. This man obviously had little patience for games, and Tommy had no desire to play.

It only took Alec a second or two to figure out where Rebecca was headed and that if he wanted to catch her before she got to Penny's room, he'd have to enter through the front door of the inn, race through the commons and up the steps to be in the hall ahead of her.

As Rebecca hurriedly closed the door behind her, she cursed her misfortune of having been spotted by Tommy. All she could do now was pray he wouldn't tell Mrs. Rind. She didn't want the woman to think she was avoiding her, that she was too cowardly to face up to her mistake. Heaving a weary sigh since it seemed her entire world was crumbling down around her and there wasn't anything she could do to stop it, she started toward the back stairs that would lead her to Penny's room. Mrs. Rind would just have to wait. She had to speak with her friend first. Maybe she couldn't stop what was happening; but she might be able to change it a little, and she'd start with Penny. If everything else in her life was ruined, she'd at least have her friend . . . hopefully.

Once she reached the top of the staircase, Rebecca paused to peer around the corner into the hallway, her heart thumping loudly in her chest. There was always the chance Alec Diamond was still in his room—whichever one that might be—and since he was the last person she wanted to see, she had to be careful not to get caught in the middle of the hall should he happen to decide to go down to the commons just now. Seeing that the corridor was empty, she guardedly stepped out into the open. Penny's room was at the opposite end of the long hallway, and once she started toward it, there would be no place to hide. Hurrying her steps, she headed toward her destination, silently wondering if she should bother to knock first, in case Penny hadn't gone down to work yet, or simply grab the key and let herself in. Deciding on the latter since it was the quickest way to get out of the hall before anyone saw her, she focused her attention on the top ledge of the framework around the door and started to run. She had just reached it and was sliding her fingers along the ridge when she heard the racing footfalls of someone on the front staircase. Whoever it was would be in the corridor in a matter of seconds! She had to find the key and open the door! Frightened, tears burned her eyes as she ran her fingers over the ledge a second time. Where was the blasted key? The footsteps were getting louder! Panic riding high, she jumped back to study the door in front of which she stood, thinking she had come to the wrong room. No. This was Penny's place. Then where . . . ?

A chill darted up her spine when she suddenly heard no other sound but that of her pulse hammering in her ears. Afraid to move or to look in the direction of the front stairwell, she just stood there, foolishly praying she would somehow become invisible. She didn't have to turn her head to know she wasn't alone in the hall. She could sense his presence. She could feel the heat of his body and of his wrath. She could smell his masculine scent and the rage that tensed every muscle in his body. In her mind's eye, she could see the hateful, dangerous look on his face. Maybe he wasn't the one who killed young Eli, but she was reasonably sure he was capable of murder at this very moment, and once the truth was told, no one would blame him. Thinking it was best to make a hasty departure without trying to explain, she gulped down her fear and took a tentative step sideways. Her only hope of survival was the narrow head start she had.

Seeing Rebecca as she stood before the door to Penny's

room had a devastating effect on Alec. She wasn't dressed as a boy with a floppy hat and dirt smudges on the tip of her nose. Nor was she the young woman who worked at the newspaper office. He saw her only as the mysterious lady of his passion, and several thoughts raced through his head. He envisioned her as she was that night: an innocent, young woman who had come to visit her friend and found more than she could handle, a virgin, a damnable, foolish, headstrong virgin! Why, in God's name, hadn't she called out? Why hadn't she resisted? Why hadn't she screamed? He would have stopped and there wouldn't have been a need for him to be standing here in the hall right now, ready to make a grab for her the second she started to run. And that's exactly what she was planning to do. He could sense it. Well, she was about to learn that running away never solved anything. It only worsened the problems. He could attest to that.

"Miss Wilde," he said, forcing himself to take another step toward her. "I think it's time you and I had a long talk."

If Rebecca hadn't been so scared, she would have laughed out loud. She sincerely doubted that all he wanted to do was talk. He wanted to strangle her, and if she screamed for help, no one would come to her aid. She deserved his ire and anything else he decided to do to her, and once a would-be rescuer saw who was being attacked and who was the attacker, that person would nod his head, say she had it coming and turn away. Her eyes wide with terror, she glanced fearfully at him for only the briefest of seconds, then spun on her heels and raced off down the hallway toward the back stairs.

He was on her in a flash, seizing the long, thick locks of her hair flying out in back of her long before she had reached the stairway. She screamed in pain and in horror when he jerked her backward into his arms, and was about to scream again when a wide hand came up to cover her mouth and stifle her second attempt to send out an alarm. His strength didn't really surprise Rebecca, but when he lifted her up off her feet and perched her on his hip as he might a sack of flour, she began flailing her arms and legs in the hope of landing a blow where it would do some good. She might deserve what was

161

coming, but she certainly wasn't going to give in without a fight!

Alec winced each time a tiny fist, elbow or foot painfully landed a blow to his ribs, stomach or shin. But his rage kept a tight grip on her as he carried her down the hall toward the door at the far end, and as they passed by Penny's room, the young woman suddenly appeared at the threshold, her big, brown eyes wide with surprise and concern. Alec didn't cherish the idea of fending off two hot-tempered females in his quest to get Rebecca alone where they could discuss her shortcomings, and accordingly sent the young redhead a warning glance not to interfere as he hurried on by with his captive. Luckily, no one else had heard Rebecca's cry for help, and since Penny had obviously decided not to intervene but rather return to her room and close the door, Alec was free to escort Rebecca to his own room without an argument from anyone. Once they were safely inside, he gave the little hellcat a shove and turned to lock the door behind them.

"If you don't allow me to leave," Rebecca gasped breathlessly, "I'll scream so loud it'll bring the entire town pounding on that door!"

"Go right ahead," Alec challenged, his broad frame blocking the way. With his chin lowered and his nostrils flared as he glared back at her, he folded his arms over his chest and added threateningly, "If you want everyone to know what happened between us, go right ahead. Scream. As loud and as long as you wish. It won't be *my* reputation that's ruined." He raised a long, brown finger and pointed at the rocking chair. "Sit!"

Some of Rebecca's spunk evaporated. Reluctant and a bit fearful, she numbly backed toward the piece of furniture he indicated and sank down into it.

Alec wasn't sure if his offer would work on Rebecca until he saw the horrified look on her pretty face. Obviously it had, and knowing her weakness was the advantage he needed. Now all he had to do was figure out whether or not she'd tell him the truth. Remembering the sudden appearance of Penny Dawson in defense of her friend gave him the

162

solution. He'd talk to this one first, then verify the story with the redhead. One discrepancy and he'd know she had lied. However, the problem he faced now was in deciding where to begin. Maybe if he threatened to get her fired from her job, she'd open up on her own. Plucking the key from the lock, he slipped it in the pocket of his waistcoat and crossed the room to stare outside at the yard below his window.

"Did Mrs. Rind approve of the story you wrote about me?" he asked after a while.

Rebecca would have liked to say yes. She would have taken comfort in knowing someone, *any*one was on her side. But the truth of the matter was that she wasn't sure. After her argument with Jon-Gregory, she had locked herself in her room and lain awake until well past midnight trying to figure out how her article had managed to appear in the *Gazette*. Mrs. Rind would have had the same questions Penny asked, and until she was convinced everything in the story was accurate, she wouldn't have printed it. Since she and Mrs. Rind hadn't discussed the facts, Rebecca was almost positive she wouldn't have included it in yesterday's edition. That left Tommy. He must have seen what Rebecca had written and assumed it was to be printed. Who was to tell him differently? She had gone off to follow Alec without giving him any instructions, and Mrs. Rind was at a luncheon. Well, maybe she was wrong about the shoe with a nick in it belonging to Alec Diamond, but there were still an awful lot of unanswered questions concerning the man. He was hiding something. She just knew it. And the only way to save her hide was to find out what it was.

"Who said the story was written about you?"

Alec's head jerked around to stare at her. "Are you saying it wasn't?"

"Was your name mentioned?" The angry frown he gave her unnerved Rebecca, but she wasn't going to let it intimidate her.

"Then who was it written about?"

Rebecca bravely shrugged a delicate shoulder as if he didn't frighten her. "It was written to raise a few eyebrows. Eli was murdered, and whoever did it should pay."

163

Alec turned to face her. "And you think I did it."

"Did you?" A faint smile parted her lips. "Penny doesn't think so. Neither does Jon-Gregory."

"But you do," he pressed.

"Let's say I'm not convinced you didn't."

Exhaling an angry breath, Alec stiffened his tall frame and walked to the dresser and the wine decanter he had instructed Ben to see brought to his room. He poured a glass full, then returned to the window where he leaned a shoulder against the framework. "Suppose you tell me why you're not convinced."

Rebecca immediately thought of the impressions in the soft soil beside the spot where Eli's body had been found. Now that the shoe print belonged to Jon-Gregory, it left only that of the cane. Her evidence had become a little thin, but she refused to dismiss her instincts. "There's a strong indication that says you were there at the scene."

Alec's eyes never left her as he took a sip of wine. "That's true. I was there twice."

Rebecca's stomach churned. My God! Was he about to confess?

"I walked near the spot the night I arrived at the docks and again yesterday afternoon. But you already know that since you followed me there."

She could feel her cheeks pinken. He wasn't supposed to have seen her. "The night you arrived . . . which night was that? The night before or after Eli was killed?"

"After."

Rebecca twisted around in the rocker to face him full front. "Can you *prove* that?"

Alec nodded. "I have several witnesses. The captain and crew of the ship I was on, and Thomas Keenan to name a few. Then, of course, there was your close friend, Penny Dawson. She seems to know everything that goes on in this town." Alec casually took another drink, then allowed his gaze to slowly and deliberately drop to her rounded bosom, on to her narrow waist and the long, slender legs hidden beneath the folds of her skirt and then back to her face. "And then there was one other. A very warm, sensuous, alluringly devious, young virgin who crawled into my bed thinking she could extract money from me."

Rebecca failed to see the trap he set. Jumping to her feet, arms akimbo, she stuttered and stammered a moment as she fought for the right words to hurl at him. "Money! What do you think I am? A courtesan? And I didn't crawl, I—" Rebecca's face flamed a scarlet hue the instant she realized what she had done. Any other woman would have turned on her heel and ran, hiding herself away somewhere to soothe her shame and injured pride. But not Rebecca. It just wasn't in her. She was used to standing up for herself, and she wasn't about to change now. Not for anyone. And certainly not Alec Diamond! Her embarrassment turned to rage. "Oh, I get it," she hissed, taking a step toward him. "You think I wrote the article to get even for your raping me."

"*Rape!*" Alec nearly dropped his glass. "I'd hardly call what happened between us rape, Miss Wilde. A disaster, maybe. Or better said, a nightmare, but hardly rape. Rape is when one party resists, when someone takes advantage of the situation, the way you took advantage of me. I was sound asleep when you let yourself into the room. *I* wasn't the one who undressed you. *I* didn't force you into bed. In fact, I don't remember you once putting up any kind of a struggle. Well, you know what I think, Miss Wilde? I think *I* was the one who was raped because if I had known what the results would be, *I* would have resisted. *I* would have screamed injustice."

Rebecca didn't know why, but she felt insulted. "Well, thank you, Mr. Diamond! I'm sure if I had given myself to *anyone* else, *they* would have been honored."

Alec didn't agree. "What man in his right mind would *want* to tangle with you?" he muttered. Then he asked more forcibly, "And why in bloody hell did you have to pick me?"

"I didn't 'pick' you, you . . . you conceited lout!"

"Who did then? Penny? Was the whole thing set up from the beginning? Did poor Rebecca Wilde, the *virgin,* want to get bedded so badly that she asked her friend to help because she didn't know how to arrange it?"

Rebecca's mouth dropped open. Her rage darkened the

pale blueness of her eyes. Her body trembled with unbridled wrath. Then, low in her chest, a growl erupted and grew in volume until it rang in Alec's ears, and before he could guess her intent, she hurled herself at him with fingers curled.

Alec never would have guessed the strength of this wildcat had he not had to defend himself against her attack. Unable to deposit his wineglass safely on the nearby table, he tossed it aside and with lightning speed grabbed her wrists before she could do him any serious harm. Or so he thought. With her hands imprisoned in his steely hold, she lashed out at him with the heel of her shoe. Zeroing in on his toe, she stomped down hard and instantly won her freedom when he bellowed in pain and let go. Thinking to remain a gentleman rather than wrap his fingers around her neck and squeeze, he hurriedly stepped away from her. But that move only seemed to infuriate her all the more when he artfully shadowed every step she took and managed to keep a safe distance between them.

"Rebecca," he growled, pointing a finger at her. "You're trying my patience."

His warning had little effect on her. "And you've broken mine, you back street rapscallion! I'll take responsibility for the insults you're so free with, but I won't stand still and listen to you degrade my friend!"

Spotting the water pitcher on the washstand next to her, she seized it by the handle and flung it his way. Her aim was off, and the brightly painted piece of porcelain crashed against the wall behind him. But the spray of water emitting from it as the pitcher flew past him caught him squarely in the chest. It splashed up into his face and totally drenched his lower torso. Ironic that its coolness only added heat to his raging temper, and had Rebecca had her wits about her, she would have recognized the fact that she had overstepped her bounds. Alec took pride in his appearance, and to be soaked from head to toe while he was still fully dressed tested his will to the limit. But then again Rebecca's patience had been shattered long ago. This arrogant demented buffoon was trying to blame her for what happened! He said *she* was the aggressor! That she *wanted* him to touch her, to make love to her. Well, right now all she wanted was to land one solid punch!

It suddenly dawned on Rebecca that the only way out of the room was through the door, and it was locked and the key was in his pocket. He couldn't open up the way quickly enough to escape before she had her chance, and she decided that his hesitation to stand his ground might play to her advantage. She'd back him into a corner and then let him have it! Gritting her teeth, she lowered her chin and advanced.

Alec was wondering what the penalty would be for ridding the town of a nuisance while at the same time considering what method to use: tossing her out the window or stuffing her in a gunny sack and dumping them both in the James River. She had no right to be angry. He hadn't done anything . . . except be in the wrong place at the wrong time. And look what she'd done to his clothes! Concentrating on his soggy attire rather than on his determined companion, he began to disrobe, thinking that as soaked as they were, it would be hours before they were dry again. He'd have to change into something else. Slipping out of the jacket, then his waistcoat, he tossed them over the back of the rocker and started to unfasten the buttons on his shirt, totally unaware of the young woman who had moved within a few feet of him. Then something pricked his consciousness, and he glanced up in time to see her clench her fists and prepare to attack.

Alec swore he would never come to understand how he had failed to realize that Rebecca wouldn't be satisfied with just dousing him with water. She was angry enough to draw blood. The deadly look in her eye confirmed it. If he was to save himself from certain harm, he'd have to prove to her that he wasn't going to simply stand by and allow it to happen. But that would be rather difficult to achieve and still remain a gentleman. In all his days, he had never laid a hand on a woman in anger, and even though she deserved it, he wasn't going to make an exception in her case. But how . . . ?

He wasn't given the chance to figure out a way to stop her,

and the startled frown barely had time to kink his brow before she was on him. Tiny fists struck his chest and shoulders. They caused little pain, but certainly bruised his ego. He raised his arms to thwart off the blows and backed away. She kept coming. She hit his ear, his forearm and landed a blow to his breastbone. He winced when that one connected, and out of desperation tried to make a grab for her. That, however, was a mistake. By dropping his guard in an attempt to seize her around the waist, Rebecca's fist managed to find the corner of his mouth. He tasted blood instantly.

"Damn it, Reb! Stop it before I—"

Rebecca wasn't listening. She continued her assault with a vengeance once she saw the dot of red trickling from his lip. It was minor damage compared to what she had planned for him. Wildly flinging her arms in any direction she felt might do some good, she hurriedly followed his every step as he backed away. In a false sense of victory, she moved in for the kill. In that instant, she felt his viselike grip on her wrists and the surprising quickness of his moves when he yanked her arms down and pinned them behind her. Her breath left her in a rush when he crushed her to him, and before she remembered how she had freed herself the last time, he had spun her around with him and threw them across the bed. The shock of being so easily subdued left her weak, and before she could regain her strength *and* her senses, Alec had rolled her beneath him and trapped her arms at her sides with his knees holding them immobile as he straddled her and sat up to gingerly touch a fingertip to his bleeding lip. His suntanned face was dark with rage, his brow furrowed, his nostrils flared and the look in his eye chilled her to the bone. It was time she made an exit. He'd had enough.

"Let me up," she demanded, straining to pull loose.

"So you can hit me again?" he snarled. "Not on your life."

"So I can leave!" she shouted.

"To do what? Go home and get a gun?"

"Don't tempt me!"

"Tempting you is *not* what I had in mind."

168

Rebecca's eyes narrowed. "Oh? And what did you have in mind? Murder? Or rape?" She tried again to wrench her arms free.

Alec glared at her a moment while he tightened the muscles in his legs to hold her still. "You have about as much sense as a two-year-old child. Did you ever once consider what the consequences might be if I *had* been the one who killed that black boy? You make a public statement that does everything but spell out my name *before* you have all the facts or even bother to talk to someone in authority. You don't even try to keep your identity a secret which leaves an open invitation for the real murderer to slit your throat." He leaned forward a little. "Think how easy it would be for me to do just that."

Rebecca hated to admit he was right. He could very easily kill her. Her dainty mouth curled unflatteringly. But more than that, she knew he wouldn't.

"As for rape," he continued, placing his hands on either side of her head and lowering his face to within inches of hers, "that, too, would be simple to achieve. There's one problem, however. I never have and never will rape a woman. But should I ever happen to change my mind, *you'd be my last choice!*"

Rebecca should have been grateful. She wasn't. Using every ounce of strength she could muster, she arched her hips, caught Alec off balance and unawares, and jerked him up enough to free her hands. In new-found rage she hammered blows against his chest and stomach, but only until he decided it was time to get off. Shifting his weight, he rolled onto his side, thinking Rebecca would jump at the opportunity to run. He couldn't have been more wrong. Instead of springing to her feet, she continued her assault, and Alec found himself at a disadvantage when she threw herself on top of him.

"You crazy wench!" he exploded, fending off the blows and trying to remove himself from her vicinity. But to no avail, Rebecca was determined to cause him great pain. "Reb, if you don't stop this instant, I'll forget you're a woman! So help me, God. Ouch!"

The last was an expression of the discomfort he endured when her knee connected with his thigh. His patience shattered, and seeing no other way to subdue her, he raised up, caught her by the shoulders and attempted to pin her beneath him again. He'd let her struggle until all of her strength was gone, and then *maybe* they could talk this out. He didn't plan on telling her everything about his personal life, but enough to convince her that he had no interest in a young, black servant named Eli. However, as he pushed himself up and started to shove her over on her back, Rebecca grabbed both hands full of his hair and tried to wrench it from his head.

"Sweet mother of God," he roared, clasping her wrists and burying his thumbs in the tender flesh to force her fingers to relax. It worked, but it didn't finish Rebecca's efforts to seriously hurt him. With the momentum of their bodies already changing directions, Rebecca pushed up with one hip, thinking to roll them one more time and place her on top. The width of the bed forbid it, and before either of them could stop, they rolled off the mattress and onto the floor. Alec's body cushioned most of the fall, saving Rebecca any great deal of pain, but having been subjected to such unnecessary abuse triggered Alec's full blown rage.

"Enough!" he bellowed, giving her a healthy shove and then jumping to his feet once he was clear of her. He had been pushed, beaten and abused to the limit. He would tolerate no more! Glaring down at her, he snarled, "Dear God in heaven, I don't know what I did to deserve you."

"Nor I, you!" Rebecca rallied as she scrambled to her feet. Her long, black hair had worked loose of its ribbon and fell in wildly tossed curls about her head and shoulders. Her cheeks were flushed. The top three buttons on her dress had popped free to expose the deep valley between her breasts, and there was a red mark on her long, slim neck. She didn't look any worse for the wear, but the flinty gleam in her eyes hinted otherwise. "I didn't ask for you to be in Penny's bed. Had I known, I *never* would have come. *She* was the one you were expecting, not me!" Tears glistened in her pale blue eyes. "And then you have the nerve to stand there and pretend its all my fault. Who do you think you are? You're intolerable! That's what you are. And you're a lousy lover!" Thinking this conversation was at an end, she started past him.

Alec had been called a number of things in his life, but never a lousy lover, and he considered asking her how she had drawn such a conclusion when he had been the first. But something else, something more important bothered him. If she hadn't come to his bed with the purpose of learning the art of love, why hadn't she cried out? Why hadn't she screamed? Anything? She had stolen into his arms then disappeared into the darkness without a sound. Well, maybe it *was* a mistake, and for that, he was sorry. He caught her arm as she moved past him.

"Reb, I'm—"

"Let go!" she snapped, digging her nails in the strong fingers wrapped around her wrist. "And don't call me Reb!"

His sympathy waned. "Damn it, woman!" He seized her other wrist, twisted her arms in back of her and yanked her forward into his paralyzing embrace. "I'm trying to apologize!"

Rebecca stopped struggling. She wanted to believe him, but since when had she trusted anything a *man* said? She cocked a brow suspiciously at him.

"I should have known the second I touched you. I should have realized you were different. I can only blame it on my being tired and having had a little too much wine." He loosened his grip on her a little but didn't let go. "If you had only said something—" He sighed heavily, thinking that this whole mess really was his fault. His gaze lowered to those tempting red lips, then on to the full swell of her bosom, and his blood warmed. Suddenly the sweet scent of her filled his nostrils, the softness of her luscious curves pressed against him burned where they touched, and before he realized what he was doing or how it would affect Rebecca, he lowered his head and tenderly kissed her.

Rebecca stiffened instantly. She had sensed his insincerity. She knew he couldn't be trusted. Men only wanted two things from a woman: her passion and her silence. Well,

Alec Diamond wasn't about to have either! Working one hand free, she was about to bring it up and claw his face when she felt herself being lowered onto the bed. The memory of those delicious moments they shared flooded her mind and sent her head spinning. He hadn't really been a lousy lover as she claimed. Of course, she had nothing to compare him with, but the titilating excitement he had aroused in her that night was slow to die. The feather mattress beneath her cushioned their descent. His lips were warm and moist and sensuous. His strong, thickly muscled body pressed against her stirred the embers of her desire, and she lost the will to fight him.

Alec felt her surrender and his pulse quickened. The fragrance of her hair and skin filled his senses and dulled his wit. He was vaguely aware of what he was doing or what the result would be, only that this little minx had poisoned his reasoning. She had sparked his passion, and the visions of the night they spent together—the bliss of it—rekindled the wanton desires to sample it again. His mouth moved hungrily over hers, their tongues clashing, their fingers slipping to the fastenings of his shirt, her dress. In a fevered rush, they slid from their clothes, and their passion ran high. Long, brown fingers traced the exquisite curve of her spine as he rolled beneath her, then his caress moved on to her buttocks and hips, while his mouth greedily tasted the sweetness of hers. His breathing quickened. His heart thundered in his chest. His flesh burned from the contact of naked bodies held tightly together, and he moaned deliriously when she trailed hot kisses down his throat, the coolness of her touch lingering over his thickly muscled ribs and taut belly. She rose above him, her lips parted most alluringly, her pale blue eyes dark with unbridled lust. Alec could feel his blood raging through his veins at that moment. She was *the* most beautiful woman he had ever seen. Long, black hair fell in thick, shiny curls about her face and over creamy, white shoulders. Full, ripe breasts tempted him to run his thumb over the rose-hued peaks, to sample the honey flavor of her flesh. Her narrow waist was small enough to encircle within his hands, and for the briefest of seconds he considered giving up his freedom and all that went with it to claim her as his own. That stunning revelation killed his desire. His blood cooled instantly. The thumping of his heart softened, and for the first time in his life, he was ashamed. Their first time together had been an accident. *This* was a mistake!

"Rebecca," he whispered with a frown as he reached up to catch his fingers in her luscious black hair and draw her down against him. "This is wrong." Gently, he rolled her onto her back and tenderly covered her with the quilt as he lifted from her. Turning, he gathered up his breeches and hurriedly donned them. "I never should have let it go this far. I shouldn't have taken advantage. . . ." Feeling sick inside, he closed his eyes and rubbed his brow to ease the pounding in his temples. All he could think of was how his mother had probably been seduced in much the same manner. Whether she had been willing or not—just as Rebecca was willing— Lora Stone had paid dearly for her transgression. She had bore a son out of wedlock and lived her life in disgrace. She had never known the love of a man, his tenderness, his caring, and Alec realized Rebecca would suffer much the same way. In time, when they discovered that their passion was all that brought them together, they would grow to hate each other. Rebecca—though headstrong and rebellious— deserved better. He took a deep breath and exhaled slowly. Now, if he could only make her understand.

She had already donned her undergarments and was tugging on her hose when he turned back to explain his untimely change of mind. He expected to see tears of humiliation and a scarlet hue staining her flawless face. He was partly right. Her cheeks were pink, but he quickly realized that it was rage that darkened her flesh not embarrassment. And it didn't take him a second to figure out her reason for being angry.

"Reb, let me explain," he cautioned. "It isn't what you think."

"Isn't it?" Her voice was icy cold. "You men are all alike. You use women and then toss them away like you would an old, dirty shirt." She made a grab for her petticoats, intending to step into them, and jumped back when Alec reached out to take her arm.

"I'm not like other men, damn it! And if you'd give me a chance to—"

"To what? Lie your way out of this?" Her blue eyes sparked flashes of pure rage as she quickly eluded his second attempt to grab her.

Alec knew this wasn't going to be easy, and had it been anyone else he wouldn't have tried. His nostrils flared a little when he exhaled angrily. "You don't know enough about me to make such an assumption. But if you'd calm down for a minute, I can make you understand why I changed my mind."

Rebecca truly wanted to hear his explanation. If he only meant to use her, it didn't make any sense for him to stop. Unless his motive was humiliation. She certainly felt *that!* With her eyes trained on him lest he move when her attention was away from him, she groped beside her for the coverlet, tore it from the bed and awkwardly covered her sparsely clad body. "Two minutes. You have two minutes to try and talk me out of telling Jon-Gregory that you tried to rape me."

Alec's shoulders dropped. "You sure are a hard learner, Rebecca Wilde."

"Well, you don't think I'd tell him any differently!"

"Why? Are you ashamed of the truth?"

Rebecca could feel the color in her cheeks growing darker. "You have a minute and a half left, Mr. Diamond," she answered, though her tone had lost a little of its tenacity. She dropped her gaze and gave him wide berth as she walked past him and went to the rocker to sit down.

Alec stood perfectly still while he listened to her bare feet tread across the rug to the opposite side of the room. He was thinking that if he were the type, he'd show her what forced seduction really was. He mentally cringed at the thought of all the bumps, bruises, scratches and verbal abuse he'd suffer in the process and quickly dismissed the idea. He liked his women to be soft, alluring, and willing as well as smart enough to know the affair was only temporary. Rebecca hardly fell into any of those categories. Yet, because of what

174

happened, he felt he really should explain. Besides, maybe she'd learn something from it. Deciding he could use another glass of wine, he rounded the end of the bed and headed for the table where the decanter sat.

"While I was growing up," he began, pulling the stopper from the bottle and pouring himself a liberal amount, "I learned what it was like for a woman to raise a child alone. Especially if she had never been married. Her real friends could be counted on one hand. Her neighbors gossiped about her. She was shunned by the 'respectable' ladies in town, and the men made lewd remarks behind her back. No one cared about the love she had in her heart for the father of her child or that if it had been at all possible, she would have married him. All they could see was a woman who had shamed herself, and they didn't want to associate with someone like her. What was really surprising was how these same people treated her child, as if it was his fault." A pained expression came over his face as he recalled some of the things Lora Stone's neighbors and the townsfolk said to him, the names they called him, but he kept his back turned to Rebecca so that she wouldn't see. He lifted the glass to his lips and downed all the wine in one swallow, then faced her. "That's why I changed my mind, Rebecca. I don't want that happening to you or to any child our union might produce. As soon as my business here in Williamsburg is completed, I'll be moving on."

A whirlwind of emotions flooded through her in those moments. Although he hadn't actually come out and admitted it, she sensed the woman and her child of whom he spoke were his mother and himself. It pained her to hear of such atrocities brought down on a young woman's head as well as an innocent child, and what amazed her about it was that it hadn't turned him into a cruel, unfeeling adult. He certainly had the right. Yet here he was expressing his concern for her future and vowing never to put her in the kind of situation that would ruin her life. *And* he was telling her that within a few days, he'd be leaving for good. Her own brow furrowed with confusion. How could she go from hating him one moment to being filled with passion, then anger, humiliation, sympathy and finally sadness in the very next instant? What could it possibly mean? Nervously aware of her lack of dress, she hugged the quilt to her and stood. Unable to look at him, she crossed back to the bed and hurriedly donned the rest of her things before turning to face him. She didn't like being wrong about someone, especially a man, but she knew she was wrong about Alec Diamond.

"I'll see that the *Gazette* prints a retraction, Mr. Diamond," she pledged in hardly more than a whisper as she moved toward the door. "And I won't be causing you any more trouble."

Alec couldn't believe he was actually feeling sorry for the little hellcat, but he was. Setting aside his wineglass, he went to the rocker and searched through the pockets of the waistcoat he had draped over the back. With key in hand, he approached her and unlocked the door. "There's really no harm done, Reb. And maybe you'll save your job by not admitting it was a mistake. Just let it go. But you *can* promise me this." He tilted his head and waited for her to look up. "Next time, *before* you jump to conclusions, check out *all* the facts. You write a helluva story, and you've got the courage it takes to become a great writer. You just need to use a little more common sense."

Hearing such a compliment coming from a man surprised Rebecca. She never dreamed any of them would see her as anything more than a woman meant to wed and bear children. That thought sobered her. There was already a chance she could become a mother, and the idea was appalling.

"Yes, sir," she mumbled, dropping her gaze away from him to watch the door swing open. She jumped when his warm, brown hand touched her bare arm, stopping her departure.

"It's truly a shame we had to meet under such strange circumstances, Reb." He smiled softly. "You and I . . . well, we might have—" He chuckled and shook his head. "Maybe not."

Rebecca couldn't comprehend the odd sensation that assailed her just then. Nor did she suspect she wanted to know. Without commenting, she turned and stepped into the hall. She had traveled several steps before she heard his door shut behind her, and by the time she had reached the back stairs, tears had flooded her eyes and were streaming down her face. Before anyone saw, she broke into a run and fled The Red Lion.

177

Chapter Eight

Penny thought her wildly pounding heart was about to explode as she leaned back heavily against the door to her room and listened to the sounds of Rebecca's hurried footsteps racing down the hall. Rebecca had nearly caught her standing outside Alec's door eavesdropping on what little she could hear of their conversation. The only thing that saved her was the delay in opening the door once the key turned in the lock. It had given Penny enough time to disappear into her own room and close herself in, and although she would have liked to talk to Rebecca right then, the bits and pieces of the argument she heard between her friend and Alec made her decide to wait until later . . . or at least until Rebecca had time to think things over and calm down a little.

Penny's first instinct was to confront Alec. Now that she knew the truth about the whole tangled mess, it was unfair for him to blame Rebecca for what happened. If anything, it was Penny's fault. Her obsession with men had turned the lives of three people upside down, and it was up to her to correct it . . . if she could. Rebecca had obviously come to The Red Lion to see her, and instead found herself in Alec's company . . . again, and almost the same way it happened that night. And if Rebecca was here to talk to Penny, it could only mean she had wanted to apologize. Rebecca seldom let a day go by after an argument without patching things up between them. Now, it seemed, the gap in their friendship may have grown a little wider. Just as soon as she finished with Alec, she'd find Rebecca and let her know that someone was on her side no matter what she had said or done. And she planned to tell them both that it was best for all concerned that he leave Williamsburg as soon as possible.

A strange tightness gripped her insides with the thought of Alec packing up his things and setting sail for home, and she couldn't decide if it was for herself that she dreaded his departure or for Rebecca. Alec had been the first for her friend, and that wasn't something a woman could easily forget . . . if ever.

"And you're forgetting how it actually happened," she muttered to herself as she pushed away from the door and untied the sash on her robe. *He raped her.* A frown drew her brows together. *Well, mabe not rape. From the sound of it Rebecca hadn't struggled or even called out . . . which doesn't make any sense. Rebecca doesn't like men, and to have one touch her—intimately—should have sent her screaming through the halls.* A wicked smile pursed Penny's lips as she dropped her robe on the chair and slid out of her nightgown. *Maybe Rebecca liked what she learned. After all, Alec Diamond would certainly be a great teacher! And if I had been given the chance, I would have been his best pupil!*

"Stop thinking like that!" she scolded out loud as she crossed to the dresser for a fresh camisole. "You're never going to know whether he's good or not. He's made a shambles of Rebecca's sanity, and it's best he's forgotton about . . . by both of us." Yanking clean undergarments from the drawer, she quickly donned them and hurried to the armoire for her favorite yellow dress. She wanted to look her prettiest when she talked to Alec. They might never see each other again, but if *she* had anything to say about it, she'd at least make a lasting impression on him.

A moment later, she had slid into her shoes, brushed her long, red hair until it shone and was opening the door to her room. Knowing Rebecca as well as she did, Penny decided she had probably gone home to hide and pamper her wounded pride. She guessed Alec had said some awfully

179

nasty things to Rebecca—some she deserved, some she didn't—and it would be a while before Rebecca would have the courage to show her face again. Maybe their little talk would change her mind. Stepping into the hall, she pulled the door shut behind her and headed for Alec's room. She wasn't really sure what she planned to say to him, only that he shouldn't blame Rebecca for what had transpired. Rebecca had been innocent . . . in every sense of the word.

A moment passed before the latch rattled and the door to Alec's room swung wide in answer to her summons, and Penny's heart beat a little faster once Alec filled the framework. He was dressed in a soft shade of blue which enhanced his darkly tanned complexion and light brown hair, and the mere sight of him—especially when she could see the bed behind him on the opposite side of the room from them—tempted her to shove him back inside, strip off her clothes and his, and spend the rest of the day experimenting on who got tired first. It was a lovely idea, one that warmed her entire body, and she had to turn her head away and not look at him in order to cool the desire.

"I think it's time you and I had a heart to heart talk," she said, "whether you agree or not. I can't let you go on thinking what you do about Rebecca."

"And how do you know what I'm thinking?"

Penny's flesh tingled at the sound of his voice. Even that part of him was seductive. She took a deep breath, let it out slowly and looked back at him. "Because I know men better than they know themselves." She cocked a brow at him, waiting. "Shall we discuss it here where everyone can listen in, or may I come inside?"

His dark eyes sparkling, Alec grinned and nodded his consent as he stepped to one side and held out his hand for her to enter. "I hope this isn't going to be a lecture," he said, swinging the door shut behind them and crossing to the rocker for his jacket. "I guarantee you that you'll be wasting your breath. You can't possibly say anything that I haven't already told myself."

"Then you're sorry about what happened?"

His tawny brows came sharply together. "Of course I am,"

180

he answered, sliding his arms into the sleeves. "For a number of reasons." He elected not to name those that weren't obvious.

"And you're not blaming Rebecca because I messed things up?"

Alec smiled softly as he straightened his collar. "And what mess do you feel responsible for? You live your life the way you choose. You shouldn't feel guilty if someone is careless with theirs."

It was nice to hear him say that he didn't think it was her fault, but at the same time, she couldn't let him accuse Rebecca. "So who do you think is guilty? Certainly not Rebecca."

"No, I didn't mean Rebecca." His voice was low and tinged with a hint of remorse as he reached for the cane he had hooked over the arm of the rocker. "If anyone's to blame, it's me."

His confession surprised her even more than hearing him admit Rebecca's innocence. "Did you, by chance, happen to tell her that?"

"I started to. Then I changed my mind."

"Whatever for? She's feeling pretty bad about herself right now, and your not telling her the truth didn't help any. I'm sure she's wishing she had never left the house that night."

"That's precisely why I didn't say anything to make her feel better. Next time she'll think twice before doing something as stupid—"

"As visiting a friend?" Penny sharply cut in. "That's really all she was doing. She got caught in the rain and came to my room to wait out the storm. I'm not sure what happened after that. I don't believe you forced her to do anything she didn't want to do—no one can—but just the same, she left my room very different than when she went in."

"I won't argue with that. But it's the reason she left the boardinghouse in the first place that was stupid," he answered. He paused a moment to let his temper cool. There was no need to fight with Penny. They were both after the same thing: Rebecca's well being. "A woman—especially one as beautiful and vulnerable as Reb—shouldn't be out running around after dark. And certainly not at the docks to investigate a murder. She was just asking for trouble. She was lucky to have found me instead."

"And you're not trouble?" came the sarcastic reply.

Alec's shoulders drooped. When he had gone over this discussion in his head, it all fit into place. It made good logic. Penny was twisting it around. "All I'm saying is that she lost her virginity and not her life."

Penny's fists flew to her hips. "Oh, and that's not important, is that it? If Rebecca ever gets married, I doubt her husband will agree."

Alec gritted his teeth. "What good is being a virgin if you're dead? And what I meant about her being lucky to have found me is that someone else might have beat her, raped her and then killed her! I'd say she got off pretty *damn* lucky, wouldn't you?" He could see he had won the debate when Penny slowly lowered her hands to her sides and dropped her gaze away from him. It didn't make him happy, but at least he felt good knowing she understood his point of view. "As for her getting married. I hope she does someday. And to the right man her virginity won't matter. If he loves her, he'll take her the way she is."

"Would you?"

Alec's brow knit. "Would I what?"

"Take her the way she is."

He couldn't help but laugh. "Reb and me? I don't think so."

Penny's temper flared again. "Then it does matter whether or not she's still a virgin. *You* wouldn't want her."

"Oh, bloody hell," he moaned with a tired shake of his head. "Now I understand why the two of you are friends. You think alike. And irrationally, I might add." Without giving her a chance to argue, he grabbed her arm, pulled her toward the rocker and shoved her down into it. He took a seat on the edge of the mattress. With his elbows braced on his knees, he stared straight into Penny's brown eyes. "First of all, Reb's ill-begotten state is my doing. So why would I care one way or the other? But even if it wasn't, she and I . . . we . . ." He frowned, wondering how to put it into words. "I'm not interested in settling down just yet. I'm not sure I ever will be. But if I were, I doubt I'd want to live out my life with a woman who'd pray for an excuse to bash in my brains. She needs the kind of man who's willing to put up with her tantrums and oddities. I'm not. I don't have the patience." He smiled lopsidedly at her. "Do you understand what I mean?"

Penny's mouth twitched. "Yes. She's a little rough around the edges."

Alec thought that that was an understatement, but decided not to comment.

"She'll grow out of it someday, I'm sure. You'd have to know what she's been through to understand why she's the way she is."

Alec thought how Penny's remark could fit his past as well and that because of it he had learned never to trust anyone, to never get too close to a person, to never allow himself to become vulnerable. With Rebecca he felt there was a chance he might. That was part of the reason he drew back from her when he had.

"You'll probably think I'm making this up," Penny went on to say when she thought Alec's silence meant he doubted there was any hope for Rebecca, "but I think she's lashing out at her father when she behaves the way she does."

"Her father?" Alec frowned, suddenly very curious . . . and sympathetic. After all, many of his actions were the result of his feelings toward his father.

"Yes," she answered enthusiastically. She could see she had his full attention, and while she did, she wanted to relate her friend's upbringing, starting with the death of her mother all the way through to her reasons for coming to live in Williamsburg. But once she mentioned Robert Gilmore and the disgusting way he was always forcing himself on Rebecca, the expression on Alec's face made her wonder if he believed her.

"Oh, I believe you," he guaranteed once she voiced her worry. "I was an unwilling witness to it."

Penny's tiny frame stiffened. "What?"

"Yesterday morning. I walked in on them at the newspaper office when I went there to place my advertisement." He remembered Reb's reaction when Gilmore kissed her and the rage he had seen in the man's eyes just before he tried to strike her. "You mean she never told you about it?"

"No." Penny frowned. "Not that I'm surprised. She's had other things on her mind. Besides, Rebecca never talked much about him to me. It's one of her faults. She's the type to hide things rather than talk about them. I guess she might think they'll go away if she does."

"Foolish idea, isn't it?" he muttered sarcastically, thinking that that was exactly what he always did . . . lock up his secrets. No one could hurt him if they didn't know his weak side. "I take that to mean this is the first time he's shown up here in town since Reb walked out."

"As far as I know. But if she hasn't told me about his being here yesterday, there might have been other times." Frowning, Penny murmured, "I wonder what he wanted."

Alec hadn't heard the entire conversation that morning between Reb and Gilmore, but he'd heard enough to know the man's lust for Rebecca hadn't changed. "Who's Lenore?"

"Rebecca's stepmother. Why? And how do you know her?"

"I don't. I heard Rebecca say that if she didn't hate Lenore so much, she'd tell her what Gilmore had said. It's my guess he'd like a different wife."

"Why, that slimy son-of-a—" Penny exploded, jumping to her feet. "Someone ought to do the world a favor and kill that viper."

A vague smile lifted Alec's mouth. "I think Reb would have if I hadn't come along when I did."

"Then you should have stayed out of the way," Penny hissed while she irritably paced the floor. "Rebecca wouldn't be in the mess she's in right now if it hadn't been for him." She jerked around and headed for the door. "I'd better go to her. It isn't safe for her to be alone."

"I don't think you really have to worry about him, Penny," Alec told her as he stood and caught her arm on her way past him. "I believe I made it quite clear to him that he should leave her alone, and Reb assured me that he's the sort to run rather than face up to someone his own size."

His pledge seemed to soothe Penny's fear a little. "Yes, I guess that's true. And if Rebecca threatened to tell Lenore, he's sure to have raced for home. If it came down to a choice, he'd take money over *anything* else." She shook her head, wishing she could somehow change things back to the way they were when she and Rebecca were children. But she couldn't and she knew it. The two of them would have to learn to accept life the way it was. "So," she said, turning her attention on her companion again. "What do we do about Rebecca?"

"Do?" Alec frowned. "I wasn't aware we had to 'do' anything."

"Why? Aren't you the forgiving type?"

Alec scowled at her. "What?"

"She made a mistake about you. She knows that now. At least give her a chance to make it up to you."

Forgiving Reb was the farthest thing from his mind. Not that he wasn't capable of forgiving her. He already had. It was the electricity that sparked between them whenever they were alone together that worried him. That mystical force bode ill. He couldn't explain it, exactly, but he sensed he'd have even a more difficult time putting her out of his mind once he decided to leave Williamsburg than he already did if he didn't start trying right now. Deliberately meeting with her would only delay it—if delay was the right word. It might ruin it.

"What is it you want me to say, Penny?" he asked as he went to the dresser and picked up his tricorn. "That she'll make some very fortunate man a good wife? She will. I just hope he has the sense to recognize it when he meets her." Coming to stand beside her, he reached to open the door, adding, "Now if you'll excuse me, I've got business I have to attend to."

Penny stood quietly staring at Alec for a long while. She had the feeling that once she walked away it would be the end of a very short-lived adventure for Rebecca, the kind of adventure that might have turned out pleasantly for her friend. Rebecca wasn't meant to spend her life alone; she was too beautiful, sensitive and loving for it all to go to waste.

Alec had even agreed. He had said she'd make some lucky fellow a good wife. Well, he didn't know it right now, but if Penny had her way, Alec would be that man. Of course, that would take some doing since he was just as mule-headed as Rebecca. But given time, Penny just might pull it off. A frown flitted across her brow and disappeared when she realized time wasn't something she had a lot of. Alec was only here on business, and when that business was finished, he'd be gone.

"All right," she finally answered, "I'll leave you alone. Go about whatever interests you more than Rebecca." She turned away from him before he could reply and headed toward the back stairs, calling over her shoulder, "I just hope you can sleep peacefully at night knowing how you've ruined a young girl's future."

Although she chose not to steal a glance his way as she hurried to the stairs, Penny sensed what the expression on his face would be. If it wasn't rage, it was sure to be a look of total exasperation. He had made it very clear that he was finished with Rebecca—whether it was for noble reasons or not—and Penny had countered by implying that his association with Rebecca Wilde had just begun. Smiling victoriously, she skipped down the stairs, rounded the corner at the bottom and nearly collided with the man starting up them.

"Oh, excuse me," she ardently apologized. "I didn't—"

But the stranger wasn't waiting around to exchange excuses. Without so much as a nod of his head in response or even a backward glance, he mounted the stairs two at a time and disappeared out of sight.

"Well," Penny scoffed. "If I ever run into you again, I'll be sure and knock you down next time. Then see if you can ignore me." With an indignant toss of her head, she turned and made her exit.

A mixture of rage, humiliation and ambivalence clouded Rebecca's mind and blinded her awareness of the direction she had taken once she fled The Red Lion through the back entrance, and it wasn't until someone shouted at her to watch where she was going that she became fully conscious of her surroundings and that she had walked herself right out of town. Standing in the middle of the road leading north to Robinson's deserted farmhouse, she halfheartedly excused her absentmindedness to the driver of the wagon who had nearly run her over and moved aside to allow him to pass. Heaving a tired sigh, she watched him drive away, wondering just how far she had come and how much farther she would have gone if the man hadn't called out to her.

Not far enough, she mused with a curl of her upper lip. She could walk to the end of the earth and still not escape the burning memories of her disastrous meeting with Alec. The only way she'd ever be able to put those thoughts from her head was if she were to fall, crack her skull on a rock and wake up later not knowing who she was or how she had gotten here. A dark brow lifted, and she fleetingly looked around for just such a piece of granite to do the job.

"With my luck, all I'd have for the effort is a bad headache," she muttered. Tears suddenly glistened in her eyes and she blinked them away. "As well as the pain in my heart."

Glancing up at the cloudless, blue sky overhead, she realized it was getting close to noon and that she hadn't gone to see Mrs. Rind yet. The woman deserved an explanation, and it wasn't something Rebecca could put off for very long. And especially not since Tommy had seen her going into The Red Lion. If he told Mrs. Rind that he had, she'd know Rebecca wasn't sick, and that would only make matters worse. With shoulders sagging, she turned around and started back toward town.

She hadn't gone very far when a pebble became lodged in her shoe. Hobbling to a rotten tree stump at the side of the road, she sat down and removed her slipper, muttering beneath her breath that it seemed her whole life was one problem after another as she shook the offending stone to the ground. First there had been Lenore, the fortune hunting witch who had cast a spell over Rebecca's father and moved in. The death of Trevor Wilde had been hard enough for

187

Rebecca to handle without her stepmother marrying that detestable piece of slime, Robert Gilmore. But then she'd had to deal with his pawing and lewd remarks until out of desperation she had left home. Next she had found out that Eli had been murdered, wound up in bed with a total stranger and had a horrible argument with Penny that would more likely end their friendship. And to top it all off, she was about to lose her job, the only kind of work she had ever longed to do.

"What next?" she hissed, jamming her foot back into the shoe. "Lose your room at Miss Abigail's?" She tossed her hands in the air and stood. "Why not? It's a perfect ending to an absolutely unbelievable nightmare."

And all because of that damnable Alec Diamond, she silently fumed as she stomped back toward the road. But just then the sound of hoofbeats coming toward her caught her attention, and when she glanced up, she instantly recognized the very man who she deemed was the cause of her most recent problems riding in her direction. Her first reaction, since he hadn't seemed to spot her yet, was to duck back behind a tree, certain he had come looking for her. But once she had, and a moment passed in which she had the time to think it through, she was sure that that would be the last thing on his mind. Wondering if he had actually seen her before she moved out of sight, she stood perfectly still, listening . . . and waiting. A few moments later, he rode on by without so much as glimpse her way, and Rebecca didn't know if she should be glad he hadn't the faintest idea she was there or if she should burst into tears over his obvious disinterest in her. However, her journalistic nature denied her even the briefest of moments to consider her choice when she suddenly realized he had no reason for being out this way . . . or did he? Guardedly moving out from the cover of trees, she stared curiously after him until the bend in the road took him out of sight, and without realizing she had, she started to run after him.

When the pain in her side became almost unbearable, Rebecca staggered to a halt a short while later, her breath coming in ragged heaves, her face flushed and her blue eyes mirroring her irritation. She'd never be able to find out what he was up to as long as he was on horseback and she was on foot. She had chased after him for more than a hundred yards or so, and she was already too winded and drained to go on. She knew she should turn around and go back to town, but if she did that, she'd never know who or what sent Alec Diamond down the road. After all, the only thing of interest for the next five miles was the Robinson place, and who'd deliberately go there? Old man Robinson had died several years ago, and without any kin to claim the property, the place had remained empty and unused. All Alec would find there were cobwebs, dust and a house full of mice. But maybe that wasn't his reason for heading this way, she concluded with a lift of one eyebrow. He had said he wanted to buy some good cropland, but since Robinson's farm was mostly woods, perhaps he was supposed to meet someone there. Her interest aroused anew, Rebecca took a deep breath, straightened her spine and started off again, only this time at a much more comfortable pace.

Alec was fairly certain of what he'd find long before he reined the mare down the narrow lane leading to the property Daniel Heller had purchased in his name. However, once he came in plain view of the place, his brow furrowed angrily, and the muscle in his cheek flexed. Whatever bit of hope he might have had about finding Heller alive dwindled rapidly the instant he saw the dilapidated log house, shed and broken-down corral. Whoever sold this worthless piece of land to his agent certainly knew what he was doing. The question was, had Heller found out he had been hoodwinked? And had he paid for that knowledge with his life? What Alec couldn't understand was how the crook could think that killing Daniel Heller would be the end of it. Heller was only an agent. The man who sent him would surely come to claim his land . . . more, once he found the one responsible.

With a disgusted shake of his head, Alec slowed his horse to a halt near the front door of the cabin and hesitated before dismounting. There really wasn't much need to go inside. He knew what was there: broken furniture, bugs and possibly a varmint that had taken up residence. But there also might be a clue. Alec doubted it, but he approached the door anyway.

Hanging by only one hinge, the portal squealed when he leaned a shoulder against it and pushed, one corner of it dragging against the wood floor. A cloud of gray, suffocating dust bellowed upward with the intrusion, and while Alec batted it away, he listened to the rustling sounds of tiny rodents scurrying about for a hiding place. If a man's life wasn't included in this mess, he might have found the situation rather amusing. He didn't, especially since his time and money were involved as well. Like Heller, he too had been tricked, and Alec never appreciated being the target of someone's scheme.

From the appearance of the room, Alex guessed it had been years since someone had lived there and a similar amount of time had passed since the last person set foot inside the cabin. Dishes were scattered over the table, on the floor and stacked haphazardly in the cupboard. Torn, dingy white curtains hung from the pair of windows. The huge stone fireplace, filled with ashes and half-burned logs, housed a black kettle hanging from a hook, and when Alec stepped closer, he could see the hardened remains of the last meal cooked in it stuck to the side of the pot. He wrinkled his nose and turned away, imagining the rancid smell emanating from the place at one time. In the far corner sat a narrow, straw-covered cot. Next to it stood a crude nightstand with a hurricane lamp, hairbrush, tobacco pouch and pipe sitting on top. Moth eaten rabbit pelts hung on the walls, cobwebs filled every corner, a thick layer of soot covered the floor and propped up against what Alec guessed the owner used as a washstand was a long-barreled, flintlock rifle. It appeared to be the only thing of real value in the entire cabin despite its rusty brass mountings and side plate, and he wondered why someone hadn't stolen it long before now until he saw the crack in the barrel.

Crossing to the small writing desk on the opposite wall, he carelessly examined the paper lying on top and contents of each drawer, finding nothing of real importance. Wiping the dirt off his fingertips and the dust from the sleeve of his jacket, he glanced about the room one more time, an irritated frown slanting his brows downward and pulling his mouth in a tight line. It seemed painfully obvious that Daniel Heller had never had a chance to inspect the results of his work, at least not the interior of this cabin, and the mystery around his disappearance began to intensify. It also became rather clear that Alec would have to start asking questions if someone didn't inquire about the advertisement he had placed in the newspaper. Thinking that he might find something of interest in the shed out back, he crossed to the door and went outside.

His hopes, as before, fell short as he stood in the opened entryway staring at the straw-covered floor, the pile of hay in one corner, a harness, pitch fork, spade and broken-handled saw hanging on the wall and the huge hole in the roof. He couldn't imagine how anyone living here could have made enough money to pay for the repairs needed on the place, let alone the seed to grow the basics to feed one's self. And the cabin, shed, and four acres of wooded land didn't promise to cover one tenth of what Alec paid for the property, *if* he could sell it. Stepping back and glancing off to his left, he decided that about the only thing this run-down piece of land was good for was offering a haven for mice and raccoons and the like. There wasn't even a stream running through the property on which to build a lumber mill. With a grim shake of his head, he turned around, intending to collect the horse's reins, mount and ride back into town. But in that same moment, he heard the mare snort as if something had startled it, and Alec quickly ducked inside the shed to hide within the shadows and wait, sensing that someone else had come to examine the property. Perhaps this was the piece of luck he had been hoping for.

Several minutes ticked away in which Alec begrudgingly thought the mare had only jumped at something it had seen crawling through the grass. Perhaps the animal had, but it wasn't the kind of snake he was praying would show himself, and he reluctantly straightened his tall frame and started to step out into the light when the snapping of a twig from somewhere close by froze him to his spot. Whoever or whatever it was, was coming his direction, and he silently cursed his decision to leave his cane back in his room. He had left himself totally defenseless except for the small advantage he had of being able to surprise his foe, and he quickly removed his coat and tricorn, tossing the latter aside.

With the jacket clutched in both hands, Alec positioned himself off to one side of the doorway, daring his adversary to move within reach. Once he had, Alec planned to toss the garment over his opponent's head and then whirl him off balance. While the stranger struggled with the coat, Alec would disarm the man. He had plotted out every detail, certain his scheme would work. Then he saw the shadow of his rival cross the stream of sunshine just outside the shed, and his surprise turned to relief, irritation and finally rage. He didn't have to see her face to know that the dark silhouette of shapely curves and full skirts belonged to Rebecca. Who else would follow him here? Who other than that witless female journalist would stick her nose in where it didn't belong? Hadn't she learned anything from their encounter on the road just the day before? Or had she forgotten already? Gritting his teeth as he watched the shadow creep closer to the doorway, he tossed his jacket aside and prepared to lunge the second she stepped into view. Maybe he should beat some sense into her.

When Rebecca had neared the lane leading to the Robinson farmhouse, she had all but decided to walk on by. There was no logical reason why Alec would go there. The place was empty and had been for years, and it hardly classified as the kind of property he was interested in buying. Yet, something in the back of her mind urged her to investigate, and when she saw his horse munching lazily on the grasses at its feet in the front yard, Rebecca was glad she had listened to her instincts, and quietly approached.

After peeking in through one of the windows to learn Alec wasn't inside, she had decided to check around in back. But now that she ventured toward the shed and could hear no sounds of his moving about, she wondered where he might have gone . . . and why. Frowning, she concluded that perhaps she was one step behind him and that he had already searched the shed and was on his way back to his horse. Worried that he might have too much of a lead on her for her to determine which direction he would take once he left the farm lane, she rushed forward as silently as possible. In the next instant, a strong hand lurched out at her from the darkness of the shed, seized her arm and yanked her off her feet. Startled by the suddenness of the attack and fearful of falling, she screamed. But once she landed in the soft mound of hay and was able to see who it was that had grabbed her, noticing that the expression on Alec's face revealed his ire, she didn't bother trying to get up. He stood too close, his feet braced apart, his fists low on his hips and a challenging glare in his dark brown eyes warning her not to move. In all likelihood he'd knock her back down if she tried to rise.

"What in bloody hell are you doing here?" he snarled.

The tone of his voice as well as the way he asked the question bruised her ego. She resented being treated like a child. Raising her nose in the air, she countered, "Might I ask you the same? What in bloody hell are *you* doing here?"

Tempted to grab her by the scruff of the neck and shake her until her teeth rattled, he took a tentative step forward, then changed his mind. "If I didn't know for certain," he sneered, "I'd swear you were a boy parading around in women's clothes. You certainly talk like one."

Rebecca's blue eyes narrowed, but she chose not to answer. Instead she brushed the pieces of hay off her skirt and started to rise.

"Unh-unh," he quickly ordered with a wag of his finger as he stepped closer. "You're going to sit there until you tell me why it is you won't allow me a moment's peace. I didn't invite you to come along. In fact I was hoping to get away from you. I was *praying* I'd never have to see you again." He exhaled a long, irritable sigh. "But here you are . . . prying into my affairs." Tawny brows crimped into an angry frown. "What is it about me that you find so interesting?"

A sarcastic sneer curled her lips. "The truth?" she baited.

Alec cocked his head to one side, doubtful. "If you can

manage it."

The leer deepened. "I can't find much about you that *is* interesting," she rallied, hoping her insult had cut just as deeply as his. "But I do find your actions curious." Before he could second guess her, she scrambled to her feet and stepped clear of him. "And being a journalist, I always act on my intuition."

Unaware that he was staring, Alec's eyes followed the slim hands brushing pieces of straw from her dress. "And what does your intuition tell you about me?" His gaze shifted to the dark locks of hair and the shafts of hay she picked from them.

"That you're hiding something . . . that you're in Williamsburg for a totally different reason than you let on."

"Such as?" he tested, one eyebrow lifted.

Rebecca shrugged a delicate shoulder. "If I knew that I wouldn't have to follow you." She frowned suddenly. "And just so you don't let that conceit of yours get out of hand, I didn't follow you here exactly."

Alec snorted and turned away from her. "Then what did you do . . . exactly?"

Rebecca didn't like the condescending manner in which he asked. "You passed me on the road, and since I saw no valid reason for you to be coming this way, I decided to—"

"Follow," he cut in.

"Check it out," she corrected.

He spun back. "I hate to be the one to break this to you, Miss Wilde, but I don't have to have a reason for going anywhere. And I certainly don't have to explain why I go for a ride . . . not to you or anyone." He stepped closer, his chin down, his brow furrowed and his nostrils flared. "But let's not look at it from my side. Let's examine the situation from a reporter's angle." His gaze skimmed the shapely length of her and up again, burning a path wherever his eyes rested. "A lovely, defenseless, *female* reporter shuns all common sense to follow her intuition, not once realizing the kind of predicament she might be putting herself into by snooping into something that doesn't concern her. She disregards her safety for the sake of a story." He continued to advance,

194

backing her into a corner where she couldn't escape him. "She thinks that just because she's a woman no one will harm her, that should the man she's following not like her prying into his business, he'll leave her alone just because she's a woman." Irked by the lack of worry in the bright blue eyes staring back at him, Alec brought up his hands and pressed them against the walls on either side of her, trapping her between his outstretched arms "In my case, she'd be right. But let's pretend it's not me she's pursuing. Let's imagine I'm a ruthless, cold-blooded—" he paused for effect— "lowlife who enjoys taking women against their will just for the sport of it."

"Alec," Rebecca warned, the muscles in her stomach turning to granite, "this isn't funny."

"It wasn't meant to be," he growled, leaning in, his nose inches from hers. "That's the kind of man you could have followed, Reb. The unforgiving type, the sort who thrives on hearing a woman scream, seeing her cry and beg for mercy. The kind who lurk in the shadows just waiting for their chance. What would you have done, Reb, if you'd found someone else in this shed instead of me? What Reb? What would you have done?"

Wanting no more of this conversation, she frowned angrily and tried to push his arm out of the way. It felt like a hard band of steel. "Let me pass, Alec Diamond!" she demanded when he wouldn't budge.

"Not this time, Reb. You asked for trouble, and this time you'll see just how deep you've gotten yourself into it." He lowered his chin and repeated, "What would you do, Reb if you had found a total stranger here in the shed instead of me?"

Realizing that he had no intention of letting her go until she complied with his demands, Rebecca gave way to her foolishness in thinking she could win this contest of wits. Her mistake was not reacting quickly enough. Long before she doubled up her fist, he read her plan in the blue depths of her eyes and easily caught her wrist in a steely hold before it came anywhere close to his jaw.

"Ouch!" she whined. "You're hurting me."

"Not half as much as *he* would hurt you." He grinned mockingly.

The rage that suddenly exploded within her masked the pain he inflicted, and without much forethought, she brought up her other hand, thinking to claw his face. He entrapped it as well. Surprised but not discouraged, her wrath goading her on, she sucked in an outraged breath and raised her foot, planning to drive the heel of her shoe into his toe. But Alec had guessed as much, and before she could carry it out, he jerked her forward into his arms, crushed her in a viselike grip with her hands locked behind her, and lifted her off her feet. She cried out in pain and fought back the tears that sprung to her eyes.

"Alec," she moaned. "You've proven your point. Let go!"

"Not yet, I haven't," he snarled, spinning with her and roughly depositing them both on the mound of hay, her tiny body held immobile beneath his, "I told you he was the kind of degenerate who enjoyed a woman's pain, her fear. He wouldn't let go just because she begged him. He likes that. Ask again."

Doubt creeped into her mind. "Alec," she half-sobbed, half-whimpered, "you're not going to . . ."

The terror he heard in her voice cooled his need to teach her a valuable lesson . . . if he hadn't already. "No," he snarled, pushing away and rolling onto one hip. "But *he* would have. I pray you realize that now. Just because you want men to think you're equal to them doesn't mean you are. Not physically, Reb. And the sooner you accept that, the better off you'll be." He jerked back out of the way when her elbow nearly hit his cheek in her awkward attempt to rise. "Maybe if you were an ugly, old crone, you might be safe, but I doubt it. Dead is dead, Rebecca, and if you go poking around where you don't belong, you could get yourself killed."

"Really?" she sneered, the look of horror gone from her lovely face. "That's where I beg to differ with you, Mr. Diamond."

Alec straightened sharply once he realized the trick she'd played.

"Men never have been and never will be *half* as smart as women." Whirling, Rebecca grabbed the pitchfork from its nail and spun back in time to laugh at the clumsy way he was trying to get to his feet. "What would I do to protect myself from a degenerate, you ask? Why, this," she sneered, launching her weapon.

Alec dove out of its path, safe from harm, but Rebecca wasn't through with him. Latching on to the handle of the wooden bucket she found sitting on the floor next to her, she swung it around and let go, hoping to bounce it off his chest, if not his skull. It too missed, but she wasn't a bit worried. Sooner or later he'd duck the wrong direction. Driven by her need to see him in pain, she averted her attention away from him long enough to select another weapon, and in that fleeting moment, Alec saw his chance. Hurling himself through the air, he caught her around the waist and tumbled them both to the floor. Rebecca let out an ear-piercing shriek, then rained him with every blow she could manage before he pinned her arms to her sides and rolled her beneath him.

"Dammit, Reb!" he howled. "I don't know why I bother with you. You're the most obstinate, hardheaded woman I've ever come across."

"And you're just like every man I've ever known," she spat back.

The story Penny had told him about Reb and Robert Gilmore flashed to mind, and Alec knew that wasn't true. Not in his case anyway. But trying to convince Rebecca of it wouldn't be easy. "If you promise not to throw something at me, I'll let you up. Otherwise we'll have to finish this conversation the way we are. Do I have your word?"

Rebecca was sure he meant it, but she didn't like having to admit he was in control, either. "I don't see where we have anything to discuss," she announced, squirming to break his hold and failing.

"Oh, yes, we do," he frowned, tightening his grip in response. "You haven't told me why you followed me here." When she started to correct his statement, he closed his eyes and shook his head. "All right," he relented. "Why you

197

thought there was a story involving me."

She renewed her efforts to be free. "Get off me and I'll tell you."

"Only if you'll give me your word you'll stop fighting," he reiterated.

Rebecca's blue eyes narrowed as she glared back at him. She hated having to give in to him, but she hated having his hands on her even more. "All right!" she yielded. "I won't try to kill you . . . for now."

A flicker of amusement lightened his dark eyes and disappeared. Gingerly, not quite fully trusting her, he eased up from her. In a burst of energy, she shoved him away and stood, dusting the straw from her skirts as she backed away several steps.

"I'll tell you why, but you're going to have to be honest with me," she scowled. "Otherwise, this is only the beginning. You're hiding something, and I don't plan to stop until I find out what that is."

Stretching out comfortably on the straw-covered floor, Alec quietly studied the beauty glaring back at him. He knew she meant every word, and because of it, he realized she'd be more of a hindrance than a help. She just might stumble across an important piece of information ahead of him, and because she wouldn't know what it meant, she might put herself in danger. It truly irritated him to have to admit that he had come to a dead end in finding out what happened to Heller and that he could use someone's help, but he did. And right now, this little hellcat seemed to be the only one he could trust. She had nothing to gain or to lose. She merely wanted a story. Since everyone in Williamsburg knew she worked for the *Gazette*, they wouldn't think much of it if she were to ask questions. And there was always the chance that she already knew something and wasn't aware of it.

"All right," he finally relented, "I'll tell you. But you'll have to understand the importance of being discreet about it."

Rebecca's smooth brow wrinkled. Whenever the word "discreet" was used, it usually meant a woman was involved, and a dull ache seemed to tug at her heart. Was Alec

198

married? Had his wife run off on him, and he had come to Williamsburg looking for her? Her stomach in a knot, she dropped her gaze away from him and crossed to the mound of hay where she spread out her skirts and sat down.

"I see," she murmured. "You're looking for someone, and you want it kept a secret. What's her name?"

Alec's tawny brows dipped downward. "*Her* name?" he repeated. "What makes you think I'm looking for a woman? In fact, what makes you think I'm looking for *anyone?*"

Rebecca could feel her cheeks redden. "You said we'd have to be discreet," she mumbled, wondering if he could guess what had made her draw the wrong conclusion.

"Yes, I did," he agreed, sitting up and draping his arm over his bent knee. "But I said it because I meant there could be some threatening results. And yes, you're partly correct in assuming I'm looking for someone." Realizing he had gotten ahead of himself in relaying the story, he paused a moment to collect his thoughts and figure out just where to begin . . . and just how much he should tell her. He also realized that by confessing his reason for being in Williamsburg, he'd be tying himself in with Rebecca, something he had earlier decided would be disastrous.

"And now you're having second thoughts, Mr. Diamond?"

The dulcet tone of her sweet voice penetrated his musings, confirming his fears that forgetting Rebecca Wilde would be a feat he'd probably never achieve. "Stone," he said aloud.

A faint line appeared between her dark eyebrows. "What?"

"My name is Alec Stone, not Diamond. I told Penny that because I don't want the wrong person to know I was here in Williamsburg." He knew he was confusing her by not starting at the beginning, and now that he had gone this far, he also realized he'd have to tell her everything. She wouldn't leave him alone if he didn't.

Rebecca sat by quietly listening to everything he said, more impressed with learning about his estate on that faraway island of Jamaica than in finding out his agent was missing. But when he admitted the Robinson farm was the property Heller had purchased for Alec, she burst out laughing.

"You own *this?*"

Her mirth pricked his ego. "I suppose to everyone else it would be humorous," he admitted, annoyed. "I, however, don't find it very funny. I paid a great deal for this piece of land, and Daniel Heller may have paid for it with his life."

Rebecca swallowed her glee almost instantly, though some of her laughter still sparkled in her pale blue eyes. "I'm sorry. I didn't mean to make it sound like Mr. Heller's misfortune should be taken lightly." She struggled with the smile tugging on her mouth. "It's just that you don't appear to be the sort who's easily duped." She cleared her throat and clamped her teeth together, willing herself to see the serious side of this situation. Deciding it would help if she got up and walked around, she stood and began to pace the floor. "So it's your thinking Mr. Heller was tricked and probably murdered once he figured it out. And you've also concluded that whoever sold this property to him might well know what happened to him . . . if indeed the man didn't actually kill him."

"It's the only answer I've come up with so far," he replied, still a little miffed by the way she had reacted to his problem. "I also figured that if I announced who I was and started asking questions about Heller, whoever's behind this would crawl back under his rock and I'd never learn the truth."

"What makes you think he's still here? In Williamsburg?" Rebecca posed.

Alec shrugged a shoulder. "Nothing. He could be in England for all I know. But on the chance that he is, I have to play this very carefully. And so do you," he warned. "You'll be able to ask questions without raising anyone's curiosity, seeing as how that's the way you spend your every waking hour, but you'll have to choose the right ones to ask and how to go about acquiring the answers. That's what I meant about being discreet." He saw the irate look in her eyes and knew his intentional attack on her character had struck the right vein. "If I'm right about this, you could wind up with your pretty, little neck wrung." His brown eyes darkened all the more. "And I don't want to feel any more responsible for you than I already do."

"Responsible?" she snapped. "For me?" No one's responsible for me and certainly not you! I can take care of myself."

"Oh, yes," he mocked, pushing himself up to his feet. "You surely can take care of yourself." He busied himself with brushing the bits of straw and dust from his clothes while he continued. "You never allow yourself to get caught in a situation you can't handle, and on those rare occasions when you can't prevent it, you always manage to come out on top." His dark eyes glanced over at her. "So to speak," he added ambiguously,

The implication was quite clear to Rebecca. Her face flamed, but more from rage than embarrassment. "Damn, I curse the day you set foot in Williamsburg."

"And I, you," he countered. "My life was relatively uncomplicated until I met you."

"And now how is it different? You'll finish up your business here and go home to your wife." Rebecca inwardly cringed with that last declaration. It sounded horribly close to being jealous.

"My wife?" He chuckled sarcastically. "I don't have a wife. I've never even thought about getting married." He cocked a brow at her. "Do you suppose I had some premonition on the subject? If I did have, I'm sure it included you." He turned away to pick up his jacket. "But that's not fair, I suppose. Not all women are like you."

"What's that supposed to mean?" she exploded, sorely tempted to club him over the head with something.

Slipping his arms into the sleeves, he hiked his coat up over his wide shoulders and adjusted the collar. "That you're the exception to the rule. I feel fairly safe in saying that most women are gentle, kind, soft spoken and prefer that their men do the fighting."

Rebecca actually hated women who were the way he described, but hearing him praise those attributes and exclude her from the group left her feeling insulted. "Maybe it just takes the right man to bring it out in me."

He laughed in earnest. "Exceptional is the better word for

him. If you're planning to find him before you're old and gray, I suggest you start looking now. He's got to be one in a million and very difficult to come across."

Rebecca could hardly believe the tears that burned her eyes and that his callousness was the cause for them. "Did you ever stop to think that maybe I like the way I am, that perhaps I behave like this because no *man* has ever given me reason not to?" She looked him up and down, from the top of his luscious blond head to the tips of his shiny black shoes. "Just because you dress in fine clothes and can afford the nicer things, doesn't make you a gentleman. Or the sort who would interest me. When the *right* man comes along, I'll be willing to change, and I'll probably do it without realizing I have!"

"I wish I could stick around that long. I'd love to see it," he grinned.

The throaty growl he heard was just enough of a warning for him to prepare himself. With the quickness of a cat, he raised his hand and caught her wrist before she could slap his face.

"Ah, Reb," he teased. "And just when I thought you really meant what you said."

"I *did* mean it, you back street rapscallion. *Every word!* But you're too cocksure of yourself to admit you might be wrong about me, that given a chance I might be just as kind and gentle and soft spoken as any other woman you might know." She squinted her eyes at him. "But then I'd be just like all the other women in your life . . . weak and simple-minded." She snatched her arm away. "Maybe that's what you're really afraid of and can't admit it. You feel threatened by someone like me, that I'll show you up, that you'll look less the man because I have the courage to say and do whatever I please."

Alec's attempt to explain the reasons why she should learn to act like a lady took a different, unexpected turn. She was absolutely right when she said she wasn't at all like the other women he had known. None of them had ever been weak and simple-minded, but they certainly were dull in comparison to Rebecca Wilde. Oh, they had nice curves and ivory skin and knew all the right words to say, enticing little promises that never failed to warm his blood and cloud his mind. And not once had he found any of them unwilling. Not even Rebecca. He shuddered inwardly at the thought, wondering just what that might mean. If she claimed no man had ever given her reason to behave like a lady, how could she justify the passion he had sparked in her? And not once, but twice!

"Well?"

Her question startled him out of his pensive state of mind. "Well what?" he barked, bending to pick up his tricorn and brush the dust from its brim.

"Tell me that I'm wrong, that you don't feel threatened by me." Her bright blue eyes gleamed with victory.

"You're wrong," he snarled, looking heatedly at her. "You're no threat to me . . . except to my sanity, perhaps." He turned away with the intention of going to his horse, mounting and riding off, leaving her behind to walk. But Rebecca caught his arm and jerked him back.

"Then tell me why this subject makes you so uncomfortable."

His dark brown gaze fell upon her, and Rebecca felt a twinge of doubt.

"You really want to know?" he questioned.

She hesitated, then nodded.

"All right. Then I'll tell you." He faced her full front and lowered his chin. "I was agreeing with every point you made . . . about not being like other women and that perhaps you are the way you are because no man has changed your mind. I was thinking that you *are* different . . . in all respects but one."

Sensing what was coming next, Rebecca moved back a step. He had a funny look in his eyes.

"That's right, Reb," he continued with a half-smile. "Whether you're willing to admit it or not, you're a very passionate temptress in bed. So much so that I have to admit I've never enjoyed a night spent in a woman's arms as much as I enjoyed being with you. The only threat I feel from you is the possibility that I'll never find another to equal you. But I can tell you this; underneath all the thorns, all the insults, all the denials, you're every inch a woman." What humor there had been laced in his words and shining in his eyes disappeared. "Would you like me to prove it?"

Every inch of her flesh tingled. "No," she quickly answered, thinking to move past him and out into the bright sunlight. But he shadowed her steps and blocked the way.

"Why, Reb? Are *you* afraid?" he challenged.

"Of you?" She laughed nervously.

"No," he softly replied. "Not of me. Of yourself."

Rebecca's fair brow crimped. "What do you mean? Why should I be afraid of myself?"

His gaze lowered to her parted lips and back up again. "You're afraid of your feelings . . . of a man's touch. You're afraid to admit you like what it does to you."

"I do not!" she snapped.

He cocked a brow. "Like what it does? Or you're not afraid to admit it?"

Rebecca's mouth opened and closed several times, but no words would come out. He had struck upon the truth, and his nearness singed her very being, melting away the hardened shell with which she had fought so hard to protect herself. He played with her mind, teased her soul, and tormented her existence. Yes, she was afraid . . . of herself, of him and of the future. Trembling, she backed away. He followed. Panic threatened to fill her eyes with tears. She swallowed hard and drew in a breath. In one last effort to convince him that this was not what she wanted, she opened her mouth to deny his claims and raised her hand to stress the fact. In the next moment, she saw him toss aside his tricorn, and while she unwittingly watched its descent to the floor, he grabbed her wrist, caught his free arm around her narrow waist and brought her full against his hardened frame. His opened mouth descended upon hers, bruising her lips as he tasted hungrily of their kiss. His probing tongue pushed inside, halting Rebecca's breath and her desire to stop him. Yes, she liked the feel of him, his moist, burning lips upon hers, the iron thews pressed against her soft breasts, the full length of his steely body molded with hers.

She liked it, and what scared her was that *he* knew it.

A gentle warning to bring this to an end before it was too late began to surface, and Rebecca found both the will and energy to fight him. Slipping her free hand in between them, she pushed with all her might and managed only to pop loose the buttons up the front of his shirt. Cool fingertips touched the warmth of the rock-hard, bare muscles across his chest, scorching her flesh and setting her entire body on fire. In a gallant effort to cool his raging desires, she tore her lips from his.

"Alec . . . don't," she begged breathlessly. "Please. We mustn't."

But Alec wasn't listening. What he had thought would simply educate her yielded a new lesson, one where he was no longer the teacher but an unexpected pupil. The feel of supple curves and warm flesh, the sweet scent of her hair and skin filled his senses and stirred the fires of passion within him. The closeness of her was intoxicating and muddled his thinking, for if he'd had the ability to reason, he would have recognized his error. Driven by an all consuming need to press her down in the soft mound of hay and sample fully of the pleasure she could afford him, he kissed her again. Slanting his mouth across hers while one hand cupped the back of her head and the other slid along her spine to her hips, he pulled her close against him to reveal the evidence of his burning desire.

His mouth left hers and trailed a molten path down her long, slender neck, a course Rebecca's senses followed unwillingly. She had neither the breath to ask nor the want to stop him any longer, and she silently damned the consequences as she dropped her head back and savored the feel of his sultry kisses against her throat. A titillating shiver raced down her spine and chilled her flesh, and when his fingers found the buttons of her dress, she eagerly helped him unfasten them and slide the garment off her shoulders. Accompanied by her petticoats, the yards of cloth floated to the ground as she stepped out of her shoes and kicked them aside. His jacket and shirt soon followed, and Rebecca's appreciative gaze roamed freely over the hard expanse of his bronze chest, thickly muscled ribs and lean, flat belly before coming to rest on those dark, lust-filled brown eyes. In silence they read each other's thoughts, saw the desire burning between them and knew this was something neither of them could ignore or deny.

Glancing over his shoulder at the opened doorway, a soft smile touched Alec's lips as he looked at her again and reached to seal in their privacy. At the sound of creaking hinges and a rusty latch catching, he bent and swooped her up in his arms to carry her to their bed of straw. Their lips met again as he knelt with her and slowly lowered her down, and the small, dusty cubicle became a world unto its own, shielding the young lovers from all else as they clung desperately, passionately to each other.

As strong hands roamed the full length of her, from the delicate line of her jaw, over her creamy-white throat, her shapely back, waist, hip and thigh, Rebecca surrendered to the glorious sensation his touch aroused. Her mind tettered on delirium. Her breath quickened and her pulse raced, and she returned his kiss with such ardor that it betrayed her want to hate him. While she caressed the iron thews across his back, his fingers worked the strings of her camisole free, exposing the soft flesh from its lacy restraints. His thumb stroked one peak until it rose and grew taut, his mouth, hot and demanding, seeking out the sweetness of hers again. Her passion soaring, she reached for the fastenings on his breeches, and while he shed them, she slid off her garters and hose, and unlaced the camisole all the way. But when she moved to slip it away from her, his hands came up to stop her, and she frowned.

"Let me," he whispered against her throat, and Rebecca's heart fluttered.

Long, brown fingers slowly eased the delicate undergarment from her, and once he had tossed it aside, he caught her in his arms and pulled her close, his opened mouth claiming a rose-hued peak of one breast. A burning fire coursed through her veins as his tongue teased the nipple then sucked greedily, and Rebecca's world careened. Pulling him back down upon the mound of hay with her, she eagerly parted her thighs to welcome him when he shifted his weight above her.

"You're a beguiling little minx, Rebecca Wilde," he murmured, his dark eyes glowing lustfully, "You'll be my ruin." His gaze dropped to her trembling parted lips. "God help me," he whispered, lowering his mouth to hers as he pressed his manhood full within her.

Rebecca instinctively arched her hips and moved with silkened grace against him, savoring that first thrust, the fullness inside her, the pleasure of responding without guilt to his sensuous lovemaking. She clawed his back, moaned in sheer delight, breathed in the scent of him and tasted of the ecstasy he alone could arouse in her. He was no evil threat as she had claimed all men were. He was her knight in silvered armor, her king among kings, her savior, the mystic warrior of her dreams. He had come to rescue her from the black demons that haunted her reasoning, to show her the passsionate, giving side of love. With her heart thundering in her breast, she closed her eyes and buried her face in his neck while he swept her away on a tide of pure desire, their bodies molded and fused as one. Then at last he breathed a shuddering sigh when their passion reached its fevered crest and exploded in a fury of blissful release. Drained of their strength, their bodies gleaming with moisture, he fell breathless and exhausted at her side, his eyes closed and a faint smile on his lips.

"You're a witch, Rebecca Wilde," he murmured a few moments later, a soft chuckle rumbling in his chest. He turned his head and looked over at her. "A beautiful one, but a witch just the same."

"And you, sir, are the devil," she answered wistfully, sitting up to slide on her camisole and hide her nakedness when the bright light of day seemed to taunt her. "I came here hating you and look how I wind up. The work of Satan must course through your veins."

"Nay." He laughed, pushing up on his elbows to watch her frenzied movements as she quickly covered those tempting breasts and narrow hips. "I doubt one could say 'tis blood that warms me, rather lust, but never Satan." Sensing her embarrassment, he reached for his breeches and slipped into them while he considered the haven they had unwillingly chosen for their tryst. "However, I must say that if I'd had my wits about me . . ." He let the statement go unfinished, certain she would agree that the softness of a feather bed was much more appealing than a mound of hay.

Rebecca misunderstood, remembering the last time they were alone together and how he had resisted, stating that their passion for each other was wrong. Perhaps it was. But there was no denying it existed. Hurt by his apparent regret over the matter, she kept her eyes averted while she gathered up her hose, petticoats and dress, quickly stepping into her shoes once she had donned the rest.

"So tell me," she dared ask, her chin held high and the soft blush in her cheeks gone as she stood with her back to him, "how do I compare?" Surely that was what he thought of their little roll in the hay . . . another conquest.

"To what?" he questioned innocently, coming to his feet as he picked up his shirt and slid it over his shoulders, unaware of his companion's turmoil.

"To those before me," she replied, gallantly masking her pain.

A pleased smile lifted his mouth as he buttoned the shirt and tucked the tails into his waistband. "There is no comparison," he dreamily admitted, crossing to where he had thrown his shoes and stockings.

Rebecca's blue eyes darkened. "That's what I thought," she hissed, heading for the door.

The stream of brilliant sunshine flooding into the small shed was the first hint to Alec that something was amiss. The resounding crack of the door as it slammed open against the wall was the second. The flash of green skirts as Rebecca raced from the shed drove the message home, but it was much too late. Having donned only one stocking, Alec hopped after her, pausing in the archway as he called her name.

"What the hell did I say?" he shouted, his tan brow furrowed as he watched her slim form disappear around the corner of the cabin. Muttering to himself as he hurriedly sat down to pull on his other stocking and then his shoes, he cursed himself for not realizing beforehand that any entanglement with that little hellcat could only end up poorly as he jumped to his feet and started to chase after her. But the sound of hoofbeats stopped him cold once he realized he would have to walk all the way back into town. With his nostrils flared, he sucked in a deep breath and let out a long, throaty roar that scared the birds from their lofty perches high in the treetops above him.

Chapter Nine

Standing on the sidewalk in front of The Red Lion, Alec's angry gaze shifted from the mare tied at the hitching rail to the Ludwell-Paradise House and then to the inn. He couldn't decide if he should go to his room and clean up first or find Rebecca and demand an explanation for her stormy departure. It had taken him more than an hour to walk all the way back, but his temper hadn't cooled a degree. In fact it had seemed to heighten with each step he took. He had gone over their conversation word for word and still hadn't come up with a sensible reason to justify her rage, and short of giving himself a headache while trying to figure it out, he realized the only guaranteed solution would be to ask her about it. Yet with the irritable frame of mind he was in, he knew they'd only wind up shouting at each other, and he turned for the front door of the inn. He'd change his clothes, splash cool water over his face and comb his hair while he mentally forced himself to calm down. *Then* he'd look for Rebecca.

The only customers in the place sat at a table near the back, and Alec paid them little heed as he crossed the room on his way to the stairs. Nor did he even notice the pair of brown eyes watching him from near the bar until he found his path blocked by Penny Dawson's tiny physique. Coming to an abrupt halt, he straightened, blinked, then frowned at her in a silent warning not to lecture. He recognized that annoyed look on her face as one that promised little peace.

"Don't say a word, Penny," he snarled. "Not a single word. I'm truly in no mood to listen."

"Then you'd better get in the mood. I just talked to Rebecca."

Alec's broad shoulders slumped. "Wonderful," he sneered. "Then you've already been told all you need to know." He nodded stiffly at her and brushed past her for the stairs.

"Mrs. Rind fired her."

Alec had climbed only a trio of steps before Penny made her announcement, and although he would have liked to race up the rest of them, he didn't. Coming to a hesitant stop, he leaned against the handrail, pausing, then turned around.

"I'm sorry to hear that," he said. "I know her work meant a lot to her, but I'm sure she couldn't have been too surprised. Perhaps she'll know better the next time she thinks about writing a story she hasn't fully investigated." He turned back to start up the stairs again, halted by Penny's next comment.

"Does that mean you're not going to do anything about it?"

Alec let his head fall back as he exhaled a tired sigh and stared up at the ceiling above him. "What have I to do with her losing her job?"

"Well, she was fired because of the story she wrote about you."

"So?"

"I just thought you might feel a little responsible."

"Sorry," he proclaimed, starting up the stairs again. "I didn't force her to write it."

Lifting the hem of her skirts, Penny hurried after him. "But surely you understand why she did."

Wanting nothing more than the chance to be alone, he didn't answer her as he headed for his room.

"A young friend of hers had been murdered, and she wanted to expose the truth. She was wrong in thinking you were the guilty party and wrong in allowing the story to get printed, but she did it out of loyalty to a friend."

211

"I can appreciate that, Penny," he replied sympathetically, "and I already told her that I didn't hold it against her. But as far as I'm concerned, my responsibility ends there."

"But she has no way to support herself now."

Alec jerked to an angry halt and spun around. "So what do you want from me? She made a mistake and now she's paying for it." He exhaled a quick breath. "It's part of growing up. We all face it sooner or later."

"All right," Penny concluded, not at all threatened by the harshness in his tone of voice. "She's paying for her mistake. Are you going to pay for yours?"

Alec's brown eyes narrowed. "Oh, I see. You're thinking to blackmail me into doing something."

"Blackmail?" Penny rallied, her own temper flaring. "How could I possibly blackmail you? Who would I tell that it would make a difference? Or are you saying you're married?"

Alec started to deny her assumption, but she cut him short.

"Or that you have a sickly mother who'd be devastated to learn what her son did? No?" She answered her own question. "Then how about an elderly grandmother, or—" she hadn't thought of this before, and the idea truly bothered her—"a fiancée?"

The vision of Meredith Stockwell flashed to mind, and he blinked it away. The young woman had often hinted to Alec that they should wed since her father and Alec were the two richest men in all of Jamaica. The joining of properties and wealth would assure them full control of the island. But going into partnership and having a wife were the farthest things from his mind.

"You're not *engaged,* are you?" Penny blurted out once she saw how the question had silenced him.

Alec raised a brow, the smile he fought to conceal tugging at the corner of his mouth. He honestly didn't think Penny was the sort to use blackmail to get what she wanted, but she had inadvertently given him a way to challenge her. "Would

212

it make a difference if I were?" he casually asked.

Penny could feel her face pale. Engaged wasn't the same as being married, but it was awfully damn close. "I . . . I guess it depends on whether or not you love her," she murmured with a frown, eyes averted as she struggled with the anguish of telling Rebecca what she had learned . . . if she *should* tell her.

Seeing that he had Penny right where he wanted her, he grinned openly and turned for his room. But once he had reached it, the humor vanished from his face; for the door stood ajar, and the lock had been broken. Stepping off to one side, his back against the wall, he motioned for Penny to stay where she was and to be quiet while he reached to swing the door slowly open. Guardedly peeking into the room to find it empty but in a shambles, he cursed beneath his breath and straightened as he moved into the archway, his brow furrowed angrily.

"What is it, Alec?" Penny worriedly asked as she came to stand beside him and peer into the room. "Oh, my God," she breathed, eyes wide.

Every drawer had been pulled out and the contents dumped on the floor. The coverlet and sheets had been ripped from the bed, his satchel lay upside down on the rug, and the doors to the armoire stood open, his clothes scattered about.

"What were they looking for?" Penny queried as she followed him inside.

"I haven't any idea," he snarled through clenced teeth. "But money would be the most obvious."

"Do you think they found any?"

"Not likely," he confessed, moving farther into the room where he squatted down to examine his belongings lying on the floor. "I carry it with me."

"Is anything else missing?"

Other than his clothes, cane and the jewelry he wore, Alec had nothing of interest to anyone. "Doesn't look like it," he replied with a shake of his head. Then, remembering the stickpin he found the night he arrived, he grabbed the satchel and pulled it open to examine the secret compartment he often used to hide important documents whenever he was forced to carry them.

"What is it?"

Alec glanced up to find Penny standing over him, her eyes trained on the jewel-studded piece of jewelry he held.

"Was the thief looking for that?"

"I doubt it," he answered as he put it in his coat pocket and stood. "No one knows I have it." Frowning, he glanced at the door and instructed, "Would you mind finding a locksmith for me? I won't get much sleep tonight if I have to keep one eye on the door."

"Oh, yeah . . . of course," Penny agreed, staring toward it. "Are you going to tell the constable about this?"

Alec shook his head. "What's the need? Nothing was taken."

Standing at the threshold, she paused and looked back at him. "I'm really sorry about this."

"Why should you be sorry?"

Penny shrugged. "I don't know. I guess because I live and work here, I feel partly to blame for not looking after things while you were gone."

"How could you? You had your work to do downstairs. You can't be in two places at the same time." He came to stand next to her and gently squeeze her elbow. "Other than having a mess to straighten up, there's no harm done." He nodded at the broken lock. "Except for that. And once it's fixed, no one but you, me and the locksmith will know the difference."

"And whoever did this," she frowned as she surveyed the damage again. "Maybe you should take another room."

A soft smile played upon his lips, thinking Penny was offering the use of hers. "Yours, perhaps?"

"Of course not!" she exclaimed. "I wouldn't do that to Rebecca."

The frown barely had time to wrinkle his brow before Penny turned and walked away.

*   *   *

214

The gray streaks of pre-dawn painted the eastern sky with the promise of another day, and Alec absently viewed the scene from his open window as he stood beside it, his tan brow furrowed and his dark eyes mirroring his aggravation. On the day he made his decision to come to Williamsburg and look for Daniel Heller, he had expected to run into problems. A man just didn't disappear off the face of the earth without someone knowing what happened. How it had occurred and who was behind it would be the difficult part to unravel. But Alec had never dreamed that in the process he'd wind up saddled with the likes of Rebecca Wilde. The problems she created for him could take up most of his time to solve, and aside from the fact that he couldn't afford even a minute out of his day for her, he truly didn't think it was his obligation to try. Reb had gotten herself into this mess on her own, and she could get herself out of it. Besides, if it hadn't been Alec she got involved with, it would have been someone else. So why should he be standing here feeling guilty?

Because it wasn't someone else, he mused, disgruntled. *I was the one she crawled into bed with.* Angry, he pushed away from the window and crossed to the armoire to get dressed. The truly annoying part of the whole situation was that he needed her help. He needed an intermediary, someone who could ask the questions for him without raising suspicion, someone like Reb. Yanking a clean shirt out of the wardrobe, he jerked it on and went to the dresser to brush his hair. Rebecca was the only person in the whole of Williamsburg he could trust. Yet, being with her caused nothing but trouble for him. Look what happened there in the shed. And in his room that very same morning! Every time they were alone together—

Alec's broad-shouldered frame straightened with an idea. *So, you just won't ever be alone with her again,* he silently concluded. And who better to see that that didn't happen but Reb's best friend? Penny already knew about their first meeting, and since she obviously blamed herself for it, he could use that guilt to his advantage. She would be their chaperone!

Brushing back his hair and tying it in place with a satin ribbon, he quickly buttoned up his shirt, stuffed the hem into his breeches and returned to the armoire for his shoes. Of course, that meant telling Penny the truth about himself. But did it really matter? Reb had probably already told her everything . . . including that little scene in the shed. Exhaling a long, wearisome sigh, he grabbed his coat and slipped into it.

The moment he discovered his room had been ransacked, he had forgotten all about finding Rebecca and asking her why she had ridden off in such a state. He hadn't thought about her again until after the locksmith fixed the door and left, and he found himself alone with his thoughts. If he hadn't come to Williamsburg under a guise, he would have dismissed the break in as a simple robbery with no results, but something in the back of his mind kept hinting that somehow the two were connected. Perhaps someone had seen him go into the courthouse, and after he'd left, they had questioned the clerk about him. They couldn't have gotten much information from the man since Alec had purposely been very cautious with his questions. The direction he had taken as he rode out of town would have pretty much told them where he was going *if* they suspected Alec's mission, and they would have then been presented with a perfect opportunity to look through his belongings while he was gone. But what were they looking for? The deed Heller had sent to him, perhaps? Obviously the document had been forged, and they might have feared Alec could somehow relate it to them. But what had put them on his trail to begin with? The newspaper advertisement? With that thought had come the image of the raven-haired vixen who worked for the *Gazette*, and Alec had spent the rest of the evening wondering what he would do about her.

He had skipped having supper in the commons since he had been relatively sure Penny wouldn't allow him to eat in peace, and instead had gone to talk with John Greenhow and confirm their business deal. Greenhow had invited Alec to have dinner with him and his wife, and Alec had quite willingly accepted on the chance the man might unwittingly tell him something useful. He hadn't, and Alec had returned to his room well after dark.

Trying to sleep had proven rather difficult if not impossible for Alec since the vision of Rebecca Wilde flared up to haunt him every time he closed his eyes. He could almost smell the sweet fragrance of her hair, the intoxicating scent of her smooth skin, and feel the silky texture of her thick, black hair as it brushed his cheek or fell against his shoulder. The memory of her hips moving under him, the stinging sensation of her nails raking his back and the touch of her warm lips on his drove him out of bed to pace the floor time and time again. Finally, out of sheer exhaustion, he had fallen asleep sitting up in the rocker only to awaken shortly before dawn, his neck stiff and the muscles in one arm cramped. He had wanted to blame his constant thoughts of her on the fact that their lovemaking had been an accident, that he hadn't wooed her into his bed the way he usually did a woman, but he knew that wasn't entirely the case. Rebecca Wilde was different. They had both said as much. What tore at his conscience was the reason she was. He could see in her the kind of traits that drew a man to a woman—long lasting traits—and it scared him. He never wanted *anyone* to have that kind of hold on him.

So, get this matter of Daniel Heller finished and go back to Jamaica, he angrily told himself as he headed for the door. *You'll forget about her once you're home again.*

That gnawing in his brain intimated otherwise.

Standing in the empty hallway outside Penny's room, Alec hesitated a moment before raising his hand and rapping his knuckles on the door. He rather doubted Penny would be up this early, but it also meant no one else would be either, and they'd have the privacy he wanted while he told her what he had planned. A few moments later, he heard her moving about inside, and he called out his name to her, adding that he'd meet her downstairs in the commons as soon as she was able.

The row of windows across the front of the building let in enough light that Alec didn't have to feel his way across the

217

room to the kitchen doorway, and by the time Penny joined him, he had already heated up some water and had two cups of tea ready and waiting at the table where he chose to sit.

"What's the matter?" she asked, pulling out a chair and sitting down. "Your conscience bothering you?"

"My conscience?" he echoed as he slid one of the cups over to her.

"Well, you're up awfully early. I figured you couldn't sleep." She raised her eyebrows at him and took a sip of her tea. "Thinking about Rebecca?"

Alec wrinkled up his face at her, inwardly wondering if she was just expressing her wishful thinking or if she had mastered the art of mind reading. "In a way, yes. But not how you'd like. I need her help."

"So why get me out of bed? I was hoping for an encore this morning, and you've pretty well ruined it. He'll be dressed and gone before I finish my tea."

Alec started to reply before he actually heard what she had said, and once it registered, he smiled instead. "My apologies. It won't happen again."

"You bet it won't," she informed him. "Because if you forget your promise, I'll just pretend I never heard you knock." Readjusting the collar on her dress, she asked, "So why did you get me out of bed, and what do you need with Rebecca?" She frowned irritably and glanced around the empty room, her hand extended. "And couldn't it have waited until the sun was up?"

"No," he replied. "It couldn't. I wanted to make sure no one heard us."

The seriousness in his tone captured Penny's full attention. "Has this got something to do with your room being broken into?"

Alec shrugged and leaned back in his chair. "It might. That's why I need both yours and Reb's help."

"Doing what?"

It surprised Alec to learn that he had been wrong about Reb. She obviously hadn't told Penny a thing about him or Penny wouldn't have asked. But before he started to relate his story to her, he made Penny promise not to tell anyone other than Rebecca about their conversation. Not only might it ruin his chances of finding the truth about Heller, but it could endanger both women; and he didn't have the time or energy to be looking out for the two of them. Once he had finished and sat quietly by while Penny digested the tale, he could see by the intense look on her face that he had made a wise decision. He was sure of it when she shook her head and muttered an oath.

"I knew there was more to you than you let on. I just couldn't quite figure out what it was. Alec Stone," she murmured. "Does Rebecca know?"

Alec nodded. "I told her yesterday." A half smile curled his lips, and he glanced down at the teacup cradled in his hands. "I guess you could say I didn't have much of a choice. She had followed me to the Robinson place and demanded to know why I was there."

When he grew quiet for a moment and got a faraway look in his eye, Penny suspected that his reason for visiting a deserted farmhouse wasn't all they had talked about. And now that he mentioned it, she remembered thinking that at the time Rebecca came to tell her Mrs. Rind had fired her, she appeared to be upset over something else as well. One corner of her mouth crimped with a half smile. Was it possible they had done more than just talk? she wondered. After all, Rebecca had ridden back into town on Alec's horse, and he was nowhere to be seen. Raising her cup to her mouth, she smiled into it as she thought how this was going better than she had hoped it would. Apparently, there was an attraction between the two that neither of them could control. All she had to do was help it along.

"So, what do you want from me?" she asked, returning her cup to its saucer while in her thoughts she mused, *I already know what you want from Rebecca.*

Totally unaware of the workings of Penny's mind, Alec failed to sense the trap he had set for himself, for if he had known, he would have packed his things and left the Colonies without ever finding out what happened to his agent. "The first thing is to establish whether or not Heller was actually in Williamsburg."

"What do you mean by that? You said he sent letters to you and that he had forwarded a deed to the property he had purchased in your name. Isn't that enough proof?"

"If he had come home, yes. But no one's seen him in over a year. And you must remember he had an awfully large amount of money that didn't belong to him."

Penny's brown eyes widened. "Are you saying he cheated you?"

"I'm saying it's one avenue that has to be explored. I didn't know Daniel Heller personally. He's the brother of a man who works for me. I have no way of really knowing if I should have trusted him, and until that fact is confirmed, I can't assume anything."

"Oh, I see," Penny murmured. "So tell me what he looks like. Maybe I've met him. How long ago did you say this all began?"

"The last letter we got from him was close to a year ago."

Penny wrinkled up her nose. "That was before my time. Reb and I didn't move here until much later."

"But you know a lot of people who were here at the time. That's how you can help . . . you and Reb." He leaned forward with his elbows braced on the edge of the table. "Once we have absolute proof that Heller was here working in my behalf, the next thing the two of you can do for me is find out all you can about the Robinson property. I've already figured out that the deed Heller sent me was a forgery, whether it was his doing or someone else's. Then we'll find out who he was dealing with and take it from there."

"Sounds simple enough," Penny replied.

"It won't be, I assure you. And I want you to remember that whoever's involved in this scheme isn't going to take kindly to your poking around. That's why you and Reb have to be very careful. Now, will you promise me something else?"

Penny nodded excitedly.

"I don't want you or that silly friend of yours to take any chances. If you think you're on to something, come and get me. *I'll* follow up on the leads. You two just ask the questions."

"You don't have to worry about me," Penny promised.

"I know I don't," he admitted. "I was actually referring to Reb. Trouble has a way of following her around."

An impish smile parted Penny's lips, but she elected not to tell him that she thought the only real trouble her friend was going to have was confessing that she felt something for Alec Stone. Rebecca had made up her mind a long time ago that there was no room in her life for a man, and she had set out trying to prove it. Then *he* showed up and ruined everything. Well, whether Rebecca cared to admit it or not, Alec had made a difference, and with a little coaxing on Penny's part, Rebecca would soon learn what that difference was.

"I think I'll start by talking to Ben," Penny announced, finishing off her tea and setting the cup aside. "He's lived here all of his life, and he'd know if there had been a stranger in town looking to buy some property. Can we meet somewhere later so I can tell you what I've found out?"

"Sure," Alec agreed. "Where?"

The only place Penny could think of that would allow Alec and Rebecca some privacy without drawing too much undue attention was Penny's room. After all, wasn't that where it all began? Smiling to herself, she pushed back her chair and stood. "My room, around noon. Is that all right with you?"

"That would be fine," he replied, coming to his feet. "I have some business to take care of with John Greenhow this morning anyway." He smiled softly at her and added, "Thank you, Penny. I realize you don't have to do this for me."

"Oh, I'm not doing it for you," she cut in before he could say anything else. "I'm doing it for Rebecca."

His rugged brow crimped suspiciously. "For Rebecca," he repeated. "How is it you've come to that conclusion?"

With a toss of her red mane, she turned and headed for the

221

stairs, calling back over her shouldesr as she went, "Think about it, Alec. I'm sure you'll figure it out."

Rebecca didn't like being anywhere near The Red Lion since there was always the chance she'd run into Alec, but the note Penny had sent her said that it was important they talk and that it was vital no one saw Rebecca going into Penny's room. Thus, she had taken the back way into the place and slipped up the stairs without being seen at precisely fifteen minutes before noon . . . just as Penny had instructed in her message. Using the spare key, she let herself in and closed the door. But the moment she had, a rush of memories flooded over her, and she very nearly turned around to make a hasty exit. She hadn't been in Penny's room since that awful night, and she doubted she'd ever be able to come here again without thinking of it. The image of that bronzed god she found lying beside her had been burned into her memory, and there would be no escaping it. She was sure it would have eased with time if she had never seen him again or learned who he was. But fate hadn't been kind to her. Not only had she seen him again *and* learned his name, but they shared the same sweet, tender moments in each other's arms as they had that night. And until Alec Stone left Williamsburg, she feared it might happen again . . . and again.

"Damned rogue," she hissed in a burst of anger as she crossed to the window to stare out at the street below. "Why did it have to rain that night? Why couldn't it have waited until I was back home in my own bed? Why did he have to pick The Red Lion for a place to stay? Why couldn't he have gone on to Boston with his crew? I'll tell you why," she snarled, taking an agitated swing at the pink lace curtains. "Because Lady Luck hates me, that's why." Growling, she whirled away and crossed to the rocker to hurl herself into it.

Without realizing it, her gaze drifted to the brass bed with its pink and white coverlet. The rage she felt eased as she unwittingly recalled the pleasure she had experienced there and again in the shed, and a smile broke the stubborn line of

222

her mouth. It amused her to think that a man like Alec, one with fine manners and a taste for elegant clothes, had stripped away both in the heat of passion to lay with her on a bed of straw, and she wondered if he had suffered as many scratches as she had. At the time it hadn't made any difference to either of them. All that filled their thoughts was the strong desire to sate that burning lust which seemed to rekindle every time they were alone together.

"I'm doomed," she moaned, dropping her head forward against her fingertips. Until he left Williamsburg, there would be no hope of her ever putting him out of her mind. And even then she wasn't so sure it would be enough. It wasn't like catching the sniffles; suffer a few days with it and then it was gone and forgotten. Alec had become a very vivid part of her life, and she'd never be able to forget him . . . not fully.

So what are you to do? she silently asked herself. *Sit here and feel miserable? Go on hiding every time you think you might see him?* An idea struck her, and she raised her head, a look of hope building up in the pale blueness of her eyes. *Of course not*, she inwardly declared. *You can't hide . . . not for long. The day Miss Abigail asks for the rent and you can't pay, she'll throw you and your belongings out on the front lawn. You need a job Rebecca, and since there's only one kind of work you're willing to do, you better prove to Mrs. Rind how fine a journalist you really are. You'll write a story that will win her respect and the praise of every person living here in Williamsburg.* A devious gleam lifted one eyebrow and pursed her lips. *And guess who'll be the subject of that story!* Giggling triumphantly, she slapped her hands together and bolted from the rocker to pace the floor in thought.

She had been so busy feeling sorry for herself after their little session in the shed when he had so callously admitted she meant nothing to him, that she had forgotten about the confession he had made to her. He had a mystery to solve, and it had all the makings of a great news article. All she had to do was solve it. And once she had, she'd get her old job back at the *Gazette* and Alec would go home . . . to Jamaica. A strange emptiness assailed her when she realized how far away that island really was, but she courageously shook it off. The truth of the matter was *it wasn't far enough.*

"So where do I begin?" she questioned aloud as she went to Penny's small writing desk and sat down. Taking the quill from its well, she began with a list of everything Alec had told her and soon realized that they never discussed what Daniel Heller looked like. She'd need that bit of information if she was to ask around town about him. Someone was sure to have seen him, talked to him, rented him a room, since Alec claimed the man had stayed in Williamsburg for several weeks. Her smooth brow wrinkled when a thought came to mind, and she slowly leaned back in the chair as she laid the quill down. What if the whole thing had been prearranged before Heller ever got to Williamsburg? The temptation to steal the kind of money Heller had been given would surely lure even the most honest of men. But if that were true, why hadn't the man sent for his wife and child? Alec had said Heller was married. It didn't make sense for him not to want to share his ill-acquired wealth with his family. She shook off that idea but didn't truly dismiss it from her mind. Once they found Heller's grave, then she'd know for certain she had been wrong.

The rattling of the doorknob lifted her attention away from her work, and she half-turned in the chair to voice a greeting to her friend once Penny stepped into the room. But when the wide archway was filled with the broad-shouldered shape of Alec Stone, her eyes widened, her pulse leaped in her veins and her head began to spin. Thinking of him and conjuring up various images of his tall, well-dressed physique suddenly proved quite lacking, for her whimsical daydreams hardly compared with the full sight of him as flesh and blood. He was taller, more muscular and profoundly more handsome than her memory allowed. And the warmth of his presence—although he stood across the room from her—reached out to caress every inch of her. Feeling the blush rise in her cheeks she blinked, swallowed her nervous-

Get a Free
Zebra
Historical
Romance

*a $3.95
value*

Affix
stamp
here

ness and averted her gaze, hoping to cool the raging fire that threatened to shatter what was left of her composure.

"If you're here to see Penny, she'll be up in a few minutes," she softly told him while she guardedly returned the quill to its well and folded up the piece of paper on which she had made her list. "I was just on my way out." Rising, she stuffed the parchment in the deep pocket of her skirt and turned for the door, her eyes still lowered. It was better for her if she didn't look at him. But the sound of the latch clicking shut ruined her plan. Frowning, she glanced up.

"I think we have a problem that we need to talk about," he announced, his own brow furrowed with a mixture of determination and mild annoyance.

He stood in front of the door with his arms folded over his wide chest, his feet apart and his tricorn held in one hand. The plum shade of his attire seemed to enhance his coppery complexion and highlighted his dark blond hair. The coat hugged his thick shoulders and accented his narrow hips. The dark breeches molded his well-muscled thighs and left little doubt of his male prowess, and Rebecca quickly pulled her gaze away from where it rested. She didn't have to be reminded. There wasn't much about him that didn't pluck the strings of her ever-growing weakness for him.

"Talk?" she jeered, deliberately turning her back on him and making a wide berth of the bed as she crossed to the window. "What could we have to talk about? It seems that every time we try, we end up arguing." *And then making love,* she added in her thoughts.

"I agree," he replied, his gaze drinking in the shapely length of her slender form and lingering on the gentle sway of her hips as she moved away from him. He blinked, silently reprimanded himself for letting his mind wander, and turned to toss his tricorn on the bed. A frown curled his brow the instant he realized where he had thrown it, for it brought back a flood of memories that twisted his insides with an unpleasant fusion of blissful satisfaction and deep remorse. Gritting his teeth, he forced himself to forget about that night and concentrated on the matter at hand. "Maybe we argue because it's the only way we can communicate. Bloody dreadful, I must say, and perhaps this discussion will have the same results, but I feel I must apologize." He shook his head, confused, and added, "For something."

Surprised to hear that he had even an ounce of conscience, Rebecca slowly turned her gaze upon him.

"I made you angry yesterday . . . there in the shed. . . ." The vision of her silkened flesh, the lust burning in her eyes, and her parted, trembling lips flared up suddenly, and he steeled himself against the image. Squaring his shoulders, he continued. "I honestly don't know what I said to send you running off like that or that I should even be apologizing, but I am. I'm sorry, Rebecca, for making you angry."

She lifted a finely arched brow at him. "And that's supposed to make everything all right?"

Not only could he see her refusal to believe him shining in her blue eyes, but in the stubborn way she held her chin. Apologizing to her was even harder than talking to her . . . or putting her out of his thoughts. "It would if you'd let it," he answered.

"And if I did, you'd be able to sleep well tonight. Is that it?"

He started to tell her that he hadn't had much trouble sleeping *last* night, remembered how he had paced the floor for hours and finally found a few moments of solace in the rocking chair, and couldn't bring himself to lie. But he certainly wouldn't admit the truth, either. He never liked seeing someone gloat. He decided on a different tactic. "If that isn't enough, then why don't you tell me what I said that was so horrible. I assure you I haven't the vaguest idea."

She tossed her silky mane and stared out the window again. "So you can deny it?"

"Deny what?" he exploded. "That at times I'm so confused by you that I wonder if I've lost my mind?" He exhaled a long breath and glared back at her. "Well, I *won't* deny it, Rebecca. Sometimes—like when you left me behind at the Robinson's farm—I'm *sure* I've gone insane."

A moment of silence followed in which Alec considered

226

asking her if she's heard a word he'd said, and Rebecca willfully refused to acknowledge that she had. Then finally, and much to his chagrin, she cast him a look over her shoulder, an icy damning look.

"'Twould be an excellent excuse for dismissing what you've done, wouldn't it? I can hear you now when you're talking to your male friends. 'I don't know what got into me. I bed the saucy wench without a thought. I must be insane.'" She stared out at the bright sunlight again, irritated with the tears that suddenly burned her eyes.

"Is *that* what this is about?" he exclaimed, crossing the room to grab her arm and force her to face him. "Were you so filled with guilt the moment you realized you had willingly given in to your passion that you couldn't deal with it and sought to lay the blame on me?" He shook her. "Well, go ahead. Blame me if it makes you feel better."

Rebecca angrily jerked free of him. "It wasn't guilt, you thick-witted oaf! I was sorry I let it happen, but only because of the things you said to me."

"What?" He nearly shouted the word. "What did I say? For all that's holy, please tell me, for I swear if I live to be one hundred, I will never figure it out."

Rebecca opened her mouth to recite every word and suddenly found that she couldn't recall a single one, only what his comments implied. She raised her nose in the air and proclaimed, "That I was no different from all those before me, that as soon as you had gotten dressed, you'd forget what we had shared. I was nothing more to you than a . . . a . . . a roll in the hay." With an arrogant toss of her head, she started to turn away, intending to leave his presence as quickly as possible, but he caught her elbow and wouldn't let go.

"Excuse me, Reb, but I think my hearing as well as my mind is starting to fail me." He tightened his grip when she tried to pull away. "But I don't remember saying any such thing. You asked me how you compared to the other women in my life, and I said there was no comparison."

"Yes! You did," she strongly agreed, yanking on his hold

227

only to wince in pain when he wouldn't release her.

"And you turn that around to mean I'm a cold-hearted—" He stumbled for the right word.

"Bastard," she supplied with a sneer.

The muscle in his cheek flexed, but he managed to keep his temper under control. "Perhaps you're the one who's thick-witted, Rebecca Wilde. When I said there was no comparison, I meant that I'd never been with a woman like you before." He rushed on when she tried to point out that that was just what she had told him. "I thought I made that perfectly clear to you. I thought you'd know it just by the way I act around you. God, Rebecca, can't you see how hard it is for me to keep my hands to myself every time we're alone?" His gaze automatically dropped to the fingers wrapped around her arm, and he quickly untwined them. "I don't know what it is you'd like to hear me say. I'm not sure you even know or that I'd be able to say it if you asked it of me. We're not meant for each other, Reb. We're two extremely different people. *If* I ever decided to settle down, I'd want a woman who wouldn't make demands on me, someone who wouldn't complicate my life. I'd never have that with you. And I wouldn't ask you to change just to suit my needs." His dark brown eyes softened, and a vague hint of smile lifted one corner of his mouth as he reached up to gently stroke her cheek. "You should stay the way you are, Rebecca Wilde. You're special. And someday the right man will come along to recognize that in you." Gently, he brushed a long, black curl from her shoulder. "I guess what I'm saying is that you deserve better than me."

What an odd thing for him to say, she mused with a frown. It had been her opinion for years that all men were the same. Then Alec Stone came into her life and contradicted everything she had been led to believe. And now he was telling her that she deserved better than him? She truly couldn't agree with that. She had never met a man before him who showed her even an ounce of respect. So how could there possibly be someone better than Alec Stone? Lowering her gaze from those hypnotic eyes, she stepped away from him. Perhaps it was merely what he wanted her to believe, that it was his way of letting her down easily. Maybe he truly wanted nothing more to do with her—he never had—and it was his way of covering up his true feelings. She had been a pleasure for a while, but now she had lost her appeal. Fighting back the sob that knotted her throat, she drew in a deep breath and defied the notion that she had been used by him simply to satisfy his male needs.

"I guess you're right," she claimed. "I *can* do better than you."

Although Alec had meant what he said, to hear her agree left him feeling a bit hurt, and that surprised him. He honestly felt that aside from their lust for one another they had nothing in common, that out of bed they would constantly be at each other's throat. And what kind of a life would that be for either of them? He rather enjoyed his freedom. And having Rebecca around, even without the bonds of wedlock, suffocated him. He was forever thinking of her, worrying she might have gotten herself into trouble, concerned for her well being. Dammit, it was the same as being married to her, only with one major difference; as soon as he decided, he'd be free to go back home without her. Frowning confusedly, he shook his head. So why was he feeling as if his life would be empty without her?

Rebecca had covertly watched Alec's reaction to her declaration, the surprise, possibly even the pain registered on his handsome face, and she took a subtle pride in knowing she had said something that stung his ego. Perhaps she hadn't been wrong about her generalization concerning men after all. It was quite obvious to her that he had expected her to discredit his claim, maybe even beg her to reconsider, and when she hadn't and had in fact agreed with him, he didn't know how to deal with her rejection. With bright blue eyes sparkling, she unconsciously turned for the bed with the intention of sitting down on it, came to an abrupt halt once she realized where she was headed and the possible results, and detoured the direction she took. More comfortable with the rocker, she eased into it, crossed her knees and leaned one elbow on the arm.

"So," she began, her voice light and tinged with devilment, "when will you be going home?"

That odd feeling of loneliness seemed to intensify with her question, and several moments passed before Alec could brush it aside and think clearly enough to answer. Shrugging a shoulder, he turned away from the window and started for the bed. He, too, came to an abrupt halt, changed destinations and took a seat at the writing desk. "I can't leave until this matter with my agent is solved," he replied, wondering why he was suddenly so uncomfortable. "I have a piece of property that isn't worth one tenth of what I paid for it, and a man I hired is missing." He stared at her a moment, then sighed and reached for the brass paperweight lying on the desk beside him. "I know I really have no right to ask it of you, Reb," he began, rolling the shiny ball over and over in his hand, "but I really could use your help." He shifted his gaze and his attention back on Rebecca. "Yours and Penny's."

"Penny?" she repeated, surprised.

Alec nodded and set the brass weight back down. "I've already talked to her about it, and she said she'd do what she could for me. She seems to know just about everyone in town, and I thought between the two of you that one or the other would be able to track down Heller's movements after his arrival. If I started asking questions, I might ruin everything. You understand, don't you?"

Oh, I understand, she silently admitted. *You'd rather have three of us looking into it so you won't have to waste time. The sooner you're finished, the sooner you can go home. Well, if you think that's going to bother me, I'll show you that it isn't.* Reaching into her pocket, she withdrew her list, saying, "I couldn't agree more. In fact, just before you came in, I was jotting down notes about the case." She glanced over at him, smiling pleasantly and wondering if she had gotten her point across that where he went and when he decided to go were of no major concern to her. The interested look on his face made her doubt she had, and she quickly dropped her gaze to the piece of paper she held. "Have you given any consideration to the possibility that Heller's the one behind this? That he saw an easy way to make some money and simply ran with it?"

"Yes," Alec admitted, truly amazed with the way Rebecca thought things through. She really had the potential of becoming a great journalist someday. "It has crossed my mind. That's why I asked Penny to see if she could find someone who had actually talked with Heller. If we can establish the fact that he was here and made contact with someone about purchasing land, then we'll be able to start looking for the man who sold the Robinson place to him."

"Well, it wasn't Robinson," she firmly assured him. "The way I hear it, he's been dead for years." Straightening in the chair, she leaned forward with her elbows braced on her knees. "Let's suppose Heller was the victim, not the criminal. How was it possible for someone to sell your agent a plot of land that didn't truly belong to him? I realize the deed Heller sent you was probably forged, but wouldn't he have checked out the property before he handed over payment?"

"I'm sure he would have. It's my guess Heller was shown a different piece of land and assumed that was what he was buying."

Rebecca's brows came together as she absorbed the information. "Then can we suppose the culprit is a wealthy man?"

"Why would you say that?"

"He'd have to be to pull off something like this. He's rich and he saw a way to get richer." Excited with her idea, Rebecca stood and began walking back and forth across the room. "A stranger in town lets it be known that he's interested in buying land and that he's willing to pay whatever it takes. Our thief decides that since this fellow is new to the area he won't know what's happening to him until it's too late. So he offers him a deal, one he can't pass up. But something goes wrong. For some reason, Heller discovers he has been cheated and the man has to kill him before he is exposed." She stopped her pacing and faced Alec. "It

231

certainly explains a lot, don't you agree?"

"Yes." Alec nodded, frowning. "But if you're correct, it leaves us without a horse to ride."

Rebecca's pretty face wrinkled. "What?"

Glancing up to see the confusion in her blue eyes, he chuckled and explained, "It's an old saying of my mother's. It means that we're left with nothing else to go on." The ticking of the mantel clock behind Rebecca drew his attention. "That's strange," he murmured, taking note that it was half past twelve. "Penny said to meet her here at noon." He shrugged it off and stood, mumbling to himself that perhaps she'd been too busy to get away.

"Oh, I'm sure of that" came the heated reply of his companion, and when Alec glanced up at her, he was surprised to see the angry look on her face. "She told me to be here at precisely eleven forty-five. You don't suppose she did it deliberately, do you?"

The sarcastic tone of Rebecca's voice and the way she squinted up her eyes told Alec that she did believe it. Although she failed to see the humor in it, Alec did, and he couldn't stop the smile that curled his mouth. "I wouldn't be too awfully angry with her, Reb. She meant well. She probably thought it was time you and I called a truce, and decided to help out." His smile softened, and he tilted his head at her. "We have called a truce, haven't we, Reb?"

Rebecca wanted to tell him that it would last only long enough for him to learn the truth about his agent and to make plans for his return trip home. After that, *anything* was fair. However, admitting it to him would be the same as playing into his hands, and she didn't want that. She didn't want him to feel that he could add her name to his collection of conquests. Forcing a smile, she nodded and headed for the door.

"I'll start asking around right away," she told him as she reached for the knob and pulled the door open. "If I learn anything, I'll let you know."

"Rebecca."

The sound of his voice calling out to her stopped her at the threshold, and she frantically tried to ignore the warm

232

sensation that raced through her entire body. "What?" she asked without looking at him.

"Thank you. For your help and your understanding. And I'm pleased that we'll be friends now."

"Friends?" She laughed sarcastically as she cast him an acid glare over her shoulder. "I don't think so, Mr. Stone. I don't think so."

In a whirl of satin and petticoats she exited the room.

Chapter Ten

Rebecca carefully avoided seeing Alec, and kept her visits with Penny to a minimum for the next two days. She had made her friend promise not to tell anyone else about her losing her job in the hope Miss Abigail and especially Jon-Gregory wouldn't find out about it. It was her want to uncover the truth about Daniel Heller, write her story and present it to Mrs. Rind, and then win her job back before anyone knew what had happened. With Jon-Gregory, she merely wished to avoid hearing him lecture and knowing that he was worried for her now that she had no income. But it was Miss Abigail that concerned her more. If the old woman learned one of her boarders had no immediate means with which to pay the rent, she might start looking for a new tenant and force Rebecca out of her room before she had the chance to prove herself. Thus, Rebecca rose every morning and ate breakfast in the dining room with the other boarders as if nothing was wrong, and left for work at her usual time. However, her destination hadn't been the same, and she soon worried someone might miss her presence at the newspaper office. To ease that possibility, she deliberately let it be known that she was working on a story, one that took her away from her desk most of the day.

She began her investigation by visiting the courthouse and examining the records concerning both the area deaths and the sale of property. The first revealed a very curious aspect to the puzzle, one Rebecca had difficulty in understanding.

Arnold Robinson had died nearly ten years earlier and left no immediate heirs to his meager estate, since both his parents were dead, he had been an only child and he had never married. The only logical conclusion she could draw from this was that the tiny farm had soon been claimed by the royal governor of Virginia acting as a representative of the Crown, when the taxes on the property weren't paid. What drew her softly arched brows together was her confusion over the discovery she made in the second ledger the clerk's assistant had given her. No mention was made anywhere of the Robinson property being up for auction, and after all these years, Rebecca figured the governor had forgotten the Crown even owned it. Yet, written on the page she had spread out before her was the transaction of that sale to one Alec Stone of Jamaica . . . through a proxy. Was the proxy Daniel Heller? Or had Heller hired the services of a solicitor? Was the solicitor the man they were after? Or was it the county clerk who drew up the deed? And could he have been acting on orders from the governor? Or paid off by someone else? There were so many possibilities that it was hard to determine the more likely candidate on what little information she had been given here, and she decided to ask the young man behind the counter.

"Excuse me," she called out to him as she laid the huge books down in front of her. "Could you spare me a minute?"

"Yes'm," he replied, leaving his desk to come to the counter.

Shoving the register toward him, she pointed at the entry concerning the Robinson farm. "It shows here that this property was purchased through a proxy. Do you have any way of knowing who that was?"

A frown gathered on the young man's brow as he readjusted his spectacles and studied the page. "No, miss. I'm afraid I don't. You see that was before I started working here."

"Would the county clerk know, perchance?" she asked hopefully.

He shook his head. "I rather doubt it. He was only assigned this job a few weeks ahead of me."

"And how long ago was that?"

"Close to a year."

"What happened to his predecessor? Did he retire? Do you know where I might find him so that I could ask him about it?"

An odd smile parted the young man's lips. "Yes, miss, I know where you could find him, but I don't think you'll be able to talk to him."

Rebecca's smooth brow wrinkled. "Why not?"

"He's dead, miss. He's buried in the church cemetery."

Rebecca's hopes sank. "Oh," she murmured, dropping her gaze.

"Strange thing, his death," the man went on as he leaned an elbow on the counter and absently stared down at the ledger.

"Why's that?" she asked, but she really wasn't interested. It truly made no difference to her how he died. He was dead and he couldn't tell her what she wanted to know.

"He was murdered."

Rebecca's head came up, and her blue eyes sparkled with curiosity. "Murdered? Why?"

The young man shrugged. "That's the strange part. No one knows for sure. He'd worked late that night, and his assistant figures he went straight home after that. But his body was found in the woods north of town the next morning."

"North of town?" she repeated, immediately thinking that that was the direction one would have to take to reach the Robinson farm. Might there be a connection? "How far north?"

The man scratched his chin while he tried to recall. "Three or four miles. Maybe farther. I don't remember for sure. It was a while back."

Rebecca scooped the second book into her arms. "But you're sure it was about a year ago?" she asked.

"Yes'm." His pale brows came together suddenly when her inquiry piqued both his interest and his suspicion. "Why do you want to know?"

"It's my job to want to know," she quickly told him once

she realized she had said too much already. "I'm a journalist and we get paid to ask questions." Hugging the ledger to her bosom, she smiled back at him and added, "Can't you see that there might be a story in this? A man was murdered, and no one bothered to find out why." The thought of Eli's death surfaced briefly and disappeared. Trying to solve his murder had had some rather devastating repercussions with no results. Hopefully, this would be different. Casting the assistant a weak smile, she turned for the table and sat down with the book opened in front of her.

Flipping to the back of the book, she scanned the pages for the list of deaths that occurred around the time the young man had said the county clerk's body had been found. If her hunch was correct, she expected to find that the man died somewhere close to the time Daniel Heller purchased the Robinson farm. That's what she was hoping for, anyway. It would mean she was on the right trail, that someone in Williamsburg knew what had happened. Yet, once the tip of her finger glided down the long column of names and dates and came to rest on the one at the bottom of the page, a chill shot up her spine. The county clerk had died the same day Alec Stone had become the new owner of a small piece of land. But that bit of knowledge soon paled in importance once she noticed the following entry, and she quickly closed the book.

"Thank you for your help," she called to the young man sitting at his desk as she laid the ledger down on the counter and turned for the door. Her next stop would be to pay a visit to Bruton Parish Church's cemetery.

"There she is," one of the two men standing across the street from the courthouse announced as they watched Rebecca hurry down the sidewalk. "Where do you suppose she's going?"

"If I knew that, we wouldn't have to follow her," his companion snarled. "Did you find someone to deliver the note?"

The first man nodded. "Paid a boy to do it." He settled his

attention on Rebecca again. "Do you suppose she found something at the courthouse?"

The second man's eyes narrowed as he studied the energetic gait of the young woman walking away from them. "If she has, you better pray you did your job well. One slip right now and we're finished. *You're* finished."

"Me?" the other echoed. "You're just as much a part of this as I am. *More,* in fact. This whole thing was your idea."

"And you went along with it . . . quite eagerly, I might add."

"Well, of course I did. What choice did I have? I was tired of sleeping in the alley and stealing food. What man wouldn't jump at the chance to earn some money?"

"Earn it?" the other sneered. "You've killed for it, but I wouldn't exactly say you've earned it."

"They had to die and you know it. It was a part of the plan, so don't make it sound like I'm to blame. You're the one who said it was the only way this would work." Angered by the way his cohort seemed to want to shirk his share of the responsibility, he added, "And if you hadn't been stupid enough to lose that stickpin, we wouldn't be in the fix we're in right now." Encouraged to speak his piece when his companion chose not to answer, he faced the other and said, "And if you'd think with your brain instead of the crotch of your breeches, we'd be back home enjoying the rewards of our effort instead of sneaking around Williamsburg."

Dark green eyes glared at him. "Are you finished?" He didn't give his companion the chance to reply. "Because if you're not, I think I should remind you how easy it would be for me to eliminate you. I don't need you any longer. In fact, I haven't needed you since the moment I met your cousin. So I suggest you watch what you say to me from now on. *And* I suggest you get that pin away from Mr. Diamond before it's too late."

Recognizing that he had been given no idle threat, the smaller of the two men nodded in his head. "I'll take care of it just as soon as I can get him alone," he mumbled. "Since I couldn't find it in his room, he must be wearing it."

"Brilliant deduction," his partner jeered. "I do believe

your cousin could have figured that out." He jerked his head in the direction of The Red Lion. "Then see that it's done right away. I'll follow her." His green eyes shifted to the trim figure clothed in light blue as Rebecca made her way down the street, unaware that she was being watched and by whom.

Long shadows moved along the sidewalk in front of Rebecca as she headed back to the boardinghouse sometime later. Her trip to the church's cemetery and a few questions asked of the groundskeeper had proven her suspicions were right. They didn't, however, completely solve Alec's problem, and she doubted he'd be willing to go home just because she had guaranteed him that Daniel Heller was dead. There was still the matter of his money.

The warm aroma of cooked meat, freshly baked bread and even the smell of apple pie drifted out across the yard in front of Miss Abigail's to greet Rebecca as she dashed up the path leading to the porch. She hadn't had a thing to eat since breakfast, and if she wasn't sitting down at the table before Miss Abigail served the first dish, she'd be forced to wait until tomorrow morning. That was one of the old woman's rules, just as it was a rule that no one be allowed into the house after ten o'clock at night. Well, she'd made it home in time to have dinner, and she'd see to it that she was home before Miss Abigail locked the front door. Just as soon as she was finished eating, she'd go to The Red Lion and talk with Alec. Freeing the latch, she stepped into the hallway.

"Rebecca? Is that you?" came the high-pitched voice from the dining room.

"Yes, Miss Abigail. I'm not late, am I?"

"No, child. But a message came for you today. I laid it there on the table in the hall. Do you see it?"

Rebecca's gaze quickly dropped to her left. "Yes, ma'am, I see it."

"Guess whoever sent it must not know ya work at the newspaper office, don't ya think? Otherwise they would have sent it there, I reckon."

"Mmmm," Rebecca murmured as she popped the seal and unfolded the piece of paper.

"Hope it's not trouble," Abigail called when several moments of silence passed and her curiosity got the better of her. "It's not, is it, Rebecca?" When the young woman failed to answer her, Abigail laid aside the silverware she had been arranging around the table and moved to the doorway, there to peek out into the hall. "Rebecca? Is everything all right?"

Hurriedly refolding the message, Rebecca tucked it in her pocket and asked, "Who delivered this?"

The wrinkles in Abigail's brow deepened. "I don't really know, child. By the time I got to the door, they were gone, and I found it laying on the mat. Why? Isn't it signed?"

Rebecca had more than once wished Miss Abigail could keep a secret. She had such a way about her for getting at the facts that Rebecca would have liked using the woman's help. But such was not the case today, and if Rebecca didn't come up with a satisfying answer for her, Miss Abigail would continue to pry. "Yes, it's signed," she lied. "I was just wondering who had been asked to bring it here." Turning for the stairs, she added, "How long before dinner, Miss Abigail?"

"Not long, so if you're thinking about taking a nap, don't. You know the rules," the old woman replied with a stiff nod of her gray head.

"Yes, ma'am," Rebecca answered. "I was just hoping I had the time to freshen up."

"Well, don't take too long," Miss Abigail instructed as she stepped back through the doorway and out of sight.

Many of the laws Abigail Beecher laid down for her boarders were of the sort that could easily be lived with. However, her insistence that the meals be eaten slowly and with practiced manners suitable for dining with the governor only added to Rebecca's frustration this particular night. She had so many things to do and very little time to accomplish them before she had to be back in the house that she truly worried she wouldn't make it by ten o'clock. And having to sit through what seemed to her to be a dilly-dallying execution of fine social conduct merely shortened

Rebecca's temper.

"Is something wrong?" Jon-Gregory asked quietly when he noticed how his friend had seemed to rush through her meal and was sitting with her hands folded in her lap, her eyes darting from one guest at the table to the next as if willing each to finish up as quickly as she had done. "You'll make yourself sick eating that fast."

Rebecca shot him a sideways glance which clearly marked her agitation. "I have things to do and can't afford to be sitting here all night."

"Well, can't it wait until morning?" He leisurely cut into his first bite of apple pie, ignoring the heated glare he received from her.

"No. It can't." She declined Miss Abigail's offer of pie and silently wished everyone else would. "I have to meet with someone."

"Tonight?" Jon-Gregory exclaimed. "Who?"

Reaching for her cup of tea, she raised it to her lips and snarled, "I don't remember sticking my nose into your business."

He straightened in his chair and scowled back at her. "And I don't recall ever having done so to you. I merely asked a question. But if I thought keeping a close eye on you would keep you out of trouble, I'd do it more often." He turned his attention back on the piece of pie. "I really feel sorry for you, Rebecca. You refuse to allow a friend to be concerned. Someday you won't have any left to badger."

She knew her stinging remark had hurt Jon-Gregory's feelings, and she would have liked to apologize. But she couldn't. He'd only pressure her into telling him who she had to meet at such a late hour, and she absolutely couldn't give in. Jon-Gregory would strongly object even if he knew the man was Alec Stone. In fact, he might even insist on going along with her. And that wouldn't do. Once she had reported her findings to Alec, she had to be on the grounds in back of the Public Hospital by nine-thirty . . . just as the note had instructed. It had also said that she was to come alone, and she couldn't risk scaring off whoever sent her the message by allowing Jon-Gregory to accompany her. She would have liked having him there beside her, since the unsigned note left her feeling a bit uncomfortable, but apparently whoever it was that had information concerning Eli's death wanted his identity kept a secret. And seeing justice served in the matter of her childhood friend's death was more important than her silly fears.

The mantel clock sitting over the fireplace in the parlor struck half past seven before Rebecca was excused from the table. Forcing herself not to race up the stairs, she returned to her room to find a shawl and to unlock the window. The Public Hospital was on the other side of town, which meant there was a strong chance she'd never make it back to the house in time to use the front door. She'd have to rely on the rose trellis again if that was the case, and as she headed out into the hall, she was wishing she could have donned some of Tommy Henderson's clothes again. It would make the tricky ascent a little easier.

Standing outside the front door to The Red Lion, Rebecca paused long enough to take a deep breath and steel her will to face Alec. From the number of horses tied to the hitching rail, she assumed Penny would be too busy to join her while she talked with Alec in his room, and Rebecca worried that their privacy would lead to other things besides discussing Daniel Heller. But her concern was unfounded once she had stepped inside and learned through Penny that Alec wasn't there. Apparently someone had inquired about the advertisement he had placed in the newspaper, and he had gone to Raleigh Tavern to meet with the man.

Nearly an hour had slipped away on her while she waited for him in his room. She had spent most of that time pacing the floor and wondering if her news could wait until morning. It was so much more important to her that she not miss her meeting at the hospital that she was about to leave Alec a note when the door latch rattled and he suddenly appeared in the framework. As always the sight of him stirred her blood, and rather than enjoy the way his cape fell in rich folds from his wide shoulders or how perfectly the breeches hugged his muscular thighs and the ivory-colored, lace cuffs of his shirt gently caressed the backs of his brown hands, she averted her gaze while muttering a weak, halfhearted greeting.

"Penny said you'd found something important," he stated as he shed the dark cape and tricorn and tossed them on the chair beside him. "I assume it's about Heller."

"Yes, it is," she answered nervously. Horribly aware of the huge bed and the man who stood so very close to it, she moved away from them both and sat down in the rocker next to the hearth. "I'm afraid it's bad news," she announced while she idly toyed with the nail on her thumb and covertly watched him from out of the corner of her eye. She'd feel a lot better if he would move away from the bed.

"He's dead," Alec concluded with a shake of his head. When she didn't respond, he sighed heavily and went to stare out the window. "How did you find out?"

Relaxing a little when it seemed he was more caught up in hearing her story than in coaxing her into bed, she lifted her eyes to look at him. He stood with his back to her, one hand resting near the window latch, the other holding back one section of the curtains while he studied something below him in the street. It was the first time Rebecca could see how the weariness of his journey had affected him, and whether or not he had ever met Daniel Heller, he obviously felt remorse. Having to tell him that Heller was not only dead but that he had been murdered was something she wished she didn't have to do.

"Since you had already found out that your agent had been tricked into buying the Robinson farm," she began, "I decided to check the records at the courthouse to see if I could determine who had sold it to him. About all I could come up with was that the governor of Virginia had claimed the land for unpaid taxes, and the county clerk recorded the sale in the ledger." She scooted forward in her chair. "The interesting part and how I discovered for certain Heller was dead was when the young man working at the courthouse told me that I wouldn't be able to question the county clerk. It just so happens that he died nearly a year ago. In fact, he was murdered on his way home after work . . . the same day he entered the sale of the Robinson property in the ledger."

Alec's dark eyes settled on her almost instantly.

"That's right," she replied to his unspoken question. "The same day. So, being the inquisitive sort that I am, I looked up the day he had died and learned that the body of a second man had been found along with the county clerk. There was no name listed, but I assumed he had been buried in the church cemetery."

"And were you correct?" Alec quickly asked.

Rebecca nodded with a bright smile. "I talked to the groundskeeper about the unmarked grave, and he told me that the man's body had been found on old man Robinson's property. Too coincidental, I'd say. Wouldn't you?"

A frown drew Alec's tawny brows together. "Yes, but it doesn't necessarily mean he was Heller."

"I thought you'd say something like that," she admitted. "So I asked him if he knew someone who could describe him to me. He said it didn't matter because the man's face had been bashed in and that there really wasn't much to identify. But he did tell me that the man was close to six feet tall with light brown hair and somewhere in his early thirties."

Alec slowly shook his head. "It still doesn't—"

"Wait," Rebecca cut in. "There's more. The groundskeeper told me that since no one in town seemed to know who the man was, his belongings—his jewelry and the like—were given to the minister to keep until somone came looking for him. It's still not positive proof, I'll admit, but with all the other circumstantial evidence we have, the watch the minister showed me pretty well convinced me he was your agent."

Alec realized that his not asking her to explain wouldn't change whatever it was she had uncovered, but he truly didn't want to hear it. Daniel's brother, Timothy, was a nice man. Alec liked him. And it had been his idea to send Daniel to Virginia. Now because of his suggestion, his brother was dead, and Alec would have to be the one to tell him.

"Well?" Rebecca questioned excitedly, failing to see the anguish in Alec's dark brown eyes. "Don't you want to know how I came to that conclusion?"

Alec turned away from her and stared out the window

again. "His name was engraved on the watch," he finished, his voice sounding tired and cheerless.

"Well, not quite," she confessed. "Only the intials DH." A frown crossed her brow and disappeared once she realized that Alec wasn't sharing her enthusiasm, and it suddenly dawned on her that he was probably blaming himself for Heller's death to some degree. "I guess there's a good possibility that the dead man isn't Heller," she added encouragingly. "I mean the man could have stolen the watch. Or his name might have been Douglas Hampton." She patiently waited for Alec to consider her proposal and was about to add something else when he turned around and smiled at her.

"I don't think so, Rebecca, and neither do you." He drew in a deep breath and crossed to the dresser to pour himself a glass of wine. "Besides, the description the groundskeeper gave you fits the one his brother gave me. And you already said the circumstantial evidence is just too much to be ignored. No, I'd say you're absolutely correct. Daniel Heller is dead, and whoever killed him has my money."

"So what are you going to do now?" she asked quietly as she drifted back down into the rocker.

He swallowed the entire amount of his drink to soothe the pain he felt and set the glass aside. "I guess I'll have to continue pretending I'm Alec Diamond for a while. Or at least until the *Constance* docks." He smiled halfheartedly at the questioning look she gave him. "The ship that brought me here."

"One of yours?"

Alec nodded. "We had a shipload of goods scheduled for delivery in Boston this week. That's why I decided to come along when I did, and why it seemed I appeared from out of nowhere that night. I had them drop me off on their way up the coast. They should be returning in a week to ten days from now."

"And in the meantime?" Rebecca asked.

Folding his arms over his chest, he leaned back against the edge of the dresser. "In the meantime I pray whoever killed Heller is still quite greedy."

Rebecca's tiny frame straightened. "What are you saying? The county clerk killed him."

He cocked a brow at her. "How can you be so sure?"

Unwittingly, she came to her feet and moved over to him.

"I realize you probably know more about business dealings than I," she began, "but I don't understand how you can think otherwise. It seems to me that once Heller figured out he had been swindled, he went after the man who was responsible."

"And killed him?" Alec challenged. "Maybe. But then who killed Heller?"

A puzzled frown knotted Rebecca's brow as she thought about it. "Maybe they killed each other." Alec started to deny the possibility, but she cut him off. "Now wait. Let's consider it for a minute. The county clerk's body was found north of town . . . the same direction as Robinson's farm and the spot where Heller died. Suppose, if you will, that the clerk followed Heller there because Heller had threatened to expose him. They struggled, Heller was killed and the clerk, who was badly wounded, managed to stumble a mile or so down the road before he died. It could have happened that way."

"It could have," Alec agreed. "But didn't you say that the county clerk was on his way home after work that night?"

Rebecca nodded.

"So what was he doing so far from home? I would think he'd have lived in town."

"I'm sure he did, and I'm sure he wanted everyone to think he was on his way home. If he had cheated a man out of a great deal of money and that man threatened to turn him over to the authorities, he certainly wouldn't want anyone to know where he was really going. He lied. It's as simple as that."

"Oh, you'll get no argument out of me, Reb." He grinned. "It's the only logical answer."

Rebecca's dark brows came together. "But . . ." she coaxed.

"But I don't think that's really how it happened."

"Why?" she clamored.

"Because it's too perfect," he calmly told her. "Call it

instinct, if you like, but I don't think the county clerk was the only one in on it."

"I'll call it stupid," Rebecca scoffed, turning her back on him.

"Then prove to me that I'm wrong. Check out how much the clerk left his heirs . . . if he had any. Reb, we're talking about a *lot* of money . . . more than a county clerk could earn in ten years. A month passed after Heller sent me the deed, yet the man you're accusing of his murder never left town. Why? He'd made his fortune. Why didn't he run with it?"

"Because he only got a share?" she questioned reluctantly, wishing she had figured it out ahead of Alec.

Smiling, he nodded his head at her. "And weren't you the one who just a couple of days ago suggested that Daniel Heller was the victim of some elaborate plan? That whoever pulled this off had to be rich and saw a way to get richer?" He waited until he saw her nod begrudgingly. "So don't you agree it all fits together rather nicely? The man who thought the whole thing up used his own property to lure Heller and had the county clerk verify it and register the sale for a share of the profit." He studied her for several minutes while she mentally argued the flaws in his idea, and suddenly found himself enjoying the smooth line of her long, slender throat, a tiny ear and the soft blush of her cheek. He blinked and forced his attention on other things. "Well? What do you think? Am I right?" he asked, turning for the window. Twisting the lock, he raised the sash a few inches, hoping the crisp rush of night air would cool his wandering desires while he prayed Rebecca hadn't noticed his restlessness.

"I suppose," she answered slowly. "But where does that leave us? How are we ever going to figure out who he is? If he even exists," she added stubbornly.

Reaching for the chair sitting beside the writing desk, he turned it around, pulled it near the window and straddled the seat with his arms folded across the top back rail. "It may take a great deal of research, but sooner or later we'll stumble across something. I think the first thing you can do for me is go back to the courthouse in the morning and find out all you can about the county clerk who got himself

247

murdered—where he lived, if he had any heirs, and whether or not he had a questionable amount of money on the day he died. If nothing's amiss, then you'll have to ask around about him: who his friends were, business associates, someone he spent a lot of time with. If we're lucky, he might have had an open relationship with his partner."

"And if he didn't?" she posed.

Alec shrugged. "I guess we'll have to figure that out when the time comes." Glancing over her head at the clock sitting on the mantel, he added, "It's getting late. You'd better go home."

Rebecca had always enjoyed debating an issue, but she so rarely found anyone willing to oblige her that once she and Alec had begun to toss ideas back and forth at each other, she had lost track of the time. Startled by the fear that she might have missed her rendezvous at the Public Hospital, she sprang to her feet and spun around to look at the clock. "Yes," she nervously agreed. "I guess I better." Bending, she scooped up her shawl from the back of the rocker and headed for the door. "I'll find out what I can at the courthouse first thing in the morning, then meet you here at The Red Lion around noon . . . in the commons," she quickly added. "If it's too crowded, perhaps we can go for a walk . . . or something."

Standing with her hand resting on the doorknob, she cast him a sidelong glance, felt that same betraying warmth that curled her insides whenever she found herself alone with him, and quickly freed the latch. Perhaps he didn't feel anything more for her than a brief moment of pleasant distraction, and she wished she could say the same, but she couldn't. Just being in the same room with him, hearing his voice or remembering what they had shared set the tip of every one of her nerves on fire. Unbeknownst to him, he had a very real and mysterious hold on her, and Rebecca doubted she would ever be able to break it. Hurriedly pulling the door open, she made her exit without another word or even a backward glance.

*　　*　　*

The last golden rays of the sun had all but disappeared behind the horizon by the time Rebecca reached the sidewalk surrounding the Public Hospital. It had taken her close to fifteen minutes to walk all the way even at a brisk pace, and although she judged her arrival to be on schedule, she had hoped to get there first. She didn't want whoever it was she was meeting to think she wasn't coming and run off out of fear instead of waiting a few minutes. Half-running, half-walking, she cut across the yard and rounded the corner of the hospital to the back, only slightly relieved to find no one standing under the solitary tree in the otherwise empty lawn.

With all that had been going on over the past week, Rebecca hadn't been able to spare even one short afternoon to ride out to Gideon Blackstock's plantation so that she could question him about Eli's death. The constable had sent someone to inform Mr. Blackstock that one of his slaves had been found dead at the Jamestown pier, but Rebecca was sure they hadn't bothered to ask him what Eli was doing there. *Everyone* in Williamsburg guessed he was a runaway and had met up with an unfortunate fall on his way to freedom, thus leaving no reason why they should give the young black boy any further thought. Well, even if Rebecca had agreed with the entire population of Williamsburg, she still would have wanted to hear it from Blackstock's own lips. Human curiosity was *the* most important trait for a journalist to have if he or she ever hoped to succeed. But curiosity hadn't been the case for Rebecca. Intuition and the fact that Eli had fallen in love with a young girl named Cela—as well as the facts concerning how he had died—had been the catalyst for Rebecca's determination to find the truth. Even if he had wanted to run away, he wouldn't have gone without Cela. And now, it seemed, she had been right all along. Someone had either seen or heard about Eli's murder, and that someone was willing to let her in on what he knew.

Please, God, she silently prayed as she nervously studied the darkness closing in all around her, *don't let him change his mind.*

The clock inside Rebecca's head loudly ticked off the next ten minutes and cruelly reminded her that she'd have to leave for home very soon. Miss Abigail waited for no one, and even though Rebecca had wisely given herself another alternative for getting into the house after ten, Miss Abigail had seen her leave. And since Miss Abigail loved to snoop, she would more than likely sit beside the parlor doorway specifically waiting for the return of her only female boarder. When Rebecca didn't come in through the front door but appeared at the breakfast table the next morning, Miss Abigail would assume in that very instant that either some-one else in the house—probably Jon-Gregory—had let her in through a downstairs window or that Rebecca had somehow gotten a duplicate key. Either way, Rebecca would be looking for a new place to stay.

"It doesn't matter," she muttered defiantly as she scanned the black shadows near the side of the brick building and those encasing the stand of trees on the other side of the road. "This is too important. Maybe no one else cares about what happened to Eli, but I do. And I'll wait here all night if I have to."

But the chilling wail of one of the residents in the hospital cut through the still night air and boldly challenged her commitment, spinning her around and sending a cold shiver up her spine. She had heard about Lieutenant Governor Francis Fauquier's desire to see that a hospital be erected for the care of those—as he called them—"miserable objects" who could not help themselves, but Rebecca had never had the courage to pay the establishment a visit in all the time she had lived in Williamsburg. The idea of mentally ill patients scared her, though Jon-Gregory had told her repeatedly that most of them were harmless. Yet here she was standing not twenty feet away from where they lived, in the dark, alone, and vowing to spend the night camped on their doorstep.

"*You're* the one who's crazy," she whispered, her round, blue eyes affixed to the only lighted window in the place as if she half-expected to see some distorted-looking creature poke his head out through the bars at her. "What woman in her right mind would do the things you do?" She stubbornly shook her head and inched farther away from the brick structure to hide herself beneath the spreading arms of the oak tree.

High above her an owl hooted. The eerie moan of a half-crazed woman pierced the quiet. A rustling from somewhere deep in the woods then silence echoed all around her, and with each new sound, Rebecca jumped, her iron will melting beneath the heat of an unfamiliar fear.

Dammit, where are you, she wanted to scream aloud at the one who had directed her here. *Is this some kind of game? A trick? Do you take joy in frightening women? Or just me? Do you know me so well that you thought you'd have a little fun with me? Send her a note, tell her you know the truth about her friend's death and watch her run blindly into your ruse. Well, I'm not going to play anymore. I've waited long enough. I'm going home.*

Grabbing both hands full of her skirts, she spun around and dashed off toward the center of town.

"Aren't you gonna stop her?" the shorter of the two men asked as the pair stood hiding behind a huge tree a safe distance away.

"Of course not, you imbecile," his partner barked. "That wasn't the idea. All I wanted out of that note was to have her away from Miss Beecher's at ten o'clock."

"Why? What good will that do."

The first heaved an irritable sigh. "Must I explain everything to you? There's only two reasons she's staying in Williamsburg; her job and because she has a place to live. Fortunately for us, Mrs. Rind took care of the first one. Her landlady will take care of the second . . . with my help."

"Oh," his companion sang knowingly. "Miss Beecher's rules." His cohort's brilliant plan made him smile until he discovered a problem. "But she could always find another room to rent."

"And who would be that stupid . . . besides you? If she doesn't have a job, she can't pay. If she doesn't have a room or a job, she'll be forced to go home."

The other thought about it for a while as they stood watching the young woman quickly head back for the boardinghouse. "I hope you're right," he murmured. "I really hope you're right."

Hidden within the shadows of the tall lilac bushes lining the east edge of Miss Abigail's property, Rebecca didn't have to be told the time to know it was well past ten. The entire first floor was dark, including Miss Abigail's bedroom, which meant everyone else in the house had gone to bed and that the old woman knew her youngest boarder had broken a rule. As she stood there staring at the two-story, wood-frame structure, Rebecca imagined the scene at the breakfast table. Miss Abigail would be all huffy and indignant and probably bar Rebecca's entrance into the dining room with her short, pudgy body, a scowl on her wrinkled face and her fists knotted on her hips.

"You can't come in, Rebecca Wilde," she'd announce. "You're not one of my boarders anymore. Now get your things and get out."

"But, Miss Abigail," Rebecca would argue, "whatever do you mean? My rent's paid until the end of the week."

"Maybe so, but you broke a rule. And you know the penalty for breaking a rule."

"Which one, Miss Abigail?" Rebecca would ask. "I don't know what you mean."

They would banter back and forth until Rebecca had her so confused that Miss Abigail would think Rebecca had actually walked in through the front door, bid the woman good-night and boldly climbed the stairs to her room. Miss Abigail would shake her head, mutter something about her needing more sleep and let the incident pass. At least that was what Rebecca hoped would happen as she darted across the open yard to the rose trellis. If it didn't, Rebecca would have a new problem to solve.

Inch by inch, rung by rung, she carefully ascended the whitewashed latticework covered with thick green vines, leaves and fragrant flowers, while trying to avoid the sharp edged thorns which threatened to prick her fingers and snag her skirts. At the top she gingerly pressed her hand against

252

the cool glass of the window and pushed upward until she had enough room to stick her fingers under the sash and lift. A moment later she was awkwardly swinging herself over the sill as noiselessly as possible, but the instant her feet touched the floor, she sensed her effort had all been for nothing when she saw that the door to her room stood open. She hadn't left it that way after she came for her shawl. In fact, she had locked it behind her which could only mean one thing; Miss Abigail had used her spare key. Squinting in the darkness that enshrouded her, Rebecca worriedly scanned the interior of the room for the dark shape of something that didn't belong.

Chapter Eleven

Startled out of a sound sleep by the insistent pounding on his door, Alec bolted out of bed and hurried toward the armoire where he kept his pistol. But long before he reached it, Penny's voice called out to him, and he changed directions. The urgency behind the summons and in the tone of her voice hastened him to hurry, and once he had slid into his breeches, he went to the door and opened it.

"We need your help," she said, shoving past him and pulling Jon-Gregory with her. "You two know each other, don't you?"

Alec's gaze fell briefly on the young man at her side before he gave the door a nudge and turned for the nightstand where he lit a candle. "Not formally. We've never been introduced, but I know who he is. He works for Greenhow, and he's a friend of Reb's. I assume one of those two qualities concerns me." He motioned for Penny to sit in the rocker, but she declined.

"There isn't time for niceties," she informed him. "We've got to find Rebecca."

Alec's gaze shifted to the mantel clock, surprised to learn it was four o'clock in the morning. He frowned back at his guests. "What do you mean 'find her'?" For a second he wondered how he had slept at all. Reb was obviously in trouble again, and he thought he had grown to sense it before it actually happened.

"I guess I better explain," Jon-Gregory offered.

Alec cocked a brow. "Please do."

Penny's suggestion that they seek this man's assistance had puzzled Jon-Gregory, since he figured Rebecca's erroneous newspaper article about him wouldn't win his lasting friendship. He still wasn't sure the man would want to help once he told him why they had come, but at least he hadn't thrown them out into the hall once Rebecca's name was mentioned. Glancing dubiously at Penny, Jon-Gregory took a short breath and began. "She was acting strangely at the dinner table, and when I asked her about it, she admitted she had to meet someone. When I asked her who that someone was, she told me to mind my own business."

Years of practice enabled Alec not to show any reaction to what the young man had said until Jon-Gregory dropped his gaze away from Alec to sigh and run his fingers through his hair. Alec had to know first if Penny or possibly Rebecca had told Jon-Gregory anything about him before Alec could admit that he was the one Rebecca had planned to meet. As he frowned questioningly at the pretty redhead, Penny shook her head, silently indicating that his secret was safe. But that bit of knowledge confused him even more. How was he to help if he was bound to silence?

"Tell him the rest, Jon-Gregory," Penny urged, her gaze still resting on Alec.

Brought out of his worried thoughts by the request, Jon-Gregory straightened and shifted his attention from Penny to the man who stood waiting to hear his reply. "Penny told me that Rebecca had come here to The Red Lion, that she was the someone Rebecca had to meet. But I don't think Penny was who Rebecca meant."

Alec's face remained expressionless. "And why is that?"

"As soon as dinner was finished and everyone was excused from the table, Rebecca ran to her room, got a shawl and high-tailed it for town. I know because I stood at the bottom of the stairs and watched her. I've never liked the kind of work Rebecca has chosen for herself. It's too risky, and she's too careless, which in my opinion is a disastrous combination. Well, apparently Miss Abigail noticed my concern because she asked me what was wrong. I usually don't tell the old woman anything since she has the tendency to repeat everything she hears, but for some reason I told her that I was worried about Rebecca. That's when I learned about the note."

Alec's brow crimped. "Note? What note?"

"Someone left a message for Rebecca at the boarding-house," Jon-Gregory revealed. "I'm surprised Miss Abigail didn't read it before she gave it to Rebecca, but she didn't. Consequently, neither of us knows what was in it or who sent it. But I can tell you this much," he added, an intense look on his young face, "meeting with Penny here at The Red Lion wouldn't have upset Rebecca. So something else did, and it's my guess it had to do with that note."

Alec was thoughtfully quiet for a moment, wondering if the message might have concerned him. But if it had, why hadn't she mentioned it during their visit? Suddenly realizing why Rebecca's two best friends had deliberately awakened him in the middle of the night, he glanced at the clock and then at Jon-Gregory, a cold, hard knot forming in his belly. "Are you trying to tell me that she hasn't been home since you talked with her at dinner?"

"Yes, sir." Jon-Gregory nodded. "I'm afraid I am."

Alec hurriedly turned for the armoire as he asked, "And would you care to tell me why you waited so long to tell someone about it?"

"I'll tell you, but I'm not proud of it," he sheepishly admitted while he watched Alec don a shirt, then grab his stockings and shoes and sit down on the edge of the bed to put them on. "I'd done a lot of heavy work for Mr. Greenhow today, and I was tired. I fell asleep waiting for Rebecca to come home and didn't wake up until a short time ago. That's when I checked her room and found it empty. I was praying she had come in while I was asleep." He shook his head and muttered, "I really hope she just decided to spend the night somewhere instead of trying to sneak back into the house."

Rising, Alec buttoned his shirt and stuffed the tails into his waistband. "Why would she have to sneak?"

"Because Miss Abigail locks the door. No one is allowed in or out of the house past ten o'clock at night or before six in the morning. If she's caught, she'll be asked to leave." He smiled halfheartedly. "Of course that never stopped Rebecca. I've seen her climb the rose trellis a number of times."

Alec felt a strange warmth touch his face as he wondered if Jon-Gregory had seen her climb the trellis the night she and Alec met. He brushed aside the thought and reached for his jacket.

"Do you have any idea where she might be, Alec?" Penny questioned. "Can we help? Tell us what to do."

Slipping on the jacket, Alec reached for his cane. "I think you should go back home," he instructed, his gaze falling on Jon-Gregory, "for two reasons. If she's spending the night somewhere with the intention of walking through the front door at breakfast time as though nothing out of the ordinary had happened *and* gets away with it, there's no sense in having Miss Abigail angry with you when she learns you sneaked out of the house. If she isn't, then someone should be there waiting to wring her neck."

"I was hoping you'd say something like that," Jon-Gregory declared. "It will be my pleasure to beat some sense into her thick head."

"As for you, Penny," Alec went on. "I think it's best you wait in your room . . . just in case she shows up here for some reason."

"What are you going to do?" Penny asked, moving toward the door when Jon-Gregory took her arm.

Following the couple into the hall, Alec pulled the door shut and locked it, then said, "I'm going to try and imagine what a scatterbrained, slip of a girl would do at four o'clock in the morning. If I'm lucky, I just might figure out where she is." Nodding his farewell, he turned and headed down the back stairs.

Alec viewed the deserted street in front of The Red Lion as well as the one that intersected with it with little more than mild satisfaction. It meant that should Rebecca be out there somewhere wandering the dark avenues alone, no harm would come to her . . . at least not until he caught up to her. But it also offered no help in locating her, since it appeared there had been no witnesses to the direction she had taken or any who might have seen her talking with someone. Although he hoped Jon-Gregory had been correct in his suggestion that Rebecca was simply spending the night somewhere, he rather doubted it. She obviously hadn't asked Penny for shelter, and since she had no money to pay for a room, he guessed that her reason for not coming home was simply because she couldn't. That conclusion slanted his tawny brows downward in a fierce frown. If something had happened to her because of him, he'd see to it that whoever was responsible would pay very dearly for their stupidity. Stepping off the curb, he headed toward the courthouse.

Rebecca had proven to him several times that she was no ordinary woman, and because of that fact and simply because he couldn't think of a better place to start, Alec wondered if she might have returned to the courthouse after their meeting earlier to reexamine the ledgers. The office would have closed long before she would have gotten there, but that wouldn't have stopped her if she had truly wanted to get inside. Glancing over his shoulder and up and down the street to make sure he was still alone, he decided that even if Rebecca hadn't gone to the courthouse, he'd let himself in and have a look at the records for himself. Rebecca had a keen eye for detail, but that didn't mean she couldn't have overlooked an important bit of information. With any kind of luck, he'd see something she hadn't, a tiny clue that would send him in the right direction.

Cutting through the side yard, Alec approached the building from the rear where it would be less likely he'd be seen should anyone happen along while he was breaking into the place. Pausing near one of the windows, he carefully scrutinized the shadows lining the perimeter of the property, then turned his attention on finding a quiet method for entering the building. A moment later he stood shaking his head when he found that all the windows were locked and that he'd have to break the glass if he wanted inside. Suddenly the image of a long-haired, feisty young woman came to mind, and he was wishing he could have been somewhere close by to watch while Rebecca climbed the trellis and let herself in to her room. It couldn't be an easy feat for her to accomplish considering her skirts probably got in her way. And just as he must do here, she would have to be very quiet lest she awaken Miss Abigail. The smile that had curled his mouth while he imagined the sight slowly disappeared when a new thought came to mind, and he moved into the shadow of the courthouse to give it some consideration. Only a few seconds later, he was whispering his thanks to Jon-Gregory and racing off across the yard.

Shivering, Rebecca huddled deeper into the mound of hay and pulled her cloak up under her chin. It would have made more sense for her to sleep in the cabin where she could start a fire in the hearth and be comfortable, but the place had been such a mess that it would have taken her until dawn before it was clean enough to suit her. Thus she had chosen to make her bed out of the pile of hay in the shed, get a few hours of rest, then attack the job in the morning. But sleep hadn't come easily for Rebecca. She had spent most of the night tossing and turning and thinking of Alec.

After Miss Abigail had confronted her there on the windowsill where Rebecca had no hope of convincing the woman that she hadn't broken a rule, Rebecca had reluctantly packed up her things and left the house under Miss Abigail's insistence. Rebecca had tried to play on the woman's sympathy, that a young girl shouldn't be thrown out into the streets after dark and that it would never happen again, but Miss Abigail would have none of it. If she let one boarder do as he pleased, then she'd have no control over any of them, and that simply wouldn't do. Rebecca's behavior was unacceptable, and the old woman didn't want someone of that sort living under her roof. As for the matter of turning her out into the streets, Miss Abigail firmly informed her that since it hadn't seemed to worry Rebecca enough to be in the house on time, it certainly wouldn't concern her now nor would it bother Miss Abigail. The loud slamming of the door behind her as Rebecca stepped out onto the porch confirmed the woman's callous declaration. The key turning in the lock marked the beginning of a new adventure, one Rebecca truly wasn't in favor of exploring.

Her first instinct was to go to The Red Lion and ask Penny to let her stay with her until Rebecca could find someplace else to live. But the closer she got to the inn, the more she realized what an imposition that would be, and she slowed her step. She had no money, so renting a room for the night at one of the other inns was out of the question. She needed a place to sleep that wouldn't cost her anything. That was when she had thought of the cabin Alec owned . . . an empty cabin with just enough furnishings to accommodate her needs. He certainly wouldn't object. After all, part of her predicament was his fault anyway. And if he said anything negative, she'd remind him of it.

The light of early morning was beginning to peek through the cracks around the door of the shed, and although she hadn't gotten much sleep, laying on the mound of hay had lost its appeal. Coming to her feet, she stretched the kinks out of her back and rubbed the tired muscles in her neck, thinking that since it would be light soon and she had nothing better to do, she'd start cleaning out the cabin. She could always take a nap later.

Her first task was ridding the fireplace of its ashes and cobwebs and sweeping the debris off the stone slab. Next she stacked fresh logs in a neat pile and set the kindling on fire. Within minutes the pleasant smell of burning wood filled the room and chased away the damp, dusty odor that had attacked her senses the second she had stepped into the cabin. The kettle she had found hanging there on a hook was filled with water and left there to simmer and hopefully loosen the encrusted remains of the last meal cooked in it. Gathering up the dishes from floor and cupboard, she placed them with those already sitting on the table. Once she had cleared off a place to work, she'd heat up another kettle of water with which to wash them.

A cloud of dust soon filled the air when Rebecca began sweeping the floor, and she paused in her labor to open the window and front door, hoping the soft, morning breeze would drift through the cabin and carry the gray fog with it. By now the water in the kettle was boiling, and she stopped her work long enough to carry the pot outside and dump it. Her logic had proven correct, for the huge iron bucket rinsed clean, and after refilling it with fresh water from the well, she returned it to the hook over the fire. The dishes would be the next on her agenda once the water was steaming.

Staring down at the narrow cot with her hands on her hips, Rebecca shook her head disgustedly. The dingy mattress would have to be restuffed with new straw and the ticking laundered if she hoped to ever sleep comfortably on it. Deciding to leave that until last, she picked up her broom and finished sweeping out the place.

By the time she had wiped out the cupboard, washed the dishes, stacked and put them away, stripped the walls of musty rabbit pelts, wiped down the furniture with a wet cloth and cleaned every corner of the room of cobwebs, dust and litter, the tiny cabin took on a healthy, fresh, livable atmosphere which brought a pleased smile to Rebecca's face as she collapsed into one of the chairs sitting around the table. Domestic chores had never been something she enjoyed and often times avoided doing, but she took special pride in what she had done here. First glance had conjured up little hope that the cabin would ever appear to be anything more than a rundown shack, but now . . . now it was worthy of being called home. Then her gaze drifted to the cot on the other side of the room, and her upper lip curled disapprovingly. She was ready for her nap, but it would have to wait until she had a bed to sleep in. Rising, she crossed to the cot, rolled the thin mattress into a ball and headed outside with it.

Morning had dawned with a flood of cheery sunshine and a cloudless blue sky. Songbirds filled the air with their melodious tunes, and the gentle breeze stirred up the sweet smell of wild flowers and the scent of pine. Dropping the mattress on a bed of green grass, Rebecca closed her eyes, tilted her head back and sucked in a deep breath, reveling in the serenity of the moment. Although her life seemed to be in chaos of late, it was moments like these that offered hope and encouragement. It gave her time to think and collect her wits, to reevaluate her goals and decide which path she should take to reach them. The events of last night had happened so quickly that she hadn't had much time to consider each one individually. Nor had she realized the state she was in until now. Turning slightly, she glanced back at the cabin. Oh, she had a place to stay; but she didn't have any money to buy food, and she certainly couldn't go out in the woods and hunt game. She had no idea how to fire a gun, and even if she did, she wasn't sure she could pull the trigger. Turning back, she glanced down at her next project, quietly admitting to herself that she would have to find work and soon . . . whether it was at the *Gazette* or taking in someone's laundry.

Lowering herself down on her knees, Rebecca reached out for the mattress and the seam at one end which she intended on pulling apart, when she suddenly noticed that the woods around her had grown ominously quiet. Perhaps it was just her nerves and the fact that she was overly tired that made her think the silence was a forewarning of trouble, but with all that had happened to her lately, she refused to ignore her instincts. Whoever had sent her the note that had resulted in her losing her room at Miss Abigail's must have had a good reason for doing it. At the time she had wanted to believe it had been a trick, that someone took delight in watching her chase after shadows. Right now she wasn't so sure. Maybe it hadn't been a ploy, and whoever sent it had meant to meet with her and couldn't for some reason. Eyes and ears alert, Rebecca slowly came to her feet. Had she run off too early last night? Had the person arrived in time to see her dashing off down the street? Had he spied on her? Had he been aware that Miss Abigail had asked her to leave the boardinghouse? Had he followed her here? Nerves atingle, she fearfully scanned the trees and scrubs surrounding her, wondering if he was out there right now watching her.

Suddenly, the sharp explosion of gunfire rent the air, and Rebecca dove to the ground with her arms covering her head, certain that at any second excruciating pain would rack her body. She had to have been hit since the gun blast was just as loud as it was frightening. Yet as the seconds ticked away and the only thing she felt was the thunderous pounding of her heart, she quickly realized that *this* time she had been spared. Cautiously lifting her head, she studied the underbrush for any sign of movement or a clue to the gunman's whereabouts. In the distance and toward the road that intersected with the lane leading to the farmhouse, she heard a horse whinny as if the animal was as equally frightened as she was, and Rebecca soon concluded that *she* had not been the man's target. Had she given it any thought at all, she should have considered herself very lucky and raced for the protection of the cabin, but as always, Rebecca's fears were pushed aside when her curiosity urged her to investigate. Slowly coming to her feet, she guardedly started down the dirt path.

When Rebecca was to think about it later, she would realize that nothing could have prepared her for what she was about to see. She would have been just as shocked, just as sickened and equally terrorized by the sight of a man bending over Alec with a pistol held in his hand while Alec lay bleeding and unconscious on the ground if she had been told ahead of time. Too numb to react, she just stood there watching while the stranger searched Alec's clothes until he had apparently found whatever it was he wanted to steal. Tucking the object in his pocket, he quickly turned, mounted his horse and rode off back toward town.

The sound of racing hoofbeats and the movement of a second steed, when the animal pranced and pawed the ground near Alec's feet, brought Rebecca out of her trance. She blinked, forced herself to breathe and stumbled forward. She had realized some time back that Alec Stone meant something special to her, but she had never imagined that she cared what happened to him. Caring meant that he had won a place in her heart, and she had always thought that she was too clever to ever let someone get that close to her. Trevor Wilde had been the only man she had ever loved, and although the love of a daughter for her father was different from the lasting kind shared between husband and wife, Rebecca had decided she would never allow herself to experience such an emotion again. The death of her father had been painful for her, and because of some twisted reasoning, she had blamed herself for his passing; because she had loved him so much she had brought about his death. Tears filled her eyes as she staggered to a stop and dropped to her knees beside Alec. If she let herself fall in love with this man, wouldn't it mean he'd have to die as well? Her chin trembling, she clamped her teeth together, closed her eyes and raised her face heavenward.

"Then I shall not love him," she declared in a whisper. "He shall not die because of me."

Having found the courage to ignore the weakness she had for him, Rebecca swallowed her tears and concentrated on what had to be done. A quick examination revealed that his attacker had been the cowardly sort and had shot Alec in the back. The lead ball had passed cleanly through his shoulder, and the fall from his horse had rendered him unconscious when his head struck a rock, for there was a large gash across his right temple. He was bleeding terribly, and Rebecca knew that she would have to get him back to the cabin in order to tend his wounds properly. That, however, would be the difficult part as she hadn't the strength to lift him, and while she fought for an idea on how to accomplish it, Alec stirred, moaned and opened his eyes for a brief second.

"Alec," she called to him as she cupped his handsome face in her hands. "Alec, please try and stay awake. You've got to help me get you on the horse. Alec, do you hear me?"

Pain darkened the eyes that slowly lifted to look up at her, and even though he didn't answer, she knew he understood.

"Don't move," she instructed, one hand held out in front of her as she scrambled to her feet. "Just lie there a minute and stay awake. All right?" She didn't expect him to say anything, nor did she really want him to waste the energy trying. But if she could get him to concentrate on her words, he might not slip back into unconsciousness until after she had him in the cabin. Gathering up the horse's reins, she guided the mare closer to him, then knelt and took his arm. "Hold on to me," she told him. "I'll help you up. Do you think you can stand?" Draping his arm around her neck, she gently but firmly pulled him up.

Rebecca hadn't realized that her tears had started anew until Alec was on his feet and leaning heavily against her. A weak smile had parted his lips as he looked over at her, and before she could get him to grab hold of the saddle, he raised a hand and softly brushed at the moisture on her cheek.

"Don't flatter yourself," she barked angrily at him. "I'm not crying because you're hurt. I'm crying because this means I have to take care of you. I was rather looking forward to a few days on my own where I wouldn't have to listen to you lecture. Now get on the damn horse," she sharply added, untwining his arm and looping it over the animal's back. Guiding his foot to the stirrup, she waited for him to balance himself and then pushed with every ounce of strength she had. Blood was streaming down the side of his face, and Rebecca knew he was close to passing out again; but somehow he managed to swing himself up onto the saddle and hang on.

What seemed like a lifetime passed before Rebecca had led horse and rider to the front door of the cabin, and while Alec leaned forward against the animal's neck, she hurriedly dragged the dingy mattress back inside and tossed it on the cot. A few minutes later, she had him lying on the bed, stripped of his jacket and shirt, and a fresh kettle of water was heating up over the fire. She knelt beside him and examined the extent of his injuries. The moment his head had fallen against the pillow, he had lost consciousness again, and Rebecca was actually rather glad he had. It would be less painful for him while she cleaned and dressed the wounds.

While she waited for the water to come to a boil, Rebecca shed her petticoats and tore the fabric into several long, narrow strips to use as bandages. The gaping hole in his shoulder bled profusely, which meant it had to be cauterized if she didn't want him to bleed to death. The idea made her stomach churn; for although she had seen the procedure done before, she had never taken part in the actual execution of such a ritual, and she wasn't positive she could go through with it.

"Yes, you can," she firmly told herself as she walked to the cupboard and selected a wide-bladed knife to use. "His life depends on you right now, and you're not going to let him die because you're squeamish." Crossing to the hearth, she knelt and stuck the instrument into the fire, tears streaming down her face. She angrily brushed them away and stood.

Dragging the table over to the bed, she carefully laid out the stack of neatly folded pieces of cloth, a bowl and the tiny piece of lye soap she had miraculously managed to find while cleaning up the cabin earlier. Returning to the fireplace, she used the hem of her dress to protect her hands as she lifted the kettle from its hook and carried it to the table where she filled the bowl with hot water. Once she had hung the pot back over the fire, she came back to the table, dipped one of the rags into the bowl, lathered it up and sat in the chair beside Alec to tenderly wash the blood from around the gunshot wound. It continued to bleed rather steadily, and Rebecca hurried her movements. Awkwardly rolling him onto his side, she rinsed out the rag, rubbed it against the bar of soap and quickly washed the area where the bullet had entered. Praying for the strength it would take to finish her task as rapidly as possible, she went to the hearth and retrieved the knife, its blade glowing a bright orange. It took her a moment to steel the queasiness she felt at the thought of what had to be done, but once she reminded herself that there was no one else to do it, she courageously returned to her place in the chair.

Alec's eyes were still closed, which Rebecca hoped meant that he hadn't regained consciousness and wasn't just sleeping. It was going to be difficult enough for her to find the strength to merely draw the blade across the wound without his lashing out at her. She wouldn't be able to hold him down *and* do the job if he fought her. Whispering a prayer that it would all be over quicky, she gritted her teeth, leaned forward and touched the glowing knife to the wound. The smell of burning flesh filled her nostrils and stung her eyes. Alec's body had stiffened, and he groaned. The knot in Rebecca's stomach slipped to her throat, but she gulped it back down. While she still had the courage to see this through, she rolled him onto his back and repeated the process. This time, however, Alec responded quite violently. His arm came up, hit hers and knocked the knife from her hand. It flew across the room and landed near the fireplace with a thud. Rebecca watched its flight for only a second before she realized she had quite a struggle on her hands. Alec wanted up, and even in his weakened condition, he had more strength than Rebecca could handle.

"Alec!" she shouted at him, throwing herself against him when he tried to sit up. "Lie still, Alec. You're hurt. You mustn't move around. Please, Alec. You're safe now. It's me, Reb. I'll take care of you, and I won't let anyone hurt you again. Do you hear me?"

Although he never opened his eyes or showed any sign of understanding a word she had said, he slowly relaxed back down on the cot and seemed to drift off peacefully again. Her face the picture of torment, Rebecca watched him for several moments. When it appeared that she'd have no further trouble with him for a while, she hurriedly set about bandaging his shoulder, then washing the dried blood from his face and over his temple. The gash to his head had been deep, but as long as she could get him to lie still, it wouldn't require stitches. She was truly thankful of that since she doubted she'd be able to calmly sit there and sew his flesh back together as if it were nothing more than a piece of cloth. She also doubted she'd find a needle and thread anywhere in the cabin.

Rebecca's next concern came after Alec was sleeping comfortably and she had covered him with a blanket she had found. She had witnessed a man attempt to kill another for whatever his victim had in his pocket. It hadn't been Alec's money that the man was after since she had found Alec's purse in his jacket. Yet, she had seen the man take something before he rode off. The question that haunted her was whether or not that tiny object was all the brute wanted from Alec. There was a chance Alec had recognized his assailant, and once that man learned Alec wasn't dead, he just might come looking for him. That was a strong possibility, one which made Rebecca quite nervous, since she had no way of defending the two of them. The only gun she had found in the cabin had been an old, rusty musket with a cracked barrel, and even then she didn't know how to load the stupid thing . . . with or without a cracked barrel.

Remembering that she had left the mare outside by the front door, she quickly came to her feet and dashed across the room. She'd hide the animal for now, just in case the stranger came back before she had made any plans. Tonight, once it was dark she'd ride into town and talk to Penny. *She* knew how to load a pistol, and it surely wouldn't take her that long to teach Rebecca. And while she was there, she'd use Alec's money to buy supplies. They'd be needing quite a bit if they intended to stay here in the cabin until he was well again.

All the while she was gone, Rebecca worried about Alec, even though she really knew she shouldn't. He hadn't stirred or opened his eyes the remainder of the day despite the cool, wet cloths she regularly dabbed across his fevered brown and cheeks. In all likelihood he'd sleep through tomorrow and possibly the next day or at least until he showed signs of healing. And if he had woken up while she was away, he wouldn't have had the strength to get off the cot. No, what really made her nervous was that she had left him alone and unprotected. Until they had the chance to talk about the man who had shot him, Alec wasn't safe.

The fire had nearly died out by the time she returned to their small hideaway. After checking on Alec to make sure he was still asleep and hadn't moved, she stoked up the fire, set about putting away the things she had purchased in town and then made herself a bed on the floor next to his cot. But rather than falling off to sleep right away, she lay thinking about the young redhead she called her best friend.

Rebecca had never liked working in the kitchen, and because Twin Oaks had a full staff of servants to see to those jobs all the while she was growing up, she hadn't learned to do much more than scramble eggs or stir cake batter.

Apparently Penny had already known about her friend's lack of experience, for it had been her suggestion that she ride out to the cabin every night with a basket full of food to last her until Penny's next visit. At first Rebecca had been reluctant, stating that she feared whoever had attacked Alec might figure out what Penny was up to and follow her. Rebecca didn't want to put her friend in any danger, nor did she want to make it easy for the stranger to find where she was hiding Alec. Penny had assured her that she'd be careful not to let anyone know where she was going or why, and that even if Rebecca didn't approve, she would come to the cabin anyway. After all, Alec was *her* friend, too, and she wasn't about to turn her back on either of them just to save her own skin. The conversation had ended there, but more was said in those few moments they stood silently staring at each other than in all the time they'd spent arguing. After a tearful embrace, Rebecca had gathered up her packages and left for the cabin under the protective blanket of darkness.

Just as her friend had promised, Penny visited Rebecca and the still-unconscious Alec the very next night after business had slowed at the inn and she could get away for an hour or so. Rebecca had been glad to see her, although she tried very hard not to show it. Her concern for Alec was weighing on her nerves, and she had needed the minor distraction to take her mind off how seriously injured he was no matter how brief the interruption. She had also longed to hear someone else tell her that it wasn't uncommon for a man in Alec's condition to sleep for such a long time without so much as muttering a sound or moving a muscle.

Besides the warm meal she brought to Rebecca, Penny also had some news to give her . . . such as it was. After their meeting the night before and learning what had happened to Alec, Penny had deliberately listened in on every conversation spoken at the inn to see if his disappearance had been noticed or if the fact that his body hadn't been found made anyone particularly nervous. Nothing out of the ordinary had been discussed, nor had Penny seen any strangers hanging around The Red Lion as if waiting for something to explode. In Penny's opinion, the man who had attacked Alec

269

didn't care whether or not he had killed him, and he had probably left town. That bit of information made Rebecca feel a little better, but she still didn't intend to let down her guard . . . not until Alec could tell her what this was all about.

The only distressing part of Penny's report was when she told Rebecca that Jon-Gregory had been pressuring her to tell him where Rebecca was and that he was worried about Alec. Penny went on to explain how she and Jon-Gregory had gone to Alec for help when Rebecca hadn't come home that night. It was Penny's guess that Alec may have figured out where Rebecca had gone and had followed her, unaware that he himself was being trailed until it was too late. When Rebecca asked her what she planned to do about Jon-Gregory, Penny had reluctantly confessed that she had already told him the whole story, but that Rebecca shouldn't be too upset. Jon-Gregory cared a great deal about her and would never say or do anything that might cause her harm. In fact, Jon-Gregory had vowed to learn as much as he could about Alec's situation in much the same method as Penny's. With the two of them working on it, one or the other of them was bound to stumble across a clue.

In Rebecca's mind, she felt the clue was whatever the man had stolen from Alec, and when she voiced that observation, Penny's face had gone horribly white. Until that moment Penny had forgotten that Alec's room had been broken into and the place turned upside down, and it was her guess that the one responsible for it was probably the same man who shot Alec. At the time, Alec didn't seem to know what it was the man was after since Alec carried his money on him and nothing else appeared to be missing, but he had shown concern over a jeweled stickpin he had hidden in the lining of his satchel. Penny remembered seeing Alec put the the pin in his jacket pocket, and when Rebecca showed her the coat Alec had been wearing at the time of the attack, Penny's eyes widened. It was the same jacket, and after a hurried search through all of Alec's things, only to come up empty-handed, the girls concluded that the thief must have been after the

270

piece of jewelry. But why? What was the importance behind it? Penny admitted the pin had several jewels in it, but its value hardly justified all the trouble the man had gone through to have it. And once Alec was back to feeling good again, the price of ownership would rise severely.

As Penny bid Rebecca farewell that night, she told her friend that maybe it would be a good idea for her to visit the jeweler's in town first thing in the morning. Although she truly doubted it, the man who had stolen the pin might have tried to sell it. Rebecca agreed that it was a slim possibility at best—if he was really after money, he would have emptied Alec's purse—but since they had no other avenues to explore at the moment, Penny might as well make the effort.

The next day repeated itself in much the same manner as the one before it. Alec still slept, although he moved around periodically as if he might be in pain or suffering from an unpleasant dream. Rebecca spent very nearly every waking hour sitting by his side and sponging his face and neck with a cool cloth to ease the fever that raged through his body and darkened his cheeks. That evening Penny came with her basket of food.

"Is he any better?" she asked once Rebecca had let her in.

"No," Rebecca answered quietly as she took the wicker basket to the cupboard and emptied it out. "He moves around now and then and moans occasionally, but he hasn't opened his eyes."

"Well, it's too soon to worry," Penny assured her, sitting down in the chair beside him and touching her fingertips to his brow. "I stopped at McKenzie's Apothecary and bought some laudanum. It's in the blue bottle. I thought you might get him to take some when he wakes up." She frowned as she examined the bandages on his shoulder. "He must be in a lot of pain."

"Yes, I imagine he is," Rebecca agreed as she set the tiny bottle on the top shelf where she could easily reach it once Alec regained consciousness long enough to take some. "But I'm more concerned about his fever. Don't you think it should have broken by now?"

Penny shrugged one shoulder. "Hard to say. He's been hurt pretty badly." Her gaze admiringly traveled the full length of his hardened physique. "But since he isn't exactly an old man, and he's obviously taken good care of himself up until now, I think he'll pull through this." She turned a smile on her friend. "Besides, he has you to look after him. Can't beat that."

Rebecca could feel a warm blush rise in her cheeks, and she deliberately turned her back on Penny to go to the hearth for the pot hanging over the fire. "Did you find out anything at the jeweler's?" she asked, pouring the hot water into two cups sprinkled with tea leaves.

"Just what we expected to turn up. Nothing." She smiled her thanks to Rebecca for the cup of tea she was given and took a sip before adding, "But Jon-Gregory found out a bit of interesting news."

Frowning, Rebecca pulled out a chair at the table and sat down. "And what was that?"

"Well, we decided that there must be a connection between the attack on Alec and his dead agent." Penny quickly raised her hand to silence her friend when Rebecca started to object. "Hear me out before you say anything." She raised her eyebrows at Rebecca as if asking her permission, and once Rebecca nodded, she continued. "Actually it was Jon-Gregory's idea once I told him why Alec was really here in Williamsburg. He thought that maybe Alec was getting too close to the truth, and that somehow that stickpin is the key to this mess. What other reason would someone have for wanting Alec dead: And why only the pin?"

A faint smile had curled Rebecca's mouth as she sat listening to Penny's idea, and rather than allow Penny to think she was laughing at her, Rebecca averted her eyes and took a drink of her tea. "It's a good idea, Penny, but not very likely. You're forgetting that Alec never told anyone his real name . . . except you and me. So who was to know he wasn't telling the truth? No one in Williamsburg has ever met Alec

Diamond or Alec Stone until a few days ago."

"Except Daniel Heller," Penny stubbornly objected.

"Penny," Rebecca criticized, "he's been dead for close to a year."

The young redhead's brow wrinkled. "Oh . . . yeah . . . I forgot."

"And even then, Alec and Daniel Heller never met face to face. Alec hired him through Heller's brother." She shook her head and stared down at her teacup. "It doesn't matter now anyway. He's dead and buried, and whether Alec could have recognized him or not wouldn't have done any good." Both girls were quiet for a moment until Rebecca remembered that Penny had said Jon-Gregory had uncovered something interesting. "So what did Jon-Gregory learn?"

Penny's enthusiasm returned two-fold. "Well, even if we were wrong about the stickpin and all, we're positive that *no one* in town ever heard of Daniel Heller or even remembered *seeing* a man of his description. Rather peculiar, wouldn't you say, since he supposedly stayed in Williamsburg for several months. He had to have eaten somewhere, and you'd surely think he'd have taken a room instead of sleeping in the alley or something."

Rebecca thought about it for a while. "Yes. That is strange. I wonder what it means."

"I guess we won't know that until we find his killer." Penny took another sip of tea. "And I don't care if you agree with Jon-Gregory and me or not. I still think that stickpin has something to do with Heller."

Rebecca started to shake her head, but Penny cut her off.

"Well, think about it. Whether Alec told anyone his real name or not, *someone* knew he had that stickpin. And it wasn't as if they saw Alec wearing it. I told you he had it hidden in the lining of his satchel . . . *hidden* in his satchel. He didn't want anyone to know he had it; yet someone did, and they very nearly killed him for it."

"All right, so that part of it is a little mysterious," Rebecca yielded. "But it still doesn't mean it's tied in with Heller's death. How could it?"

"I don't know exactly. Only Alec does, and he can't tell us right now. But it makes me think that somewhere along the way, you or I or Alec slipped up, that we accidentally told someone why he was here either by the questions we asked or the way we behaved . . . something. Otherwise, they would have simply assumed he was here to buy some property . . . like he told everyone he was."

"I suppose it could be related," Rebecca grudgingly admitted, "but it still seems a little remote to me. So if you don't mind, I think I'll wait until Alec can fill in the details before I go running off chasing someone's fantasies."

"Since when?" Penny rallied. "Since it wasn't your idea to begin with? I remember a certain newspaper article you wrote by following your instincts, and this makes more sense than that did."

"It also got me fired," Rebecca reminded her. "This could get me killed."

Penny had no argument for that one. It had become painfully obvious that any association with Alec Stone would have its drawbacks . . . serious ones. But Penny also knew Rebecca was in too deep to turn her back on it. And then there was the man himself. Maybe Rebecca didn't realize it, or perhaps she wasn't willing to admit it; but she was in love with this blond-haired, handsome man from Jamaica, and anyone who posed a threat to Alec would have to deal with her.

"What happens after this mess is cleared up and Alec's free to go home?" Penny baited, her eyes focused on the cup she held rather than on Rebecca.

"What do you mean 'what happens'?" came the puzzled reply. "He'll go home. What else would he do?"

"And you won't stop him?" Penny casually asked.

"Stop him? Why should I?"

Finishing off her tea, Penny leaned forward to set the cup on the table, her gaze shifting from the delicate piece of pottery to the blue eyes staring confusedly back at her. "Because you're in love with him."

"I am not!" Rebecca stormed, bolting from her chair. Making an angry grab for Penny's teacup, she carried it to the cupboard and roughly set it down along with her own, refusing to say another word about it.

Penny had been relatively sure about her suspicions concerning Rebecca's feelings for Alec. Having seen her reaction when confronted with the possibility rather confirmed it. What puzzled Penny, however, was how adamantly Rebecca denied it. There was nothing wrong with falling in love with a man. Glancing briefly at the sleeping topic of their conversation, Penny left her chair and went to stand next to her friend.

"What are you afraid of, Rebecca?" she asked quietly.

Shooting her a fierce glare, Rebecca spun away and crossed to the hearth where she knelt and jammed the poker into the fire several times, continuing her silence.

"Are you afraid he won't love you back? Well, I think you're wrong. I think just about any man could fall in love with you . . . if you'd let him."

"Penny," Rebecca hissed, warning her that she had already stretched the bonds of their friendship to the limit.

"Penny what?" she challenged, following Rebecca to the fireplace. "Keep still? Don't talk about it? Why? Do you like feeling miserable? If you let him go without telling him how much you care, you'll spend the rest of your life regretting it. He isn't an ogre, Rebecca. He's a man, and judging from the way he reacted when he found out you were missing that night, I'd say he cares more for you than he realizes. Rebecca? Are you listening to me?"

Icy blue eyes glared up at her. "No. I'm not." Shoving the poker back in its stand, Rebecca rose and went to the door. "It's getting late. You'd better go before you're missed and someone starts asking questions."

Penny opened her mouth to continue her assault and changed her mind. She knew how stubborn Rebecca could be. If she didn't want to discuss something, then she wouldn't. Penny could talk all night long . . . to herself. Rebecca would ignore her. She might even walk out on her just to prove a point. Sighing resignedly, Penny picked up the empty basket and headed for the exit. But once she reached the opened doorway, she paused long enough to stare at her friend until Rebecca was forced to look at her.

"You know I'm right," she softly told her. "I just hope you come to realize it before it's too late." With that, she quietly left the cabin.

Rebecca stood there unmoving until long after the sounds of hoofbeats faded in the distance, unaware of the dark, brown eyes watching her.

Chapter Twelve

Rebecca had spent a restless night, falling asleep just before dawn, and even then the bed she had made for herself there on the floor seemed to have developed numerous lumps in it. On the edge of wakefulness the entire time, she finally sought out what comfort she could find sitting in the rocker before the dying fire, a blanket thrown over her shoulders and the first light of day stealing in through the window to fall caressingly all around her.

Her conversation with Penny the night before hadn't made her angry because she disagreed with what her friend had said, but rather because Penny had struck upon the truth. She *did* care what happened to Alec, and the thought of his retuning home with the chance she might never see him again tore at her heart and left her hurting. Yet, she knew it was something she had to face. She couldn't tell him that he had unknowingly raised doubts about the way she felt toward men, that his mere presence stirred unfamiliar desires deep within her, and that the thought of losing him made her feel empty inside. Loving someone was too risky. She had loved her mother more than anyone else in her young life, and her mother had died. Feeling lost, she had turned that love on her father, a man who she thought adored her, and not only had he proven that he could share his love for her with someone else, but because of her selfishness, he had died as well. Then Alec Stone walked into her life, and here he was lying unconscious and near death.

And all because of her. She had no right to care about someone. Her possessiveness destroyed those who were close to her. No, she mustn't ever let him think her feelings for him went any deeper than lust. She had to make him hate her.

The cabin took on a chill despite the warming sunshine which steadily chased away the shadows and filled every corner of the room with its cheerful greeting. Tossing aside her blanket, Rebecca rose and started for the wood box, only to come to a disgruntled halt once she saw that it was empty. She had never watched someone chop firewood, let alone picked up an ax in her entire lifetime. Yet knowing it had to be done, she turned around and started for the door, thinking to find the tool she needed out back in the shed.

An hour later Rebecca entered the cabin with an armload of freshly cut logs, a pleased smile on her face and dirt smudges on her chin and the tip of her nose. The work had been tiring, and she had not only torn her dress and pinched a finger, but a splinter had become embedded in the palm of her hand. Yet in spite of it all, she had a good feeling about herself. She had finally accomplished a job meant only for men, and the idea of it made her laugh. Given enough time and willpower, she'd be able to overcome any obstacle put in her way. She'd prove to herself *and* to Penny that she could get along just fine without a man to complicate things. She could learn to take care of herself in every sense of the word. A frown contradicted that declaration as she bent and dumped the logs into the wood box. Maybe she'd better start by learning how to cook.

Once she had the fire going again, Rebecca grabbed a bucket and went outside to fill it with water. Warm sunshine peeked down through the thick, leafy branches overhead and boldly drew her attention to the tear in her skirt and the fact that she hadn't changed her clothes in all the while she had been here. At the well, she noticed how dirty her hands and arms had become from all her work, and she didn't have to look in a mirror to know what a mess her hair must be. She needed a bath and to launder out her things, the latter of which being a job she detested.

A silly smile curled her mouth as she lugged the heavy pail back to the cabin, wondering if Penny would agree to do her laundry if Rebecca learned to cook. Shaking her head with certainty that Penny would never call it an even trade, she stepped through the doorway and carried the bucket to the hearth where she poured the water into the kettle hanging over the bright flames. Just as soon as it was warm, she'd wash her hair and soap herself down as best she could since old man Robinson hadn't seen fit to own a tub . . . providing of course that he even bathed.

With her head down while she concentrated on unhooking the buttons up the front of her dress, Rebecca turned away from the hearth after kicking off her shoes and blindly approached the cupboard where she intended to select the largest bowl she could find to do the job. Upon reaching it, she paused and slipped out of her dress, letting the garment drop to the floor as she stepped out of it. Bending, she scooped up the yards of cloth and carelessly tossed the dress at the rocker. In that moment while she watched its flight, she suddenly realized what she had done without the slightest hesitation. She had stripped down to her camisole, garters and hose, and hadn't given a thought to the fact that she wasn't the only one using the cabin. Apprehensively, her cheeks burning with embarrassment, she slowly turned her head to look at the cot and the man who lay there. Warm brown eyes smiled back at her, and although his cheeks were flushed with color, Rebecca *knew* it had nothing to do with her lack of attire. Unable to move, not knowing if she should cheer his recovery or curse his silence for not letting her know he was awake, she just stood there, mouth agape, blue eyes wide, and the heat of her humiliation scorching every inch of bare flesh.

"How . . . how long have you . . ."

The smile that glowed in his eyes softly parted his lips, "Not long enough to see anything I haven't already seen," he answered quietly, his eyes drifting shut. "And I realize you think the worst of me, Reb, but let me assure you that I haven't the strength to take advantage of the situation." He shifted uncomfortably, grimacing at the pain in his shoulder and asked, "Could I trouble you for a drink of water?"

His request and seeing the agony he suffered from just moving an inch spurred Rebecca into action. Plucking one of the blankets from her makeshift bed on the floor, she whirled it around her shoulders and took down a cup from the shelf, filling it with water from the pitcher sitting on the table. Hurrying to his side, she knelt, slipped her hand behind his head and lowered the cup to his lips. He drank nearly all of it before he settled back down on the pillow, his eyes still closed and the crease in his brow marking his distress.

"Penny brought some laudanum," she offered. "Why not take some? It will help you—"

"Sleep?" he cut in, smiling and opening his eyes again. "I think I've slept enough, don't you?"

Rebecca wondered if he could see by the expression on her face how glad she was that he had finally come around. It didn't really matter to her if he could. She truly didn't care who knew it. Alec was alive and getting well, and maybe that meant the curse which seemed to follow her had finally been broken. Or maybe it was because she had vowed to keep her feelings about him a secret.

"Sleeping is the best cure," she told him, her eyes sparkling. Touching the backs of her fingers against his cheek, she frowned slightly and left his side to collect a bowl of cool water and a rag. Pulling up a chair, she sat down, set the bowl on the floor next to her and dipped the rag in the water.

"How long have I—" he began, wincing at the effort it took just to speak.

"Almost four days," she answered, wiping his brow and cheeks with the wet cloth. "You were hurt pretty badly." Gentle fingers brushed aside his hair to examine the cut and bruised flesh near his temple. It was healing nicely. "You lost a lot of blood, and I'm sure the headache you must have came from falling off your horse. Your head hit a rock when you landed." She rinsed out the cloth again and tenderly pressed it against his forehead. "I'm lucky you regained consciousness long enough to help me get you into the cabin. I don't know what I would have done otherwise."

"I remember," he quietly replied. "You were crying." His dark eyes slowly traced the smotth curve of her cheek and jaw. "Because you didn't want to bother with me, you said."

Rebecca remembered, too, and she remembered the reason she had lied. "I guess it wasn't so bad after all." She grinned. "You've slept the whole time. Are you hungry?"

Alec closed his eyes, his lips forming a negative reply but no sound escaping them.

"Alec," she said after a moment, "that man who shot you, did you know him?"

"I'm afraid I never saw him. I heard the gunfire, felt myself falling and woke up to find you bending over me."

"Penny thinks he stole your stickpin."

His brow furrowed, but Rebecca knew it wasn't from the pain in his shoulder. "Did you look in my coat pocket?" he asked, glancing up at her.

Rebecca nodded. "It's gone. And the curious thing is that he didn't take any of your money."

"Then I'd have to agree with Penny."

"Why? What did he want with it? Was it worth a great deal, enough to warrant shooting a man and leaving him for dead? Penny asked around in town about someone trying to sell it, but it seems he *and* the pin are gone. Do you think—"

Laughter rumbled in his chest, ending in a moan when the movement hurt him. A moment passed while he waited for it to pass and he could draw a breath to respond. "Always the journalist, aren't you, Reb?"

He smiled at the color that instantly stained her cheeks and reached out to cover her hand with his. It was cool to the touch and reminded him of how sick he'd been and how it would be some time yet before he was completely well again. He had a lot to thank her for—he knew that. If she hadn't found him when she did, he would have died. And if solving this mystery was all she really wanted from him, then he'd give her all the help he possibly could. But not now. The

281

short time they had talked left him weak and exhausted. Letting go of her hand, he closed his eyes.

"Take your bath," he instructed in a whisper. "We'll talk later . . . after I've rested."

Rebecca would have liked to finish their discussion right then, but she knew he had spent more energy than he could afford already. "All right," she yielded. "You sleep. I'll get cleaned up, and we'll have some tea later . . . when you're strong enough." Within moments Rebecca could see that he had drifted off again, and although she expected to feel disappointed over having to wait to learn the facts about his assailant, she wasn't. She was happy . . . extremely so. Alec was going to get well, and at the moment that was all that really mattered to her.

The noon hour came and went. Rebecca had washed her hair, taken a quick bath, changed into fresh things, mended the rip in her skirt with the needle and thread Penny had thoughtfully supplied her, and done some laundry, hanging it outside in the sunshine. Then she ate a little something. All the while Alec slept, and once Rebecca had finished her work, she drew up a chair beside him and sat contentedly watching the gentle rise and fall of his chest. The fever had finally broken, and his color had turned a little pale; but that was to be expected. He slept peacefully, and had it not been for the bandage covering his shoulder, it would appear to anyone that he was merely taking a nap after an exhausting day spent running a huge plantation. That thought stirred Rebecca's curiosity. What had he left behind when he came to Williamsburg? Might there be a woman waiting for him? He had claimed he wasn't the type to settle down and get married, but it didn't mean that he couldn't have a mistress . . . one of those darkly tanned island girls eager to fill his needs whenever he wished companionship. A tinge of jealously arose and kinked the soft line of her brows, and she quickly blinked away the feeling *and* the vision of him locked in a young woman's arms, a beautiful, long-haired, smooth-skinned, *willing* girl. Rebecca knew that she would not be the last woman in his life, the one to change him, win his devotion, his respect, his loyalty. How could she be? He was young and virile and possessed all the qualities of a healthy, free-spirited stallion set loose to mate with however many sleek and graceful mares he could find. What would he want with someone like her? Frowning, she mentally tallied up the number of women Williamsburg had to offer and concluded that she had merely been a pleasant distraction from his usual fare. She hardly fit in the category of half-naked girls. Nor had she been willing. It made perfectly good sense that he had found the difference enjoyable and attractive. But once the novelty wore off, he'd go home to those giggling, scantily clad, brainless twits who'd chase after him and throw themselves at his feet, begging, "Take me. Take me."

Rebecca nearly fell off her chair when she realized how she had let her imagination get control of her, and she jerked upright to clear her mind and set her thoughts on something else. Embarrassed and fearing Alec had awakened long ago and had seen the questionable expression on her face, she quickly glanced over at him, found him still asleep and bolted from her chair. It would never do—no, it would be disastrous for her if he ever suspected what went on inside her head. He'd laugh at her and tell her how right those thoughts were. Angered, she went to the hearth and poured water into the kettle. She'd busy herself with other things and deny those awful thoughts the chance to upset her. True or not, she'd never think on them again. Once he was gone, she'd forget all about him . . . him and his little harem of trollops.

Alec slept most of the day, and when he awoke sometime in midafternoon, he was feeling much better than he had earlier. Although he still suffered from a burning sensation in his shoulder and an occasional twinge of pain, he found that he was actually hungry. And he was tired of lying on that hard, lumpy cot. A quick look around the room told him that Rebecca must have gone outside. He would have liked her help in sitting up, but since she had done more than her share already, he decided it was time he started caring for himself. Shoving the blanket aside, he gingerly swung his legs off the bed and slowly pushed himself up with his good arm. The minor feat brought sweat to his brow, and he collapsed back against the wall, his eyes closed and a pleased smile on his lips. He had always hated being so ill that he had to depend on others just to feed him and see to his basic needs. He liked it even less knowing that that responsibility had fallen on Rebecca's shoulders. She had enough problems of her own without having to deal with his. Well, that would change. It might take him a while to get around, but Reb no longer had to sit at his bedside.

Once the wave of nausea passed and his face was cool and dry again, he opened his eyes and quietly studied the interior of the cabin, amazed to learn that the once disheveled, filthy room stood a chance of resembling a comfortable place to live. He was used to the spacious, immaculate chambers of his mansion back home with its high ceilings and marble floors and tall, opened windows letting in the sunlight and the fresh, cooling breeze scented with the smell of the sea. Yet this place, this tiny one-room house reminded him of the small stone building he had shared with his mother as a child. Those memories were usually painful for him whenever he recalled how difficult it was for his mother to see that they had enough to eat. But today, for some reason, he felt the love and happiness that had balanced out the dreadful times, and without realizing it, he smiled while he absently toyed with the ring on his little finger.

A shadow crossed the stream of sunshine pouring into the cabin through the opened front door to his right and stilled his thoughts of childhood. Relaxing back against the wall behind him, he appreciatively watched Rebecca's trim figure hurry into the room with her arms full of firewood and race for the hearth where she knelt and rolled the logs to the floor. His first instinct was to help, but the second he tightened the muscles across his chest to boost himself up, the pain in his shoulder changed his mind. He'd have to be content to watch, knowing that at least his manners hadn't failed him.

"I'd do that for you, but I'm afraid the only thing willing is my mind," he apologized, smiling when Rebecca jerked around clumsily to look at him.

A disapproving frown marring her pretty face, she scolded, "You shouldn't be sitting up."

Alec chuckled, then grimaced, "I got tired of counting the cracks in the ceiling. Besides, I'm hungry, and it's easier swallowing if everything goes straight down." Shifting carefully, he drew up one knee and rested his foot on the edge of the cot. "Would it be asking too much for you to fix me a cup of tea and anything else you might have that's palatable?"

"Not at all." She smiled softly as she brushed off the dirt from her dress and stood, pleased that he was feeling good enough to think about eating. A few minutes later she handed him a small serving of the food Penny had brought them the night before and drew up a chair to sit beside him and hold his cup of tea until he was ready for it. "I don't know which was worse," she admitted while she watched him eat, "seeing your face flushed with fever or how pale it became once the fever broke. I must say you look a lot better now."

"And so do you," he teased, exchanging the empty plate for the cup of tea. He grinned at the confused look she gave him. "Your face is clean," he explained before taking a drink of the hot tea.

The image he must have had of her earlier this morning as she stripped off her dress and tossed it aside flashed before Rebecca's eyes, and she laughed. "Yes, I suppose I did look a sight."

"A good one," he promised, resting his head back against the wall while he enjoyed the way sunlight stole into the room and fell softly against her fair skin. "I don't think I've ever seen you smile before."

Feeling her face warm under his steady gaze, she lowered her eyes. "I guess I never had much reason until now."

Alec took another sip of tea. "I would think you'd have less reason to smile now. Didn't Miss Abigail ask you to leave?"

Rebecca's brow wrinkled. "How did you know that?"

"Simple deduction. Jon-Gregory told me about the woman's rules and that you hadn't been home all night." His own brow furrowed. "He also mentioned a note. Mind telling me what that was all about?"

Rising, she set the plate on the table and proceeded to fix herself a cup of tea. "I'm not sure. At first I thought it was sincere. Then I decided someone had an odd sense of humor." Pulling out one of the chairs at the tables she sat down. "The message said that I was to meet whoever wrote it at half past nine in back of the Public Hospital and that I was to come alone. It said he had information about Eli's death. But no one ever showed up. I waited as long as I dared, then went home." She smiled halfheartedly. "Miss Abigail was waiting for me. I was late."

"And you came here to spend the night," Alec concluded.

Rebecca nodded sheepishly. "I was afraid to ask Penny to let me stay with her."

"You should have," he quietly reprimanded. "Or at least told her what had happened and where you were going. She and Jon-Gregory were very worried about you."

"I know," she admitted ruefully. "Penny told me as much." Not wanting to hear another lecture, she decided to change the subject. "But what about you? Have you figured out what someone would want with your stickpin?"

Leaning, he set his empty cup on the chair beside him. "It wasn't mine."

Rebecca's eyes widened. "What? Then whose was it?"

Alec shook his head. "I would guess it belonged to the man who shot me."

"So how did you happen to have it, and how did he know you did? Penny said you had it hidden in your satchel, that she'd never seen you wearing it."

Alec silently recalled the incident there at the pier and remembered having had the feeling he was being watched. Maybe his instincts had been correct. It certainly appeared that way now. "I found it the night I arrived," he said aloud. "I had intended to tell someone about it because of its value. I figured whoever owned it would appreciate having it back. I never imagined just how much or I wouldn't have forgotten about it."

"Where?" Rebecca asked excitedly. "Where did you find it?"

"At the pier." He started to add that it had been near where the young boy's body had been found and suddenly wondered if in some bizarre way the two were connected. But what had Eli's death to do with him?

Rebecca had seen the suspicious look on Alec's face. "What? You've figured something out. What is it, Alec? Tell me. Let me help."

He was quiet a moment longer, trying to discredit the idea and couldn't. His instincts were working again. "I found it near where Keenan said Eli had died. I was just wondering if—"

Rebecca could feel her face whiten. "If it belonged to whoever killed Eli?"

Alec nodded.

"But how did he know *you* had it?"

Frowning, he admitted, "I can't be absolutely sure, but at the time I thought someone was watching me. I had just picked up the pin and put it in my pocket when I heard a noise . . . a snapping of a twig or leaves rustling from within the woods ahead of me. I never saw anyone or even an animal, but I sensed someone or something was there. It would certainly explain how someone knew I had the pin."

"But Eli died the night before. His body wasn't found until the next morning. Why would his killer wait so long to look for the pin?" Rebecca observed.

"The obvious answer would be that he simply didn't realize he had lost it until much later. I would also guess that that pin is very special to someone."

"How so?"

"If the right person saw it, they'd know who it belonged to and that its owner had killed your young friend."

Rebecca had to agree that was logical. "Then you were merely an innocent bystander? If someone else had found the pin, *they'd* have been shot instead of you?"

"Maybe," he replied, his eyes darkening as he considered another possibility.

"But you're not convinced," she speculated, leaving her place at the table to sit down on the bed next to him. "Why, Alec? What are you thinking?"

He glanced over at her and smiled. "I might be making more out of this than there really is, but there's still your conviction that Eli was murdered. If we go on the assumption that he was—backed up, I might add, by the note you received—then the question is why. If he wasn't a runaway, then what was he doing at the pier?"

Rebecca suddenly understood. "Are you saying he might have known something and had to be silenced before he could tell anyone?"

"I might be stretching it a bit, but yes, that's what I'm thinking."

"And that something was the identity of the man who hoodwinked your agent?"

Alec nodded.

"Well, it certainly fits, but why would Eli have waited nearly a year to tell someone? And who was he going to tell?" Rebecca wanted to believe it was that simple, but there were too many flaws in the idea. "Furthermore, why did he feel he had to say something? He was only a slave. He wouldn't have been a threat to whoever killed him."

"Obviously, they thought he would. As for why he waited so long, maybe he only just found out about it and that whoever tricked Heller was planning to do it again and those plans involved Eli. You knew him. Was he capable of murdering someone?"

"No! Absolutely not!" she exploded. "He was just a boy, a gentle, loving boy. He'd never kill anyone. Why would you even suggest it?"

"Because I'm trying to rationalize his running away. Maybe he was unwillingly involved in Heller's murder and simply refused to help out again."

"Gideon Blackstock," she breathed, excitement growing inside her. "I think you're right, Alec. I've never met the man,

288

but I've heard he's a little strange. He keeps to himself—doesn't socialize—that sort of thing. And he's rich, *very* rich." A bright smile parted her lips and glowed in her blue eyes. *"He* owns a huge plantation—the sort that could be used to trick someone into handing over all their money." Eager to find out if they were right, she bolted off the bed and headed for the door.

"Where are you going?" Alec called, stopping her in the doorway.

"To the courthouse," she advised. "I've got a hunch that the records will prove Mr. Blackstock came into a large sum of money about the time Heller died. Then we'll have him. We'll know he killed Eli and who has your money."

"Reb, wait!" Alec shouted, but she had already made up her mind. She was going to the courthouse whether Alec liked it or not. She was determined to prove Eli had been murdered and see that the man responsible for it was forced to admit it. Her only regret was that she knew Blackstock wouldn't hang for what he'd done to Eli, but if everything worked out the way she hoped it would, he'd face the executioner to account for Daniel Heller's demise. Either way, justice would be served, and Eli's death would be avenged.

"Rebecca, I don't mind telling you that I think this is the stupidest thing you've ever talked me into doing," Penny snapped as their carriage rounded the last bend in the road and gave them a clear view of the Blackstock plantation. "What do you hope to prove? That you've completely lost your mind?"

"I already told you," Rebecca hissed through clenched teeth.

"And I told you that you're making things up. Why would Blackstock kill one of his own slaves? Especially Eli. You heard Jon-Gregory say that the man cared very deeply for Eli . . . almost like a son. What you're suggesting doesn't make sense."

"Then talk to Alec. This was his idea."

Penny started to challenge her friend's suggestion, but instead quickly clamped her fingers around the edge of the seat when the carriage hit a rut and nearly toppled her from it. "I hope you'll forgive me for saying that I find that hard to believe. I can't imagine Alec asking you to visit Gideon Blackstock if he thought the man was capable of murder." An angry frown slanted her brows together as she studied the huge manor house laid out before them with its tall, white columns adorning the face and its monstrous oak trees lining each side of the drive. "And speaking of Alec, is he well enough to leave alone?"

"We won't be gone that long," Rebecca grumbled as she guided the rig onto the lane leading to the front door.

"I hope not," Penny crisply remarked. "I don't like traveling on the road after dark." She shifted her attention from the stately mansion to the fiery sunset off to her left. "But of course, I guess there isn't much I can do about it now, unless I sprout wings and fly home." Another thought struck her, and she scowled at her companion, asking, "Did you really ask Jon-Gregory to come with us?"

Rebecca dared not look at her. "Yes," she lied. "But he couldn't. He said he had too much work to do."

Her answer seemed to appease Penny, and she relaxed a little, knowing that once Penny found out the truth—that Rebecca hadn't even *seen* Jon-Gregory, much less talked to him—everything would be over and done with, and all Penny could do then was gripe. Rebecca would have preferred the young man's company on the long ride out of town, but she knew he'd get very upset if she told him why she had to speak with Gideon Blackstock and that he'd try to stop her from going even if she told him Alec had been the one to figure it out. Maybe it *was* stupid on her part, but alone or with someone, she was going to the Blackstock plantation.

The records at the courthouse had revealed exactly what she had thought she would find. Around the same time Heller's body had been found, Gideon Blackstock purchased a large number of slaves, not enough to equal the amount of money Alec had lost, but a tidy sum that raised Rebecca's curiosity. She didn't plan to come right out and accuse Mr. Blackstock, but if she worded her questions just right, she might trick him into saying something he'd rather be kept secret. Then she'd have him, and Penny would be her witness. They could go to the constable with their proof, and Gideon Blackstock would have to stand trial. A sadness came over her then when she realized exactly what that meant. If she recovered Alec's money, he'd have nothing to keep him from going home.

A black slave hurried toward them to grab the mare's halter and allow the women to safely descend the carriage once their rig had rounded the circular drive and stopped at the sidewalk leading to the front door. Another met them on the porch, and once Rebecca had requested a moment of Mr. Blackstock's time, the butler showed them into the manor and directed them to the parlor to wait. Both Penny and Rebecca sat quietly on the mint green upholstered settee while the servant went to inform his master that guests had arrived, for they were too numbed by what they saw to carry on any kind of conversation. In the center of the ten-foot-tall ceiling hung a huge chandelier with hundreds of candles and multi-faceted, teardrop crystals. The thick oak walls were richly enhanced by deeply carved molding and large oil paintings hanging over the white marble fireplace. A pale green and white Persian rug partially covered the dark wood floor. A bouquet of white chrysanthemums adorned the end table positioned between two mint-green wing chairs. A brass wood box sat beside the hearth. Along the mantel were various alabaster figurines. Fine crystal bowls, vases, tiny bells and porcelain music boxes were artfully arranged on all the remaining tables, and a gold-framed mirror hung on the wall opposite them. There was more wealth contained in this one room than either girl had seen in a long while, and they both suddenly felt unworthy of sitting on such an exquisitely manufactured piece of furniture.

"I feel like I'm waiting to see the king of England," Penny

291

breathed, leaning forward, her hand outstretched and fingers expectant of the smooth, polished surface of the figurine she was about to touch. Suddenly fearful that some unseen force would knock it to the floor and break it in hundreds of pieces, she pulled back, knowing it would take a month's pay to replace it . . . or more.

"I know what you mean," Rebecca agreed. "I'm not even sure the Governor's Palace can match this." Her gaze settled on the black-lacquered, covered box with tiny clusters of diamonds in its lid sitting in front of her. "I didn't realize being a planter paid so well."

"Maybe he's got his hand in other things," Penny suggested.

"You mean besides hoodwinking total strangers?"

Penny shrugged. "Well, it sure makes a person wonder. Maybe he's into slave trading." Her brown eyes lit up. "Maybe he's a spy for the British and they pay him handsomely for his information."

Rebecca smiled. "You're beginning to think like me, Penelope Dawson. Maybe we shouldn't see so much of each other."

Penny was about to respond when the thick, oak door in the room suddenly swung open on well-oiled hinges, and without realizing it, both young women quickly stood up as if they were about to be presented to Colonel Washington. Who they saw instead not only sent a shiver of disappointment through them, but one of revulsion as well. Neither Rebecca nor Penny had ever seen Gideon Blackstock before today. They had heard his name mentioned many times in connection with money and power; but he had always been somewhat of a recluse, and his reason was suddenly quite clear. He was shorter than both Penny and Rebecca and was nearly as round as he was tall. His white periwig sat strangely on the top of his head, and it was easy for them to guess he had very little, if any, hair of his own. His black, bushy eyebrows contrasted sharply with the wig and shadowed his very narrow set, bulging gray eyes. His chin hung in folds, his lower lip curled downward, and his nose was broad through its bridge and pointed on the end. But the purple birthmark that covered half his face was more distracting than any of his other unattractive features, and although his clothes were made of rich cloth and diamond rings adorned three of his fingers, it was difficult for the girls to notice anything beyond the dark blemish which seemed to pucker his left eyelid. Everyone had a fault or two that they would have loved to correct, but Rebecca was thinking this man had more than his share. Penny, on the other hand, was thinking that this was *one* man she'd rather just talk with than entertain in bed.

"Mr. Blackstock?" Rebecca said, forcing a polite smile and stepping toward him with her hand extended. "I'm Rebecca Wilde, a reporter for the *Gazette*." She released his hand, briefly thinking how wet it was, and turned to acknowledge her companion, failing to see the glimpse of recognition darken his eyes. "And this is Penelope Dawson." She waited until they had exchanged a greeting and he had instructed them to sit down again before she continued. "I apologize if we've interrupted anything, sir, but it was most urgent that I speak with you."

"Urgent?" he repeated in a gravelly voice as he took a seat in one of the wing chairs across from them, his feet barely touching the floor once he had settled his wide girth into it. "What concerns me that could be urgent?" He squinted his narrow eyes at her.

"It's about Eli, your manservant, sir. It's my belief he was murdered, and I'm trying to gather information that would prove it."

"I'm afraid I can't help you, Miss Wilde," he was quick to reply. "What happened to Eli doesn't interest me." He started to rise. "You've wasted your trip."

Rebecca prayed the smile that tugged on her lips didn't show itself in her eyes as she stared back at him. His hasty denial had all but confirmed her suspicions about him. Of course he'd say something like that. He didn't want *anyone* to prove Eli had been murdered because it would lead to much bigger atrocities . . . all of which involved him. However, the constable wouldn't arrest him just because of

Rebecca's instincts. She had to have more.

"But, sir," she said after glancing briefly at Penny and coming to her feet, "I understand you cared very deeply for Eli. I would think you'd *want* to know what happened to him . . . if not for personal satisfaction than simply to be reimbursed for the cost of a good and faithful slave."

"I'm sorry, Miss Wilde, but I'm afraid you've been misled. I don't really care anymore. You see, I sold Eli a little more than a week ago. His new owner is the one you should be asking." He started toward the door.

"Sold him?" Rebecca blurted out. "But I thought—"

"Eli had become difficult to handle, Miss Wilde," Gideon interrupted. "And when a slave becomes difficult, you get rid of him. I believe that's why your stepmother sold him to me." He opened the door and stood to one side, silently telling them that this conversation had come to an end.

Rebecca had to bite back the truth about why Lenore had sold Eli. This wasn't the time or the place to discuss it. "May I, at least, ask the name of the man who bought him?"

Gideon Blackstock's narrow eyes moved from Rebecca to Penny and back again. "I don't see where it will help, but yes. His name is Nathan Blackstock, my cousin. He, however, lives in Georgia, and I would guess Eli escaped him before my cousin had the chance to take him home. Now, if you'll excuse me, I have a lot of work to do." He held a directive hand toward the door.

It wasn't uncommon for a slave owner to sell one or more of his slaves, but in Eli's case it didn't ring true. Jon-Gregory had often talked with the boy whenever he and his master visited Greenhow's store, and Jon-Gregory had many times remarked on how devoted the young man was to his master. He was happy living with Gideon Blackstock. The man *never* beat him, but gave him his own room in the manor house and many liberties few other slaves enjoyed. Therefore he had no reason to cause Blackstock any trouble. Blackstock had to be lying. Otherwise, it simply didn't make any sense.

"I'm sorry to be rude, sir," she apologized in advance as

294

she came to stand beside him and reach to swing the door shut again. "But I'm afraid I don't believe a word you've said."

"Rebecca!" Penny exclaimed aghast. Her friend's boldness and the fact that Rebecca may have put them both in serious danger frightened her. Maybe Rebecca didn't care what happened to her in the process of learning the truth, but Penny did. She faced Mr. Blackstock. "Please excuse her, sir. Sometimes—"

"Penny, stay out of this," Rebecca warned. "I'm not leaving here until I have the truth." Although she spoke to her friend, Rebecca's eyes never left Gideon's face, and she was glad they hadn't. Otherwise she might have missed the glimmer of worry that briefly wrinkled his brow. "As you've already admitted in an obscure way, Eli was no stranger to me. But in case you're not aware of it, he and I were childhood friends. I probably knew him better than anyone else . . . except, perhaps, Cela." She raised her brows at him, silently asking if he recognized the name. At his continued, apparently nervous silence, she explained. "Cela was Eli's girl. He loved her, and I would imagine they planned to get married someday. So why would Eli do anything to jeopardize that?" She didn't wait for him to answer. "He wouldn't. Furthermore, he *couldn't*. Eli didn't have it in him to be rebellious. He was a dedicated servant . . . to whoever owned him. And that includes my stepmother. She sold him to spite me and for no other reason." She cocked a dark brow at him and turned to sit down in one of the wing chairs. "So your claim that you sold him because he was rebellious just doesn't quite settle right with me."

Gideon's eyes narrowed to fine slits. "Do you think I care whether or not you believe me?" he snarled. "I don't. Eli was a troublemaker."

"Really? Is that why you treated him better than any of your other slaves? Is that why you gave him his own room here in the house? Is that why you took him everywhere you went?" Rebecca's rage led her blindly on. "Is that why you killed him?"

In shock, Penny staggered backward and leaned heavily against a small table, her eyes wide, her face pale and her entire body trembling, certain she was about to die.

"What?" Gideon raged. "Who do you think you are to come in here and accuse me of murdering Eli? His body tightened, and tears sprang up in his eyes. "I loved Eli! He was the only one in my life who didn't cringe the first time he saw me, the way both of you did. He made me laugh. He made me feel good about myself. He really liked *me."* A pudgy hand jabbed at his chest. "The me who's trapped inside this grotesque body, the man who can only *dream* about being accepted for what he really is, a man who will forever long for a woman's touch, her gentle words, her kindness. Eli saw it in me. No one else did. *They* only saw my wealth, a way to have the things they couldn't have. Yes, I treated him better than any of my other slaves because he deserved it! Eli was better than *everyone,* including *you,* Miss Wilde."* Tears streaming down his face, his round, little body shaking, he seized the doorknob and yanked the portal open. "Get out!" he demanded, a gnarled finger pointing the way. "Get out of my house immediately!"

Rebecca numbly came to her feet. She hadn't expected to hear such a confession, and now that she had, she knew she had been wrong about Gideon Blackstock. "I apologize for my insensitivity, sir, and the only right I can claim for coming here and making such inaccurate statements is simply because I cared about Eli, too. He was the only friend I had who understood my desire to be a journalist. All I really want is to find out what happened to him. I believe you'd like to know that, too," she added softly as she watched the crippled-up, little man lower his head and turn away from her to wipe the moisture from his face. "You didn't really sell him to your cousin, did you?"

Gideon's frame shook as he fought to control his grief. "No. I . . . I only said that . . ." He shook his head and mumbled, "It doesn't matter why. You wouldn't understand anyway."

"Try me," Rebecca gently encouraged. "Not everyone is as

hardhearted as you'd like to believe. We're ignorant at times, even cruel without realizing it. But I cared for Eli, and I want someone to pay for killing him."

Still unable to look at her, Gideon kept his eyes averted as he returned to his chair and sat down. "I have no idea what happened to him, and I probably never will. But I can't help blaming myself for his death."

"Why?" Rebecca frowned, coming to kneel beside him and tenderly cover his hand with hers.

A moment passed while he swallowed his tears and steeled himself against the pain he felt over his loss. "He came to me that morning and asked my permission to go to Williamsburg. I could see in his eyes that something terrible was bothering him, but I didn't have the time right then to talk it over with him. I'm afraid I was a little short with him . . . like I am most of the time with everyone else who works for me. I told him no, that he'd have to wait until later." A defiant tear spilled down his rough cheek, and Gideon quickly brushed it away. "He pleaded with me, which only made me angry, and I ordered him to get to work. It wasn't until that night that I discovered he had run away. The constable came the next afternoon to tell me Eli was dead."

"And rather than let anyone know you blamed yourself for what happened simply because deep down inside you felt you could have prevented it, you made up the story about selling him," Rebecca guessed.

Gideon's gray eyes glanced at her then closed. "Yes," he whispered.

"Mr. Blackstock, I'm sure everyone who liked Eli felt the same thing," she reassured him. "I'm blaming myself for his death, too. That's why I'm here. I won't rest until I know what happened and who was responsible. And I apologize again for accusing you." Rising, she took the chair beside him, motioned for Penny to sit down and asked, "Did you ask any of his friends if they knew what was bothering Eli?"

"Yes. As soon as I found out he was gone, I questioned everyone here. But no one knew a thing."

"So you have no idea what drew him to Williamsburg or even if he was planning to meet with someone."

Gideon shook his head.

"Mr. Blackstock, are you missing a jeweled stickpin?"

The man's brows came sharply together, and he stared confusedly at Rebecca, then Penny and back again. "If you're trying to imply that Eli stole something from me, let me assure you that that's the last thing Eli would ever do. I gave him all he could ever want." Gideon's short frame seemed to grow two inches as he straightened himself and jerked clear of the chair. "I'll have you know I was planning to buy his young woman so they could be married. He knew it, too. So why would he steal from me?"

"Are you missing a jeweled stickpin?" she calmly asked again.

"No!" came the outraged reply. "And I think it's time you left, Miss Wilde. I've told you everything I know about poor Eli." He quickly returned to the door and held it wide.

Penny, still convinced the strange, little man planned to murder them both, quickly hurried across the threshold and out into the hallway. Rebecca wasn't as eager. Nearing the exit, she paused, her eyes lowered, a frown on her smooth brow and one finger tapping her chin.

"Mr. Blackstock," she said, turning on him, "would you mind answering one more question?"

The man gritted his teeth and the muscle in his thick cheek flexed, but he chose not to reply.

"I did some research at the courthouse this afternoon, and I learned that about a year ago you purchased a rather large number of slaves. Would you mind telling me where you got the money to make such a purchase?"

"Oh, my God," Penny moaned. Until two seconds ago, they had a chance of leaving here alive. Rebecca had just destroyed what little hope Penny had. And since her friend didn't seem to care about her own life, Penny decided to take charge of hers. Jerking forward, she clamped on to Rebecca's wrist and yanked her away. "We'll be going now, Mr. Blackstock," she called over her shoulder as she pulled

Rebecca with her toward the front door which the butler had opened for them. "Thank you for seeing us. We *won't* be bothering you again."

"Dammit, Penny, let go!" Rebecca howled, stumbling on the stone sidewalk as she fought to free herself from Penny's unrelenting grip. "I must hear his answer." She practically collided with the redhead when Penny stopped suddenly and swung around.

"It's none of your business, and if you persist in provoking that odd little man . . ." Pausing long enough to glance past her stubborn friend at the closed front door, she heaved a quiet sigh once she realized Gideon Blackstock wanted nothing more to do with them, and turned her attention back on Rebecca. "You've taken on more than you can handle, Reb," she warned, "and I suggest we get our tails back in that carriage and go home before Blackstock changes his mind. He *isn't* the one you're after. Can't you see that?"

"I can see he's hiding something," Rebecca rallied.

"What if he is? Do you think he'd confess to you just because you asked him?"

"Not really," Rebecca hesitantly admitted. Taking a breath to add something more, she frowned instead when Penny cut her off.

"Well, praise the Lord," she mocked. "You've finally said something that makes sense. Now let's go home." She turned for their carriage waiting at the end of the sidewalk, and Rebecca had to run to catch up.

"What I meant," she said, grabbing Penny's arm and denying her the opportunity to climb the rig's step when she yanked her off balance, "was that if I'd badgered Mr. Blackstock long enough, he'd say something he'd prefer not to admit out of sheer frustration."

"And then what?" Penny snapped, jerking her arm free of Rebecca's hold. "Would we just stand there while he loads a pistol and shoots us both dead?" She gave Rebecca a challenging look and hurriedly ascended the carriage. "No, thank you. I'm not *that* curious." Grabbing the reins, ready to crack them across the horse's rump, she gave her friend one last chance. "Are you coming?"

Rebecca wanted to say no, that she wasn't leaving until she had the truth, but she realized it would be a rather long walk home if she didn't leave with Penny, and Mr. Blackstock had probably said all he was going to say. Glancing over her shoulder at the closed front door, she wrinkled up her face at it, then begrudgingly turned to pull herself up into the seat next to her friend. She had to admit that it wasn't as though she had wasted her trip. Gideon Blackstock had, in a roundabout way, confirmed her feelings that Eli hadn't been a runaway. What puzzled her and left her very suspicious was why Blackstock tried to hide that fact. There had to be more to it than that, and she was determined to find out what that was.

The two girls rode in silence as Penny guided the rig down the lane toward the main road. But long before they reached it, she veered the small carriage off to the left and in the direction of the James River marked by a thick line of trees.

"What are you doing?" Rebecca demanded, when the wheel hit a bump and jarred every bone in her body. "Are you trying to get us killed? I thought that was the reason you wanted to leave Blackstock's . . . so we wouldn't get killed. Turn back to the road this instant."

"It's shorter going this way," Penny argued, her attention riveted on the path she chose for the horse to follow. "I told you I didn't like riding alone after dark."

"You're not alone," Rebecca contended, eyes wide, her body tense, certain that at any second she would be thrown from the carriage.

"I might as well be," Penny rallied. "You certainly don't care what happens to me."

"And you think we're safer cutting through the field? It will be pitch black soon, and you won't be able to see. The horse could stumble and the carriage—"

The thought had barely formed into words when the front wheel hit a hole. The frame moaned, dipped downward, rattled loudly and came to a sudden stop when the splintering of wood told the girls that they would either be walking home or riding double.

"Penelope Dawson!" Rebecca fumed as she jumped to the ground to inspect the damage. "Look what your foolishness has done."

"*My* foolishness?" Penny countered. "You're the one who thought it was so damn important to talk to Blackstock that it couldn't wait until morning or at least until someone could go with us." Furious, she grabbed her skirts in one hand, yanked them aside and stepped to the ground.

"And if you'd stuck to the main road, this wouldn't have happened."

"That's right, blame me!" Penny howled as she rounded the back of the carriage to confront her companion.

"You were driving, weren't you?"

"Yes! But it's rather difficult to concentrate on what one's doing when someone else is criticizing every move you make!"

"Then you shouldn't have tried," Rebecca hissed, her fists on her hips, her jaw set and her nose close to Penny's.

Several moments passed while the two stood flaring at each other, each silently wanting to blame the other for the predicament they were in and soon realizing that no matter what the situation or given circumstances, Penny Dawson and Rebecca Wilde could turn it into a fiasco. A glimmer of humor surfaced in Rebecca's blue eyes and tugged at the corner of Penny's mouth. They fought to reinforce their anger, each wishing that for once she could prove the other wrong. But the years of friendship they had shared and the honest desire not to ruin it soon gained the advantage, and within seconds they both burst out laughing.

"Someday, Penny," Rebecca promised, her arm draped around her friend's shoulders, "you and I will figure out a way to behave like ladies."

"God forbid!" Penny exclaimed, joyful tears running down her cheeks. "Wouldn't life be boring?"

"Oh, I don't know," Rebecca challenged playfully, falling back against the side of the carriage, her eyes bright with devilment. "A lady has servants to do things for her. She has expensive gowns to wear, balls to attend, hordes of gentlemen callers—"

"Oops!" Penny cut in. "I guess that makes me a lady."

Knowing exactly what Penny meant, Rebecca laughed again. "Not the same. A gentleman caller doesn't crawl into bed with a lady before dessert is served."

"What do you mean?" Penny chaffed. "That *is* dessert."

Although Rebecca had heard similar comments from Penny countless times before, they were still nonetheless shocking. Gasping in astonishment, she pushed away from the carriage, stared open-mouthed at her companion for a few moments, then shook her head resignedly. "Well, if you plan to be on someone's menu tonight, we better get this horse unharnessed and start for home." A worried frown marred her brow as she moved to do as she suggested. "I need to check on Alec."

"What do you mean unharness the horse?" Penny wailed, "You're not implying we're to *ride* the beast, are you?"

"Well, I certainly don't intend to walk, do you?" With practiced hands, she unhooked the straps and freed the horse from its restraints.

"I do if the only choice I have is sitting on top of that nag," Penny stubbornly declared her face flushed, her red hair glowing in the last rays of dying sunlight and her small frame rigid with conviction.

"I can't believe you've never ridden horseback in your entire life, Penelope Dawson," Rebecca remarked sometime later as the horse they rode cantered parallel with the stand of trees hiding the river from view. "And don't hang on to me so tightly," she added, prying at the fingers clamped in a steel-like grip around her waist. "I won't let you fall."

"I know *you* won't," Penny assured her, eyes closed, her body molded against the one in front of her, and her arms wrapped around Rebecca as if she were clinging to life itself. "I'm just not too sure about the horse."

A smile creased Rebecca's cheek, and she was about to reply when the faint sound of men's voices drifted up from the river bank. She yanked back on the reins to bring the horse to a stop and motioned at Penny to keep quiet. Had she been alone on the mare, Rebecca wouldn't have worried about her safety. But Penny wasn't skilled at riding bareback, and the double weight the horse had to carry would slow them down. It was best, therefore, that they stand perfectly still until the danger had passed.

"What is it?" Penny whispered.

Rebecca pointed toward the river, then pressed a finger against her lips to silence her companion.

"Who do you suppose they are?" Penny persisted, unaware of how easily her voice could carry in the still night air.

Reaching back over her shoulder, Rebecca clamped her hand over Penny's mouth. Maybe now she'd understand. She didn't.

"If you're scared," Penny hissed once she had knocked Rebecca's hand away, "then why don't we run for it?"

"Because they don't know we're here," Rebecca snarled. "At least they didn't!"

"But—"

"It doesn't matter who they are. The point is we're two women alone." She twisted to look Penny in the eye. "Get my meaning?"

A frown wrinkled Penny's face, and she nodded, knowing exactly what Rebecca meant.

Although she couldn't actually see the men, Rebecca recognized the sounds of oars stroking the water and could only conclude that the men had chosen to travel by boat. What drew her brows together thoughtfully was their reason for doing so at night. Shaded on both sides by tall, thick trees, the surface of the river darkened long before the sun went completely down, making the journey upstream that much more difficult. Only a fool or a— A chilling thought struck her, and without explaining to Penny, she quickly slid off the horse and tiptoed closer to the river's edge where she hid herself behind a huge tree to watch and listen in on their conversation. It surprised her to see three boats filled with boxes and crates and a dozen men or so.

303

"I'm tellin' ya he ain't gonna be expectin' us this soon," one of the men in the first group vowed. "We're a day early."

"So what would ya have us do?" his companion snarled. "Take a room at Raleigh Tavern? You idiot, we can't be seen. Someone would start askin' questions. And you can bet your share of the profits, ol' Blackstock wouldn't even know who we are. He'd let us rot in gaol before he'd put himself at risk."

Mouth agape, Rebecca fell against the tree and quietly slid to the ground. So that was how Gideon Blackstock made his money. He was a smuggler! That certainly explained his sudden wealth a year ago when he purchased all those slaves. And it explained why he didn't want anyone poking his nose in where it didn't belong. He couldn't take the chance of being found out just to learn who killed Eli.

"Well, Mr. Blackstock," she whispered, "that leaves you in the clear." A disgruntled frown darkened her eyes. "And it leaves Alec and me right back where we started."

Chapter Thirteen

"I don't see why you're so angry," Rebecca snapped as she knelt before the hearth, stoking the fire. "Nothing happened, and I found out what we needed to know."

"At the risk of your own life," Alec pointed out. "And if that wasn't bad enough, you insisted Penny go with you."

"Would you have preferred I go alone?" she hissed irritated that he wouldn't at least, thank her for what she'd done.

Wincing from the pain in his shoulder when he moved too quickly, Alec forced himself to rest back against the wall as he sat on the foot of his cot. "I would have preferred *no one* went," he replied as calmly as he could manage. "It could have waited until I was well enough to check into it myself."

Rising, Rebecca dusted off her hands and gave him a scalding look. "Are you saying you could have done better?"

Alec drew in a breath to correct her misinterpretation and changed his mind. Winning a point with Rebecca Wilde when she had her mind set was just about as difficult as keeping a ship on course in the midst of a gale. If she didn't want to hear it, she wouldn't, and he truly didn't have the strength to argue with her.

After her abrupt departure earlier, Alec had wanted to go after her. In truth he had pushed himself up from the bed and staggered to the door, hoping he could stop her before she rode off since he knew what she was planning. But that simple trek exhausted his strength, and he had been powerless to deter her from going. He had spent most of the time worrying and cursing his inability to do for himself. He hated being so weak that it left him vulnerable to any circumstance he came across, and his rage only seemed to worsen his disposition as well as tire him out all the more.

He had napped for a short while then managed to find something to eat and even wash his face and hair. He would have liked to shave and change his clothes, but since all of his things were still back in his room at The Red Lion, he'd had to be content with donning the shirt Rebecca had washed and mended for him. That little bit of exercise had chased him back to bed, but it had also helped keep his mind off Rebecca and what she was doing.

By the time the sun had disappeared and left the cabin in darkness save the flickering light of the dying fire in the hearth, Alec feared the worst had happened, and he had unwittingly sat on the cot with one knee drawn up, his arm draped across it and his face the expression of anguish, both mental and physical. He stared blankly at the wall opposite him while his mind defiantly conjured up images of how Rebecca's fate had been decided. He had never been a religious man—while growing up and watching the way his mother suffered, he'd doubted there was a supreme being—but at that moment, he found himself asking God's help in keeping Rebecca safe from harm. What surprised him more than realizing he was actually praying was the reason why he found it necessary. And that reason truly unsettled him. Aside from Lora Stone, no one else in his life had ever meant anything to him. Although he had loved his mother, he honestly doubted what he felt for Rebecca could be called the same thing. He felt responsible for her and that if anything happened to her it would be his fault, but he simply couldn't believe he loved her. He had imagined that that kind of love would leave a man feeling all tingly inside, that his thoughts would constantly be filled with visions of her, that he would live each day wanting to be near her, to hear her voice, see her face. He enjoyed Rebecca's company, and their moments in bed were quite exquisite, but he couldn't see spending the rest of his life with her. They were too different. If they weren't making love, they'd be arguing. A twinge of pain had stabbed at his shoulder then, reminding him of why and how he had come to be sitting alone in this cabin, thankful to be alive and who was responsible for that fact. It was Rebecca, that rebellious, high-spirited, sharp-tongued vixen named Rebecca Wilde.

Brought out of his musing by the sensation that someone stood beside the cot, Alec quickly masked the perplexed expression he was sure showed on his face and looked up at her.

"Well?" she asked again. "Are you implying you could have done any better?"

Studying the fiery spark in her blue eyes for a moment longer, he awkwardly pushed himself up from the bed and crossed to the bucket of water sitting on the cupboard where he scooped out a dipper full and took a drink. "No. I'm not," he finally replied, setting aside the ladle and turning for one of the chairs sitting around the table. "The result would have been the same." He sat down and lifted brown eyes to look at her. "What I meant, Rebecca, was that it was my responsibility to question Blackstock, not yours. None of this concerns you." He quickly raised a hand to silence her when she sucked in an outraged breath to debate the issue. "It was *my* money someone stole. It was *my* agent they killed. *I'm* the one who got shot. Your only connection was that Eli had been a friend. I don't think he would have approved of your risking your neck on a hunch any more than I did. You can't change the fact that he's dead. And finding out who killed him won't bring Eli back. So what difference would it have made if you had waited a day or two? None. That's all I meant, Reb. I wanted you to wait. I wanted to go with you, to be there in case someone—"

"To protect me," she cut in. "You're saying I can't take care of myself, is that it?"

Alec closed his eyes and dropped his head forward to rub his brow and consider just how he should answer her. "If that's what you want to believe," he said after a while, "then

307

I can't stop you." Rising, he headed back toward the cot. "It's a shame, Rebecca," he added once he had lain down with his ankles crossed and his head resting back on his arm tucked behind him for a pillow, his eyes staring up at the ceiling above him, "that you have to be so mule-headed. You might not be so unhappy if you allowed someone to care what happened to you. There are times when we all need a friend." Closing his eyes, he settled himself more comfortably on the straw mattress and quietly bid her good night. He had said all he was going to say on the subject, and as far as he was concerned—for Reb's well being, anyway—the matter of his agent's death and where his money had gone was closed. From this point on, Rebecca was out of it. If he was to learn the truth, he'd do it on his own.

Morning dawned clear and bright, and for the first time since his injury, Alec felt good enough to insist he return to Williamsburg. Rebecca argued the point, saying that he was still too weak to care for himself, but Alec disagreed. By returning to his room at The Red Lion, he would be able to sleep more comfortably on a feather bed and enjoy the luxury of three hot meals a day, which he was sure Penny would gladly serve to him in bed. The insinuation behind that remark—though Rebecca knew Penny would never do something like that to her friend—hurt Rebecca very deeply. It was his subtle way of telling her that what they had shared no longer meant anything to Alec, that he was ready to move on. She should have been grateful he felt that way since it was what she had planned as well—he would leave, and they'd never see or think of each other again—but just the same the mere idea that another could so easily take her place tugged at her heart and threatened to fill her eyes with tears. What she didn't know was Alec's real reason for saying it.

The closeness of the small, one-room cabin had started to close in on Alec. It reminded him of home, his mother, her death, and the fact that he shared the privacy with the one woman who had turned his life upside down. Even though his shoulder was stiff and ached a great deal, he found himself more concerned with his desires to pull Rebecca down on the narrow cot with him. If they didn't go their separate ways and soon, he feared the wild passion she stirred in him would cloud his mind and distort his reasoning. And Rebecca deserved better than that. She was meant to be loved, to marry and have children, to live out her life knowing what it was like to be happy, truly happy. They would say their good-byes and get on with their lives . . . the way they should be lived.

"I want you to stay here for as long as you like," he quietly told her once he had awkwardly climbed into the saddle and sat looking down at her while she stood in the opened cabin doorway. "The property and house belong to me, and since I feel partly to blame for your dilemma, it would ease my conscience knowing you had a place to stay." Noticing what he thought might be tears shining in her eyes, he steeled himself against the urge to go to her and sweep her up in his arms. Drawing in a long breath of cool, fresh air, he turned his head to stare, unseeing, at the road. "Thank you, Reb, for all you've done for me. There haven't been many in my life who would have given my problems a second thought, let alone give up everything to help solve them. I truly can't count a handful as my friends, but of those I do—" he shifted his attention back on her—"of those I can, your name will always come first. Good-bye, Rebecca Wilde." He thought he saw her chin tremble, and his strong will crumbled a little. If only he could explain. . . .

"Good-bye, Alec Stone," she replied, her voice hardly more than a whisper. She wanted to tell him that what she had done for him hadn't been done out of friendship or concern or anything else along those lines. She wanted to tell him it had been a part of her job, that the mystery surrounding Eli's death and Daniel Heller's disappearance offered the best story of her life and that she would have done *anything* to report it. But deep down inside she knew that was a lie. She also knew she couldn't tell him the truth. If she opened her mouth right now, nothing would come out.

She was already struggling with her tears. Unless she deliberately went to see him at The Red Lion, *this* would be the end of it; once he rode off, she'd never see him again. Mustering up all the courage she could find, she forced a smile, waved farewell and went inside the cabin. The sound of the horse's hooves against the dried earth as the mare started down the lane reverberated in her ears, and she angrily clamped her hands to the sides of her head to block out the message of his departure, her eyes closed and tears streamed down her face.

You'll be all right, she silently vowed. *You'll get through this. A week from now you'll have forgotten all about him.*

Yet, once she had gathered a small measure of composure and opened her eyes, the room began to spin; and before she could reach out a hand to grab the back of a chair and steady her balance, blackness claimed her vision, and she slumped, unconscious, to the floor.

With each new day that dawned Alec grew stronger. The wound in his shoulder and the gash on his head had healed nicely, and he was able to leave his room and eat downstairs in the commons by the second day. He hadn't seen Reb since leaving the cabin that morning, and although he was tempted to ride out and pay her a visit just to see how she was doing, he didn't. Nor did he allow himself the benefit of asking Penny about her. They had said all that needed to be said, and spending even a moment more with each other would ruin the uncomplicated break they had already made. Yet despite his conviction, thoughts of her continued to haunt him.

A lot had happened to him during his stay in Williamsburg, so much so that while he shaved and donned fresh clothes, he suddenly realized that he had forgotten about Geoffrey Synder and the *Constance*. They were due to sail into port any time soon, and rather than worry his good friend, Alec decided that once he had finished breakfast, he'd ride out to the pier. He had also come to the conclusion that it was best he packed up his things and moved into one of the other inns. He simply couldn't risk seeing Rebecca, and with Penny living and working at The Red Lion, it was a strong possibility.

"Does this mean you're going home, Mr. Diamond?" Ben had asked later when Alec requested a bill for his lodgings and the meals he had eaten.

"Soon," Alec had replied, deliberately avoiding a more definite answer. Ben was sure to tell Penny that Alec had left The Red Lion, which meant she'd tell Rebecca, and he'd feel better thinking they had drawn the wrong conclusion.

Although Alec ususally preferred his privacy, the bustling activity at Raleigh Tavern promised to help keep his mind off the dull ache in his heart. It also gave him hope that someone in the crowded commons might know something that would interest him. Since Reb, Penny and their friend Jon-Gregory had kept their word and not revealed Alec's true identity to anyone, he felt safe in continuing his search for the culprit behind all of Alec's problems. Having paid for his room in advance and after carefully putting away his things, he picked up his tricorn and cane and headed for the stable where he had taken the mare.

It surprised Alec to actually feel invigorated riding horseback all the way to the wharf since he normally chose the comfort of a carriage with thick leather seats. The only conclusion he could come up with was that he appreciated just being alive. The vision of the dark-haired beauty who had helped him stay that way tormented his thoughts, and he quickly pushed it aside. She was a part of his past now, and it never did anyone any good to dwell on anything other than the present. And right now he had to contact Geoffrey Synder.

His instincts told him that he should board the *Constance* and go home, that he should consider the loss of his money as a very costly lesson. But as always his honor stood in the way of common sense. And he wanted revenge—for Heller's death and against the man stupid enough to steal from Alec Stone. Readjusting his tricorn down over the frown that marred his brow, Alec set his attention on the busy wharf once it came into view, his gaze quickly taking in the sight of the huge frigate anchored at the end of the long pier, the number of men unloading its cargo and the fact that it wasn't the *Constance*.

"Good morning, Mr. Diamond," Thomas Keenan gleefully called out to him while Alec reined the mare in alongside the hitching rail and dismounted. "Haven't seen you in a while. Thought maybe ya left Williamsburg."

"I take that to mean the *Constance* hasn't docked in the last few days?" Alec asked, rather than give Keenan an explanation he didn't deserve.

"No, sir. This here's the only one this week," Keenan replied with a jerk of his head toward the ship his men were tending. "Why? Was ya expectin' her to dock?"

Alec shifted his attention on the dark waters of the bay as if half expecting to see his frigate gliding toward shore. "Yes. I'm just not sure when." He looked back at Keenan again. "Could I trust you to get a message to her captain should the *Constance* drop anchor when I'm not here?"

"Part of my job, Mr. Diamond." Keenan beamed proudly. "You're gonna be shippin' goods here, aren't ya?"

Alec hid the smile that threatened to part his lips. He truly disliked the sort who'd say or do anything to win favor in a man's eyes—especially if that man was wealthy . . . like Alec. "Just tell him that I'm staying at Raleigh Tavern and that I'd like to speak with him."

"Yes, sir," Keenan answered enthusiastically. "You can count on me."

Suddenly realizing that Geoffrey would have no idea who Keenan meant when he told him Mr. Diamond wanted to see him, since Alec had chosen the name *after* the *Constance* had set sail, he quickly changed his instructions. "No. Perhaps it's better if you just send one of your men for me. I gave the captain orders not to leave the ship." He could see the puzzlement in Keenan's eyes and went on to explain, "We're not looked on with much respect from the British, if you know what I mean. Captain Synder has orders to weigh anchor should a British ship sail into port."

"Ohhh," Keenan sang. "I get it. I guess being neutral has its drawbacks, huh?"

A faint smile sparkled in Alec's brown eyes. "You could say that," he agreed, remembering his earlier days when *he* captained the *Constance* and how many times he had cheated King George by smuggling goods into England. His only regret was that he hadn't been a part of the excitement last December in Boston. He would have truly enjoyed disguising himself in feathers and war paint and helping the patriots dump English tea in the harbor—not because he necessarily agreed with the rebellion, but simply because it pleased him to tweak the royal nose of Britain's ruler.

He thanked Keenan for his help, told him that he'd wait around the docks for a while on the chance his ship might sail into port, and excused himself from the man's presence. The warm sunshine on his face felt good, and the fresh sea breeze helped clear the fog from his brain as he idly walked toward the pier. He had never really liked being forced to stay inside, no matter what the reason—business, storms, illness and the like—and while he stood savoring that odd sense of freedom he got by simply being in the open, he absently watched the activity going on around him. Keenan's men worked quickly and efficiently as they stacked the crates and boxes into flatbed wagons bound for one of the general stores in Williamsburg. Witnessing how effectively they handled the merchandise with a minimum of debate and fewer accidents convinced Alec that he had made a wise choice in electing to expand his trade to include Williamsburg. He also concluded that if John Greenhow wasn't able to buy all Alec could ship him, then he'd seek out other merchants in Richmond. The James River would supply an easy method of delivering the goods rather than by wagons, which practically guaranteed to raise the risk of damage. Once he finished up his business here, perhaps he'd take the time to go to Richmond and check out the prospects.

He was rudely jolted out of his musings when a broad, well-muscled shoulder struck him squarely in the back and nearly knocked him off his feet. A quick hand on Alec's arm saved him from stumbling to the ground, and the intruder's immediate apology cooled Alec's temper over the man's clumsiness and helped soothe the sharp pain their collision had induced in Alec's sore shoulder.

"I hope I didn't hurt you, friend," the tall, dark-haired stranger vowed once he saw the way Alec clutched his arm. "I'm afraid I wasn't watching where I was going." A warm and sincere smile stretched his lips, and his dark eyes sparkled once he'd been assured his apology had been accepted. "Too anxious to stand on solid ground again," he admitted, jerking his head back in the direction of the frigate moored to the pier. "Been at sea too long, I guess. Forgot my manners as well." A concerned frown appeared the instant he realized that Alec continued to hold his arm tightly against his chest. "You sure you're all right?"

Ordinarily Alec would have cut the conversation short and moved on, since he'd never lain eyes on this man before today and Alec never trusted strangers. But something about his easygoing manner and the sincerity in his voice tempted Alec to make an exception. "Yes, I'm fine. This happened several days ago." He nodded at his shoulder. "And there's really no need to apologize. I shouldn't have been standing in the middle of the walkway. A wise man would choose to do his thinking where it's safe."

"You know, I'm always telling my brother the same thing." The stranger laughed. "Only it's more like, thinking never gets you anywhere except deeper into trouble . . . or mischief, depending on your reasons." He frowned, though it had a playful curl to the way it drew his brows together. "Or is it Dane who's always saying that to me?" He shrugged as if totally confused, then tapped the brim of his tricorn with a fingertip as he repeated, "Again, my apologies, sir, and if we run into each other again, I hope it isn't as painful."

Before Alec had a chance to reply, the man bowed slightly and stepped around him on his way to Thomas Keenan's office. Turning, Alec watched him walk away and took a minute to appraise the stranger's tall, muscular build, the

314

fine cut of his clothes, and the way he carried himself with a sure and somewhat cocky air. He might have just stepped off the ship, but he certainly didn't look like a sailor. Alec raised one brow and smiled softly, thinking that he, too, didn't look like the type to have ever sailed the seas.

Maybe that's because it wasn't really what I wanted to do, he mused. *I'd rather find whatever it takes to bring peace into my life so that I can live out the rest of my days quietly.*

Unconsciously thumbing the ring on his little finger, he was silently wondering if learning his father's identity was enough to still the restlessness in his soul when, for some unexplainable reason, the image of Rebecca Wilde came to mind. He straightened, scowled darkly and, cursing beneath his breath, jerked around and headed for the place where he had left the mare.

Alec paid the courthouse a second visit that afternoon in the hope of uncovering another clue that would lead him to his money, a subtle hint that would send him in the right direction. However, if his guess that the county clerk had been a part of the hoax was correct, it also meant that the dead man had probably covered up any reference to his partner, and right now Alec was sure there had to have been at least two, possibly three people involved. He simply couldn't believe Daniel Heller could have been that easily tricked. A search through the records and a short, guarded conversation with the young man at the counter awarded Alec nothing, and he set off toward John Greenhow's store feeling a bit defeated and frustrated.

Later, as he took a seat at one of the few empty tables in the commons of Raleigh Tavern, his curiosity about Daniel Heller's trip to Williamsburg brought a frown to his brow. Ordering his supper, he settled back in his chair to think. He'd had the good fortune to run into Jon-Gregory, once he had finished his business with Greenhow, and although he had intended only to be polite and return the young man's greeting before leaving the place, Jon-Gregory wouldn't let

315

him. Motioning for Alec to follow him, Jon-Gregory led him around in back of the building where they wouldn't be overheard and quietly asked if Penny had told him the interesting bit of news Jon-Gregory had learned about Heller. Since Alec hadn't talked to Penny in several days, he suggested the young man repeat it, and once Alec heard that no one in town had heard of Daniel Heller or rented him a room in all the while he supposedly stayed in Williamsburg, Alec had to agree with Jon-Gregory that it raised a whole new angle to Heller's disappearance and subsequent death. They discussed various possibilities to explain the mysterious aspect of Heller's lodgings, concluding that perhaps Alec might have misinterpreted the man's letters or that whoever was behind the deception had fed and housed Heller until it became necessary to do away with him. Jon-Gregory liked that idea and volunteered to ask more questions since he realized Alec wouldn't be able to do it himself. Alec thanked Jon-Gregory for his willingness to help, but insisted he not get involved any further than he already had. If the culprit had murdered one man to hide what he'd done, he wouldn't hesitate to do so again. The return of his money wasn't worth the cost of another man's life. Then Jon-Gregory said something that reluctantly changed Alec's mind.

"You realize, of course, that Rebecca won't stop until she's figured this out, don't you?" he asked. "You'd have to bind and gag her and lock her up somewhere to stop her. But then Penny would only let her loose again, and you'd wind up having to worry about them both. I'm simply offering my help as a way to protect Rebecca. I figure if you and I can settle this matter by working together on it rather than just you, we might have it taken care of before anything could happen to that hardheaded, little spitfire."

Alec had smiled at the young man's choice of words in describing Reb and agreed that he was right . . . on all counts. However, there would be a few conditions before Alec would give his full consent. First, Rebecca was never to know he and Jon-Gregory had talked this over. Nor was she to learn that he was helping Alec. The third provision was a bit tricky. Alec wanted Jon-Gregory to spy . . . on Rebecca. In order to keep her safe, they had to know what she was up to, and the best way to accomplish that was for Jon-Gregory to pretend allegiance to her. If she asked his help in any way or gave him information that would benefit Alec, he was to come to Raleigh Tavern where Alec was staying. These rules, of course, applied to Penny as well since Alec felt the girl's friendship was stronger than any loyalty Penny might have toward him. Jon-Gregory had given his guarantee to do as Alec requested and backed it up with a firm handshake. Alec had started to walk away then, pleased with the prospect of having this taken care of sooner than if he'd had to do it alone, when Jon-Gregory touched his arm and brought his attention back on the young man's boyish good looks.

"I'm sure I haven't been told everything," he confessed, his tone quite serious and a look of brotherly concern darkening his gray-blue eyes, "nor am I asking to be told. But I sense a lot happened between you and Rebecca, and I think you should know that she's special to me. It's the reason I'm willing to stick my neck out. It's also the reason why I feel I should tell you that I wouldn't look kindly on it if you hurt her in any way."

Alec had recognized the subtle threat, but rather than be angered by it, he had smiled appreciatively. "She's special to me, too, Jon-Gregory, and because she is, I can tell you that I'd never do anything to deliberately hurt her. In fact, once this mess is cleared up, I'll be going home." He had gone on to tell him that that was the real reason he had taken a room at Raleigh Tavern and why he had avoided seeing both Penny and Rebecca . . . and why he had been hesitant in accepting the young man's help. He had wanted Rebecca's life to return to normal, and that meant not having Alec around to complicate matters. Jon-Gregory had seemed to understand and more importantly approve, though he hadn't actually said anything. Alec had seen it in his eyes and the soft smile that broke the hard line of his mouth.

They had parted then and Alec had come here to the tavern to have supper and reflect on the events of his short stay in Williamsburg. He hoped those to come would be less turbulent and that he'd be going home soon. But that notion oddly saddened him, and he deliberately turned his attention on the couple sitting at the table next to him, hoping to clear his thoughts of the young woman who constantly disrupted his peace of mind.

He assumed the man and woman were married by the comfortable way they talked and laughed together, and from the looks of them, he guessed they were old enough to have grandchildren by now. Their style of clothing hinted they had wealth, and he wondered if they were residents of Williamsburg or just visitors. Whatever their background, he decided, they appeared quite happy with each other, and he found himself envying their oneness. Until the death of his mother, he had never fully realized how truly alone he was. He had no one with whom to share his excitement, his sorrow, his tragedies, his innermost secrets. He had never trusted anyone to that extent, and oddly enough, as he sat by quietly observing this couple, he wished he had . . . or at least that he could come to learn to trust someone. He knew he was bitter about his childhood, about growing up with only his mother's love and being denied even the honor of knowing who his father was. Lora Stone must have had a good reason for not telling him, but he would never understand what it was. What harm could have come from it? If his father was already married, Alec wasn't the type to just suddenly appear on the man's doorstep. Lora had taught him differently. He respected a man's privacy, . . . just as he expected his own to be respected. All he truly wanted to know was *why* the man had abandoned his son. He wanted to understand how *anyone* could pretend his own flesh and blood never existed. *He* could never do it.

A new thought struck him, and he frowned. Maybe his father didn't know about him. Maybe Lora never told him. Was that possible? Heaving a long sigh, he braced an elbow on the table and cradled his forehead with his fingertips, eyes closed. It was quite possible. Lora had kept the man's identity from Alec for twenty-seven years. She certainly could have kept the birth of her son a secret from the man who sired him. And what if that was the reason he never came around? Would that have changed things? If his father had learned about Alec's existence some other way, would the man have tried to contact him? The lines in his brow deepened with his resignation. It was something on which he could only speculate. Lora was dead. There was no way of ever finding out.

Opening his eyes, he was compelled to look at the couple sitting near him again, and he suddenly imagined them to be *his* mother and father and why they were here at the inn. Their children were grown and living their own lives, and they now had time for each other. Maybe they were even celebrating the anniversary of their wedding. A soft smile played upon his lips with that thought. Had his father married Lora, Alec might have had brothers and a sister or two. He, himself, might be married with children of his own. The image of Rebecca flared up in his mind's eye, and he blinked, the idea of the two of them settling down together sending a chill up his spine. If that were the case, would there ever be a day in his life when he didn't sport a black eye or some other bruise because of her? He wanted to dismiss the idea from his head, but instead continued to ponder the possibilities. Maybe some of her wildness would fade if she were married. The responsibility of a husband and home would fill her hours and use most of her energy. And if there were a baby to care for, well. . . .

Sweet Mother of God, he moaned silently. *What the hell is the matter with me? Rebecca Wilde is nothing but trouble, and you know it! Yet you continually allow yourself to think about her as if there's a future in it!* Gritting his teeth, he snarled and angrily shifted his chair in a direction that put his back to the unsuspecting couple who, he felt, had brought it all on. But in doing so, he presented himself with a clear view of the barmaid serving drinks to a group of men, a redhead with freckles. Just seeing her reminded him of Penny, and that in turn made him think of Reb. Moaning, he shook his head and closed his eyes again. If only he could finish up his business here and leave, he'd soon put the incident behind him and get on with his life. Or would he? She had carved a notch in his very existence, and he truly doubted there would ever come a day when he wouldn't—in some way—be reminded of her. *Maybe I should strangle her. I couldn't think about her if she were dead,* he mused sarcastically. His upper lip curled. *Oh yes, I would. Her ghost would haunt me. So what do I do about her?* It was a question he wasn't given the time to consider, for in that moment the sound of something hitting the table top jolted him out of his thoughts, and he opened his eyes, frowning at the tricorn he saw lying there.

"I thought I'd give you fair warning this time," the deep voice beside him said, and Alec glanced up to find the stranger from the docks smiling back at him. "You seemed to be deeply engrossed in something, and I figured if I touched your arm, you'd more than likely take a swing at me without first bothering to ask what I wanted. Not that I don't deserve some sort of retaliation for what happened back there at the pier. However, I've always been opposed to pain . . . especially my own." He grinned broadly and held out his hand. "The name's Brad Remington, and was wondering if I might share your table. The place is a little busy, and I'm very hungry."

The man would never know just how grateful Alec was for the interruption. It was all he needed to get his mind off Reb. He quickly rose to his feet and took Brad's hand. "Alec Diamond, and I'd welcome the company." He nodded at the chair opposite him.

"From Jamaica?" Brad asked as he watched Alec sit down again while taking his own place across the table from him.

Alec nodded with a puzzled frown. There weren't many in town who knew that.

"Thomas Keenan," Brad explained, smiling. "The man loves to tell me all about my competition. And I try to tell him that there's enough business to go around for twenty more suppliers." A devilish twinkle lit up his brown eyes, and

320

he quickly glanced over one shoulder then the other and leaned in to add, "The fool actually thinks that's all that matters to me."

Remington's lighthearted nature was infectious. "And it's not?" Alec asked, his throat tight with laughter.

They were interrupted for a moment when the barmaid set down two mugs of ale and waited while Brad ordered his meal. Once she had left them alone again, Brad pulled out a cheroot, offered it to Alec, who declined, and lit it for himself. "Nothing better than a good cigar," he sighed, watching the white smoke curl above his head. "And no, running supplies up and down the coast isn't what excites me."

Alec rarely liked a man until after he'd had time to get to know him. Brad Remington's case was different, and he'd be horribly disappointed if he found out later that his first impression had been wrong. "I'm almost afraid to ask," Alec teased as he raised the mug to his lips. "What really excites you?"

Brad cocked a brow and peered over at him through a haze of white. "Aside from a robust, willing wench?" he countered, his dark eyes sparkling. The humor faded while he intently studied the man sitting across from him as if measuring his worth or trying to decide whether or not he could be trusted. He flicked the ash off the end of his cigar into the dish sitting in the middle of the table and picked up his drink. "Living in Jamaica must mean you haven't an interest in the Colonies' problems, I suppose."

"I do when it affects my trade," Alec easily revealed. "But if you're asking if I'd pick up a musket and fight—for either side—the answer is no. The people of England never did me any favors when I was growing up, and I have no ties with the Colonies." Pale blue eyes and raven-black hair clouded his vision of the man listening to him. He blinked it away and took another drink of ale.

"Where in England?"

"Near London."

"Really?" Brad replied with a grin. "So did I. Or I should

321

say my brother and I grew up there."

Suddenly the Remington name held more importance than it had a moment ago. "The Wrenhaven Estate?"

"Yes," Brad excaimed. "Don't tell me we were neighbors."

"Not exactly," Alec corrected. Although Wrenhaven wasn't far from the cottage he shared with his mother, Alec would never fool himself into thinking they were neighbors, not by his definition. No one from Brad's family ever paid them a visit, and the Stone's kept their respectable distance. Those of wealth never mixed with those who had nothing. "One wouldn't have to be a neighbor to have heard of Wrenhaven."

Brad chuckled and took another drink. "Yes, I must admit it was quite a place." The smile disappeared from his lips. "I miss seeing it."

"How long has it been since you were there?"

Brad shrugged his wide shoulders. "Years. I've lost track of how many."

The barmaid appeared then with their meal, refilled their mugs, flirted a moment or two with Brad and then left. In the short time the two teased each other, Alec got the impression that Brad Remington wasn't a stranger to Williamsburg and voiced that observation while they ate.

"I don't really call any place home now. I have a cousin who owns a plantation a day's ride north of here, and my brother and his wife live in Philadelphia with their three sons. I guess you could say I live on my ship when I'm not spending time with Beau or Dane."

"Have you considered going back to Wrenhaven?"

"Can't," Brad replied, cutting his meat into bite-size pieces. "After our father died, we sold the estate and came here. Besides, I don't think I'd be too welcome in England anymore."

Smiling, Alec wiped his mouth with his napkin. "I know what you mean. I was never one of her favorite sons. That's why I chose to live in Jamaica."

"Are you married?"

322

The vision of Rebecca with golden sunlight shining in her hair crossed his mind, but this time he wasn't so quick to push it away. "No. Being tied to one woman doesn't really interest me."

"You like variety, is that it? Kinda like me, I suppose." Brad chuckled.

Alec shook his head. "No, it's nothing like that. I'm just too busy to get involved right now. I have some matters to settle before I think about marriage. And I'm not really sure I'll want to even then. I don't think I have the temperament to put up with a woman's moods."

Brad wrinkled up his face. "Oo-o-o. Sounds like you've been burned."

"Burned?" Alec laughed. "That's not quite the right word for it. I *tangled* with one who nearly beat my brains in for something I said."

Brad's attention was momentarily drawn to the newcomers entering through the front door of the inn. "Reminds me of someone I know," he absently replied as he watched the group of men take a table in the back. Their arrival disturbed him, although they seemed not to have noticed his presence. He carefully watched them a moment longer before he settled his gaze back on his companion again. He wasn't in the mood for trouble, and since he'd lost his appetite, he decided to cut short his conversation with Alec and pay Patrick Henry a visit before going to his room. Picking up his napkin from his lap, Brad wiped the corner of his mouth with it then laid it aside, concentrating on what had been said before the men entered the tavern. "She's a pretty, little thing, but take my advice, friend. If you ever have the occasion to meet Rebecca Wilde, don't waste a second running the other way."

Alec couldn't stop the smile that parted his lips, and Brad didn't miss it.

"Don't tell me you've already had the honor?" he moaned, falling back in his chair.

"I'm afraid so," Alec admitted with a chuckle as he lifted the mug to his lips. "I met her the first night I arrived."

Unable to think of any comforting words, Brad just sat there, open-mouthed and staring. Finally, he shook his head. "And I suppose that means you've met her friend, Penelope Dawson?"

Alec nodded. "They're quite a pair."

"*I'll* say," Brad agreed, finishing off his ale. "Insult one and it's the same as insulting the other. I ought to know. I made that fatal mistake . . . once."

He got a faraway look in his eye then, one Alec noticed right away. But rather than question him about it since it really wasn't any of Alec's business, he pretended to be enjoying the last of his ale.

"Well, Alec Diamond," Brad announced suddenly, "I thank you for allowing me to share your table and for the company. But I've got to pay a friend a visit before it gets too late." He pushed back his chair, stood and extended his hand. "Hope we have a chance to talk again."

Rising, Alec accepted the man's warm handshake. "Me too," he replied. He remained standing while he watched Brad walk away and wave a friendly farewell to the barmaid before he made his exit from the place. If someone had told Alec as a child that someday he'd meet a man like Brad Remington and that they'd actually have something in common, Alec wouldn't have believed it. They came from two very different backgrounds, the kind that set men apart. But Brad wasn't like all the other arrogant aristocrats Alec had met over the years. Wealth didn't seem to matter to him when it came to making friends. *That* was a sobering thought, one that crimped Alec's brow and lowered him back into his chair. He hardly knew Brad Remington, and he was already considering the man as a friend.

Overwhelmed by the discovery, he smiled, shook his head and reached for his ale only to find the mug empty. Disappointed, since the first one had gone down so easily and had tasted exceptionally good, he raised the mug in the air to catch the barmaid's eye. In that same moment, he noticed that an argument had broken out among the group of men at one of the tables near the back. He was too far away to hear much of what they said nor did he truly care, but in all appearances it seemed one man was being held back when he tried to leave the table. He complained that his cohorts didn't care that his brother's murderer had just walked out of the tavern since the dead man was no kin of theirs, but that he wasn't about to let Remington get away with it.

As the argument grew in volume, the other patrons quieted down, and Alec turned his gaze away from the men simply because he didn't want any of them to think he was interested in their conversation. It was then he noticed that Brad hadn't finished his meal before departing and that he had seemed to be in a hurry to leave. Maybe he truly wanted to visit his friend as he had said he did, but Alec rather doubted that that was all there was to it. He had seen Brad's reaction, his clandestine interest in the men when they walked in. He hadn't thought much of it then, but now he understood why Brad had covertly watched them . . . and why he chose to make a hurried exit. Only a fool would take on a crowd.

Brad had only walked the distance of a few hundred feet before he heard the angry voice of a man call out his name. He didn't have to turn around and look to know who it was. Most of his last two visits to Williamsburg had been spent avoiding a confrontation with Elliot Greenwood. The man wanted to kill him even though the constable had told Greenwood that his brother's death had been an accident and he shouldn't blame Brad Remington. After all, the younger Greenwood had tried to rob Brad, and the gentleman had only defended what rightfully belonged to him. But Elliot hadn't seen it that way. Just because a man was hungry and saw no other way to obtain the money he needed to feed himself didn't mean he should die for it. Besides, Remington was rich. He wouldn't have missed the few coins Charlie wanted to steal. In Elliot's eyes Remington was the criminal, and he was going to pay for murdering his brother.

"Turn around, you coward!" Elliot shouted. "Face me like a man."

Unfortunately for Brad, the streets were rather deserted at this hour since nearly everyone else had sat down to eat. Otherwise, he might have tried to ignore Elliot Greenwood by disappearing into a crowd or taking a detour into a nearby store. As it was, he could do nothing but comply. Once he had, he truly regretted not having given his alternatives a little more thought, for there standing only a few yards away was Elliot Greenwood surrounded by four of his friends.

"I don't want any trouble, Greenwood," he said calmly while his gaze quickly took in the scene spread out before him. "What happened between me and your brother was unfortunate, but nothing you can do will bring him back."

"Maybe not," Elliot sneered as he slowly cut the distance separating them in half. "But at least his death will be avenged once I kill you."

"Is that why you had to bring help?" Brad challenged, hoping to shame the man into evening the odds. If Elliot was anything like his brother, he hadn't the courage to face Brad one on one and the result might be different.

Brad had been on his way to visit his cousin that day when Charlie Greenwood ambushed him on an empty stretch of road late in the afternoon. Brad could tell by the way the young man's hand shook as he pointed a pistol at him that he wasn't used to robbing people, and Brad had taken advantage of that. Dismounting in response to Charlie's orders, Brad waited for the boy to move within reach with his hand extended to accept Brad's purse and grabbed the youth's pistol once Charlie's full attention focused on the reward of his effort. In one fluid movement, Brad laid his fist to Charlie's jaw, rending the young man unconscious before he hit the ground. The tragedy came when Charlie's head smashed against a rock in the fall, killing him instantly. Brad truly hadn't meant for that to happen since he never liked killing anyone and had told the constable as much.

"He's just riffraff, Remington," the sheriff had said.

"Don't let it worry you."

The announcement hardly appeased Brad's regret over the matter, but he had managed to put the incident behind him until Charlie's older brother made known his want for revenge. Another would have to die before this was over, and Brad vowed it wouldn't be his body they laid to rest in the church cemetery.

"I don't need help in watching you bleed to death," Elliot snarled, pulling a pistol from his belt.

The black bore zeroed in on Brad's chest, and he cursed his decision to leave his own gun behind on his ship. He had foolishly forgotten about Elliot Greenwood, and that mistake promised to cost him his life. Every muscle in his body turned to granite as he watched Greenwood's thumb cock the hammer.

"Are ya sweatin', Remington?" he sneered, his small eyes squinted half shut. "Ya should be. Say your prayers if ya think that will help, 'cause you're about ta meet your Maker."

"And you'll be second in line," the deep voice behind him guaranteed.

Greenwood's partners quickly scrambled out of the way once they saw the blond-haired stranger standing behind them with his pistol aimed at Elliot. None of them had wanted to be a part of this to begin with, but Elliot had disgraced them into believing they owed it to him and his brother. However, now that they were faced with a threat to their own lives, they felt no obligation to either Greenwood sibling.

"I suggest you carefully release the hammer and lay the pistol down," Alec firmly instructed. "Otherwise you won't be given the opportunity to think about how stupid you are."

Elliot hadn't moved, but he had heard his friends' rapid departure and knew he stood alone. He could only assume the man behind him had a weapon trained on the middle of his back, and although he would have liked to pull the trigger and watch his enemy writhe in agonizing pain once the lead ball tore through his flesh, he had to admit he didn't want to die alongside him. Yet the vision of his little brother lying in a casket clouded his judgment, and he spun around, intending to eliminate Remington's savior first before finishing what he came here to do. It was his plan. However, the stranger wasn't about to comply so easily. The explosion of gunfire pierced the quiet, first one shot then a second close behind it, and once the white puffs of smoke had dissipated, Elliot Greenwood lay facedown on the sidewalk, a puddle of blood slowly encircling his head.

"That was a helluva chance you took back there," Brad finally said after a long silence, while the two men sat sharing a bottle of wine in the commons at Raleigh Tavern.

They hadn't spoken a word to each other in all the time it had taken to summon the constable and the undertaker, explain what had happened and what had brought it about, listen to Greenwood's friends verify the incident and then stand idly by as they watched the dead man's body being put in the back of a two-wheeled cart. Nor had they said anything once the crowd that had gathered had slowly moved on, leaving them alone. If asked, neither Brad nor Alec would have been able to say whose idea it was to return to the tavern, only that they both had apparently thought it was a good idea, for they had concurrently turned and walked that direction without a verbal suggestion.

"You could have been the one loaded in that cart," Brad added, a frown on his face while he stared at the glowing fire in the hearth.

Hiding his smile behind the glass he raised to his lips, Alec replied, "You're welcome." He downed a healthy swallow, then settled his gaze on the man's startled expression. "Isn't that what you're trying to say? Thank you?" He smiled broadly and reached to refill his glass.

"Of course I thank you," Brad replied, his frown deepening. "I'm well aware of the fact that I might not be sitting here right now if it wasn't for you. But what I don't understand is why you did it. We only just met, and Lord knows you don't owe me anything."

What Alec didn't want to tell Brad was that he'd been asking himself that same question for the past ten minutes, and he honestly didn't know the answer. It wasn't his custom to stick his nose in other people's business, especially when the obvious result would lead to someone's death. All he could attribute his blind heroism to was simply that he liked Brad Remington and he couldn't just sit by without doing something when he knew Brad was outnumbered. He took a second drink of the fine wine Brad had ordered and set the glass down.

"I guess I knew I wouldn't sleep well tonight if I had ignored what I knew was going to happen," he said with a shrug as if his choice of action was an everyday occurrence and it meant very little to him.

Brad cocked his head to one side, his expression one of doubt. "You helped so you could get a good night's rest?" he mocked. "Please, Alec. Give me more credit than that. What really made you do it?"

A bright smile parted Alec's lips. "Haven't any idea," he confessed. "And if I had stopped to think that there were five of them and two of us and you without a pistol . . . well, things might have been different." He grinned devilishly. "Let's just say we were both lucky."

Brad's dark eyes stared back at him for a long while. "I'd have to say *I'm* lucky," he softly contradicted. "I was lucky to have run into you on the wharf this afternoon."

"Fate?" Alec teased, making light of Brad's sincerity. For some reason this conversation made him uncomfortable. He'd never done anything like this before, and he wasn't sure if he liked the unfamiliar feeling it aroused. Or was it simply because he didn't understand it? Wishing to change the subject, he picked up his glass and asked how long Brad was planning to stay in Williamsburg.

Although he had to admit that he truly didn't know Alec Diamond all that well, Brad sensed that Alec was having difficulty in accepting Brad's gratitude and decided to let it drop . . . for now. "A few weeks," he answered, while he openly watched his companion in an effort to understand him. "How about you?"

Absently studying the contents in his glass, Alec replied, "I'm not really sure. I'm here looking to buy some property, and that could take a while."

"Good," Brad proclaimed. "Then you'll have time to accept my invitation." He focused his gaze back on the dancing flames in the fireplace.

Alec's tawny brows crimped. "An invitation to what?"

"To spend a few days with me at my cousin's place. You haven't *lived* until you've tasted Cinnamon's cooking." Sensing Alec was about to decline, he rushed on, "I won't take no for an answer. And besides, if anyone in this area knows of property for sale, it's my cousin Beau. So, you'll be doing me a favor and helping yourself at the same time."

Alec took a moment to agree since he didn't want to appear too anxious. It might raise Brad's curiosity when only a second ago he seemed determined to stick to his decision. Yes, he'd be doing Brad a favor since he so obviously wanted to show his appreciation in some way, but little did Brad know that he'd be doing Alec an even bigger favor. With any kind of luck at all, Beau Remington might hold the key that would unlock the door to the mystery Alec so desperately wanted to solve.

Chapter Fourteen

A worried frown drew Penny's coppery brows together as she pulled back on the reins and brought the buggy to a stop near the front door of the cabin. This was the first time she had paid her best friend a visit that Rebecca hadn't heard her coming and met her at the front door. Shading her eyes with one hand, Penny looked up at the bright blue sky overhead as if trying to convince herself that Rebecca was probably still asleep since it was rather early for company. Penny usually waited until mid-morning to leave the Red Lion and Ben alone with the few customers they had at that time of day, but the news she had to tell her friend was too important to postpone for even a couple of minutes, let alone an hour or two. Lifting the hem of her skirts out of the way, Penny stepped down from the buggy and hurried to the cabin's door.

"Rebecca!" she called, letting herself in. "Wait until you hear what happened last . . . night . . . " Her excitement dissolved into surpirse then alarm once she saw Rebecca kneeling on the floor with her head bowed over a bucket. "My God, Rebecca, what's wrong? Are you sick?"

Her answer came in a way Penny would have preferred not to hear; for in that same moment, Rebecca's body tensed, and she retched what little she had in her stomach into the wooden bucket. Penny never had been any good at caring for sick people, but since Rebecca was her friend, she forced herself to try. Rushing over to her, she knelt down next to her and rubbed Rebecca's back.

"Can I do something?" she asked, wishing she had the magic potion that would cure whatever ailed the poor girl.

Reaching for the wet cloth laying on the floor next to her, Rebecca wiped her face and rolled onto one hip. "I'll be all right in a few minutes. I usually am," she confided as she leaned back against the cot, her eyes closed.

Penny's frown deepened. "What do you mean? Have you been sick like this before?"

Rebecca nodded. "For a week now. But it goes away after a while, and I'm fine for the rest of the day." She sighed and managed a weak smile. "I guess I ate something that didn't agree with me."

"For seven days in a row?" Penny scoffed. "I don't think so."

Rebecca's weary blue eyes opened to look at her. "Then what is it?"

Penny thought her friend was only playing with her. The look on her face told her differently. "You really don't know?" she asked hesitantly.

"No," Rebecca replied, her brows cocked suspiciously. "Do you?"

Pushing herself up from the floor, Penny crossed to the hearth where she intended to stoke the fire and heat some water for tea, silently hoping she was wrong. No magic potion would fix what bothered Rebecca. "It depends," she said, purposely keeping her back to her. "Have you been feeling light-headed and dizzy? Perhaps even fainted for no reason?" She prayed the answer would be no.

"Yes," Rebecca told her, remembering the morning she had said good-bye to Alec. "I fainted once, but that was because of Alec."

So is this, Penny mused drily.

"Why do you ask, Penny? What does it mean?"

Willing herself the courage it would take for her to say the words, she turned around and went back to sit on the floor beside her naive, little friend. "I'm afraid, Rebecca," she tenderly began as she reached for Rebecca's hand, "that it means you're going to have a baby."

Eyes wide and her face pale, Rebecca jerked her hand away. "I can't!"

"Well, there's only one way you can't, and that's if you didn't," Penny snapped, irritated by Rebecca's refusal to accept her sympathy. "Are you saying you didn't?"

Rebecca's face flamed a bright red before she was able to scramble to her feet and hurry away. "I mean you're wrong. It wouldn't do for me to be . . . be . . ." Tears flooded her eyes when she realized the shame she had burdened on her unborn child. She knew Penny was right now that she thought about it. The time for her monthly curse had come and gone. "Oh, Penny," she sobbed, "what will I do?"

Bolting to her feet, Penny raced over to envelop her friend in her arms. "Do?" she repeated. "I think that's rather obvious. You'll tell Alec, and the two of you will get married."

"No!" Rebecca exploded, shoving Penny away. "He isn't to find out. *Ever!* I won't tell him, and neither will you."

"Why not, for heaven's sake? He has a right to know."

"No, he doesn't. Besides, he . . . he isn't the father."

Penny burst into laughter. "Who is then? Brad Remington?"

The girl's suggestion not only hurt Rebecca but surprised her. "Whatever made you think of him? He hasn't been around in months, and even if he had, you know he and I don't get along. I'd never—well, it's an insult to even imply there was a chance. *You're* the one who'd like to crawl into bed with him, not me. And it was purely by accident that Alec and I . . . that we . . . oh, damn!" she howled, violently throwing the rag at the cupboard.

"Rebecca, I'm sorry," Penny apologized. "That wasn't what I meant. I was being sarcastic. It was my way of saying that I don't believe for a minute that any other man on the face of this earth could be the father of your child *except* Alec. So don't go trying to tell me otherwise."

Rebecca's lower lip trembled. "But why Brad Remington? You know he flirts with every other woman but me. He thinks I'm a brat. He said so."

Penny couldn't stop the laughter that escaped her lips.

"That's because you're the only woman who won't flirt back. You hurt his ego." Remembering the purpose of her early morning arrival, she reached out for Rebecca's arm and pulled her down on one of the chairs beside the table. "And the reason why his name came to mind is because Elliot Greenwood tried to kill him last night."

"Oh, my God," Rebecca breathed as she rubbed the tears from her face. Her problem suddenly didn't seem as immediate as before. "Is he all right?"

"Yes, thanks to Alec."

"Alec?" she questioned, puzzled. "What did he do?"

Since Penny was sure she didn't have the entire story, she repeated what details had been told to her by several of the customers that morning and finished by saying that someone had seen Alec and Brad ride out of town together shortly after breakfast. It was Penny's guess that they wouldn't be coming back for a while, if at all, since Penny had heard that Alec had taken his things with him. She hadn't meant to be so blunt and hadn't realized the effect it would have on Rebecca until her friend rose suddenly and walked to the window to stare outside.

"It's for the best," Rebecca murmured after a moment.

"The *hell* it is!" Penny stormed, jumping to her feet. "You're carrying his baby, and he deserves to know he's going to be a father, for God's sake. How can you say it's for the best? The two of you have to get married now. *That's* what's for the best."

"No!" Rebecca exploded, spinning around and glaring back at Penny's startled expression. "I don't want to marry him! I don't want to marry anyone. He isn't to know about this, do you hear me? You're *not* to say a word . . . to anyone! I mean it, Penny," she threatened when she saw the challenging look in the girl's eye. "If you breathe a word of this to anyone, I'll run away. There are plenty of other newspapers around where I can find work."

Penny simply couldn't understand Rebecca's hostile determination. "Oh, really? Do you honestly think it'll be easier for you to get a job somewhere else than it was at the *Gazette*? Do you think they'll welcome you—a pregnant you—with open arms? Don't be stupid. And who, might I ask, will take care of you while you're having the baby? You know how they look down on a woman who's about to give birth without the benefit of a husband."

"I'll say I'm a widow," Rebecca declared, her blue eyes brimming with tears and her small frame trembling. "I'll wear my mother's gold wedding ring. Who'd know the difference?"

Penny tilted her head to one side, her arms akimbo. "Oh, I can think of one," she announced.

Rebecca's eyes widened, believing Penny meant herself and that she wouldn't keep it a secret. "You?" she sobbed angrily.

"No, not me," Penny barked. "The baby. Would you continue to lie when the child got old enough to ask questions about his father? Would you deny him the chance to meet Alec? And what about Alec? Have you given any consideration to the chance that maybe Alec would *want* to be a part of raising his son or daughter? Rebecca," she urged when the other turned away from her, "this baby isn't just yours. It belongs to Alec, too. He has a right in helping to decide his child's future. You must tell him."

Rebecca defiantly shook her head. "There's more to it than who has rights or not, don't you see that? *My* life's involved in this, *my* happiness as well as the baby's. Must I offer myself up as a sacrifice just to do what's proper and honorable? Is it written somewhere that a woman must be the only one to suffer?" She slammed the palm of her hand against the table top. "If it is, you can bet a *man* wrote it." She whirled around to face Penny, hot tears streaming down her flushed cheeks. "Well, I won't do it! I won't bow my head and crawl on hands and knees to him, begging him to take me in! I won't! I'd *kill* myself first."

Rebecca's outburst and chilling promise stabbed at Penny's heart and truly frightened her. Mouth agape, for no words would pass her lips, Penny struggled with her emotions. She had never seen her friend so distraught nor could she understand the violence of her refusal to do the right thing for everyone involved. Rebecca was a crusader, a modern day Joan of Arc fighting for a cause, for truth and justice. This simply wasn't like her, and Penny could only hope that once Rebecca had time to think it through, she would do what she knew in heart was right. Blinking back her own tears, Penny slowly crossed the room and tenderly wrapped her arms around Rebecca's quivering body, pulling her closer and softly murmuring words of encouragement.

Alec wasn't sure exactly what he expected to see once he and Brad guided their horses down the lane that would lead them to Raven Oaks, but whatever it was, he soon realized his vision of it fell far short. On each side fields of young cotton and tobacco plants dotted the black soil as they stretched skyward for the bright sunlight that would soon fade into darkness. On the horizon stood a mill, tall and statuesque, while spread out before it were rows upon rows of small, one-room cabins, obviously used by the many slaves and indentured servants Brad had told Alec his cousin used to run the place. Scores of people bustled about with some duty or another to perform, and from the blacksmith shop, the ringing of an anvil filled the air. Alec was quite impressed with the size of Raven Oaks and the amount of money it must have taken to get it that way, and he said so to Brad.

A band of small, barefoot children, their faces smudged with dirt, ran up to greet them as Alec and Brad approached, and many of the workers waved a cheerful greeting to the dark-haired man, who didn't hesitate to return their warm welcome. An odd sense of coming home hit Alec, although he'd never set foot on Raven Oaks before today, and he wondered at the feeling as he watched Brad tease a young, blond-haired girl. These people liked him, and Alec found himself envying the man's good fortune and wishing *he* could be received as enthusiastically. But then Brad Remington had a way about him that invited people to like him, and Alec knew he was too private and cautious to encourage such an outward show of affection . . . from anyone.

The lane veered off to the left suddenly, and at the far end, nestled among a stand of huge, black oak trees, a magnificent two-story, white-pillared mansion came into view. A wide veranda ran the width of the front, and white, wrought-iron furniture sat clustered in groups along the railing. The house radiated a warmth and friendship, and even though Alec had accepted Brad's invitation to spend a few days as his guest for a different reason than Brad had assumed, Alec looked forward to his stay. Greeted by two groomsmen at the end of the sidewalk, Alec and Brad dismounted, and Brad ordered their things taken inside.

"Well, what do you think?" Brad grinned with one hand extended toward the manor. "Not too bad a place to spend a couple of days, is it?"

"Not at all." Alec chuckled.

Brad wiggled his eyebrows. "I just hope we're not late for dinner. It's really the only reason I come here so often. But don't tell Beau. He thinks I come to see him."

Alec doubted any of that was true but elected to keep his thoughts to himself.

Suddenly the front door was hurriedly opened, drawing both men's attention to it, and the most beautiful young girl Alec had ever seen came bounding through it, her long black hair flying out behind her, a bright smile on her lovely face and her arms outstretched as she raced the distance to the man standing next to him.

"Uncle Brad," she shrieked.

"Hello, Victoria." He laughed, catching her up in a strong embrace and whirling her around, her skirts and starched petticoats rustling noisily. "How's my favorite niece?" he teased, giving her a hug and kiss.

"Oh, Uncle Brad," she frowned once he had set her down again. "I'm your *only* niece. How can I be your favorite?"

A big hand flew to his chest as if her question had shocked him. "But of course you are. How silly of me." He wrinkled up his face. "Maybe I should say you're my least favorite niece. Would that be better?"

For being only thirteen years old, Victoria had the charm and grace of a young lady. Her deep brown eyes stared challengingly at him for a moment then narrowed. "I think

Papa's right, Uncle Brad. You *are* a tease. And if you're not careful, *I'll* be the only woman in the world willing to marry you."

Brad threw his hands in the air. "Now don't you suppose that's the reason I'm the way I am? I can't imagine loving anyone more than I love you."

Victoria's cheeks pinkened slightly, and she boldly turned her head to look at the stranger who had silently witnessed their exchange. "He think's I'm playing with him, but I'm not," she confided in Alec. "He's really not my uncle, you know. He's Papa's cousin, and I could marry him if I really wanted. But I'm not really sure anymore. He's getting old."

"Old!" Brad exploded, his dark eyes sparkling as he made a halfhearted grab for the flash of blue satin heading back off toward the house in a rush of giggles. "Come back here, you little imp."

Both men watched her race up the stairs and across the porch, only to come to an abrupt halt when a tall, well-built figure of a man stepped through the doorway and blocked her path.

"Now you're going to get it, Victoria," Brad promised. "Your father's going to tan your hide for being impudent."

Big, brown eyes peeked out from around her father's side as Victoria hid herself protectively behind him.

"Impudent?" Beau questioned, twisting to look at his daughter. "My Victoria?" A smile teased his strong features, and Alec quickly realized that the young girl was safe from any parental guidance Brad would have liked to see her get. "And who do you suppose taught her to be impudent?"

His questioning gaze fell on Brad, and he in turn looked at Alec. "See why I only come here to eat?" he mocked in a loud whisper. "If anything goes wrong, *I'm* the one who gets blamed. Even if I'm not here!" He gave his companion a playful nudge. "Maybe we ought to saddle up and ride back to Williamsburg where we're appreciated."

"No!" Victoria shouted, darting out from behind her father. "Don't go, Uncle Brad. You only just got here." Her youth denied her the recognition that her father and his cousin were only bantering words. "Please, Papa, make him

338

stay," she begged, grabbing her parent's hand.

Beau raised a dark brow. "Are you sure, Victoria? I can send him on his way if you wish." He winked at her, and the young girl suddenly understood.

"Well," she began, unable to hide her smile, "maybe if he promises to behave."

"I promise," Brad pledged with his hand over his heart. "I'll do whatever you say, my sweet Victoria. Besides—" he jerked his head toward Alec—"you wouldn't want to turn away the man responsible for saving my life, would you?"

Victoria's dark eyes widened as they shifted to the stranger. "Really?" she questioned in awe as she descended the steps and walked closer. "Did you really save his life?"

"I suppose you could say that." Alec grinned, suddenly wishing he could be around in a few years to see what a beautiful woman Victoria Remington promised to be. "But had I known *he* was the one to steal your heart, I might have given it a second thought. Now it seems I'll have to fight him for your hand." Taking his tricorn from his blond head, he bowed politely. "Alec Diamond at your service, Miss Victoria."

Blushing softly, she curtsied in response, reached out to take his arm and lead him toward her father for a formal introduction, and glanced back over her shoulder at Brad. Knowing no one but he would see, she stuck out her tongue at him then turned back to present an air of perfect manners, missing the wide smile that parted Brad's lips.

"Father," she said once they had ascended the steps and stood facing him, "this is Alec Diamond. Mr. Diamond, my father, Beau Remington."

"I'm honored," Beau admitted as he shook Alec's hand. "And even though there have been times when I've been tempted to beat some sense into my cousin's thick head, I'd never wish him any real harm. Thank you for seeing that that didn't happen."

"My pleasure"—Alec nodded—"though neither of us have figured out what made me do it."

Beau threw back his head and laughed loudly as he unknowingly clasped Alec's good shoulder and moved toward the door. "Welcome to my home, Alec Diamond. You'll fit in just fine."

Beau led his guest to the parlor where he instructed Victoria to fetch her mother, tell Higgins that they had guests and have him bring a bottle of their finest wine. With his attention away from Alec, Beau failed to see the surprised look on the man's face or how quickly he masked it.

"Is that ol' reprobate still here?" Brad asked once the three men had gone into the parlor and sat down.

"And where do you think he'd go?" Beau challenged playfully. "It's much more peaceful working for me than playing cabin boy to you. He's a gentleman, and he doesn't relish the idea of getting shot at." Picking up a finely carved wood box from the table next to him, Beau opened the lid and offered a cheroot to Alec and then to his cousin before taking one for himself. "And speaking of getting shot," he continued once they enjoyed the pleasurable taste of their cigars, "who was it this time, Brad? An outraged husband?" He grinned at Alec. "I should warn you, Alec. If you have a beautiful wife somewhere, you'd best keep her hidden from this rogue. A gold wedding band makes no difference to Brad."

"That's not fair, Beau," his cousin argued, eyes twinkling. "I only entertain married women who wish to be entertained."

Beau raised his brows. "Is that what you call it?"

Brad ignored him. "And it wasn't a jealous husband. It was Elliot Greenwood."

The humor vanished from Beau's face as he stated, "I think it's time we did something about him."

"You don't have to," Brad guaranteed him. "Alec took care of that."

Beau's gaze shifted questioningly to Alec.

"I would have liked it to end differently," Alec explained. "But he left me no choice. I had to kill him."

Beau could see by the expression on Alec's face that he truly meant what he said. "Well, don't let it get to you, Alec. Greenwood had been asking to get killed for a long time. If it hadn't been you, it would have been someone else. He was a

340

troublemaker, the kind who's always looking for someone to push around. Everyone knew that. Even his friends . . . what few he had."

The serious moment was broken when Victoria appeared in the parlor doorway anxiously tugging on a woman's hand who seemed not to be highly enthusiastic about interrupting.

"Victoria," she lightly scolded when the men hurriedly came to their feet, "don't be so rude."

"I'm not rude, Mama," she argued with a hurt look on her face as she pulled her mother to where Alec stood. "I just wanted you to meet him." She smiled prettily at Alec, then nodded at her mother. "Mr. Diamond, this is my mother, Alanna Remington. Mama, Alec Diamond."

"How do you do, Mr. Diamond." She smiled.

"Please," he corrected, while he silently attributed Victoria's stunning beauty to her mother, "call me Alec."

"On one condition," she posed, her expression warm and sincere, "that you call me Alanna."

"I'd be honored," he replied, his attention suddenly drawn to the gray-haired gentleman who entered the room carrying a silver tray, bottle of red wine and four glasses. Only Beau seemed to acknowledge his presence when he instructed the butler where to set down the tray, for Alanna had focused her charm on her husband's cousin. While the two teased each other, Higgins filled the glasses, unaware of Alec's watchful eyes or how nervous the guest was when the man came to him and offered him a glass. The older gentleman never bothered to look Alec in the eye or say a word, for which Alec was glad. If by some sheer stroke of luck this Higgins was the one who had attended Lora Stone's funeral, he might accidentally reveal Alec's true identity to the Remingtons; and he wasn't ready to explain his deceit, nor was he sure he should.

Higgins wasn't all that common a name, Alec silently admitted while he watched the man serve Beau, but there were other considerations that made him suspicious. Alec had been a young boy the last time he remembered seeing Edwin Higgins, so he wasn't that familiar with the man's appearance. Yet he recalled him to be rather short and stocky built and going bald . . . as this man was. And dark hair could and often did turn gray. Then there was the fact that Edwin Higgins left London for the Colonies . . . to visit relatives. Yes, he was supposed to have gone to Boston, and this was a long ways from there; but the man could have easily settled in Williamsburg. Or was Alec just hoping where no hope existed?

"Higgins!"

Brad's exclamation brought Alec out of his thoughts and settled his full attention on the two, a puzzled frown crimping his brow as he watched the older man straighten sharply and turn back to the one who had called him.

"It's me, Brad," he proclaimed, his voice filled with amazement. "Don't tell me I've been gone *that* long that you don't even recognize me."

Higgins started to respond when Beau cut in with an explanation. "He would have if he could see you."

Brad's gaze shifted to his cousin. "What are you talking about?"

Beau casually took a sip of wine as he lounged in his chair. "His eyesight is failing."

"Well, for heaven's sake," Brad growled, frowning at the butler. "Why don't you get yourself a pair of spectacles?"

"Oh, he has them," Beau continued. "He just won't wear them. He'd rather stumble into things than admit he's getting older."

"Well, I think he looks distinguished in them," Victoria defended. "Like Mr. Franklin."

"Thank you, Miss Victoria," Higgins replied with a slight nod of his head. "Coming from you or your mother, that's a compliment. If I listened to your father or this good-for-nothing pirate, I'd—"

"Pirate?" Brad exploded. "I'm not a pirate, Edwin Higgins, and you know it. Just because you're hanging on to your old ways and refuse to see what the people of the Colonies are trying to do and why they're fighting to change things, doesn't make me a pirate." He took a short puff on his cheroot then added, "And if you really disapprove, why don't you return to London?"

"If your father was still alive, I would," he declared, his nose held loftily in the air. "And if you father was still alive, he'd be ashamed of you."

"Ha!" Brad loudly denied. "Aric Remington would be sitting right here beside me arguing with you, and you know it. He often times told Dane and me how he thought King George only cared about himself and not the people of England."

"Often times," Higgins fumed beneath his breath as he started to walk away. Then in a burst of anger, he turned on the young man who was bold enough to make such a claim. "How many times was that, Brad Remington? Once? Had he been drinking? Was he feeling lonely? You know he blamed anyone and everything for the death of your mother. If he'd had his wits about him, he never would have spoken out against the Crown. He loved England."

"And so did Dane and I," Brad countered, his manner and tone softening. "But things change, Higgins. It doesn't mean we've abandoned our homeland. It means we want something better out of life." He smiled lopsidedly at the man. "And I apologize for making you angry. I know how much you miss living there. But you've made yourself a new home . . . here with Beau and Alanna. If you'll let yourself, you'll come to love it here even more than you did living in London."

"No, I won't," he muttered, turning for the door. "It gets too hot here." Without looking back he crossed the threshold, murmuring, "There's no early morning fog, and these Colonials are murdering the king's English."

The inhabitants of the room sat quietly listening to Higgins' footsteps fade down the hall, each focusing his attention on something else rather than admitting they had witnessed the exchange. Finally, Victoria broke the silence.

"Why do you always argue with him, Uncle Brad?" she asked. "Higgins is such a sweet man."

"I know, Victoria," he agreed. "And I'm sorry I ruined everything. But you must understand he feels as if *he's* the one who's abandoned his homeland by coming here, and he's taking it out on me. I don't mind, since it makes him feel

343

better. I'm glad I can help." Frowning, he gazed at the empty doorway a moment. "To tell you the truth, I think there's more to it than that."

"You do?" Victoria asked, coming to sit on the edge of Brad's chair. "Like what?"

"I think he ran away from something." He smiled crookedly at the young girl staring back at him. "I think he wanted to escape some very painful memories, and he realized the only way he could do that was to leave England."

"How do you know?"

"I can see it in his eyes. He's not the same man who helped raise Dane and me. He's hurting. I just don't know from what."

Alec had a good idea, but he realized he couldn't voice it. Brad would ask how he knew, and Alec wasn't willing to tell him . . . not yet. He had to be sure about the Remingtons before he could confide in them. Besides, he still hadn't quite accepted his good fortune in finding Edwin Higgins so easily. It almost seemed as if some unearthly being had had a hand in it, and that thought made him uncomfortable.

The conversation turned to Brad's voyage back from Boston and the supplies he had delivered, his visit with Dane and his wife, and how Brad and Alec had met. The men wisely chose not to go into the details of the episode with Elliot Greenwood since Victoria appeared to be hanging on every word they said, but once Alanna heard about it, she voiced her gratitude for helping out her husband's cousin. Again Alec felt a twinge of envy over the love this family shared for each other, wishing that he'd had cousins and sisters-in-laws and the likes of Victoria to care about his health. Nodding his acceptance of Alanna's appreciation, he took a sip of his wine and silently concluded that perhaps Edwin Higgins would change all that for him.

When the topic of business matters came up, Alanna politely excused herself to go to the kitchen and ask Cinnamon to fix their guests something to eat. Victoria stayed behind, electing to sit on the red velvet settee next to her father where she had an indiscriminate view of both Brad and Alec Diamond. She had never met a man with blond hair and such intriguingly handsome features before, and she stared openly at Alec every time he spoke. She was even more impressed to learn he lived on an island in the Caribbean and that he wasn't married. She had vowed at a very young age that someday she would become Brad's wife, but the more she listened to this charming, handsome man from Jamaica, the more she wondered if she'd made the right decision. Her mother had told her several times that she was too young to understand what real love was all about, that she was only infatuated with her father's cousin, and maybe her mother was right. What she was beginning to feel for Alec Diamond was different.

They adjourned out onto the wide veranda where Alec and Brad were served a very delicious meal while Beau, his wife and daughter enjoyed a cup of tea sweetened with honey. The men tasted a second cheroot, and everyone fell quiet as they sat there on the porch savoring the beauty of the golden sunset. Higgins never showed himself again, which pleased Alec, for he feared the man might appear before him wearing his glasses and spoil this special moment. He planned to confront the man before he left Raven Oaks, but he wished to do so at a time of his choosing and when the two of them could be alone. This was a matter that didn't concern the Remingtons.

"I imagine this isn't at all like living on a tropical island, is it?" Beau asked, once Alanna had taken the reluctant Victoria off to bed.

"There are a lot of similarities, but no, it's not the same. For one, my place sits close to the shore, and I spend my evenings watching the surf wash up on the beach."

"Are you anxious to go home?"

Alec shrugged. "Yes and no," he replied, thinking that once he left the Colonies, he would never see Rebecca again. That was his only reason for not truly wanting to leave, even though he knew he must. "It might seem to someone who's never lived on an island that it would be something close to paradise, and it is. But even paradise can become a little boring after a while."

"That's probably because you live alone," Brad remarked

offhandedly as he raised his glass of wine to his lips.

Alec chuckled. "That's an odd thing to say for a man who isn't any more committed than I am."

"Committed," Brad grumbled. "That's a good word for it. Get married and commit yourself to the Public Hospital. A man would have to be crazy to want to get married." He sat up and leaned forward to look past Alec at his cousin sitting in the next chair. "No offense, Beau," he added.

"None taken." Beau smiled. "But if you don't mind, I'll remember what you said and remind you of it on the day you get married."

"Ha!" Brad exclaimed, falling back in his chair. "You should live so long."

"I probably will . . . and longer." His cousin laughed. A moment of silence passed, then he asked, "So what about you, Alec? Isn't there one woman in your life that's tempted you to settle down?"

"Not after meeting Rebecca Wilde," Brad cut in. "You remember her, don't you, Beau? She's the newspaper journalist at the *Gazette*. Got one of the hottest tempers of any woman I've ever known." His brows came together while he gave that statement a little more consideration. "Except for Brittany. Or Alanna." He smiled one-sidedly. "And probably Victoria when she gets a little older." He sat forward in his chair again and looked over at his cousin. "What's wrong with us Remington men that we're attracted to such mean-spirited vixens?"

Beau's dark eyes sparkled as he stared out at the horizon. "Because they're the only ones who can handle us, I suppose."

"Or maybe they're the only ones interesting enough to attract a man's attention," Alec speculated, thinking that that was part of the fascination he had for Rebecca. All of the other ladies he'd been with were soft-spoken, gentle, feminine . . . and boring. Without realizing it, he smiled.

"Uh-oh," Brad moaned, a devilish twinkle in his eye as he sat with one elbow propped on the arm of his chair, his jaw resting on his fist and his gaze centered on Alec. "I think Alec's been associating with us too long already, Beau. He has that stupid look on his face." He raised his eyebrows inquiringly when Alec turned a puzzled frown on him. "Are you going to deny what—or I should say who—brought that silly smile to your lips? It wouldn't be Rebecca, now would it?"

Alec could feel a warmth slowly creeping up his neck. He didn't appreciate getting caught thinking of her, nor did he like how easily Brad had come to the right conclusion. Averting his gaze, he took a drink of his wine and silently refused to confirm Brad's guess.

"No answer is the same as an answer, Alec ol' boy," Brad continued to tease, glancing over at Beau and winking. "Is that why you're not in any rush to go home?"

Uncomfortable, yet not at all upset over the man's prying, Alec absently studied the dying sunlight and said, "You're the one doing all the talking. Suppose you tell me."

"All right," Brad agreed, taking up the challenge. "Let's see if I can figure this out." He straightened in his chair and raised a fingertip to tap his chin as though the feat promised to be quite involved. "You left your home some weeks ago—or paradise as you called it—because it had become boring. You aren't married, which means there are no women in Jamaica worth your time. You come to Williamsburg on business and visit the newspaper office to place an advertisement, and low and behold, you meet the most gorgeous woman you've ever seen in your life. You make a pass at her, but she's offended. Maybe she even slapped your face for trying." He grinned mischievously at Alec and asked, "How am I doing so far?"

Alec shrugged, noncommittal.

Truly enjoying his little game, Brad left his chair to pace the veranda in front of Alec. "Not one to be put off so easily, you ask around town about this young, black-haired beauty and learn her name and that she's unattached. What you don't learn is why—which should have been your first question. You would have lost interest if someone had told you how much she despises men. But you didn't, so . . . you take a room at The Red Lion where Rebecca's best friend works and lives just on the chance of seeing her again without it looking like you planned it." He stopped his pacing and looked at Alec. "Right?"

The muscles in Alec's throat tightened as he fought to control his laughter. "Not even close."

"You shouldn't have told him that, Alec." Beau chuckled. "He loves this sort of thing, and he won't let up until he has the truth . . . whether he makes it up or you confess."

"Well, he dared me," Brad replied in his own defense. "If he really wanted to keep it a secret, he'd have told me it was none of my business."

"Maybe he's being polite." Beau grinned. "Or maybe he likes watching you make a fool of yourself. Lord knows you've done that often enough." Leaning closer to Alec, Beau nudged his arm while he continued to stare at Brad. "Did he tell you about the time he tried to woo her into bed and how she very nearly took his head off? He had the biggest black eye I've ever seen. Tried telling me he was thrown out of his bunk during a storm at sea. But I never believed him. Besides, Penny told me all about it later."

"Penny Dawson?" Alec asked, surprised Beau knew her.

"Yes. I had supper at The Red Lion shortly afterward. I never quite figured out why, but Penny wanted to apologize for what had happened." His grin widened. "I told her not to bother, that Brad always got what he deserved when it came to women. And you know what she said to that? She told me that that was why she stayed away from him."

"Un-oh," Alec warned, mimicking his friend's earlier playfulness. "I think you struck a raw nerve with that one, Beau." He pointed at Brad, whose expression had changed from one of merriment to something akin to hurt. "Looks to me like his ego has been dented."

"Dented, possibly"—Beau laughed—"but never destroyed."

Giving them both a disapproving sneer, Brad returned to his chair and sat down. "Has it occurred to either of you that perhaps what Penny Dawson thinks of me really matters? I might be a rogue, but I do have feelings."

"Good Lord, Brad," Beau exclaimed, pushing forward in his chair so that he could look him in the eye. "Don't tell me

Penelope Dawson has somehow managed to get you to see women in a different light? Since when have you ever cared what they think of you?"

"She's a friend," Brad firmly argued. "That's all. Everyone needs a friend now and then. I happen to like her, and I wouldn't want to do anything to ruin it."

"So you make a pass at her best friend?"

"That was before. I haven't tried since, and I never will. Not now. Not since I know Alec is interested."

"Whoa there!" Alec quicky interjected. "Who said I was interested? If Rebecca Wilde is your type of woman, then go right ahead and do whatever you please . . . with my blessing. As soon as I've finished my business here, I'm going home. I didn't come to America looking for a wife. I came here to buy some property. Nothing more!"

A long silence passed between the trio while they each stared across the spacious front lawn at the last glimpse of the dying sun. A puzzled frown curled Brad's dark eyebrows, and a look of firm conviction crimpled Alec's rugged features while a devilish smile played upon Brad's lips. Sneaking a peak at his friend from out of the corner of his eyes, Brad finished off his wine and cleared his throat to keep from laughing out loud.

"You really don't have to sound so adamant, Alec," he finally announced as he pushed up from his chair. "I'd believe anything you'd say. But then perhaps *I'm* not the one you're trying to convince." He grinned broadly at Alec when the man sucked in a quick breath to respond, and started for the door before he could utter a sound. "I don't know about anyone else, but I'm tired. I think I'll go to bed." Pausing at the entryway, he looked back and asked, "Anyone else?"

Irritated, Alec came to his feet. "I think it's a good idea. That way I won't have to listen to your inane babbling."

Deep, heartfelt laughter filled the wide hallway as Brad draped his arm across Alec's shoulders and guided his friend up the long, winding staircase to the balcony and their rooms above. Whether Alec cared to admit it or not, Brad had seen that special gleam in the young man's eye every time

349

Rebecca's name was mentioned, and it could only mean one thing. Something in Alec Diamond's comfortable life was about to change no matter how hard he might try to stop it.

Alec awoke the next morning shortly after dawn, feeling refreshed and oddly content. A rooster crowed from somewhere close by in the yard below his opened window, and the sweet smell of fresh, spring air floated into the room, luring him from the warmth of his bed. Slipping into his breeches, he raked his fingers through his hair as he crossed to the French doors leading out onto a balcony. He couldn't remember the last time he looked forward to spending the day doing absolutely nothing, and the idea made him smile. Lifting the latch, he stepped outside to enjoy the view and clear his head.

The pastels of sunrise danced across the sky and mirrored their reflection in the pond he saw nestled within the border of huge willow trees just beyond the mill. A dozen or more ducks and geese glided effortlessly across its smooth surface, and tiny ripples marked the direction they took. Behind them trailed their offspring, and Alec was suddenly reminded of home as he savored the serenity of the moment. There had been a pond not far from the cottage where he lived as a child, and he had always gone there to be alone with his thoughts whenever something troubled him. A frown spoiled the mood when he realized how often he had sought out that solitude; for as a young boy, it seemed a great deal had plagued his mind, and now as a man full grown, he had yet to find the peace he so strongly yearned to have. His problems had taken on a different tone over the years, but they were still just as real and just as vexing as they had been for the bastard son of Lora Stone. His only hope now was that Edwin Higgins would be the one to lay those heartaches to rest.

The sound of children laughing brought Alec out of his reverie, and he turned his head to watch three dark-skinned youngsters scamper off down the lane that would take them to the mill. The smell of burning wood in cook stoves suddenly reached him, and he reluctantly realized that he shared the early morning with several others. Conscious of his informal dress, he moved back inside to shave, wash his face, comb his hair and don the rest of his clothes. Perhaps now would be the time to seek out Edwin Higgins—before breakfast was served and before any of the Remingtons were up.

He quietly closed the door to his room behind him and started down the long staircase, wondering where he might find the butler at this time of the morning, when he suddenly became aware of the exquisite oil paintings and plaques hanging on the wall beside him. Obviously he hadn't noticed them the night before while Brad playfully jostled him up the steps or he would have taken the time to comment on them. Several were landscapes, a few were portraits of people he didn't recognize, and he smiled to himself as he thought that perhaps he had found a buyer for his Rembrandt. Then his gaze fell on the one at the foot of the staircase, the plaque that sent a chill through him, and he half stumbled down the remaining stairs in his haste to get a better view.

Because of his lowly station in life, and more pointedly because his father never married his mother, the Stone's never had a family crest. He'd seen several of them now that he had the wealth that put him in touch with the upper class of people who prided their heritage, but none of them ever impressed him. This one did, however. The name of Remington, in raised gold lettering, ran the width of the bottom. Delicately carved twigs of bronze with softly painted green buds curled around the outside and haloed the fragile shape of a tiny bird with its wings outstretched in flight. It could have been the likeness of a raven, he concluded, and that Beau had used that aspect of his family's crest in naming his plantation. But the thought vanished as quickly as it had surfaced when he unknowingly stroked the ring on his little finger, and the obvious pieces began to fall into place. His stomach churning, he slowly raised his hand to study the black onyx and the figure carved in it. What he had once thought was only an ornamentation now became the same tiny, budding twigs surrounding the bird in flight.

And the winged creature he had wanted to believe had no specific classification suddenly took on the shape and appearance of a wren.

Filled with a sudden, indefinable rage, Alec clenched his fist, raised his chin in the air and gritted his teeth, eyes closed. Of course it was a wren! And Beau hadn't been influenced by the family crest when he chose a name for his plantation. Aric Remington had! Sweet mother of God, Aric Remington was his father!

"Alec?"

The sound of his name on someone's lips jolted Alec out of the paralyzing trance he was in, and he jerked around to find Edwin Higgins staring back at him, the old man's face twisted with surprise and confusion, his spectacles resting on the bridge of his nose.

"My God, it is you," he breathed, tears suddenly glistening in his eyes. His gaze shifted away from Alec to the balcony above the winding staircase as if he couldn't understand how the young man had found his way here or that perhaps he didn't want anyone else in the house to know he was. Chin trembling, he looked back at Alec. "How did you find me? How did you know where to look?"

"I didn't," he growled, his wrath focusing in on the only living being who knew the answers to the secret Lora had taken to her grave. "I'm here because Brad invited me and for no other reason. I came to enjoy a pleasant holiday away from all my troubles, and I seem to have only stirred them up. I walked blindly, unsuspectingly into a den of liars. Only the joke is on them. They don't know who I really am. But you do, don't you, Edwin Higgins? You've known for years, but like my mother, you chose to keep it from me." His nostrils flared as he sucked in an angry breath. "Why, Higgins? What possessed you to hide the truth from a young boy who only wished to know his father's name?"

"A promise, Alec," Higgins confessed. "A promise I made to your mother on the day you were born. I did it for Lora and *only* because she made me swear an oath." His aged frame shaking he nervously glanced up the staircase, then back at Alec, begging, "Please, Alec. No one else knows. Not

Brad or Dane or any of the others. Your *father* didn't even know. Lora wanted it that way." He motioned toward the parlor. "I can't hide the truth from you any longer, but please, let's discuss it in privacy. You owe that much to your mother's memory."

Alec wanted to shout that he didn't owe anything to anyone, that *he* was the one who had suffered all these years, and that if for once something hadn't gone his way, he probably never would have learned the truth. He wanted to say it, but he couldn't. He knew his mother had suffered just as much as he had . . . possibly even more. With a quick jerk of his head toward the parlor, Alec turned and led the way.

Bright morning sunshine stole into the room, but it failed to cheer Alec's dark mood as he crossed to one of the wing chairs and sat down, his brow furrowed, his deep brown eyes riveted on the man who couldn't bring himself to look at Alec. Instead, Higgins paced the floor for several minutes, trying to collect his thoughts and settle on the best way to begin.

"Start at the beginning," Alec suggested as if reading Higgins' mind, his tone sharp and laced with bitterness and anger. "See if you can make me understand why a father and son should be denied the knowledge of the other's existence. Explain why my mother slept with a married man. Or was it rape?"

"No!" Higgins exploded. "It wasn't rape! Mr. Remington wasn't the sort to take a woman against her will. You didn't know him. And I won't allow you to shame your mother's name by implying she was a harlot. She wasn't! She loved Aric Remington. She loved him so much she kept your birth a secret."

Alec glared at the old man for a long while, his elbow resting on the arm of his chair while he tapped the first knuckle on his fist against his chin, his dark eyes snapping with hatred for a man he never met. "Why?" he finally asked. "Was she afraid to tell him? Would he have killed her to cover up his mistake?"

"Never!" Higgins shouted.

"Then what?" Alec cut in. "I'm sure a wealthy man like

353

Aric Remington wouldn't have any qualms about ridding himself of an embarrassment—especially if his wife heard about his unfaithfulness. I hardly think she'd allow him to bring his mistress and bastard son into her home. Or wasn't it the first time? Had he sent all of his mistresses away once he learned they carried his child, and Lora knew it? So rather than be forced out of her home, she hid the truth?" His eyes narrowed as he spat, "If you call where we lived a home. It was hardly more than a shack, no better than the log cabins Beau Remington uses for his slaves. With one big difference, however, his slaves are better fed."

"Alec, please," Higgins begged. "If you'll just allow me to explain, I can—"

"Yes, Higgins, please do," a deep, angry voice from the doorway interrupted, and both men turned to find Brad standing there, his brown eyes dark and challenging, his nostrils flared and his broad frame stiff with rage. Shifting his attention from the older man to the younger one, he hissed, "Explain to me why I shouldn't beat this son-of-a-bitch to death with my bare hands for the insults he's thrown at my family."

A strange sensation raced through Alec once he realized that the one who threatened his life was his half brother and that all his longing for a family he could call his own had finally come true. He had another half brother named Dane, and *he* had three sons, Alec's nephews. He had a sister-in-law and a cousin. And after all these years, he knew his father's name. He should have been overjoyed with the discovery, but he wasn't. He never felt more alienated, more alone than he did right now. "I have no quarrel with you, Brad," he declared softly and turned his gaze back on Higgins.

"You insult a man's family, his name, and you expect no retaliation?" Brad snarled. He moved farther into the room, the muscle in his jaw flexing as he gritted his teeth. "Do you honestly think I'll just stand by calmly and allow you to continue? I asked you here as a friend. I invited you into my cousin's home, and you, in turn, slur the Remington name. All you deserve, Mr. Diamond, is to be thrown off this property with no explanation whatsoever. But that would be the same as ignoring your accusations . . . which I'm honor bound not to do. Aric Remington loved his wife and *never* had a mistress." He glared hatefully at Alec. "Or a whore."

A sudden, blinding fury enveloped Alec. In a fit of rage, he catapulted off the chair and hurled himself at Brad's midsection, burying his shoulder in the man's stomach and shoving him backward until they crashed into the wall. Paralyzing pain shot up Brad's spine, but he ignored it to interlock his fingers and land his fists with a staggering blow to the middle of Alec's back. Shaking off his pain, he watched Alec drop to his knees, stunned and hurting, but Brad wasn't about to let it end there. Grabbing a handful of Alec's hair, Brad raised the man's head and brought up his knee, smashing it into Alec's jaw and sending him sprawling backward into one of the end tables. The hurricane lamp, ash tray and porcelain figurine sitting on top crashed to the floor, and the sound of shattering glass echoed throughout the manor.

Dazed and feeling the renewed pain in his healing shoulder, Alec shook his head to clear his vision. In that same split second, he saw Higgins race from the room and realized that his foe intended to continue the assault. Rolling onto one hip, Alec lashed out a foot to catch Brad in the ribs when he bent to make a grab for him. The blow toppled Brad over the back of the settee and spilled him to the floor, and Alex quickly followed through with the attack. Springing to his feet, he raced forward, grabbed Brad's shirtfront, and hauled him to smash his fist into the man's face. Blood spurted from his opponent's nose, but it in no way slowed his reflexes. A second later Alec's head snapped to the right with the force behind Brad's fist landing on Alec's chin. A second blow found its mark, and Alec could feel the soft flesh inside his mouth split open. The third attempt to separate Alec's head from his shoulders was blocked when Alec raised his arm, and he returned the assault with a stinging punch to Brad's stomach. He followed with a backhanded hit across the man's cheek, which opened a large gash near Brad's eye and sent him flying backward through the doorway and into the hall where he stumbled to the floor.

Exhausted but not willing to admit defeat, Brad came up on one knee, the other bent and his elbow braced on it while he gasped for air and studied his opponent standing in the doorway. Obviously Alec was feeling the effects of their fight as well. He was leaning forward with his hands braced on his knees for support, and every breath he took seemed difficult to draw. Praying this would be his one last attempt to overpower his adversary, Brad awkwardly came up on his feet and charged. Leading with his shoulder, he crashed into Alec, caught him around the waist in a steellike grip and squeezed with all the strength left in him, intending to break Alec's ribs. But his foe refused to cooperate even after Brad lifted Alec off his feet. With his arms pinioned to his sides, Alec was left with no other recourse but to crack his forehead against Brad's. The impact stunned them both, and Brad unwillingly let go when his vision suddenly began to spin. Alec staggered back a step or two to catch his breath *and* his balance, and to summon up the energy he needed just to stand up, as well as to finish off his opponent. However, once he focused his eyes on the man and started to move in on him, Alec was suddenly jerked sideways by arms that imprisoned him in a much stronger, more determined and unrelenting grip than before, and he halfheartedly tried to break free, only to be roughly hurled back against the wall.

"Don't move!" Beau's angry voice ordered. "Don't even think about it or I promise you, you'll regret it."

More than willing to call a truce, and because he had no argument with the man or the strength to fight even if he had, Alec nodded weakly. Swaying once Beau let go of him, he leaned heavily against the small table next to him while he gulped for air and rubbed the blood from his mouth on the back of his hand.

"And *you!*" Beau raged, turning on his cousin with one finger pointing at the settee. "If you're going to act like a couple of hot-headed boys, then that's how I'll treat you. *Sit!*"

Brad clumsily obliged his angry cousin, but more out of a need to sit down rather than out of respect. Every muscle in his body ached, his head pounded and he was almost certain

Alec had broken his nose. His mind might have been willing to continue the battle, but his body had begged for surrender long ago. Falling onto the soft cushion, he laid his head back and closed his eyes, unaware of the terrified look on Alanna's face as she stood in the doorway behind Higgins observing the scene.

"Would one of you mind telling me what the hell brought this on?" Beau demanded, his fists on his hips as he looked from Brad to Alec and back again as though he were the father and they were his unruly children.

"I'm afraid, sir," Higgins spoke up, "that Master Brad misunderstood something he overheard and reacted before I could explain."

"Misunderstood?" Brad repeated sarcastically as he peered over at the butler through one half-opened eye. "He accused my father of being unfaithful and said that he'd buy his way out of any trouble he might have gotten himself into." Lifting his head, he looked straight at Alec. "I don't think I could have misunderstood him. I *heard* him!"

"Is that true?" Beau growled. He knew his cousin well enough to know Brad wouldn't lie, but he liked this young man and truly didn't want that to change.

The heated glowers he received from the two men had little effect on Alec. After all, they were cousins . . . full-blooded cousins. *He* was the outsider. How else would they react? He pushed himself up from the table and straightened his jacket and ascot. "What other conclusion could I have drawn?" he asked, wincing at the stiffness in his shoulder and wondering if Brad had indeed cracked a few of his ribs. "What conclusion would either of *you* have drawn if you had grown up the bastard child of a woman who—until the day she died—refused to tell you anything about your father?"

Sitting up, Brad dug through his pockets for a handkerchief and blotted his nose with it. "And *that* justifies accusing Aric Remington of unfaithfulness?"

"No!" Alec countered. "*This* does!" He jerked the ring from his little finger and threw it at Brad. "Recognize it?" he hissed once Brad had a moment to study the black onyx and the delicate carving etched on its surface. "You should. If I'm not mistaken, it belonged to your father."

"Where did you get this?" Brad hotly demanded, the ring clutched in his fist and his jaw set in a hard line.

Alec glanced over at the gray-haired man who stood trembling in the doorway. "I suggest you ask Higgins."

With everyone's attention centered on him, Edwin Higgins felt as if he'd been accused of murder and was about to be led to the gallows. Gulping down his nervousness, he lowered his gaze and moved into the room. "I stole it the day Aric died and gave it to Alec's mother."

"Why?" Brad exploded. "What right did she have to it?"

"She had every right," Higgins replied, the features of his face looking drawn and tired. "If you will allow me, I'll explain everything. But you're not to interrupt. What I have to say mustn't be heard in bits and pieces. Will you give me your word?" He waited for Brad's reluctant nod, then indicated that Alanna was invited to hear the story as well. Once she and her husband had sat down, Higgins turned to Alec. "We've never really met until now, not really, although I used to see you now and then with your mother. Until his death, I was Aric Remington's personal manservant and trusted friend. I helped raise Brad and his older brother after their mother died. It was a hard time for them." He changed his attention to Brad. "It was harder on your father. He loved her very much, and the loneliness afterward was more than he could bear. He took to drinking for a spell, trying to drown his sorrow so-to-speak, and he spent most of his nights in a pub away from his memories and his empty bed. You wouldn't remember that because you were too young. Master Dane might." Higgins paused a moment to collect his thoughts and figure out just how to continue, and the vision of a beautiful, innocent, young, blond-haired girl came to mind. He shook off the image, saddened by all that had happened over the years, and drew in a breath to speak.

"It was in one of those pubs that he met a lovely, young lady by the name of Lora Stone. I know because I was with him. I was always with him." Gray brows slanted downward with the memory. "She was a barmaid there, and I think the similarities between Miss Stone and Aric's dead wife were

358

what drew him to her. Well, needless to say, he used her to forget his pain, not realizing that she had fallen in love with him. I could see it. Aric couldn't. And it didn't take Lora long to realize what had brought them together. She also recognized the fact that Aric would never love her, that his wife was the only woman he could ever care about. She told me later that that was why she decided to call an end to their . . . relationship. A month later, she found out she was carrying his child. You, Mr. Stone," he said, nodding at Alec. He sighed and looked at Brad to find him staring blankly at something across the room from him, his eyes dark, his brows knotted tightly, and Higgins changed his mind about making it perfectly clear that Alec and he were blood relatives. Brad already knew.

"I liked Lora Stone very much, and whenever I had the chance, I'd visit her. She never told me who the father of her child was. She didn't have to. I could see the resemblance to Aric in the baby's eyes and mouth. What she did ask of me was that I never tell Aric what happened to her after the day she walked out of his life. I never did—out of respect for her. It was my decision," he admitted reluctantly, "to give her Aric's ring after he died, claiming that on his deathbed he had begged me to find Lora and give it to her. I lied to her, Mr. Stone. But in doing so, I made her happy." Suddenly, a pained expression crimped his brow when he thought of something, and he couldn't bring himself to look at Alec anymore. "I know it wasn't fair to you, son, and it probably wasn't fair to your father. Aric would have loved you just as much as he loved Masters Brad and Dane. But it was what Lora wanted, and I would have done anything in the world for her."

A long silence hung in the room like an early morning fog waiting for the first bright rays of sunlight to chase it away. For Brad, it was a time for accepting the truth no matter how much he wanted to deny it. But he had known Edwin Higgins all of his life, and he knew Higgins wouldn't lie . . . not about something as important as this. Beau and Alanna were thinking much the same thing, that once the initial shock had passed for Brad and he could look at the situation objectively, he would happily welcome Alec to his family. That was the way Brad was. Alec, on the other hand, was having a bit more difficult time adjusting to what he had learned. For years he had hated his father for all the wrong reasons, and it was hard for him to lay those feelings aside just because of something someone said. Higgins' comment that Aric would have loved his bastard son as much as he did his other offspring had he known about Alec didn't help. He was feeling more cheated than ever. But he also discovered a new respect for Lora Stone. She had known Aric didn't love her, and she had given up her happiness for his by not forcing him into a marriage he didn't want. He admired her for that, and he admired the strength it had taken for Edwin Higgins to keep her secret. Thinking of the man, Alec glanced up at him. Whether Higgins cared to admit it or not, Alec was sure this gray-haired, polite Englishman had been in love with Lora Stone. How sad it was that he had never told her. But then, maybe she had known it all along.

A movement to his left brought Alec out of his musings, and he turned his head to watch Brad leave the settee and approach, his eyes lowered to the object he held in his hand, and his expression solemn.

"I believe this belongs to you," he said quietly, holding out the ring to Alec. "I'm sure Father would have wanted you to have it had he known about you." He continued to stare at the ring while he watched Alec slip it on his finger. "And I must agree with Higgins when he said Father would have loved you just as much as he loved Dane and me. That's the kind of man he was. I realize that's little comfort now." He finally lifted his eyes to look directly at Alec. "And just as soon as I've had a little more time to adjust to the idea, perhaps I can make it up to you . . . Dane and I, that is. You may have been denied the kind of upbringing you deserved to have, and nothing I can do now will change that; but you're a part of the Remington family now, and I'm sure I can speak for my brother as well when I say we wouldn't turn our backs on you just because—" He sighed heavily as if his thoughts were difficult to put into words. "Well, you're Aric Remington's son. So am I." A twinkle appeared in his dark eyes, and a second later a slow smile parted his lips. "Besides, I always wanted a little brother to kick around the way Dane always did me." The smile widened as he held out his hand. "And who knows? Maybe you'll want no part of us once you learn what an odd bunch we are."

Alec had waited his whole life for this moment, for the chance to be welcomed as an equal, to have a family, to share the things he'd missed growing up. Reaching out, he took Brad's hand and firmly shook it as he said, "Not a chance, Brad Remington. You'll not get rid of me that easily."

They stared at each other in silence for several moments as if really seeing the other for the first time. Finally, Brad broke the spell when he turned to the couple who stood anxiously off to one side.

"Cousin," he announced, "I'd like to introduce you to a relative of yours." His dark eyes fell on Alec again. "Beau, this is my half brother, Alec Dia—" A puzzled frown crimped his brow when he suddenly realized Higgins had addressed him as Mr. Stone. His gaze shifted questioningly to the older man, but before any reference could be made to that one's sagging memory, Alec cut in.

"The name's Alec Stone," he confessed. "And if you'll allow *me* the chance to explain—how it is I happen to be here, how I managed to find Mr. Higgins, and the reason I couldn't tell you who I really was—perhaps we all can help each other."

Brad was more than willing to listen, since he had the same curiosity about his newly discovered half brother as Alec had for him, and because Beau had sensed from the start that something else had brought Alec to Williamsburg—most rich planters used an agent to purchase land for them rather than doing it themselves—he suggested they meet on the patio in back of the house where they could enjoy the morning sunshine. But first he wanted to get dressed since he hadn't had the time earlier to don anything more than his breeches when Higgins came pounding on his door. He also suggested that perhaps Alec and Brad would want to change and wash the blood from their faces. Everyone agreed, and Alanna stated that she would go to the kitchen and instruct

361

Cinnamon on what to serve for breakfast. Inviting Higgins to join them for the discussion since he had always been a part of the Remington clan and because he knew Aric Remington better than any of them and could therefore answer any questions Alec might have about his father, the four men left the parlor amid good-natured gibes and warm laughter.

"You know, Alec," Beau said sometime later once the whole story had been told and the group sat enjoying the memory of their delicious meal and the taste of the tea they drank, "you took an awful chance coming here with Brad. From your point of view, *I* could have been the man you're after."

A smile graced Alec's rugged features, and his eyes sparkled as he absently studied the teacup he cradled in his hands. "Would you like to hear my reasoning on that respect?" He glanced up at Beau, saw him nod, then fell back in his chair to stare out across the luscious green grass at the line of willows in the distance. "I figured a relative of Brad's couldn't be involved in something like this."

Brad's brow wrinkled. "Now *that's* a crazy assumption to make. We hardly knew each other. We *still* don't." He looked playfully at his cousin. "In fact there's still a good chance he's the one you're looking for. I always wondered how he earned his money."

"Not the way you do," Beau countered with a grin as he picked up his teacup.

"Will you two behave?" Alanna cut in. "This is serious. Someone tried to kill Alec, stole his money, and murdered his agent. You shouldn't make light of it."

"That's all right, Alanna," Alec assured her, smiling warmly. "I've never had anyone before today with whom to share my problems, and I really don't mind the teasing. It feels good." He shifted his attention on Brad. "And yes, it was crazy for me to think such a thing, but something about you told me that I could trust you."

"That's me," Brad joked. "Ol' trustworthy."

"Except where women are concerned," Beau corrected, his mouth twitching with suppressed laughter.

362

"Beau!" Alanna admonished.

"I'm sorry, darling," he apologized to his wife. "But I just couldn't pass it up." He leaned toward her, kissed her cheek then settled his gaze on Alec. "I wish I could help you, Alec, but I can't. For as long as I can remember there hasn't been a plantation up for sale or I certainly would have bought it. I'm afraid whoever tricked Mr. Heller did a very good job of it. As for the County Clerk . . . I remember the day his body was found and that of a stranger's. But no one connected the two. Maybe someone should have. Or at least asked a few questions. Too much time has passed now for it to be of any help. I will, however," he added, "pass this along to some of my trusted friends and see what any of them can come up with. Other than that . . ." He shrugged and sadly shook his head.

"I'd appreciate anything you can do for me," Alec replied with a sigh, "although I truly don't expect anything to come of it. I've reached a deadlock. The money *and* Mr. Heller are gone, I'm afraid. I just wish I didn't have to tell his wife and son."

"The poor dear," Alanna murmured, then added encouragingly, "but I'm sure after all this time, she expects the worst has happened. It will still be hard for you to tell her, but it won't be quite as much of a shock."

"Perhaps," Alec agreed quietly.

"So what are you planning to do about Rebecca?"

Alanna's bold assumption that there was anything at all he had to finish with Rebecca surprised Alec, and he could feel the blood drain from his face. "I . . . I don't know what you mean."

A soft, somewhat sympathetic smile curved Alanna's mouth upward. "Why, Alec, I'd have to be blind not to have seen how much you care for her. Surely you don't plan to leave without telling her how you feel."

Alec's gaze quickly moved from Alanna to Beau and finally to Brad, all of whom had questioning looks on their faces. He'd been caught, and there was no sense in trying to deny what he had only recently wondered about himself. Resting back in his chair, he idly toyed with his teacup. "I care," he admitted, "but not enough to want to change how I live. I quite enjoy the freedom I have by not being married, and I doubt I'll ever regret it. I expect to receive word in the next day or two that the *Constance* has docked, and once it has, I intend to be on it when it sails for home." He frowned suddenly and picked up his cup, muttering, "I've wasted enough time already chasing shadows. I'm needed back home."

No one argued the point or voiced an opinion on what he should or shouldn't do. Not that it would have made a difference. Alec had made up his mind, and no one was going to change it. He would spend a few more days with the Remingtons and then return to Jamaica . . . alone.

A strange emptiness tightened its hold on his heart.

Chapter Fifteen

Dark brown eyes glowed as they watched the man enter the pub and take a seat at one of the tables near the back. Penny had been told he was the captain of the *Constance*, which could only mean that Alec hadn't left Williamsburg for good . . . yet. It also meant she'd have time to put her plan into action, and while she watched him doff his hat and stretch out his legs under the table, she prayed he had enough sense to figure out what it was she was trying to tell him. Running her hand up the back of her head to smooth out her hair and catch the stray tendril, she squared her shoulders and reached for the tray laying on the bar at her elbow.

"Good morning, sir." She smiled brightly at him while she cleared the dishes left by her last customers. "What can I get you?"

The troubled expression on Geoffrey Synder's face vanished once he glanced up and saw the pretty redhead staring back at him. He couldn't remember the last time a beautiful, young woman had acted as though she was glad to see him, and although he knew it was part of her job, it made him feel good anyway.

"Well, it's a little early, I know, but I've got an awful thirst I need to quench. How about a mug of ale?"

"As quick as Ben can pour it," Penny assured him, turning to call to the old man behind the bar. "Ben, this gentleman wants your best ale."

"Coming right up, Penny," Ben replied with a wave of

his hand.

"Penny," he murmured. "That's quite an unusual name. Can't say I ever heard it before."

"Short for Penelope," she answered, thinking this was going better than she expected. "But I'm not really a Penelope, so my friends call me Penny. What do your friends call you?"

Geoffrey knew she was flirting with him, and her reason didn't interest him. "Geoffrey, I guess," he answered with a slight shrug.

"You guess?" Penny laughed. "Does that mean you guess they call you Geoffrey or you guess you have friends?"

"A little of both, I suppose." He chuckled lightheartedly.

The young woman excused herself for a moment to fetch his ale and take the dirty dishes to the kitchen, and Geoffrey boldly watched the sway of her hips as she walked away, thinking that if Alec were here with him, she probably wouldn't have given him a second glance. Alec Stone had a way of attracting the stares and attention of beautiful women, although he never really seemed to notice. That was the strange thing about Alec. He could have his choice of women; yet he never seemed interested, and Geoffrey thought what a shame that was. A man like Alec Stone should be married and raising a family. It was probably the reason why he appeared to be so lonely. The image of Meredith Stockwell came to mind with that observation and he frowned. Miss Stockwell, according to rumor, had made it quite clear to every available woman on the island that she and Alec would wed one day and anyone who thought differently would pay the price. "The price," as far as Geoffrey was concerned, meant that Miss Stockwell would pout and whine to her father until he couldn't stand it anymore, and he'd have a talk with the father of the young woman foolish enough to think she could steal Alec away. If that didn't work, the elder Stockwell got their attention by using a different method. By exploiting his wealth and his influence, Stockwell would see to it that the family of the young lady would suddenly find itself in a bit of financial bind.

The only thing that had saved Alec these past few years was that he didn't like Miss Stockwell all that much and marriage wasn't on his list of priorities. Miss Stockwell may have eliminated the competition, but it did her very little good. In Geoffrey's opinion, Alec Stone intended to stay single for the rest of his life . . . that was, of course, as long as he never met the one woman who could change all that. Focusing his attention on the pretty redhead again as she gathered his mug of ale from the bar and started toward him, he realized that as long as Alec continued to live on the island, he'd never escape Miss Stockwell's conspiracy or have a chance to come into contact with the kind of woman Alec deserved.

"How long will you be staying in Williamsburg before your ship sets sail again, Geoffrey?" Penny asked as she set down his drink. She laughed at the surprised look she received in return, and as she pulled out a chair beside him and sat down, she explained. "I've been working here long enough to recognize a sailor when I see one." Leaning forward, she crossed her arms on the table and watched him take a long swallow of his ale. "And I'll bet you're the captain."

"Right again." Geoffrey smiled. "And if you can name the ship, I'll really be impressed."

"Sorry." Penny laughed. "That I can't do offhand. But if you gave me a few minutes, I'm sure I could find out. There isn't much that goes on around here that I don't hear about sooner or later." She was hoping to trick him into asking about Alec, and as a result she could play upon his curiosity when she acted as though the name had a special meaning to her.

Once Ben had told her that Alec had paid his bill and left The Red Lion, Penny called in a few favors from some of her . . . "friends." Within the hour she had learned that he had taken a room at Raleigh Tavern. By late afternoon she was told of the places he had visited and that he had gone to the wharf where it appeared he had accidentally made Brad Remington's acquaintance. She assumed he had gone there to ask Thomas Keenan if the *Constance* had docked, and after he had been told that it hadn't, he left word with the manager that Keenan should send someone to Raleigh Tavern with a message when it had. Then the episode with Greenwood happened, and Alec had left the next morning with Brad Remington for Raven Oaks. It had been through sheer luck that she learned Jon-Gregory had somehow gotten involved, and she deduced the reason Alec had asked his help in contacting Geoffrey Synder had been simply because he was the only one Alec felt he could trust. At any rate, Penny had hired a young boy to stay at the wharf and wait for the *Constance* to dock. It was his mission to get to the captain with the note she had written before Jon-Gregory was able to reach him. Apparently the youngster had been successful. Otherwise, Geoffrey Synder wouldn't be here.

"I'm not sure how long I'll be staying," he admitted. "I'm to meet someone here on . . . business. After that I hope to be setting a course for home."

"And where is that?" Penny knew the answer before she asked, but she had to make Geoffrey think he was a stranger to her. If not, her plan wouldn't work, and her best friend might never speak to her again.

"Jamaica," Geoffrey replied. "If you could call that home, I spend more time on my ship." He had unconsciously looked away from her while he answered to take another sip of ale, and when he looked up again, he straightened sharply in surprise to see that the young woman had abruptly decided to leave his company without so much as a word of explanation or backward glance. Totally confused, he fell back in his chair to watch her angrily walk away. He'd never had much luck with women and had obviously managed to keep his record intact, though he had no idea what he had said or done to turn her against him so quickly. Everything had been going along smoothly, he thought, until he mentioned where he lived, and she seemed to have taken offense to that. With a shake of his head, he decided not to bother trying to make sense of it as he pulled the old watch from his pocket and checked the time. The note he had been given said he was to come to The Red Lion and wait. A young man by the name of Jon-Gregory would meet him there with information about his employer. The mystery surrounding the message led Geoffrey to believe that Alec was all right but that while the *Constance* was in Boston, Alec had uncovered the truth about his missing agent, and they needed to take precautions before meeting publicly. A frown gathered on his brow as he lifted the mug to his lips again. At least he prayed that was what it meant.

"Penny," Ben scowled, his voice low as he handed her the tray full of drinks she had ordered for the newly arrived customers sitting near the window, "you're not ignoring that gentleman, are you?" When she looked up at him, he nodded toward Captain Synder. "I'm sure he's ready for another drink. He might even be hungry. Go ask him."

Yes, she had been ignoring the man but not in the way Ben thought. She wanted Geoffrey Synder's curiosity to get the better of him. *He* had to be the one to say something first, otherwise Rebecca would know Penny hadn't kept her word. "I'm sorry, Ben," she apologized, sounding as if she had truly forgotten she had other customers. "I'll serve these men and then take care of him." Smiling brightly at Ben, she took the tray from him and turned around. But the second she had her back to him, the smile disappeared. She had to make Captain Synder think she was upset should he happen to be looking her way . . . which he was.

Geoffrey would have liked another mug of ale, but he was afraid to ask. The young woman appeared to be angry with him, though he didn't know why. Maybe he should just step up to the bar and ask Ben to refill his mug. He could certainly avoid trouble that way. But just as he was about to rise, Penny headed for his table, and he froze.

"Would you care for another, sir?" she asked stiffly, her eyes averted.

"Aye," he replied hesitantly, his brow furrowing as he watched her turn, with empty mug in hand, and walk back to the bar. A moment later she was setting his drink on the table in front of him, and out of reflex action he caught her wrist. "Penny, I don't know what it is I did to make you angry, but I apologize," he heard himself saying long before he realized he had. He normally wasn't the type to care what anyone thought about him, but he liked this young lady with the reddish-auburn hair and big brown eyes.

Penny had difficulty in hiding the smile that tugged at her mouth. The poor fool had walked right into her trap as though he'd been coached to respond the way he had. Staring back at him for a moment—she wanted him to think she was giving his apology some consideration—she feigned a long, weary sigh and slumped into the chair beside him.

"It isn't your fault," she cunningly told him as she folded her arms along the edge of the table and lowered her gaze. Deliberately biting the inside of her lip, she briefly glanced up at him with tears shining in her eyes. "It's just—" She sighed again and started to push up from the table. "Oh, you don't want to hear this."

"Of course I do," he begged, reaching out to touch her hand and draw her back down on the chair. "Maybe I can help."

More than you know, Geoffrey, my friend, she mused excitedly while she urged a tear to spill down her cheek. Brushing it away, she cast her gaze from him and murmured, "It's silly really, and once you hear it, you'll probably agree."

"I doubt that, but tell me anyway," he coaxed.

Penny waited a moment to reply just for effect. He had to be made to think he had forced the confession from her. "It's about a friend of mine. She's . . . in trouble, if you know what I mean."

He didn't, but he didn't want to interrupt to ask her to explain either. She seemed terribly reluctant to confide in him, and if he said anything at all, he feared she might change her mind and walk away. His heart seemed to do a flip-flop in his chest when she turned sad, brown eyes on him and begged him not to say a word of this to anyone. But before he could make a pledge, she rushed on.

"My friend—the one who's in trouble—well, she met this man, a very handsome man . . . from Jamaica, and she . . . well, she fell in love with him." Penny tried to force another tear to fall; but the first one seemed to be the only one she could summon, and she sniffed instead, hoping to sound as though she barely had herself under control. "I think he loves her, too, and if he knew—about her condition, I mean—I'm sure he'd ask her to marry him. But she won't tell him, and she made me promise not to say a word." Grabbing the corner of her apron, she dabbed at her eyes and stole a peek at Geoffrey. His color seemed to have whitened a bit, and his chin was sagging as he stared blankly at the table top. *Bless your heart,* Penny wanted to say, certain the man had pieced everything together in its proper order. Now for the final clue. "I just don't know what to do. She's my best friend, and if I broke my word to her, she'd never forgive me. But he's leaving soon . . . for Jamaica, and once he's gone . . . well . . ." She sighed again and added, "So you see, when you told me *you* were from Jamaica, I was reminded of my friend's predicament. Silly, isn't it."

Of course, he could be wrong, but Geoffrey doubted it. And then there was the chance that Penny's friend had seen a way to get herself a rich husband. Alec had had that problem one other time and had finally had to confront the girl's father with her accusations before she'd tell the truth. So which was it? Was Penny talking about Alec, and had he actually fallen in love, or was this a ploy to get at the man's money? Well, first things first. Before he jumped to any conclusions, he had to know if Penny meant Alec Stone.

"No, it isn't silly, Penny," he said quietly. "I can understand your sorrow for your friend's plight. And I can understand the dilemma she's put you in." He raised the mug to his lips and took a drink. "Has she told her parents?"

A frown crossed her brow and disappeared. That was an odd thing to ask. She thought sure he'd be more interested in finding out the man's name rather than if Rebecca had told her parents. "They're both dead. She lives alone." Miffed by the captain's stupidity, she mocked, "For a while, anyway."

A few moments of silence passed between them while Penny cursed the time and energy she'd wasted on this fool, and Geoffrey wondered how he'd get her to tell him the man's name. But before either of them could make a decision on what course of action to take next, the door to The Red Lion was thrown open, and Jon-Gregory's tall, lanky frame

371

rushed in. His fierce gaze instantly fell on Penny, and for the first time in all the while she had known him, Penny felt a twinge of fear. He didn't have to tell her that he knew who had undermined his efforts to speak with Captain Synder first. She could see it in his gray-blue eyes.

"Excuse me, Captain," she hurriedly announced. "I think I'm needed in the kitchen." Scooting off her chair, she raced in that direction before Geoffrey had a chance to stop her or question the purpose of her rapid departure, but more so before Jon-Gregory could lay his hands on her.

"How long have we known each other, Geoffrey?" Brad chuckled as he reached for the bottle of wine to refill everyone's glass. "Four, five years?"

"About that," Geoffrey agreed. "We met the first time I delivered goods to Boston for Alec, and I've been with him close to five."

"And to think," Brad continued with a shake of his head as he came to where Alec stood staring out the porthole at the other ships anchored in the bay, "Alec and I were that close to meeting each other all that time. Of course, it probably wouldn't have made a difference. He didn't know about the ring until a few months ago. It could have, however, made it a little easier on us both once we learned we were related." He poured a full measure of wine into Alec's glass, then added playfully, "Damn if you didn't break my nose."

Smiling crookedly, Alec retorted, "Consider it a favor that I didn't. It might have made you uglier than you already are, and Penny would be sure not to give you a second look."

Geoffrey didn't hear Brad's reply to his half brother's quip, if indeed he said anything at all. The mention of Penelope Dawson's name had reminded him of what had to be done and how little time in which Geoffrey had to do it. Alec wanted to leave for Jamaica in the morning, and if something wasn't said before then, Geoffrey would always wonder if he'd made a mistake by not confronting Alec with the truth.

And what was the truth? he mused as he absently stared

into his glass. Alec had yet to speak Rebecca's name or tell him anything about her while he related his experiences leading up to his meeting Brad, which made him think he had been right all along and the young girl was nothing more than a fortune hunter. Yet something about the way Alec behaved gnawed at his insides and let the doubt creep back in. Granted, any man would act differently if he'd learned he had two half brothers, a cousin, sister-in-law and three nephews after all these years. But there was more to it than that. Underneath all the laughter and jokes was a hint of sadness. Geoffrey had seen it in his eyes the second Alec introduced Brad as his half brother a short while ago, and his sorrow had nothing to do with Daniel Heller's death. Geoffrey might have asked Alec about it right then if he hadn't been so taken aback by Alec's news. Now all he could do was wonder . . . or make up his mind to challenge Alec.

After his talk with Jon-Gregory that day, Geoffrey had spent the next three waiting for Alec in his cabin on board the *Constance*. According to the young man's report, Alec was spending a few days with Brad Remington on his cousin Beau's plantation, and he wanted Geoffrey to stay put until he returned. It seemed Alec had given up hope of ever recovering his money since Daniel Heller was dead and his trail had grown cold. Therefore Alec could see no reason for staying in Williamsburg, and Geoffrey had had to agree. But while he waited, he spent a lot of time speculating . . . about Daniel Heller and what could have become of Alec's money. Geoffrey had never met Heller before the day he boarded the merchant ship on his way to Williamsburg, but in the short time he spent with the man, Geoffrey grew to dislike him. Heller was a complainer . . . about his lowly station in life, his wife, how he hated having to take orders and most of all his intolerance for sailing.

"Give me a pocket full of money, fine clothes and a country estate in England," he had said. "*That's* the way a man should live."

Geoffrey hadn't given Heller's claim much thought at the time since most everyone dreamed of better things, but once he'd reflected back on the conversation, he was tempted to tell Alec that he suspected Heller had Alec's money. Of course Alec would only laugh at the idea since Heller was dead, but Geoffrey simply couldn't put the thought from his head. Maybe his death assured his elimination as a suspect, but the fact that he had been murdered raised other possibilities, ones Geoffrey wondered if Alec had even considered. Maybe he had decided to take his undeserved wealth and flee to England to live the way he wanted and foolishly bragged to the wrong person or persons about his plans, and they killed him for it. He had voiced that supposition to Jon-Gregory the next evening when he ran into the young man at Raleigh Tavern where he was having something to drink before going home to bed. Jon-Gregory quickly contested the theory when he reminded Geoffrey of the letters Heller had sent and the purchase of the Robinson property, asking why a man would go to so much trouble if he intended to leave the Colonies. And if Heller had been as dishonest as Geoffrey wanted to believe, then Heller wouldn't have wasted a single coin on such a plan. He would have taken them all and fled. Geoffrey had had to agree, though begrudgingly, and the two men fell quiet as they each pondered various other ideas. That was when Jon-Gregory mentioned Rebecca Wilde and *her* efforts to solve the puzzle. The name hadn't been familiar to Geoffrey, and once he questioned Jon-Gregory about her and was told she was a friend of Penelope Dawson's, the little scene at The Red Lion relived itself in Geoffrey's mind.

Penny's sudden decision to end their discussion over her friend's delicate situation had baffled Geoffrey until he looked up and saw the tall, blond-haired, young man glaring angrily at her from the doorway while she made her hurried departure. The pair obviously knew each other, and Geoffrey concluded the man's rage had to do with him . . . or the fact that he had caught Penny talking to a stranger. Then Jon-Gregory introduced himself, and it all fell together. Alec had gotten himself into one of those "fixes" again because of his wealth and good looks, just as Geoffrey had guessed, and the young man had somehow been made aware of what Penny and her friend were scheming and didn't approve. Geoffrey hadn't asked him about it at the time, but now that they were relaxed and sharing a mug of ale and had seemed to accept each other as allies, he casually commented on the incident at The Red Lion and how he'd gotten the impression Jon-Gregory didn't trust Penelope Dawson or Rebecca Wilde. He strongly disagreed and began to relate everything that had happened to Alec since Gerald Haugen rowed the long boat to shore and dropped Alec off, changing Geoffrey's opinion of Rebecca Wilde considerably. She had lost her job and a place to live because of her involvement with Alec, and yet she had unselfishly cared for him while he recovered from his wounds. She had possibly even saved his life to hear Jon-Gregory tell it, while putting her own in danger to help Alec find out what had become of Daniel Heller, and had then quietly stepped aside when nothing more could be done. Hardly the actions of a conniving woman, Geoffrey concluded. Yet Jon-Gregory had seemed to think so or he wouldn't have been so angry when he found Penny talking to him, and he posed that observation to the young man. He could hardly believe his ears once Jon-Gregory told him his anger had come from Penny's meddling and not because of some scheme she had thought up to bilk Alec out of some of his money, and Jon-Gregory couldn't imagine what had made Geoffrey accuse her of such a thing. Geoffrey didn't bother to explain but instead apologized when Jon-Gregory appeared to be offended. They had finished their drinks in silence after that, but when Jon-Gregory got up to leave, he paused a moment, then quietly offered his guess that Rebecca Wilde cared more for Alec Stone than she'd ever be willing to admit. He had started to say more, but instead turned on his heel and left the tavern with his shoulders sagging.

Geoffrey hadn't been able to get the young woman off his mind after that, even though he knew it really wasn't any of his business. Perhaps she did love Alec. Maybe she was expecting his child. But unless Alec said something, unless he showed the slightest hesitation about leaving, Geoffrey didn't feel it was his place to say anything. Geoffrey knew what it was like for a man to be in a loveless marriage, how confining it was, how miserable every day turned out to be, because he had lived such a life. His only escape had been his wife's decision to leave him for a man with twice Geoffrey's wealth, and he had celebrated long and hard for several days afterward. No, he wasn't going to be responsible for placing Alec in such an arrangement. If Alec wanted Miss Wilde to share his life with him, then he'd have to be the one to decide without any coaxing from anyone. But then, what would happen to Rebecca?

The silence in the cabin suddenly closed in on him, and he blinked, straightened in his chair and looked up to find both Brad and Alec staring back at him.

"We thought we'd lost you." Brad chuckled, totally ignorant of the thoughts that had been going through Geoffrey's mind. "I realize this has been a bit of a surprise to you, but think how I felt when I learned I had a half brother."

Without realizing how it would sound, Geoffrey muttered, "I've learned a lot of surprising things about Alec Stone in the last few days. I'm getting used to it." Raising the wine to his lips, he finished off his drink and fell back in his chair to stare blankly off into space, the empty glass dangling from his fingertips.

"Do you get the feeling he's upset with you, Alec?" Brad teased with a playful nudge in Alec's ribs as the two men stood side by side a few feet away from the captain.

Alec had expected that his announcement about Brad Remington being his half brother would come as a shock to Geoffrey, especially since Geoffrey had known Brad for several years and often looked him up to have a drink together whenever Geoffrey was in Boston. But the various expressions he had seen on the man's face and how drastically they changed while his thoughts took him elsewhere truly puzzled Alec. He saw no reason for Geoffrey to disapprove of Brad since he'd spoken so highly of Geoffrey Synder once Alec mentioned that the man worked for him. Yet the emotions that mirrored themselves in Geoffrey's eyes hinted of turmoil, possibly even rage, and Alec felt he owed their years of friendship the courtesy of asking what bothered him. Moving closer, Alec rested a hip on the corner of Geoffrey's desk, folded his wrists over his thigh and waited for him to look up.

"What is it, Geoffrey?" he asked solemnly.

The other frowned once he realized how careless he had been and that because of it Alec would hound him until he explained what had put him in such a pensive mood. "I don't know what you mean," he lied.

Brad, too, suddenly sensed that something perplexing was on the captain's mind. Joining the two men, he set his glass and the half-empty bottle of wine on the desk and replied, "You're supposed to be helping us celebrate. Yet you look as if we told you Alec had only a few days to live. Are you trying to tell us that of all the men in the world, why did *I* have to be his half brother?"

"No!" Geoffrey exclaimed, heaving himself from the chair. "It's nothing like that, I don't know how you could even think it. You and I have been friends for years. I couldn't have picked a more honorable, deserving half brother for Alec than you."

"So why the long face?" Brad pressed. "Or is this something you'd prefer to talk about in private?"

"Private?" Geoffrey laughed mockingly. "I'd hardly call it private when nearly everyone in Williamsburg knows about it."

The siblings exchanged a curious look before Brad asked, "I don't. Do you?"

Alec shook his head. "Why not let us in on it, Geoffrey, since Brad and I seem to be the only ones who haven't been listening to gossip."

"Gossip?" Geoffrey exploded as he stormed across the cabin to take up the vigil Alec had abandoned. "If I listened to something Miss Dawson told me, would you call that gossip?" When neither Alec nor Brad replied, he quickly faced them and asked a second time, "Well, would you?"

"It depends," Alec responded hesitantly, his brow furrowed. "When did you speak with her?"

"Does it matter? The point is, I did."

"And?"

Geoffrey's frame stiffened as he lowered his chin. "And she told me an interesting story about a friend of hers. She never mentioned the young lady's name or the man with whom she was involved. But it didn't take me long to figure out who that man was. Not long at all."

Brad could see by the look on Alec's face that he wasn't all that eager to have Geoffrey repeat what he'd heard. Brad was, however, since it was quite apparent Penny had been talking about Alec and Rebecca. "So spit it out, man. What did she tell you?"

With his eyes narrowed, Geoffrey stared at his friend until Alec suddenly decided that sitting still was more than he could manage right then. Leaving his place at the desk, he crossed to the map in the middle of the room and halfheartedly rearranged the papers lying on top, obviously ill-at-ease.

"It seems this friend of Miss Dawson's," Geoffrey began, his gaze still riveted on Alec, "got herself in a bit of trouble—the kind that won't go away just because the man responsible for it goes back home to Jamaica." Geoffrey cocked his head to one side and folded his arms over his chest when Alec's shocked and questioning look suddenly fell on him. "Oh, I see I have your attention now," he added sarcastically. "Does this mean it wasn't gossip I heard?"

Alec couldn't imagine why Penny would say such a thing if it wasn't true, but he had to be sure. "I don't really know. But I question why Penny told you and not me, since the matter is *my* responsibility.".

"Oh, that's quite simple. First of all, Miss Dawson didn't really want to tell me, but I forced her into it; and secondly, her friend made her swear an oath not to tell the expectant father."

"Bloody hell," Brad moaned as he fell back against the desk. "I guess this means you won't be leaving for Jamaica in the morning." He chuckled to himself while he rubbed his hand along his jaw, muttering, "Unless, of course, we can talk the minister into performing the ceremony tonight."

Alec shot Brad a murderous glower.

"That might come harder than you think, Brad," Geoffrey

378

announced. "I got the distinct impression that the bride-to-be has no desire to wed."

"Well, that's understandable," Brad remarked. "Who'd want to get stuck with him for the rest of her life?"

Insulted, Alec started to argue the point, but the two men who shared the cabin with him acted as though they had forgotten he was there.

"But then again, I think they deserve each other. Rebecca Wilde is just as hard-headed as Alec," Brad went on as he poured himself another drink. "And now that I think about it, they just might be what the other one needs. They'd be too busy with each other to make everyone else's life miserable." Rising, he took the bottle and Geoffrey's glass with him as he crossed to where the captain stood. "Have you ever met her?" he asked, continuing once Geoffrey shook his head. "She's very beautiful, but she's got the meanest disposition of any woman I've ever met. Of course, maybe that will change once she becomes a mother and has to raise the child on her own. That's quite a responsibility for a woman alone. Yet somehow I don't think she'll stay that way for long. Some smart man will see through all her anger and sweep her off her feet. He'll marry her and—"

The slamming of the cabin door interrupted Brad's speech and brought a devilish smile to his lips as he handed Geoffrey the glass and filled it with wine.

"A toast," he declared, holding his own up in a salute. "To the newlyweds."

Tears of anger and frustration spilled down Rebecca's cheeks as she stood staring at the charred remains of what she had planned to eat for dinner. It had been her second attempt to fix her own meal, and both efforts had ended with the same result, even though she had read Penny's written instructions very carefully. How hard could it be to cook palatable food? she had silently declared while refusing to accept Penny's invitation to live with her until after the baby was born. She would have to learn sooner or later, if not for her child's sake, then for her own. And until

Alec had left Williamsburg for good, she couldn't risk running into him . . . which was sure to happen if she moved in with Penny. Uttering a low growl, she scooped up the smoldering pot of burned stew and headed for the door, thinking that some poor, starving animal in the woods wouldn't mind chipping a tooth. At least one of God's creatures wouldn't fall asleep hungry, thanks to her.

It had been close to two weeks now since the time Alec mounted his horse and rode off, and with each new dawn she rose believing that this would be the day Penny would come to the cabin to tell her he had gone. She was sure that once he had, she could begin to forget him. But the moment she lifted her head from the pillow, her stomach would churn, and she'd race for the bucket, cursing under her breath at the blackguard who had made such a shambles of her life. Before long her retching would stop and her tears would begin. She wanted to forget him, but she knew she never could. His child grew inside her, and until the day she died, she'd always be reminded of him.

As she stood in the yard outside the cabin, the handle of the pot dangling from her fingertips, she stared off at the lengthening shadows of evening while she absently ran her hand over her flat belly. Unknowingly, she allowed her imagination to conjure up images of the newborn baby she would hold in her arms before long. Might he have tuffs of black hair and deep brown eyes? Or would it be a blue-eyed, blond-haired little girl? Would she have Alec's nose and her personality? Or Alec's silent nature and her stubbornness? Would the baby boy have a desire to express his thoughts and ideas on paper? Or would he exhibit his father's talents and become a planter? Suddenly a tear trickled from the corner of her eye and spoiled the mood. What did it matter? Alec would never know his child even existed. Her chin trembled, and she raised it proudly in the air and closed her eyes while she told herself again that even *if* Alec knew, he wouldn't care. He felt nothing for her, so why would he love his child? And if somehow he found out about the baby and came for her, what kind of a life would they have? He'd hate her for trapping him. And her dreams of being a journalist would fade.

The distant beat of horse's hooves against the road jolted Rebecca out of her sadness. She hurriedly brushed away her tears and fidgeted with her tangled hair before remembering the pot she held. Certain her visitor was Penny, she quickly hid the evidence of her disastrous attempt at cooking behind a huge rock and raced to stand near the cabin door as if nothing bothered her. Then horse and rider came into view as they turned onto the lane, and her brave façade crumbled.

"Good evening, Rebecca," Robert Gilmore sneered as he reined his horse in close and leaned forward with his crossed arms resting on the pommel. "I see doing menial chores agrees with you. You're as beautiful as ever."

Rebecca's blue eyes shot sparks of pure hatred. "What are you doing here?" she hissed.

"My, my," he mocked, swinging a leg over the horse's rump and stepping to the ground. "Is that any way for a young woman to talk to the man who could take her away from all this?" His hand swept out to indicate the small cabin and run-down shed. "Or are you going to try and tell me you *like* living here?" Without being invited, he moved past her and went into the cabin.

"What I'd like," she growled, following him through the door, "is for you to get back on that horse and ride out of my life. I never thought Lenore was very smart, but I certainly gave her more credit than to fall for the likes of you. You're evil, Gilmore, and maybe *she* enjoys having you around, but I don't. I can't even stand to look at you."

He had expected her to say as much, and since he'd heard it all before, he wasn't really offended. Ignoring her request that he leave, he strolled arrogantly around the room, examining what few trinkets or items of value he saw before settling himself in one of the chairs by the table. Crossing his knees, he smoothed a wrinkle from his breeches and set cold, green eyes on her.

"Don't you think it's time you gave up this foolishness and came home?" he calmly posed.

"Home?" Rebecca laughed sarcastically. "*This* is more my home than living on Twin Oaks." She squinted her eyes and asked, "And you know why? Because I'm not afraid I'll find you lurking around some corner just waiting to grab me. As long as you and Lenore are staying at Twin Oaks, I'll *never* go back. Can't you understand that?"

"Yes, Rebecca, I do," he easily admitted. "And I also know what it is you're really trying to say." The cocky smile had disappeared from his face, and in its place was a look that chilled Rebecca to the bone. "You're afraid to be around me because you know that sooner or later the fact that I'm married to your stepmother won't make a difference." He ignored her shocked gasp and continued, "Well, I can fix that, Rebecca. I can get rid of Lenore, and you can come home to live . . . with me."

Rebecca couldn't believe what she was hearing. "You're insane," she breathed as she fought to control her mocking laughter. "I don't care if you're married to Lenore or to a hundred different women all at the same time! *You're* the reason I won't go back to Twin Oaks. I despise you. You're the poorest excuse for a man I've ever had the misfortune to meet. And believe me, I've met a lot of them." She could see by the angry expression on his face and how his body had gone rigid that he had finally grasped the fact that there would never be any hope of her changing her mind about him, and she used that to her advantage when she added, "Besides, you viper, even if I didn't hate you more than anything else in my life, I still wouldn't agree to come home. I can't. I'm getting married."

The color drained from his face as though he'd been shot and every ounce of his blood had oozed from his body. Weak, he awkwardly pushed himself up from the chair and leaned crazily against the table. "To whom?" he demanded through a raspy voice. "Certainly not Alec Stone. You can't. I won't let you."

Rebecca had hoped her announcement would send him racing off in a fit of rage, back to his wife and the plantation neither of them deserved to claim as theirs. She had lied because she figured that sort of declaration would be the only way she could get rid of him . . . permanently. His reaction, however, wasn't anything like she expected it to be.

And his threat to not allow her to marry Alec revealed a much deeper determination to have her all to himself than she had ever imagined he felt. The hair on the back of her neck stood on end, and a chill darted up her spine as she stumbled back a step, hoping to stay out of his reach when he started to advance. Fear clouded her mind or she might have questioned his choice of a candidate worthy enough of her consideration as a husband, or that he knew Alec's last name was Stone. She also might have asked how he knew where to find her and what made him think anything about her situation had changed to the point that he felt he needed to come to her rescue. But those subjects never crossed her mind. All she could concentrate on at the moment was escaping him, for the crazed look in his eye guaranteed her that he intended to carry through with his threat. He would kill her before he'd let anyone else have her.

A whimper trailed from her lips when she backed into the door frame, which temporarily ended her departure. In that same moment, Gilmore made a lunge for her, and she screamed when his fingers caught the sleeve of her dress. But she wasn't about to surrender so easily, and when he reached out his other hand to grab her by the throat, she rammed her opened palms against his chest and shoved him backward, allowing her the time and the space to slip past him and through the door. Rebecca knew she wouldn't be given the chance to mount his horse before he was on her, nor would she allow him the use of the animal to catch up to her while she fled on foot. Rebecca waved her arms in the air and shouted at the top of her lungs while she raced from the cabin, and the steed bolted, reared up on its hind legs, then turned and galloped off down the lane ahead of her. Seizing the thick folds of her skirts in her hands, she raised the hemline to her knees and never looked back as she raced down the dirt path in the stallion's wake. Tears blurred her vision of the animal's frantic retreat and clouded the sight of the path she took, and she forced herself to listen to the horse's hooves striking the earth ahead of her for a hint to the direction she should take.

By the time she neared the end of the lane, which

intersected with the road into town, her legs were beginning to cramp, and the pain in her side was almost unbearable as she dragged air into her tortured lungs; but she refused to slow her pace. She could sense Gilmore's presence close behind her and that his rage would distort his reasoning if he caught her, and she begged for mercy. Yet she knew she couldn't last much longer, and she had to come up with a plan to insure her escape. Realizing that he had a clear advantage as long as she stuck to the road, she suddenly veered off into the woods. The way became more difficult to travel since she had to dodge tree trunks, scrubs, broken limbs and rocks laying in her path, but it also meant it would slow Gilmore down as well. Foolishly taking the chance to look over her shoulder at him, the muscles across her chest tightened with the scream she suppressed when she saw that he was only a few steps behind her, and she pushed blindly onward. A jagged tree branch pierced the thin fabric covering her arm and jerked her off balance. She stumbled, went down on one knee and felt the thorns of the scrubbery which cushioned her fall scratch her face and hands when she tried to catch herself. But that discomfort hardly compared to the agony she suffered when Gilmore's fingers locked their hold in her hair above the nape and she was dragged to her feet.

"You bitch," he growled, yanking down cruelly on the silky mane until Rebecca had to lean heavily against him to keep from falling backward. "I gave you every chance. I even killed for you. You could have had it all, but your pride, your arrogance wouldn't let you see what I could offer you. No. You thought I wasn't good enough for you, so you flaunted yourself at Stone. What has he got that I don't have?"

"A gun, for one" came the threatening declaration from behind them, "and it's pointed at your head."

"Alec!" Rebecca sobbed, the irony of how good it felt to hear his voice escaping her tormented thoughts.

"Let her go," Alec demanded, "or so help me, I won't even blink when I pull the trigger."

Panic raced through Gilmore. He had voiced a confession, though not clearly, and feared all his efforts would go to waste because of his careless slip of the tongue. Perhaps he could bargain with the man who held his fate in his hands.

"All right," he vowed, gingerly releasing the thick strands of hair entwined around his fingers and holding up his hands once Rebecca had darted away from him. "Don't shoot. I wouldn't have hurt her. I only wanted to scare her. She belongs back home with her stepmother and me, not living here the way she is. But if that's what she wants, then I won't interfere again. I swear." He kept his back to Alec, praying he had guessed right about him and that he was too much of a gentleman to kill an unarmed man . . . especially when that man wasn't facing him. "Just allow me to leave, and I won't cause you any trouble. You have my word on it."

Alec had to fight the strong desire to put a lead ball into the man just for the pleasure of seeing him bleed. He'd only met Gilmore twice, and both times he had foiled the man's attempt to force himself on Rebecca. He didn't deserve to simply walk away with an apology and a promise never to intrude upon Rebecca's life again. He deserved to suffer a little or at least experience the humiliation he had forced on Rebecca.

"I hope you'll understand when I say I don't believe you," Alec replied with a half-mocking smile wrinkling one cheek. "But I'll tell you what you can do to convince me."

"Anything!" Gilmore pledged. "Anything at all. Just name it."

"Get down on all fours" came the hissing command, and Gilmore forgot about his assumption that Alec wouldn't shoot him in the back as he spun around to face him, his brows slanted together and his mouth hanging open.

"What?"

Alec motioned at the ground with his pistol. "I said to get down on your hands and knees. I'll have to see you crawl before I'll believe you're really sincere."

A black rage darkened Gilmore's eyes. At that moment he wanted nothing more out of life than to be given the opportunity to kill this man. But the odds were against him. Chances were that if he didn't comply with Stone's demands, he'd be dead the second he took a step toward him. Shifting his hate-filled glower on Rebecca, he silently vowed his revenge, first on her lover and then on her. They would both suffer . . . a slow, agonizing torture, and he'd save Rebecca until last. She'd be forced to stand back and watch while he maliciously ended Alec Stone's life.

"Now!"

The sharp command echoed in the stillness of the woods, and Gilmore dropped to his knees. Not only did Stone have the advantage of being armed, but Gilmore knew he was no physical match to the man. Nor was it in Gilmore's nature to fight fairly. Women and boys were his specialty or anyone else who couldn't defend himself. He'd swallow his pride . . . for now. He'd leave them alone . . . like he promised, but only for the length of time it would take him to get his gun and plot out a way to catch Alec Stone off guard. He'd be back . . . and sooner than anyone expected.

The muscles in Alec's hand ached before he realized how tightly he held the pistol and how much willpower it had taken for him to not pull the trigger while he watched Gilmore fulfill his demand. During the years he sailed the Atlantic with a shipload of slaves, he wouldn't have thought twice about killing a man for much less than what Gilmore had done. But that was a long time ago, and he wasn't the same heartless renegade he was then. Not that the man wasn't begging for some sort of retaliation for what he'd done—being denied his self-respect in front of a woman hardly seemed just punishment—but Alec had Rebecca to think of. She had been through enough already, and he wouldn't add to it by killing him right before her eyes. If need be, Alec would deal with him later . . . when Rebecca wasn't around to witness it.

Remembering his reason for being here, he shifted his attention to her. She stood with one hand covering her mouth, her eyes wide and brimming with tears, and her tiny frame trembling as she watched Gilmore crawl away. The sight of her caused Alec's own emotions to take a sudden turn. He had left his half brother and Geoffrey Synder feeling totally confused, and the closer he rode to the cabin, that perplexity changed to anger. The idea of her refusing to tell him about the baby infuriated him. She had no right to keep that a secret from him. It was *his* baby, too. Maybe he didn't honestly want to be tied down with a wife, but he would never, *never* force a child of his to live the kind of life he'd been forced to endure. Then he'd stumbled across the sight of a man with his hands on Rebecca in such a way that Alec knew she had been threatened, and his rage exploded. Rebecca had done a lot of foolish things, aggravated him to no end, but *no one* would be allowed to threaten her with harm, and Alec had made that very clear to Robert Gilmore. Yet, now that the immediate danger had passed, Alec's temper rose again. Stepping closer to her, he roughly took her arm and pulled her toward his horse where he jammed his pistol in his waistband, caught her in his arms and swung her up into the saddle before she had time to object or question his intent. With reins in hand, he pulled himself up behind her and turned the animal toward the lane.

The trip back to Williamsburg passed in silence, and neither of them spoke a word when Alec directed the horse past the road leading into town and headed toward the docks. They continued their silence all the way to the wharf where he reined the animal to a halt and dismounted, then helped her to the ground and firmly led her to the ship moored at the end of the pier. After helping her ascend the lowered gangplank. Alec escorted her to the captain's quarters and didn't bother to knock before lifting the latch and opening the door. For some reason he had assumed Brad and Geoffrey would have the good sense to allow them the privacy of the cabin, and he inwardly thanked them for their discretion. It spared him the awkward moment of introductions and the uncomfortable task of telling them that he wished to have a moment alone with Rebecca.

Still quite upset over the events of the past hour, he frowned while he watched her cross the room and pause near the portholes as if whatever she saw just beyond them held a special interest. Frustrated when it appeared she had no intention of discussing their problems, he turned and swung the door shut with a loud bang.

"I hope you have a very good explanation for why I had to

learn about your condition from someone else," he declared.

"My *condition?*" she mocked, keeping her back to him. "And what *condition* is that?"

"You know what I mean," he barked, storming the distance between them to grab her elbow and jerk her around to face him. "I'm asking why you didn't come to me when you learned you were carrying my child."

Rebecca's blue eyes narrowed. "Who says it's yours?"

Alec had known this wouldn't be easy—anything involving Rebecca Wilde wasn't easy—but he never expected her to be flippant. "Whose is it then? Gilmore's?"

Her hand came up instantly to strike his face, but he caught her wrist before any harm befell him and squeezed the delicate bones until some of the fire in her eyes faded. "Shall we stop playing games now and discuss this like two adults?" he asked through clenched teeth.

Rebecca jerked her arm free. "There's nothing to discuss. This is *my* problem, and I'll handle it, thank you." She started to move away, but he stepped in her path.

"It's not just *your* problem, Rebecca. The baby is mine as well, and I have an obligation to it."

"Obligation?" She laughed mockingly. "Is that how you see it? An obligation?" She tossed her silky mane and brushed past him. "What do you propose then? A generous allotment of funds for the child's welfare and a visit from you every now and then just so he doesn't forget you're his father? I don't need your handouts, Alec Stone. I can take care of myself . . . and the baby."

"You weren't doing a very good job of it a short while ago. If I hadn't come when I did—"

"It won't happen again," she rallied hotly. "I'm planning to leave Williamsburg and go someplace where no one will find me."

"Including me?" he asked, his temper simmering.

She spun around to glare at him. "Especially you!"

The days he had spent away from her hadn't cooled the strong desires she had awakened in him from the first moment they met. If anything, her absence had tormented his sanity. And seeing her now—with her thick, black hair falling in wild disarray about her face and shoulders, her icy blue eyes snapping with anger, and the blush in her creamy white cheeks—only strengthened the knowledge that he would never be able to put her from his mind. He had been willing to try—he was planning to leave for Jamaica in the morning without her—but because of the baby, he refused to desert her. Aric Remington's excuse for not caring for his son had been simply because he hadn't known about him. Such was not the case with Alec. Rebecca probably wouldn't like his solution, but as far as he was concerned, she had no choice.

"I was planning to return home in the morning," he announced with a sigh as he turned to stare blankly out the porthole, "but that's all changed now."

"Not on my account, I hope," she hissed rebelliously. "You may leave right now for all I care."

Alec turned his head and looked at her askance. "No, not on your account. I've changed my mind because of the baby. But when I leave, you'll be going with me."

"I will not!" she shrieked. "*You're* not going to be the one to make all the decisions. It's *my* life, too, you know, and I don't want to live in Jamaica. If you want to see your child, you'll have to come to me. I've got more pride than to allow myself to be put on display as your mistress."

"You won't be my mistress, Reb," he snarled. "You'll be my wife."

The declaration caught her so off guard that she wasn't able to draw a breath at first, much less respond. Then, with her temper flaring, she spat, "Just like that? Because *you* decide we should wed, that's how it will be?"

Alec faced her, his hands low on his hips and a challenging look in his eyes. "Yes. That's how it will be, and you're not going to argue. For once in your life, Rebecca Wilde, you'll do as you're told. If you haven't the sense to do what's best for that baby, then I'll do it for you. But one way or the other—as mistress or wife—you'll be coming with me to Jamaica. I won't allow you to force the kind of life I had to live on my child because of your stubbornness."

Numb, Rebecca just stood there staring at him, her

emotions churning confusedly in her head and weighing down her heart. She wanted to laugh at him and call his proposal absurd. She wanted to ask what would become of her once the baby was born, since she didn't think being his wife would matter to him then. And electing to become his mistress would be even worse. He'd have no reason to keep her around once she gave him his son. She also wanted to remind him that she wasn't the type of woman to cower to his demands. Nor was she willing to give up her dream of being a journalist just because she was expecting a child. Yet aside from all that, what truly pierced its sharp talons into her pride and left her bleeding was the emptiness of his offer. He was honor bound to marry her. He had decided out of responsibility to the baby and nothing more. There had been no words of kindness, no remorse or hint that he felt anything at all for the mother of his child. He didn't love her, and that recognition left her feeling cheap and terribly hurt. Blinking back her tears, she averted her eyes. She hadn't been able to admit it until now, but all Rebecca really wanted was to have her love returned. She'd have that from her baby, but it was a man's love she needed. She needed Alec.

"For how long?" she quietly asked, turning away from him.

His frown mirrored his puzzlement. "How long for what?"

"How long will you expect me to stay with you?"

Alec couldn't explain the sensation that came over him then. Her question was the same as saying she wouldn't stay any longer than she absolutely had to, and the thought that someday she'd walk out of his life as turbulently as she had walked into it stunned him. He hadn't offered marriage as a temporary means to solve her problem. He meant it to be lasting. *He wanted it to be lasting.*

"What's that supposed to mean?" he barked, no longer able to keep his temper under control. "Are you saying you'll agree to come with me if I give you a time limit? Well, I won't. I've never asked a woman to marry me before—I've never even thought about doing it—but I certainly wouldn't offer if it wasn't meant to be forever. What could you possibly be thinking? That as long as the baby needs a mother, I would need a wife, then I'd pack your things and send you back to Virginia? Maybe I'm not your idea of a husband, Rebecca Wilde, but I'm a damn sight better than your having to raise the child on your own." Outraged, he threw his hands in the air and took two agitated steps then halted. "I don't believe it!" He faced her again. "If I'd wanted a nanny for my child, I would have hired one . . . not married her."

His harsh words angered her. "I really see no difference . . . except that it wouldn't be proper to bed the hired help."

Alec's tawny brows came together in a fierce scowl. "But a lot more pleasurable!"

Rebecca brushed off the insult to counter, "I'm sure it would be. You'd rather make love to some starry-eyed, brainless twit who hasn't the courage to open her mouth than a—"

"A hot-headed, sharp-tongued, spoiled brat?" he cut in challengingly, his head lowered and his body stiff with rage. "You're damned right I would." He moved closer. "What man wouldn't? I can't even begin to imagine the kind of man who'd willingly crawl into bed with a bad-tempered wench knowing there was a chance she'd bash in his head."

Never having backed down when aspersions were directed her way, Rebecca straightened her spine, raised her nose in the air and met him in the middle of the room. "A fool, perhaps?" she cunningly suggested.

Failing to recognize the insinuation behind her remark, Alec quickly agreed. "Yes! A fool."

A slow, sarcastic smile curled her mouth, and the accusing gleam in her blue eyes said more than if she'd spoken the conclusion she had drawn; and hardly a second passed before Alec realized the trap he had fallen into. With nostrils flaring and brows lowered, he heaved an exasperated sigh.

"The biggest of all," he hissed, shooting out his hands to catch her arms and pull her roughly into his embrace.

That same all-consuming fire of passion erupted in the pit of Rebecca's stomach the instant his mouth swooped down to capture hers, and without any hesitation, driven by a delirious, overpowering need, she threw her arms around his neck and returned his ardent kiss. Her mouth moved greedily against his, their tongues clashing, their hearts beating wildly and thunderously, and tears glistened beneath her dark lashes and threatened to spill down her cheeks. He might not have actually said the words she so longed to hear him say, but his subtle confession that he cared enough for her to offer marriage—even though it be under the guise of honor—revealed more about his feelings toward her than anything else he might have said. He could have abandoned her, but he chose not to, and in turn laid to rest her fear that she had only been a momentary hunger he must sate. Perhaps with the dawning of another day, she too might concede to the complexity of their souls and come to realize the faint hope that they could ever live in harmony. But for now . . . it didn't matter.

The sweet smell of her skin and fragrant hair filled Alec's senses and sent his mind reeling. Her willingness, her eager response and the luscious curves of her supple body pressed against him nearly took his breath away and clearly reminded him of what brought them together time and time again. Passion clouded his judgment as it always did and seemed to be the root of their problems. Because of his weakness for her, they had created a child, a lasting bond that could not be denied. But was it truly the knowledge that she carried his baby that brought him running back into her arms? Or was it merely lust? Nay, it was something else entirely, and that realization was what frightened him. How could he tell her that loving her was what he truly feared? That opening his heart and soul to someone, being vulnerable was what he'd spent his life avoiding? He hadn't wanted to suffer the way his mother had, yet for the first time in his life, Alec understood the woman's intense feeling for the man who deserted her. Love was unconditional.

The touch of her fingertips across his shoulders as Rebecca slid the jacket from him destroyed his last hope of denying what he felt in his heart, and he forgot all else save the burning desire to possess her. In an urgency born of lust, he helped her strip away his shirt, but brushed her hands aside when she started to unbutton her dress. The yards of cloth floated to the floor, joined with stockings and shoes, and while he trailed hot kisses down her throat, he reveled in the sound of her rapid breathing and the pleasurable moan that escaped her when his hand came up to cup her breast, his thumb gently stroking its hardened peak through the gauzy fabric of her camisole. Quick fingers caught the satin ribbon and nimbly untied the knot to expose the full swell of her bosom hidden beneath the lacy cloth. Lifting his head, his eyes dark with desire, he studied Rebecca's face for any sign that she had changed her mind. His unspoken question was answered for him when she took his hand and gently laid it on her naked breast, her eyes locked on his, her lips parted and silently begged to be kissed. In all his dreams, he had never imagined total surrender coupled with words of love could ever be like this.

Their lips met again but with a savagery and fierceness that belied their gentle beginning. His mouth twisted against hers, bruising and eager, while he trapped the long strands of her black hair at the nape of his fingers, his tongue thrusting inside to meet hers. In his frenzy, he pulled down on the silkened tresses to draw up her chin and began smothering her throat with hot, sultry kisses, burning a path all the way to the valley between her breasts. Her moan of ecstasy was music to his ears, driving him on in blind passion. He captured one rose-colored taut peak and teased it hungrily with his tongue while his fingers stripped away her chemise. Again their lips met as he caught her around the waist with one arm and pulled her full against him, drinking in the heady brew of her satiny flesh touching his bare chest while his other hand, the fingers fanned wide, cradled her jaw.

Rebecca felt as if every inch of her was aflame, an intoxicating pleasure that made her head spin and her body crave more. His hardened frame pressed against her, his thickly muscled arms enveloping her, the masculine scent of him and his demanding kisses turned her blood into a raging fire that coursed through her with every beat of her heart. Delirious with passion, she drew her nails down the sinewy ripples across his back, then on to the fastening of his brecches. Together, they tore away the rest of his clothes in an intolerable impatience to feel flesh against flesh. Yet, even that was unfulfilling. Desperate to have him deep inside her, she took his hand and pulled him with her to the bunk, there to fall together upon its feathery softness.

Legs and arms entwined, their bodies touching full length, her opened mouth, moist and hungry, found his as he rolled her beneath him. Bracing himself on his elbows, he parted her trembling thighs with his knee and touched his hot, probing staff to the soft flesh of womanhood. A moan escaped her lips when he held back, and she opened her eyes, fearing he was having second thoughts. The lust that smoldered in his dark eyes assured her that he wasn't, and she reached up, caught his handsome face in her hands and pulled his lips to hers, calling out his name in a breathless whisper.

He came to her then, his throbbing manhood penetrating deeply as he moved within her. Rebecca met his thrusts with a wild abandonment, her back arched, her legs enlaced around his. The rapture which encased them carried them to greater heights, each plateau more sensuous and stirring than the last until their minds and bodies reached a heavenly summit neither ever wanted to leave. Then an explosion of tiny, white lights set their souls on fire and suspended them in blissful infinity, draining their passion and sending them back to earth on the gentle wings of enchantment, breathless and contented.

Snuggling deep in the protective crook of his arm, Rebecca lay quietly listening to the rhythmic beat of his heart, her fingertips tracing the smooth, well-defined outline of muscles covering his ribs, his magnificent body gleaming with perspiration. She felt no regret over what she had done, only happiness. Maybe he would never allow himself to fall in love with her, but knowing he cared enough to ask her to marry him would satisfy her need to feel wanted and at the same time assure her that no harm would come to him. He would have to love her back in order for the curse to work . . . the way it had with her father.

Her thoughts were suddenly interrupted by the sound of

his laughter, starting low in his chest until his whole body shook with mirth. She pushed herself up, a frown crimping her smooth brow and a look of worry in her blue eyes as she stared down at him, trying to understand the source of his merriment.

"I'm sorry," he apologized, fighting to hold back his glee. "But I was just thinking about something Brad said earlier." He pulled her back down into the encompassing circle of his arm and brushed his lips against her temple, stirring up the sweet scent of her hair. "He told me that I'm just as hard-headed as you are and that we deserve each other. What do you think?"

"I suppose I'd have to agree when it's put that way." She smiled. "Neither of us is too willing to admit the other one is right."

"Does that mean you'll come to Jamaica with me?"

"Do I have a choice?"

Alec chuckled. "Not really. I'd already made up my mind that if you wouldn't come willingly, I'd have you bound and gagged. Would have made for a very long trip, but sooner or later I would have taken pity on you and turned you loose, and we would have spent the rest of the voyage in bed. We always seem to wind up there after an argument, don't we?" he added almost as an afterthought.

Suddenly aware of her nakedness and feeling oddly uncomfortable with his, she moved to leave the bunk and retrieve her clothes. But he interrupted her plans when he reached out long, lean fingers and entrapped her wrist.

"Why weren't you going to tell me about the baby?" he asked in all seriousness.

She stared at him for a moment before lowering her eyes and sliding off the bed. "Isn't it rather obvious?"

A perplexing frown crimped his brow while he absently viewed the tempting sight of willowy legs and shapely curves until Rebecca covered most of them from his devouring gaze. "Maybe I'm not too bright as well as being hard-headed, but no, it's not obvious. Not to me, anyway. You weren't thinking I'd deny responsibility, were you?"

She chose not to answer in the hope he'd assume the

wrong reason.

"Reb," he called, pushing up from the bunk and dragging the coverlet with him to wrap around his hips. "I'd never do that . . . not to you *or* the baby. I know what it's like growing up without a father. I had to watch my mother work herself to death just so I had enough to eat. I'd never put a child of mine through that . . . nor his mother, not when I have enough money to see to their welfare. I've done a lot of things in my life that I'm not too proud of, but deserting my child and his mother would never be counted as one. You realize that now, don't you?" he asked worriedly as he touched a fingertip to her chin and pulled her gaze to meet his.

"Yes," she answered softly, while in her thoughts she wished his reason for showing up at the cabin had been because he loved her and had realized he couldn't leave Virginia without her. But that would have made things difficult. This way she could love him, live with him, bear his children and never worry about the future. A smile broke the down-turned line of her mouth, one Alec misread, for she had suddenly realized that being a journalist was no longer on the top of her list.

"So what do you think, my good man?" Brad grinned devilishly at the one sitting across the table from him. "Should I go rouse the minister?"

Geoffrey shrugged. "You know Rebecca better than I do. Will she agree to marry him?"

"I think it's better said, will Alec let *her* decide?"

Geoffrey thought about it for a moment, and while a slow smile parted his lips, he shook his head. "Not if his mind is made up." Pulling out his gold watch, Geoffrey checked the time and snapped the lid shut again. "As for rousing the minister, I think we should wait until morning. Besides, we're not sure if Alec brought her back to the ship or not. They might still be out at the cabin."

A silly smile curled Brad's mouth. "And if that's the case, then they're sure not to want us disturbing them until morning."

"So what do we do until then? Drink ourselves unconscious?"

Brad's eyes twinkled. "Doesn't sound like a bad idea to me."

"Well, I'm afraid you'll have to do it alone," Geoffrey announced. "I've had too much excitement for one day. I could fall asleep right here in the chair." He pushed himself up and reached for his tricorn. "I'll do my celebrating tomorrow, if you don't mind."

"Fine with me," Brad replied. "You going back to the ship?"

"No. I'd rather sleep in a nice, soft bed that doesn't rock back and forth all night. I'm going to see if I can get a room at the lodging house one of my crew told me about. It'll be a little quieter there than staying here at the Raleigh." Plopping his hat on his head, he nodded at Brad and bid him farewell.

Grissell Hay Lodging House was located three blocks west and one street north of where Geoffrey and Brad had eaten their supper, and offered the kind of solitude Geoffrey needed right then. He had returned to Williamsburg hoping that Alec had found Daniel Heller safe and sound and that whatever had prevented the agent from going home had been resolved. Instead, Geoffrey learned that not only was Heller dead, but he'd been murdered; Alec had found out the truth about his family, and a good friend of Geoffrey's was Alec's half brother; and on top of all that, Alec Stone had gotten involved with a woman who, according to Brad, was probably the only female to have the distinction of winning the young man's love. It was almost more than one person's mind could handle in such a short period of time, and Geoffrey looked forward to crawling into bed and shutting it all off until morning. He always thought more clearly over a plate of scrambled eggs and biscuits. Moving off the steps, he turned to his right and started down the street.

The crowded sidewalk impeded his progress and made Geoffrey decide to turn the corner at the end of the block. If he cut over to Nicholson Street, the way would be less traveled this time of night since few pubs graced that avenue.

But just as he was about to step around the group of men standing in his path, another man and his companion chose to do the same before Geoffrey could change direction and avoid bumping into him. An apology parted his lips a second after their shoulders struck, but the words instantly vanished and surprise widened his eyes once he looked up into the man's face. Had Geoffrey been allowed to think about it later, he would have sworn an endless span of time elapsed while they stood staring at each other, since it seemed neither of them could believe his eyes. Then the cold, hard muzzle of the other's pistol was rammed in Geoffrey's ribs, and the threatening demand that he come quietly, while the second man moved in behind Geoffrey, warned him to do as he was told if he hoped to survive. Forced at gunpoint to leave the safety of the crowded sidewalk, Geoffrey reluctantly allowed the pair to lead him down a dark, deserted side street.

Chapter Sixteen

"Like I was telling Mr. Remington here," James Galt restated, directing his speech to the man who stood beside the body laid out on a long table, "your friend was dead before they brought him here to the hospital. There wasn't anything I could do for him. I hope you realize that, sir."

Alec had been told that Geoffrey Synder's death was the result of a robbery, that his money and pocket watch were missing when his body was found, and that the man they thought had done the evil deed was already sitting in the public gaol awaiting trial. But even so Alec felt partly to blame. If he hadn't wanted to come to Williamsburg, his friend and trusted employee would still be alive.

"Yes, I understand," he finally replied in a quiet, tight voice.

Unaware of the pain and guilt the stranger suffered, Galt went on, "Even if he'd been alive when he got here, I doubt even Dr. de Sequeyra could have fixed him up. He'd been hit on the back of the head and stabbed several times. A gruesome way to die, but his killer's gonna pay for it. They'll hang him quicker than you can spit." Dropping his gaze, Galt shook his head and turned for his desk as he added, "Of course, the beggardly wretch claims he didn't do it, that the only reason he took the money and the watch was because Captain Synder was already dead when he found him." He plopped down in the chair and opened the top drawer. "Like anyone's gonna believe that lie." Lifting a box from inside, he set it on the desk top and shoved it toward Alec. "Constable said to give you the money and watch since you're the one claiming the body. He also wants to know if you want him buried here or if you'll be takin' him home."

Home, Alec thought bitterly as he studied the ashen face of his friend and curbed the desire to touch him. The *Constance* was Geoffrey's home more than anywhere else. Perhaps he should bury him at sea. Geoffrey probably would have liked that.

His thoughts were disrupted when a gentle hand gripped his shoulder, and Alec looked up to find Brad standing beside him.

"I'll take care of it, Alec," he offered solemnly, "if you'll let me. I could take him to Raven Oaks. I know Beau would be honored to have Geoffrey buried in the family cemetery, and that way you could privately pay your respects to his grave whenever you visit Beau."

Alec started to object since he felt this was his responsibility, but Brad quickly interrupted before he could.

"He was my friend, too, Alec. If I had gone with him or insisted he stay with me last night, this could have been avoided. I know 'if' is a big word in a case like this, but seeing that he's laid to rest in the cemetery on Raven Oaks will help ease the guilt I feel."

A sympathetic smile parted Alec's lips. "It just so happens that I was standing here feeling much the same way." He looked back at the lifeless body of Geoffrey Synder and sighed. "It isn't often a man can claim the honor of having more than one friend. But he had many. He'll be missed . . . by all of us." Raising his chin in the air, he took a deep breath and exhaled slowly before he turned, retrieved the box from the desk and quietly left the room.

So much had happened to Rebecca over the past several weeks that it was difficult for her to comprehend it all. The most staggering of events was the reason she found herself standing at the rail of the *Constance* watching the small dot of land in the horizon grow and take shape. A new life was forming inside her, and by the end of the year she would be a mother. It was a fact she had trouble adjusting to, since she had never seen herself as the motherly type. But then she had never imagined she would fall in love and get married, either. A soft smile sparkled in her eyes as she thought how she hadn't accomplished those steps in their proper order, but that the result would be the same.

Her only regret had been the dark cloud that had enshrouded her wedding day. She had never been honored with making Geoffrey Synder's acquaintance, but she knew by Alec's reaction to the man's death that he was someone special and someone who it was her misfortune never to have known. It had been her decision not to accompany Alec and Brad and the crew of the *Constance* when they took Captain Synder's body to Raven Oaks for burial simply because she would have felt out of place, almost as though she would have been intruding on something private and personal that had nothing to do with her. Yet that was only a part of the reason she begged her leave. She had wanted some time alone with her friends before she had to say good-bye.

Jon-Gregory had volunteered to go with the girls when they went back to the cabin for Rebecca's belongings, and while they were there, Rebecca took the opportunity to tell her two friends about Gilmore and what Alec had done to him. Only because Rebecca hadn't been harmed could the pair see the humor in the situation, and all three of them laughed wholeheartedly at the vision they conjured up of Gilmore crawling on his hands and knees. Jon-Gregory remarked that a dog should be made to run with his tail between his legs, and Penny said she had a better word for him but that she wouldn't say it in front of Jon-Gregory.

The group had dinner together that night, and afterward Jon-Gregory carried the boxes containing Rebecca's clothes, trinkets and heirlooms onto the *Constance*. It wasn't until then that any of them truly realized what was about to happen and that once the ship set sail it would be a long time before Rebecca came back to visit. Choked with emotion, none of them could speak, and they had ridden back to town in silence.

The next morning Jon-Gregory knocked on the door to Rebecca's room at The Red Lion before she had a chance to go down for breakfast. He explained that his unexpected and rather improper visit was due to his need to speak with her alone . . . away from Penny's influence. He wanted Rebecca to assure him that she was marrying Alec Stone because she wanted to and not because he had forced her. His fair face reddened a little while he stumbled for a respectable way to tell her that he knew about the baby, and his words became even more labored when he tried to tell her that he cared enough about her to marry her and raise the child as his, if becoming Alec Stone's wife wasn't what she really wanted. In all of Rebecca's twenty years, she had never felt more honored or touched so deeply as she was at that moment. But rather than tell him, for words didn't seem to be enough, she had put her arms around his lanky frame and hugged him close, tears of joy and sorrow streaming down her face. She would surely miss Jon-Gregory Cole.

When Penny told Ben that Rebecca would be getting married the following morning then leaving with her new husband for Jamaica, he insisted Penny take the day off from work to spend with her friend. They went for a walk, reminisced about their childhood days, talked about men, politics and the weather, and they cried. That afternoon they bought yarn and knitting needles, and Penny taught Rebecca the art of making baby clothes. They dined with Jon-Gregory that evening, then the three of them went for a carriage ride. The fiery sunset seemed different to the trio somehow, but no one commented on the discovery, for in their hearts they knew why.

The wedding ceremony turned out to be more than Rebecca expected. Shortly before noon, Brad and Alec rode into town followed by an expensively built landau carrying Beau and Alanna Remington and their daughter, Victoria. Once Alec had announced his plans to wed, the Remington clan insisted they not be denied the opportunity to witness it. What surprised Rebecca even more than learning that Brad was Alec's half brother and Beau was his cousin was Alanna's request that Rebecca wear the woman's wedding gown, since Alanna was sure there hadn't been time for Rebecca to have her own made. Tears had flooded Rebecca's eyes as she accepted the lady's kind offer, realizing that none of her family would be in attendance.

Somehow Alec had convinced the minister to marry them in the church rather than in Reverend Jones' parlor, despite the improprieties, and Alanna had used her influence to see that the organist filled the chapel with music. It didn't really matter to Rebecca that the pews were empty, for in her mind the people who really meant something to her were there . . . including her mother and father, if only in spirit. Although Alec never said anything, she was sure he felt the same. His mother and father might not have been seated in the front row, but the rest of his family was.

Rebecca had asked Jon-Gregory if he'd walk her down the aisle, for which he declared it would be his honor. Penny helped her to get dressed, and once the task was completed and Rebecca held her mother's tiny, white leather Bible in her hand, the two friends embraced and said their good-byes. The ceremony had gone by in a blur, little of which she could remember even now. But what she did recall was the conversation she had overheard between Jon-Gregory and her new husband as the group moved outside on the church steps. She remembered thinking it was curious how firmly the young man had drawn Alec away from everyone else, but once she heard what he had to say, she understood and loved him for it.

"If I had any sense at all," he had admitted, "I probably wouldn't be standing here threatening you. But I mean it when I say you'd better take good care of her. It's a long voyage to Jamaica. One I pray I'll never have to make."

Unfortunately it was at that moment when Brad decided he wanted to kiss the bride—or his half sister-in-law as he jokingly called her—and before she was able to hear Alec's reply, Brad swept her into his arms and kissed her full and long on the lips. The sound of someone clearing his throat in disapproval forced Brad to release her, but the second she saw the devilish twinkle in his eyes and realized that her husband had been the one to show an objection, she knew

403

right away that Brad had done it to deliberately provoke Alec. It truly amazed her to see how much of a brotherly bond had formed between the two men, given the length of time they had known each other, and she wished she could be assured that such a commitment would develop between her and Alec. Perhaps it would . . . once they had settled in to married life and the baby arrived. Right now, it appeared doubtful, and the excitement she had felt a moment ago when land had been sighted faded into the uncertainty and sadness she had experienced during the entire voyage.

Raking her fingers through her hair and pulling the stray tendrils back off her brow, she studied the long stretch of white beach and thick stand of palm trees running the length of the shoreline while she tried again to understand why Alec had chosen not to share her cabin for a single night. She wanted to believe it was merely because he wished to save her the embarrassment of knowing each and every crew member was well aware of what was going on behind the locked door. Yet she knew that wasn't it. The crew of the *Constance* had probably already guessed why Alec had married her, and that was more embarrassing than having them exchange lewd remarks about a husband and wife retiring to their cabin. Besides, there were other things that made her wonder. Although they dined together, Alec's silence and the faraway look in his eye hinted that he might be thinking he had made a mistake in marrying her. He never put his arm around her or kissed her. He hadn't once inquired about her health, which led her to believe that he wouldn't have cared if someone had told him she had spent the first three days retching—whether it was from seasickness or because of the baby, she didn't know. But just the same, she had come to the conclusion that if she fell overboard, he wouldn't miss her until the ship docked in Jamaica and he saw someone carrying off boxes that didn't belong to him.

The sound of Alec's voice as he issued orders to the crew turned Rebecca around. Since the *Constance* had lost her captain, Alec had taken over the duty of navigating the huge merchant ship homeward and had given Rebecca cause to wonder if he had used that as one of his excuses for being too busy to have time for her. She would have liked to think otherwise, but while she had watched him studying his maps and charts and peering through a spyglass, she had gotten the distinct impression that he rather enjoyed the task and perhaps even missed the life of a sailor. Her mere presence might even have clearly reminded him that no matter how much he would have liked to take up sailing again, he couldn't. He was going to be a father soon, and that meant staying home where he was needed.

The anchor crashed into the sea and sent a fine mist showering upward as the crew went about its work hoisting sail, climbing the riggings and tying off the canvas with lanyards. The huge ship swung around and pulled against the restraining chains that held her steady in the water, while the longboat was lowered and several crewmen began loading it with the trunks and boxes from Rebecca's and Alec's cabins. Captivated by the speed and efficiency with which the men proceeded, Rebecca failed to notice the large group of people gathering on shore until a strange, high-pitched moaning sound rent the air and spun her around. There standing on the tallest rock in a cluster of three was a dark-skinned, half-dressed man with a horn of some type held up to his lips, and Rebecca concluded that it was used to signal the arrival of ships to the island.

A hand upon her elbow made Rebecca jump, and she smiled halfheartedly when she looked up to find that Alec had come to escort her to the longboat. His expression, as always of late, was solemn, and when he didn't speak but nodded his head toward the side of the ship, she followed obediently. She was about to enter his world, and until she was comfortable in it, she planned not to cause any problems.

Shouts went up from those on shore as the boat glided closer, and it wasn't until then that Rebecca truly studied the group. There weren't as many island girls as she had imagined there would be, which truly didn't disappoint her, but a new worry aroused when the crowd seemed to part under some unspoken command and the way opened up to reveal the presence of an older man and the young woman at his side. Unaware that she was staring and that she had ignored the gray-haired gentleman, Rebecca's gaze first took in the cut of the woman's gown and the rich cloth from which it was made. The tight bodice and low neckline accented her full bosom and the narrowness of her waist. Ash-blond hair, styled in long ringlets, graced the finely chiseled features of her face and slim throat. From this distance, Rebecca wasn't sure what color her eyes were, but she guessed a dark shade of green. And when she took the man's arm and moved closer to the shore, she appeared to float on a cloud of peach satin and lace. An unfamiliar twinge of jealousy seized Rebecca when the woman smiled and affixed her eyes to the man who helped Rebecca from the boat. Alec didn't appear to have noticed the blonde's presence as he turned to his men and issued instructions for them to take the trunks and boxes to the house, but Rebecca's mind went to work anyway. There was a certain look, a gleam in the woman's eye that hinted to Rebecca there was more to her feelings for Alec than just being glad he was home safely again. There was a subtle meaning behind the way her gaze devoured Alec, claimed him, declared he was hers, and Rebecca suddenly found herself fighting off the strong desire to lunge at the blonde and claw out her icy green eyes, to mar that flawless face and tear the shimmering gown to shreds.

"Mrs. Stone, are you all right?" the voice beside her whispered. "You look a little flushed."

Of all the men in Alec's crew, Gerald Haugen had been the only one who seemed to care whether or not she was comfortable on the long voyage to her new home, and apparently he still cared. "I'm fine, Gerald," she whispered in return. "Thank you."

But no sooner had she declared good health when that statement was put to the test. Letting go of the older man's arm, the blonde rushed forward and unashamedly threw herself into Alec's reluctant grip. Before he could react and set her from him—if indeed he might—she kissed him much too familiarly to suit Rebecca's standards. Blue eyes wide, mouth agape, she just stood by helplessy watching this stranger attack her husband, certain that once Alec gained control of his senses, he would push the brazen wench away and firmly reprimand her behavior. Tears stung Rebecca's throat when all he did was stare at the trollop in surprise once she loosened her hold on him, and out of pride, Rebecca steeled herself against feeling anything at all.

"Oh, Alec," the blonde sang sweetly as she ran long, well-manicured fingers along his cheek. "We were beginning to worry about you. You've been gone so long." Slipping her hand into the crook of his arm, she stepped around to present Rebecca with a view of her back and guided Alec to the older man who didn't seem the least bit upset over the woman's lack of modesty. "But you're home now," she went on, "and Papa and I have a big party planned in your honor."

The gray-haired gentleman laughed and held out his hand to shake Alec's as he commented, "And you know Meredith, Alec. She'll use any excuse she can find to have a party. Welcome home."

"Thank you." Alec nodded, turning with the pair and walking toward their carriage a few yards away.

Rebecca's tiny frame stiffened when it seemed Alec had forgotten all about her, and she entertained the thought of finding a rock large enough to throw at him. With any kind of luck she'd hit him in the head. If she was really lucky, her aim wouldn't be that good, and she'd bounce the rock off the blonde's stylish coiffeur.

"Was your trip successful?" the older man questioned.

"Tragic would be a better word, Randolph," Alec admitted with a heavy sigh. "A lot of things happened that I wish could have been avoided."

Does that include marrying me? Rebecca thought acidly as she watched Alec assist his shapely, overbearing companion into the carriage. Refusing to be ignored any longer *or* subjected to her husband's open flirtations, she turned to Gerald Haugen and asked if he'd kindly take her to the house, since she was tired and dirty and wished to freshen up. A frown curled his brow, and she could see the perplexity in his eyes. But when he raised a hand and started to call out to Alec, she stopped him, saying that there was no need to interrupt her husband. He was too busy to deal with her right then, and she'd be perfectly happy to have Gerald accompany her. He hesitated, and Rebecca was sure he was thinking how he hoped he wouldn't be overstepping his bounds with Alec. In Rebecca's opinion, Alec would probably thank the young man for taking her off his hands, and she expressed that thought to Gerald, only in a more courteous manner. It seemed to appease Gerald, and once he'd instructed one of the other men to inform Mr. Stone that he'd taken the man's wife on ahead, Gerald guided Rebecca to a second rig not far from the first.

"Who is she?" Rebecca asked as pleasantly as she could force herself to sound once they had left the others a safe distance behind.

"Miss Stockwell?" Gerald queried with a smile. He snapped the reins and chuckled at the same time. "A pain in Mr. Stone's—" He caught himself before he had voiced the word he'd chosen and finished a bit more respectfully, "Neck. She's been trying for years to get him to marry her, but until he met you, he wasn't the marrying sort. I must say it surprised all of us when he announced that his bride would be coming with us."

Rebecca was sure Gerald meant that the crew was surprised Alec had married someone just because she was carrying his child, but she elected not to expand on his statement. Instead she murmured, "Do you think Miss Stockwell will give up trying now?"

Gerald's round, pale green gaze fell on her. "Well, I certainly hope so. It would be a waste of time if she didn't. Of course, she's already been wasting her time beforehand. Mr. Stone never would have given in."

"Why not?"

"He doesn't like her."

That's what he'd like you to believe, she thought sarcastically as she cocked a doubtful brow. "It certainly didn't look that way to me. He appeared to be enjoying her crass form of saying hello."

"Oh, *that.*" Gerald grinned as he reined the carriage off the hard-packed stretch of beach and onto the wide dirt road that wandered crookedly through a grove of palm trees. "I wouldn't let that worry me if I were you. It meant nothing to Mr. Stone. He's a married man now, and he'll remind Miss Stockwell of it every chance he gets."

"How can you be so sure?"

"Because I know him. He's a man of honor, responsibility and pride. He'd never do anything to jeopardize that."

Not openly, anyway, she thought. After all, wasn't that the reason he married her? Hadn't he claimed several times that the baby and its mother were his responsibility? He never once said he loved her or that he'd grow to love her. It hadn't been a part of his pledge. And now she understood why. By marrying her, he'd have everything he could possibly want; respect, his honor, a wife and baby, and . . . a mistress. Tears moistened her lashes and she quickly closed her eyes and turned her head away from her companion. That was why he hadn't come to her in the middle of the night and why he was so withdrawn during the entire voyage. He had been thinking of the woman who waited for him, and worrying over how he would break the news to her that he was married. Was he telling her right now? Or would he wait until *after* they had made love.

Every room in the manor that faced the ocean had two sets of exceptionally tall, French doors which opened up onto the veranda. Fragrant sea breezes poured over the white, sandy beaches and rustled the floor-length, gauzy curtains which hid the exits when the doors were closed. For as far as one could imagine, the endless blue waters of the Atlantic stretched out and gently kissed the azure sky, obscuring the horizon in one flowing mass of color until a defiant white cloud drifted into view and spoiled the otherwise flawless masterpiece.

Visitors to the island who experienced the artistry for the first time usually stood in awe of what they saw. For Rebecca it clearly defined how far away from home she was and how hopeless it would be for her to consider running away. Alec's island paradise had become her prison, and the brightly painted room, elegantly decorated and richly furnished, was her cell. She would live out her life going through the motions of a woman who appeared to have everything she could want, then die heartbroken and alone.

Gerald Haugen had seen to it that she was introduced to the household staff, given a tour of the huge, one-story mansion, then shown to her room after making sure that a bath was prepared for her before he begged his leave. Because of Geoffrey Synder's death, Alec had asked him to be in charge of the *Constance*, and he had duties to perform as her captain before he could spend any more time away from the ship. Rebecca had assured him that she understood, thanked him for his help and kindness and made him promise to come and visit her whenever he could, then waved farewell from the veranda as she watched him climb back into the carriage and drive away.

After her bath and a short nap, she went outside for a walk while the maid unpacked the few belongings Rebecca had brought with her, and put them away. She ate a light supper alone since Alec had yet to come home, then returned to her room where she sat in a rocking chair, working on the sleeper she was knitting for the baby. The gold-painted clock on the dresser struck nine before she set aside her project and decided to retire. Stripping out of her dress, she slid into her white, lacy nightgown and crawled, exhausted, into bed. The sweet smell of freshly laundered sheets filled her nostrils, and while she settled herself comfortably in the middle of the huge, canopied bed, she forced her thoughts on other things rather than on the awful chance that her husband might be doing the same thing somewhere else. But a moment later, hot tears stained her cheeks, and she rolled over onto her stomach, buried her face in the pillows and cried herself to sleep.

The smell of the salt air and the thunderous crashing waves against the shore played host to Rebecca's first notion of early morning on the tropical isle. Rolling onto her side, she dreamily opened her eyes and glanced out across the veranda at the cloudless blue sky and the rolling white caps which dotted the endless plain of the ocean. The squawk of sea gulls pierced the quiet as they soared then swooped downward, their curved beaks poised and ready to scoop up their first taste of breakfast from the watery depths of the sea. A warm breeze filtered into the room through the opened French doors, and for a moment she wondered how anyone could be unhappy living in such a place. Then the vision of Meredith Stockwell with her arms locked around Alec flashed before her eyes, and she quickly squeezed them shut, hoping to block out the image. Instead, the sound of the couple's laughter as they frolicked in bed rang in her ears, and she angrily sat up, threw off the thin sheet covering her, and dropped her feet to the floor. The only way for her to forget about them was to keep busy. She'd have breakfast, don a short-sleeved cotton dress and go exploring. After lunch, she'd have someone take her into town where she could visit the shoppes and maybe purchase a few things for the baby. But just the thought of eating made her stomach churn, and while she frantically scanned the room for something to serve her purpose, she gritted her teeth and covered her mouth with her hand. Spying the washstand and the bowl sitting on top of it, she flew off the bed and raced across the room for it.

Several minutes passed before Rebecca was able to lift her head and splash cool water on her face. The better part of a year was a long time for a woman to have to suffer this way, and for a moment Rebecca wished someone had warned her what the price would be for letting her passion and curiosity get the upper hand. She might have been able to execute a little self-restraint had she known that every dawn would start out the same for her . . . with her head in a bowl. And had she guessed the end result would bring her to this point, she most assuredly would have flown the stranger's sweet caresses that night in Penny's bed.

"Sweet caresses," she muttered sarcastically into the towel as she dabbed the moisture from her skin. "I wonder if he was thinking of *her* the whole time." Angry, she tossed aside the piece of white linen and turned around while she

411

reminded herself not to think of her husband and the harlot, Meredith Stockwell. But the moment she lifted her eyes and took a step back toward the bed, her mouth dropped open and her face paled considerably; for there sitting up in the middle of the huge mattress, his bare chest gleaming golden in the sunlight and the white sheet pooled around his hips, was Alec, and she trembled visibly at the frown she saw marring his handsome face.

"What was that all about?" he asked, his tone etched with disapproval.

Certain he questioned her remark and that he had read her thoughts and took offense to her derogatory name-calling, she fleetingly decided ignorance was her best defense. "What was what?"

He nodded at the washstand.

Rebecca trembled all the more.

"Do you start out every morning in that manner?"

Just since meeting your mistress, she rallied bitterly, though her answer never formed into a verbal reply. She bit her lip and stiffled a gasp when it appeared he intended to rise. Until now she never would have guessed he'd get physical with her, but then she had never attacked his mistress before, either.

"You should have told me," he went on as he flipped off the covers and reached for his breeches lying on the chair. "My mother had a remedy for that kind of illness. Although she never would explain what it was she was making, it didn't take me long to figure out its purpose. She was sort of the hamlet's doctor at times when the women were too poor to pay for a real one."

Confusion wrinkled her brow as she tried to sort out his comments, and she hardly noticed the strong hand on her elbow as he guided her back to bed.

"Lie down and don't move," he ordered as he drew the thin sheet up over her. "I'll see if Harold has the right herbs. If he does, I'll be right back. But it's important you don't move. That's the trick."

The faint line between Rebecca's dark brows deepened as she listened to the door swing quietly shut and mark his exit.

He didn't seem at all angry with her for what she had said or for the thoughts that had raced through her head. Was it some plot aimed at getting her guard down? Once he had her thanking him for his kindness, did he plan to announce how things would be between him and that . . . that vamp? Rebecca's awe turned to slow, smoldering rage. Well, he had another thing coming. She wasn't about to play the dutiful wife while he flaunted his mistress around the island. And he had a lot of nerve sneaking into her bed as if it were his rightful place. Not after he'd been with her! *How dare he!* Vowing to let him know her feelings in a very clear, unmistakable way, she threw off the sheet and stood up. The second he walked back through that door, she'd hit him with the first thing she could lay her hands on. However, her decision to cause him bodily harm was suddenly forgotten when her stomach tied itself into a knot and the muscles in her throat constricted. Eyes wide, both hands over her mouth, she flew across the room to the washstand.

"Here. Drink this," the firm voice beside her ordered once the retching had stopped.

She wanted to ask if it was poison since that seemed the easiest method to rid himself of both child and wife. But the instant she opened her mouth to speak, she felt his strong fingers clamp onto her chin and the touch of cool glass to her lips as he forced her head back and raised the container high. Whatever was in the concoction tasted bitter as if he had deliberately spiked the warm milk with pepper or vinegar. Yet the second it hit her stomach, its ingredients soothed her nausea and brought a weak smile to her face.

"How long have you been suffering from this?" he asked concernedly while he helped her back into bed.

"Since the beginning," she answered faintly as she laid her head on the pillow and closed her eyes.

"And Penny didn't know anything to ease it?"

She slowly shook her head.

"All the more reason I should have been told about the baby right away," he muttered. Turning, he crossed to the French doors and pulled them shut, then drew the thin curtains over them to block out the brightest rays of the

413

morning sun. "I want you to rest awhile longer. I'll have Amanda serve you breakfast in bed once you're feeling up to it."

The mention of food didn't turn her stomach this time, a discovery that both surprised and pleased Rebecca. She hadn't been able to eat breakfast in weeks, and she was never one to skip a meal if she didn't have to. She wanted to thank him for making her feel better; but her pride had been hurt, and she really didn't want to give him the satisfaction of knowing he had helped. Sensing that he had moved to another part of the room, she opened one eye just enough to steal a peek at him and found that he had gone to the armoire and had opened the doors. The sight of *his* clothes hanging inside next to hers brought her straight up in bed.

"This is *your* room!" she raged.

Puzzled by her observation and wondering if pregnancy caused a woman's moods to swing from one end of the scope to the other, he slowly turned his attention on her. "Yes. It is."

"But it was supposed to be *mine*," she wailed, tossing off the cover and jumping to her feet. "I think you'd better have a talk with your help. They're obviously very incompetent." She stormed the armoire and began yanking her things from inside.

"What are you doing?" He frowned as he stood in awe and watched her collect an armload of dresses and under-garments.

"I'm taking these to *my* room." She shot him an icy glare. "If you'd be kind enough to show me where that is."

Alec cocked his head disgustedly. "You're standing in it."

"Oh, no, I'm not," she hissed. "We might share the same last name, but we'll *not* share the same bed. What gave you the right to come sneaking in here in the middle of the night? Who said you could crawl into bed with me? Under what illusion did you think I'd welcome you?"

The anger faded from his brow, and total bewilderment replaced it. "No illusion, Reb. You're my wife, and unless I'm mistaken, a husband and wife usually share the bedroom . . . plus a lot of other things."

She jutted out her chin at him and narrowed her eyes. "Well, you're mistaken, Mr. Stone. This is one wife who refuses to share anything more than a name." She tossed her head and sent the long, silky black hair shimmering down her back as she turned away from him and stormed the door.

In the time it took her to awkwardly readjust the garments in her arms and seize the doorknob, Alec searched his mind for a cause to her sudden change of heart. He'd had difficulty in persuading her to marry him, but once she understood the necessity and the fact that he'd have it no other way, she had willingly walked to the altar with him. Now that they were wed and beginning a new life, she obviously had her own ideas about the manner in which it would be achieved. Was this what he had to look forward to? Or was it just something to do with her condition. Suddenly, he thought he understood the problem. Most of the women he had known were a little vain when it came to their appearance; and although he had never seen it in Reb, perhaps the realization that her slender shape would soon begin to change was an embarrassment to her, and this was her way of hiding it. If that was all there was to it, then he'd deal with it. He'd let her have her way . . . for now.

"Reb," he called before she had pulled the door all the way open. "If this is really what you want, then I won't argue. But you're to stay here . . . in my room. I'll have my things moved down the hall. This is the largest of them all, and it seldom gets very warm in here. You'll be more comfortable, I assure you." When it appeared he had convinced her, he crossed the space dividing them and gently took the bundle of clothes from her arms, then directed her back to bed. "Lie down and rest. I'll send Amanda, and she'll straighten up in here for you. All right?"

Even though it was what she had deliberately led him to believe, in her heart she was wishing he would object, that he'd take her in his arms and kiss away the pain and anger she felt. She wanted him to swear that Meredith Stockwell meant nothing to him, that he had spent last night telling her good-bye and that he loved his wife and would always remain faithful to her. But he didn't, and Rebecca choked back her tears as she climbed into bed and pulled the sheet up under her chin, eyes closed.

"Yes," she murmured after a moment. "That will be fine."

The soft click of the latch seemed to sharpen the ache in her chest.

"Are you out of your mind? You can't go to Jamaica! What if you're seen? It will destroy everything we've done so far!"

Green eyes glared at the one who spoke. "And if I don't, it won't make a difference, will it? Her birthday is in a few weeks, and if she lives to see twenty-one, the property will legally belong to her."

But she doesn't know that. She was never shown the will. Besides, she's married now. What would she want with it? Her husband's rich enough to give her everything she could possibly want. She wouldn't need it. Just forget about it. She's gone, and I doubt she'll ever come back."

"Are you honestly willing to take that chance? And what about her husband? He's not some English dandy whose only thoughts are what color of breeches he should wear. He's a businessman. He'll start asking her questions she can't answer, and when that happens, he'll come here and start snooping around again. If her body's found washed up on shore, he'll have no reason to suspect it as anything more than an accident."

"As long as you're not seen. It's too risky. Be satisfied with what you have."

"Would you be?" he raged, pushing away from the table and grabbing his tricorn from the chair seat next to him. "Besides, I have a score to settle with Alec Stone, and what better way than to cheat him out of a beautiful wife?"

"Then send someone else to do it."

"You?" he challenged.

The other shrunk back, fear widening his eyes.

"I didn't think so. You're too much of a coward. No, I'm the one to do it, since we can't trust another soul with our secret." His eyes narrowed into fine slits, and hate glowed in their green depths. "Besides, I want to be there to hear her beg for her life. I want to see her crawl." A long moment of silence followed while he envisioned the sight. Then with an evil smile curling his mouth, he turned and strode from the tavern, unaware that part of their conversation had been overheard by a member of Brad Remington's crew.

Amanda Hames was probably one of the nicest women Rebecca had ever had the pleasure of knowing. Although she was in her late thirties, she still had the figure, manner and disposition of someone half her age and the wisdom and compassion it would take to be queen of England. She liked Rebecca from the first moment Gerald Haugen introduced them, and she hadn't tried to hide it. Her charm and poise had won her countless friends, and Rebecca had been included in that list almost instantly. She had seen right through the rough exterior of the young bride Mr. Stone had brought home with him, but experience had warned her not to push too soon. It was much easier to step back and wait for the right moment. Now, it seemed, was that time. A week had passed since the young woman's arrival, and even though she no longer suffered with early morning nausea, Mrs. Stone seldom left her room. It was time Amanda had a talk with her.

Sweeping into the bedroom with a breakfast tray balanced in one hand and a sewing basket in the other, she crossed to the nightstand and set down the tray. "Good morning, Mrs. Stone," she sang sweetly as she deposited the basket on a chair, turned about and headed for the French doors without breaking stride. Pulling the curtains aside, she seized the ivory handles and swung the portals open to let in the cooling breezes and bright sunlight of early morning. "It's going to be a glorious day," she announced, her auburn hair shining like spun gold as she tilted her head back and breathed in the fresh air. "And it's just the sort of day to go for a carriage ride."

Yawning, Rebecca sat up in bed and stretched the kinks from her neck and back. "A carriage ride?" she questioned, a tiny fist knotted against her mouth to stifle a second yawn. "Are you planning a visit somewhere, Amanda?"

Bright green eyes sparkled when the maid spun back around and walked toward the bed. "I most certainly am. You and I are going into town to buy the fanciest, most expensive piece of fabric we can find."

A soft frown crimped Rebecca's brow. "Whatever for?"

"Well, can't you guess?" Amanda teased while she bent and fluffed up the pillows against the headboard of her mistress' back. "So that you'll be the most stunning beauty there."

"There?" Rebecca repeated. "What are you talking about?"

Motioning for her to sit back, Amanda placed the tray across Rebecca's lap and handed her the linen napkin while she replied, "At Lord Stockwell's party the day after tomorrow. Now hurry up and eat your breakfast. I'll need every minute of the next two days to finish your gown." The young woman's reaction was exactly what Amanda had expected. Before she had even completed her sentence, Rebecca was shaking her head. "Now, don't you dare say no, Mrs. Stone," Amanda scolded as she set aside the sewing basket and pulled up the chair. "I've watched you closet yourself off in this room long enough. You need fresh air, sunshine and companionship. You can't spend the rest of your life locked up in here. *And* you're going to show Meredith Stockwell why Mr. Stone chose *you* for his bride and not her."

Despite the horrifying prospect of coming face to face with Alec's mistress, Rebecca's appetite flourished. Spreading butter over the lightly browned slice of bread, she acknowledged, "I'm sure everyone on the island knows *that* reason."

"Pooh," Amanda grunted. "I didn't mean the baby. Even if there wasn't one already on the way, Mr. Stone would have married you."

Chewing on a mouthful of food, Rebecca gave the maid a dubious look.

"Is that what this is all about?" Amanda exclaimed.

"Have you been spending every waking hour telling yourself that Mr. Stone only married you *because* of the baby?"

Rebecca smiled sarcastically and picked up a fork with which to sample the cheese omelet on her plate. "I really don't have to tell myself that. I know it as fact. If Alec hadn't found out about the baby, he would have left Williamsburg without me."

"Maybe," Amanda relented. "But not for long. He would have—"

"Don't bother trying to speculate on something we have no way of ever knowing for sure, Amanda," she interrupted. "It's nice to dream about, but that's all I'll ever be able to do . . . dream." Reaching out, she patted the maid's hand and silently thanked her for her kind words.

Amanda had never come across anyone as set in their ways as this young lady, but she wasn't about to let it discourage her. There had been a subtle change in Mr. Stone, one Amanda hadn't really noticed until a few days ago, and it had nothing to do with Captain Synder's death or the wonderful news that Mr. Stone now had two half brothers and the chance to learn all he could about his father. That in itself would alter anyone's character, but Amanda guessed that this little lady was the reason for his peace of mind. He no longer snapped out orders or exhibited a short temper. He smiled a lot, whistled and even joked with the members of his staff. He worked hard and long both in his study as well as overseeing his many projects, and whenever she caught him sitting alone on the veranda late at night, he wasn't scowling as had been his usual mood. The only thing that seemed to herald his full attention was making sure that his wife was being cared for, a responsibility that had fallen on Amanda's shoulders. Every time she bumped into him during the day, he asked about Rebecca and if she had hinted that she might like to speak with him. The negative reply to the latter always appeared to disappoint him, and it had been the spark that prompted Amanda into seeing what she could do to correct it.

"All right," she proclaimed while she watched Rebecca finish off her breakfast with a zeal that indicated she could have eaten more had she been given a second helping. "We won't argue about whether or not he would have come back for you. What we should be discussing is how you intend to prove to Miss Stockwell that she's to keep her hands and her comments to herself. Mr. Stone is *your* husband—no matter what the reason—and she's to forget about trying to change that."

"I don't know why she would even give it a second thought, Amanda," Rebecca sighed forlornly. "It seems to me that she has everything she could possibly want."

"Except your husband," Amanda corrected, her brows knotted in a frown.

Oh, you're wrong there, dear lady, Rebecca thought. *Maybe it's not in the way you think she'd like to have him, but she has him just the same.*

"Mrs. Stone," Amanda called when she noticed how Rebecca had appeared to drift off in thought, "I think I should warn you about Meredith Stockwell. She isn't the type to give up just because he's married. She's been after him for years, and every hopeful, young girl on the island was warned to look somewhere else for her man or pay the consequences. If you plan to stay married to him, you're going to have to show her that you're wise to her games and that you won't tolerate them for a second. Am I making myself perfectly clear?"

Rebecca started to debate her chances of keeping Alec when she never really had him in the first place, but Amanda cut her off.

"If Mr. Stone had wanted to marry her, he would have long ago. She isn't and never will be what he wants in a wife. She's too brazen, and if you're not careful, she'll move right in and steal him out from under your nose. What I'm trying to say as delicately as possible is that she's a tramp, and she'll use every womanly trick she can pull to win him over."

"And what happens then . . . if she wins him over, I mean?" The question sounded as if Rebecca had a sincere interest in knowing the answer, but in her thoughts she had already surrendered the contest simply because she had never been given the opportunity to fight.

"If it's not what you want—and I assume it isn't just by the look on your face—then let down your hair, bare your claws and show the little tart what you're made of. Seduce your husband right back into *your* bed."

Rebecca still wasn't convinced. "It might work for a while. But what happens when I'm fat and cranky? Miss Stockwell would only have to wag her finger at him."

"With an attitude like that, you can count on it," Amanda snapped. "You talk as though it's already too late."

"It is," Rebecca unwittingly admitted as she handed the woman her tray and slid out from under the covers to get dressed.

Amanda sat in stunned silence for several minutes while she watched her mistress change out of her nightgown and don a pretty blue, cotton dress with white lace trim, then wash her face, pat it dry and sit down at the dressing table to brush out her hair. It shocked the woman to hear that Rebecca had already given up without any attempt whatsoever at showing Meredith Stockwell that for once in her spoiled, pampered life she wasn't going to have something she wanted. Then, suddenly, what Mrs. Stone had said finally registered. Frowning, she roughly set the tray on the nightstand and came to her feet.

"I know it's not my place to ask," she admitted, a bit peeved, "but would you mind explaining that last comment?"

Blue eyes glanced up at the reflection in the mirror of the woman standing behind her. "What comment?"

"That it's already too late. Mrs. Stone," Amanda went on without giving Rebecca a chance to explain as she moved around to look the young woman in the face, "if you're saying that your husband is being unfaithful, you're wrong." Rebecca drew a breath to speak, but Amanda rushed on before she could. "You may tell me to mind my own business, and I might even make you angry with what I'm about to say; but I feel I must say it. You can't possibly know if he's being unfaithful since you haven't left this room or even talked to him since the day you arrived. But I'll tell you this; if you continue to behave in this manner, you'll push him into her arms. He's an exceptional man, but even the strongest of men have their weaknesses. He cares a great deal for you, but if you don't show him that it matters, you'll turn that love against you."

"Love?" Rebecca laughed. "I really don't think—"

"That's right," Amanda interrupted. "You don't think . . . or listen or observe. If you did, you'd know I was telling you the truth." Suddenly frustrated and realizing that she had lost her temper—something she seldom did—Amanda decided it was time she left her mistress alone. Rushing to the nightstand, she picked up the tray, grabbed her sewing basket and started for the door.

"Where are you taking that?"

Rebecca's question stopped Amanda just as she was about to reach for the ivory knob. Puzzled, she looked back over her shoulder at the young woman. "To the kitchen."

Rebecca shook her head as she rose and walked the distance to her maid. "I mean that," she said, nodding at the wicker basket. "Won't you need it to take my measurements?"

The surprised look on Amanda's face slowly turned into an excited smile. "Yes, Mrs. Stone, I certainly will," she beamed, positive now that everything would be all right.

The two women spent the next two days in preparation for the Stockwell party, locked away in Rebecca's room from early morning until late at night. The only reason Alec hadn't been too concerned about their strange behavior was because Willy, the houseboy, had told him of the trip into town the women had taken and the number of packages they had brought back with them, some of them being satin fabric, lace, thread and needles. He guessed they were merely working on a new wardrobe for Reb; but their secrecy began to irritate him, and out of an undeniable curiosity, he had several times stood outside the door eavesdropping. All he could hear, however, were muffled voices and a few occasional giggles. It had been a long time since laughter filled the quiet mansion, and the sound of it made him smile, since all he really wanted for his wife was for her to be happy. Apparently, because of Amanda, she was. Yet feeling like a little boy being cheated out of something exciting, his desire to know just why it was they had to hide their work from him soon became a question he had to have answered, and during one of those rare times when Amanda left his wife's room, he asked her about their project.

"You'll see soon enough," she told him. Then with a bright smile lighting up her eyes, she walked away leaving him more anxious than before.

His inability after a day and a half to find out just exactly what was going on behind the closed door finally sent him to his study where he sat at his desk trying to concentrate on the entries in the ledger. But before very long the figures blurred into one mass of blue ink, and out of total frustration, he laid aside his quill and leaned back in the chair, thinking that if the women were hoping to drive him mad, they were close to success. He simply couldn't understand why they were treating him this way unless Reb felt he deserved it for some reason. Frowning, he left the chair and walked to the opened doors looking out over the long stretch of beach and the white-capped waves rolling inland while he searched his memory for a clue as to what he might have done to upset his wife. With the exception of those few moments when they had argued over whether or not they would share a bedroom, they really hadn't spoken to each other since— One tawny brow lifted once he realized just how long it really had been, and he heaved an irritable sigh as he walked out onto the veranda and casually perched one hip on the railing.

"Since we boarded the *Constance*," he murmured with a shake of his head while he silently cursed his stupidity *and* his lack of foresight. How would he ever convince Rebecca that he hadn't deliberately ignored her when it seemed that way to him now that he thought about his behavior for the past several weeks? Would she believe him if he explained that he simply couldn't get Geoffrey Synder's death off his mind or the curious, questionable way he had died? Or that because of Robert Gilmore, he worried for her safety and had had to ask Brad to look into the matter for him while he took her home? Would she understand how upsetting it was for him to have to decide just how to tell Daniel Heller's widow and child that he had visited the man's grave? Everything about his life had changed over the past months, and it would take some getting used to. He wasn't made of granite and couldn't just let disturbing news bounce off him. He was a man, flesh and blood, with feelings like everyone else. Sometimes he just managed to hide them better than others could. But he still hurt. And his wife's rejection bothered him most of all.

A noise behind him jolted him out of his musings, and when he turned his head, he found Amanda standing in the opened study doorway. The disgusted look on her face and the rigidness of her slender frame as she stared at him with arms akimbo clearly told him that he had done something wrong . . . again. Rising, he walked toward her, his brows cocked questioningly.

"Don't tell me you've forgotten?" she scolded.

Apparently he had, for he had no idea what she meant.

"Lord Stockwell's party," she replied. "It's in one hour, and you're not dressed for it."

"Oh . . . that." He frowned. "I haven't forgotten. I'm just not going."

"Fine," she answered, turning her back on him and crossing the room to the exit. "Then I'll ask Gerald Haugen to escort your wife to the party."

"My—" The shock over learning that not only had Rebecca planned to leave her room but that she wanted to attend a party with him left him speechless, and while he groped for the right words to express his delight, he rushed forward and hooked Amanda's arm. "You mean she's—"

"Well, of course she is," Amanda snapped. "What did you think we were doing cooped up in her room all this time? We were making the kind of gown that will turn Meredith Stockwell absolutely green with envy. But . . . if you don't want to go . . ."

Alec's dark brown eyes glowed, and a wide smile parted his lips. "Try and stop me," he threatened enthusiastically as

424

he jerked the woman toward him and roughly kissed her brow. "Just try and stop me."

Laughter teased the corners of Amanda's eyes and tightened the muscles in her throat as she watched him bolt past her and hurry from the room. "Yes, sir." She chuckled. "Everything's going to be just fine."

"Well? What do you think?" Rebecca asked excitedly while she gave Amanda a front, side then back view of the satin gown she wore. "Will he like it?"

"Like it?" Amanda contradicted. "He'll love it! And if you're not careful, he just might decide to keep you at home."

Rebecca could feel her cheeks pinken, but she didn't really mind that the woman's comment had embarrassed her. The thought that she could once again be the center of Alec's affection pleased her. "Perhaps," she teased, "but he'll just have to wait. The whole idea was for Miss Stockwell to see the competition in her best form."

"Well, that you are." Amanda smiled as she unashamedly appraised the work she'd done. "I do believe mauve is your best color. It adds just enough blush to your cheeks and highlights your ivory complexion. A man would have to be blind not to see how beautiful you are."

"And if you continue with the compliments, I'll start thinking I don't have any flaws." Rebecca laughed as she turned to study her reflection in the mirror.

It pleased her to see that she hadn't lost her narrow waist as yet, though she had to admit the style of the gown could have concealed it quite nicely if she had. The low-cut neckline trimmed in mauve lace and the puffy elbow length sleeves detracted one's attention away from any hint that she might be with child, and the full skirts billowed out in just the right place to hide her slightly rounded tummy. Dainty slippered feet peeked out from under the hemline, and the rustle of petticoats challenged the idea that Rebecca had ever had the occasion to don a ragged shirt and baggy breeches.

425

Her thick, raven-black hair, piled high and pulled severely off her face, fell in soft, shimmering ringlets down the back of her head, and her pale blue eyes sparkled with excitement. She was ready to prove to Meredith Stockwell, her husband and the world that she was deserving of a man's love. She'd make Alec proud of her.

Chapter Seventeen

The docking of a huge frigate from the Colonies always stirred the interest and excitement of the people working at and living near the docks. For Ivy Heller it gave false hope. Although she had been told that her husband was dead, out of habit she came to watch those on board the visiting ship disembark, praying that this time he would be among them. But just as it had been for the past year, none of the men who descended the lowered gangplank were Daniel, and she had to force herself to turn away. She knew it was senseless to come to the pier time after time, but something in her heart wouldn't allow her to give up the hope that Alec Stone was wrong.

Fighting back her tears, she pushed her way through the crowded wharf and headed up the narrow path which cut through the trees back toward town and the tiny house she had shared with her husband, knowing that their son would be there waiting for her to fix their supper. Little Peter Andrew was too young to understand what death truly meant, and she'd have to give him the same answer she had always given him after she had gone to the docks to meet a ship.

"No, son, your papa didn't come home today," she would tell him. "But soon."

How long could she keep up the lie? she wondered, nodding politely at someone she knew as she left the path and started down the busy street toward her home. Perhaps she could ask a favor of Mr. Stone and journey to Williamsburg on the next of his ships going there. If she visited Daniel's grave and talked to those who had met him, maybe then she could accept what happened.

Turning the corner at the end of the main street in town, Ivy stepped off the curb and cut across the cobblestones toward the whitewashed, one-room house Daniel had built for them when they were first married. Seeing the tiny structure brought back fond memories and renewed the pain in her heart. Unable to face her son right away, since he would question the tears running down her face, she took a sudden turn and headed out toward the beach and her favorite rock on which to sit and watch the tide slap against the shore. She and Daniel had spent many sunsets there, dreaming of better things and knowing it would never come true. Daniel, for all his good points, was lazy and hadn't the ambition to work for what he wanted. He had always felt he deserved more than what he was paid and refused to break a sweat on his brow until he was. But Ivy loved him anyway.

Leaving the density of the trees and underbrush, she headed toward the cluster of rocks near the shoreline. Since the spot was still a fair distance away, she failed to see that someone else was already there enjoying the scenery and solitude, until the figure rose and moved farther down the beach. Startled to learn that she wasn't the only one who visited this particular place, she came to an abrupt halt as she watched the man walk away. Fading sunlight silhouetted his tall shape and masked his identity, but there was something about the way he carried himself that sent a shiver up her spine. Out of curiosity and an uneasy feeling, she hesitantly set off to follow him.

"You do understand, don't you, Mrs. Stone?" Gerald Haugen asked again as he guided the carriage down the road toward the Stockwell estate. "It couldn't be helped. Your husband *had* to meet with his accountant before the shipment was loaded. He asked me to assure you that it wasn't intentional and that he'll join you at the party later . . . just as soon as he's finished—"

"I understand, Mr. Haugen," Rebecca calmly interrupted, the look in her eyes cold and suspicious. "More than you know." Feeling that man's worried gaze on her, she glanced over at him and smiled. "And I'm honored that you agreed to accompany me in his stead."

"My pleasure, ma'am," Gerald softly replied as he turned back to watch the road. Alec had warned him that Rebecca might be hard to convince, since women never seemed to think business was more important than social functions. But she *had* seemed to understand, even though there had been an icy edge to her words.

It surprised Rebecca that she didn't feel the pain knot itself around her heart or that the unshed tears which usually burned her eyes with the thought that Alec was with another woman hadn't tightened her throat. Perhaps it was because she truly wanted to believe Gerald Haugen's story or because Amanda had sounded so convincing in her pledge that Alec wasn't interested in Meredith Stockwell. Or perhaps it was because Rebecca had finally found the strength not to care what her husband did. She had also come to the realization that she didn't want anyone feeling sorry for her, and that hiding herself away in her room would certainly make people think that she was weak and had no control over her life. Well, after tonight they'd know differently.

The Stockwell mansion sat atop a knoll enshrouded with palm trees, ferns and thick beds of brightly colored flowers. The lane narrowed as it twisted and turned toward the front door, and dotting the roadside, torches lit the way through the darkness, their glowing flames sputtering and the smell of oil pungent in the strong breeze. The sweet strains of violins and merry laughter floated out from the well-lighted house to greet Rebecca as the carriage swung around and rolled to a stop. Two black servants hurried forward; one to help her descend the rig's step while the other held the horse's bridle. A moment later Gerald Haugen's hand cradled her elbow as he led her to the opened front door, and she experienced a twinge of uncertainty. She had never backed down from a fight in her life, but she had always been on familiar ground then. She was a stranger here. Miss Stockwell wasn't. And all of the guests inside were *her* friends. If she chose to challenge the woman, Rebecca would have to do it alone.

The wide foyer with its marble floor, French styled furniture and numerous paintings hanging on the walls appeared as cold and as overdone as Rebecca remembered Meredith Stockwell to be, and for a moment Rebecca wondered what Alec saw in her besides her beauty. Charm, grace, an inner warmth and total devotion were the qualities for a lasting relationship. All the jewels, fine clothes and priceless belongings in the world couldn't stop a man's eye from wandering. Or so Rebecca wanted to believe. Apparently with Alec it was different, and she had to grit her teeth, raise her chin in the air and prepare herself to present a gallant façade that would seem to everyone who met her in next several minutes that despite her knowledge of her husband's infidelity, she had the courage not to let it bother her. She choked back a tear as Gerald led her through the opened double doors to their left and into the grand room filled with dozens of people.

Randolph Stockwell was the first to greet them, and had he not been Meredith's father, Rebecca decided she might have liked him. His enthusiasm over finally being able to make her acquaintance seemed sincere, but inwardly she doubted he truly meant it. Rebecca had stolen something his daughter wanted.

A flurry of faces and names were presented to her in the following moments, many of whom failed to penetrate her memory as she covertly looked about the ballroom for the one person who promised to test the smile on her lips and the polite manner she bestowed on those who congratulated her on her marriage and welcomed her to the island. Many asked where her husband was, to which she replied simply that business had delayed him. No one seemed to question the excuse, even though Rebecca suspected it wasn't true, and she suddenly realized that Alec had a lot of friends who were willing to look the other way if he chose not to behave in a

430

manner befitting a married man.

The quartet of two violins, a viola and harpsichord began to play a minuet which quickly filled the dance floor with eager couples and left Rebecca alone with Gerald Haugen and Mr. Stockwell. The latter suggested they move out onto the flagstone patio to their right where it was cooler and a table of food and drink had been set up. Rebecca would have preferred making her apologies for the headache she felt coming on and then asking Gerald to take her home, but Amanda had gone to too much trouble for her to back down now. Reluctantly she accepted his invitation, but declined a plate of fancy finger food and settled for a glass of wine instead.

"Where's Miss Stockwell?" Gerald casually asked as the trio stood sipping their wine and watching the couples float across the floor, and Rebecca fought the urge to kick him.

"I'm not really sure, Gerald," Stockwell admitted. "She prides herself on being late to every party we have, but she's outdone herself this time." One of the servants carrying a tray of refills for the table passed by, and Stockwell called out to him. "Does anyone know what's keeping my daughter?" he asked.

"Not precisely, sir," the man replied. "But I heard someone say a message was delivered to her earlier and that shortly afterward she ordered a carriage brought 'round."

"What?" Stockwell exploded, the lines in his face deepening and his neck showing signs of red. "Where did she go?"

"That's all I know, sir," the servant assured him. "Perhaps you should ask Arnold. He's the one who delivered it. He might know something, sir."

Outraged, Stockwell waved the servant away and stood chewing on the end of his cheroot while he contemplated the form of punishment he'd inflict on the young woman. He suspected where she had gone despite his warnings that she end the affair, and because of her defiance, he'd see her locked in her room for disobeying him. Then he'd settle the matter with her lover once and for all, and he didn't care what the repercussions might be. Excusing himself from his

431

guests, he walked angrily away.

The man's abrupt departure brought a frown to Rebecca's pretty face as she watched him elbow his way through the crowded dance floor and leave the ballroom. It appeared to her that he didn't have to be told where his daughter had gone. He already knew, and it greatly displeased him. Thinking to ask Gerald if he knew what it was all about, she turned to voice her question and straightened in surprise to see the devilish smile on his face.

"You did that on purpose, didn't you, Gerald?" she posed.

Gerald's green eyes twinkled, and he forced down the grin by taking a drink of his wine.

"Why? Don't you like Mr. Stockwell?"

"I don't like his daughter," Gerald whispered when the song came to an end and the other guests started to pour out onto the patio. "She's always thought she was better than everyone else, and I take extreme pleasure in showing her that she isn't."

"Then you know where she is? You knew about the message she received?"

Gerald shook his head. "Just a lucky guess. But from her father's reaction, he obviously knows exactly where she is; and I'd say she's with her lover. She's been the talk around the island for sometime now, but no one knows for sure who the man is. She's managed to be very discreet."

The glass in Rebecca's hand shook. She turned her head away as hot tears stung her eyes, and she blinked repeatedly to keep them from spilling down her face. Her heart thumped agonizingly in her chest. A whimper worked its way to her lips; but she held it back, and it soon changed to a tormented, wrathful scream begging to be let free. Rebecca was only slightly aware of the young couple who joined them and that she had acknowledged their presence with a polite nod of her head. But once they had engaged Gerald in a conversation, the topic of which was foreign to her, she covertly moved away unnoticed by any in the group. She needed the time to gather her composure and deal privately with her emotions before she could present any of them with the pretext that she was as ignorant of the name of Meredith

Stockwell's lover as they were.

Beyond the edge of the flagstone patio outlined by torches, a narrow path of hard-packed sand wound in and out of the tall, slender palm trees and dense shrubs at their bases. Moonlight trickled down through the broad, flat, leaves and clearly marked the way in silvery patches of ashen light, though her tears were already beginning to blur her vision. A soft breeze smelling of salt and fragrant flower blossoms brushed against her cheeks and teased the satiny fullness of her skirts, but Rebecca hardly noticed. Her only want at the moment was to get as far away from civilization as she could possibly go.

The thick underbrush and line of trees suddenly opened up in front of her. Ahead lay the smooth plain of the sandy white beach where it caught and caressed the turbulent waves of the ocean as they crashed to shore. In a trance, Rebecca stared at the peaceful serenity spread out before her, allowing its sounds and smells and hypnotic allurement to soothe her tormented soul and dull the pain in her heart. Suddenly its tranquil beauty offered a solution, and without hesitation she kicked off her slippers and started toward the edge of the water. So intent on her purpose, she failed to see the movement within the shadows of the trees to her right; how it stirred, then seemed to grow and take the shape of a man; how he searched the darkness for any who might see him or the swiftness with which he left the protective cover of his retreat and raced across the beach in her direction. The steady lapping of water as it rushed toward the shore then splashed and ebbed hurriedly away masked the sound of the man's approach and left her totally unaware of the danger that would soon be upon her. Her only thought was to find a quiescent release from the torment she suffered. But just as she reached the dank sand and felt the chilling wetness encircle her feet, she realized with startling certainty that her death would serve no purpose. By doing so she would also kill her unborn child, an innocent victim of this charade in which she found herself, and at the same time would free her husband of all restraints. Meredith Stockwell would win in the end, and that was the last thing she wanted to let happen.

They were the ones who should suffer, and only she had the power to see that they did. With new conviction, she turned around.

"Hello Rebecca," Robert Gilmore sneered, his green eyes glowing demonically. "You're a hard woman to catch alone, but it seems that at last I have."

Rebecca wondered for a moment if she'd had more than the one glass of wine to drink. She certainly couldn't be seeing who she thought she saw. "What . . . what are you doing here?" she asked, too numbed to think rationally. If she had, she wouldn't have wasted time on pleasantries.

"I came to wish you a Happy Birthday," he leered.

Rebecca's frown deepened, and she foolishly looked past him at the long stretch of deserted beach. "Is Lenore with you?"

Gilmore's laughter rang above the crashing surf. "Oh, really, Rebecca. Do you honestly think I'd spend any more time with that hag than I had to? I didn't marry her because I loved her. I married her for Twin Oaks. Who could love a face that's scarred?"

If someone had asked Rebecca two minutes ago if she thought she'd ever feel sorry for her stepmother, she would have said no, that whatever the woman got she deserved. However, after hearing Gilmore's confession, Rebecca decided *no one* could ever possibly warrant the kind of treatment Robert Gilmore was capable of giving. Lifting her dampened hemline, she started to move past him. Whatever reason brought him here didn't interest her, and being alone with him was even less appealing.

"You're a beautiful woman, Rebecca," he said, quickly stepping in her way. "It will be such a waste."

Although she didn't understand what he meant, the chilling look in his eye and the unspoken threat that he had no intention of letting her pass raised the hair on the back of her neck. "What will be a waste?" she asked while she covertly judged the distance across the beach and into the safety of the trees, beyond which were dozens of partygoers.

"Killing you," he admitted with an evil smile.

Rebecca's entire frame trembled, but somehow she

managed to hide her fear. "If you feel it would be a waste, then why do it?"

"Because you've left me no choice." Reaching in back of him, he pulled the pistol from his waistband and pointed it at her while he cocked the hammer.

Unable to lift her gaze from the black bore aimed at her stomach, she gritted her teeth and swallowed hard before saying, "I'm afraid that whatever I've done is a complete mystery to me."

"Yes, it is," he agreed. "That's the way Tanner and I wanted it."

"Tanner?"

"Lenore's cousin," he offered. "But then I don't believe you two have ever met, have you?" He shrugged indifferently. "It doesn't really matter anyway. Once I have what I want, I'll get rid of him, too. And Lenore."

"What is it you want, Robert?" she asked nervously.

"Robert, is it?" he mocked. "You've never called me by my first name before. I guess when a person knows he's about to die, he'll try anything to save himself. But it's too late, Rebecca. You went and married Stone and ruined everything."

Rebecca had realized from the start that her only hope of getting out of this alive would be if Gerald Haugen came looking for her, and in order to give him enough time to figure out where she had gone, she'd have to keep Gilmore talking. "What did I ruin? And how does my marriage fit into it?"

"It means you can't marry me," he boasted.

"You? Why would I want to marry you? How could I? You already have a wife."

Gilmore chuckled evilly. "I could always get rid of Lenore. She's never been the problem. Making you fall in love with me was. You see, Rebecca, Lenore knew how much you hated her, and after your father died, she was afraid you'd throw her off Twin Oaks if you knew about the will." He laughed again at the puzzled look on her face. "All your father left her was a monthly allowance. *You* were to inherit Twin Oaks on your twenty-first birthday, which I believe is in a few days? But with you dead, she'd have everything. However, she didn't have the courage to dispose of you. Then she met me . . . with her cousin's help."

Rebecca could feel her knees weaken. The tale was so bizarre that it was almost unbelievable, and listening to it took nearly all of her energy. Needing to sit down, she started to walk toward the pile of rocks a few feet away from them, but Gilmore caught her arm in a cruel grip and yanked her to him, the muzzle of his gun buried in her side. The suddenness of his move frightened her, and a whimper trailed from her lips, a sound that seemed to snap the small shred of what was left of Gilmore's sanity.

"I could have given you everything, you arrogant bitch," he hissed, heartlessly knocking her to the ground. "I wanted to share my life, my wealth with you, but you'd have no part of me. Tanner was right. I should have slit your throat the same day I married Lenore, but I couldn't. I wanted you . . . as much as I wanted Twin Oaks. If I had only known about the will *before* I married Lenore, things would have been different. I would have courted you the way a gentleman courts a lady. I would have won your heart and your hand. Instead, I was forced to tolerate that scar-faced old nag's pawing and whining while I pretended to care. I had to put up with her cousin's constant chatter about my taking so long to follow through with our plan. As if he really thought I'd sell the plantation after I killed Lenore and then split the money with him. The fool! He'd served his purpose once he'd told me about his rich, widowed cousin, but he was so stupid he couldn't see that. And then there was Eli."

Stunned by the story he told, Rebecca remained half sitting, half laying in the sand staring up at him while he ranted on, afraid that any movement on her part might startle him and he'd shoot her with the gun he still held pointed at her. But with the mention of her childhood friend, Rebecca's fear faded. "What about Eli?" she dared to ask.

A strange, crazed gleam appeared in the man's eyes then vanished, and he almost seemed rational again as he admitted. "Eli's woman overheard a conversation I was having with your stepmother about how I'd come up with a plan to make your death look like an accident. Once I realized the damage she could do, I followed her to the barn. But I arrived too late. She had already told Eli and he was on his way to warn you. I had to stop him before he could."

The shock of his admission tore through her as painfully as if he had pierced her heart with the cold blade of a knife. "You bastard!" she snarled. "You killed him." In a rage and no longer thinking of herself, Rebecca scrambled to her feet.

By the time his carriage rounded the bend and the Stockwell mansion came into view, Alec had already made up his mind that once he had put in his appearance, he would take his wife home to the privacy of their bedchambers where they could celebrate in a manner more befitting a bride and groom. He had tried to finish up his business with the accountant as quickly as possible while he silently cursed the man's untimely intrusion into his personal life and at the same time hoped Gerald had been able to convince his wife that it couldn't be helped. He rather doubted the man's success, but as the rig rolled to a stop and he hurriedly descended from inside, he vowed that if Reb would let him, he'd make it up to her. Yet just as he was inwardly promising Rebecca that nothing else would interfere with their reunion this night, his walk up the front steps was delayed a moment when he heard Thomas Heller calling out his name. Turning, his questioning look changed to puzzlement once he saw the anxious way the man escorted his sister-in-law up the footpath from around the corner of the house.

"I saw him!" Ivy cried excitedly before Thomas had a chance to apologize for intruding or to explain what had brought them to the Stockwell home uninvited.

"Saw who, Mrs. Heller?" Alec asked, reaching out to take her hands in an effort to calm her.

"Daniel! He's alive! I saw him," she wept hysterically.

Alec started to assure her that grief sometimes plays a cruel trick on a person who has lost a loved one but changed his mind once he saw the hopeful expression on Thomas's face. "Did you speak with him?" he tested, thinking that he might talk Ivy Heller into admitting she had made a mistake.

Unable to speak, she shook her head.

"Then how can you be sure—"

"Because I *saw* him," she wailed. "He was down at the beach, near the rocks where we used to watch the sunset and dream. I didn't recognize him right off—you told me he was dead, and I wasn't expecting to ever see him again—but when he got up and walked away, I knew!"

Alec could understand the woman's want to believe her husband was still alive—he caught himself thinking that way about his mother—but he didn't want to encourage her fantasies, either. "Mrs. Heller, I gave you his watch, and I visited his grave. I know how much—"

"I don't care about the watch, and how do you know my Daniel was buried in that grave?" she argued. "I saw him. He's alive!"

Realizing the uselessness in debating the issue, he asked, "Where is he now?"

But before she could answer, the thunderous clatter of a carriage racing toward them pulled the trio's attention away from the conversation they held. A second later the rig slid to a stop at the end of the sidewalk, and a rather spindly built man was roughly thrown from inside to stumble and fall unceremoniously at Alec's feet.

"I'd wait until after I heard his story to decide about helping him up," the voice from within the shadows of the carriage warned, stopping Alec just as he was about to lend the little stranger a hand. "He deserves a lot worse than he's gotten so far."

The carriage rocked when a well-polished, black boot was placed on the step as the one from within moved to make his exit, and Alec's jaw slackened once he saw his half brother's wide frame unfold through the narrow door and step to the ground.

"Brad?"

"I'll explain once you tell me where Rebecca is," he promised.

Alec jerked his head toward the house. "Inside with Gerald Haugen. Why?"

"Because this little reptile would like it a whole lot if you said we were too late," Brad replied as he placed the heel of his boot on the man's rump and shoved him flat on the ground again.

"What are you talking about? Is Reb in some sort of danger?"

"If she's with Gerald, no. But we'll have to find this one's partner if we want it to stay that way." Bending down, he grabbed the little man by the scruff of the neck and hauled him to his feet. "You want to tell him or should I?"

The one questioned shook so badly Brad knew he'd never be able to get two words out of his mouth, and they really didn't have the time to waste waiting on him.

"It seems this little rodent had a score to settle with his cousin after she threw him off her property when he came begging for a handout. That's when he came up with a plan to get even, but he needed a man with money and the courage to kill to have more. He met that man in a tavern in Williamsburg. But the money his partner had on him wasn't his; it belonged to someone else." Brad paused a moment to see if Alec had guessed the partner's identity, and when Alec frowned, slowly shook his head and lowered his gaze, Brad knew he had. But so had the man standing next to Alec.

"Are you saying that man was Daniel Heller?" Thomas asked, his voice etched with anger. "Because if you are, more than this man's word will have to convince me of it."

Brad looked questioningly at Alec. He didn't know either of the two people staring back at him and wondered if he should wait with his report until he and Alec were alone.

"Brad, this is Thomas Heller, Daniel's brother, and Ivy, Daniel's wife."

"Oh," Brad murmured, suddenly uncomfortable.

"You might as well tell it, Brad," Alec went on. "They'll have to hear it sooner or later."

What Alec said was true—Brad knew that—but it didn't make the task any easier. He apologized in advance for the pain they were about to suffer and continued as gently as possible. "Daniel and this one shared a few drinks and exchanged their woes. Daniel complained about being poor and said that he wished he could keep the money he'd been entrusted with to buy a cotton plantation, that he'd always dreamed of living in England. This one said he knew of a way if Daniel was willing to share some of the profits. He told Daniel about his widowed cousin and the plantation she had inherited and that if Daniel were to marry her, then kill her, the place would be his."

"No!" Ivy exploded. "It's not true! Daniel loves me. We have a son!"

"Hush, Ivy," Thomas demanded as he held her securely in his arms. "Let him finish. Then we'll know if it's true or not."

Her outburst had been heard by some of the guests in the house, and a crowd started to gather on the veranda behind them; but Brad paid them no heed as he continued, "Knowing that you'd come looking for your agent and your money, Alec, Daniel had to figure out a way to cover his tracks. Thus the letters telling you about a plantation that was for sale and how he'd have to wait around to buy it. That was done to give him the time to persuade this one's cousin to marry him, and once she had, he bought the Robinson farm, sent you the deed and killed the county clerk, not only to cover up the truth but to make you think Daniel had been tricked and murdered for his money."

"Who's buried in the grave?" Alec asked, his temper rising. "Someone who looked like Heller?"

Brad nodded. "He was a stranger just off a ship from England."

"And Daniel planted his watch on him, knowing I'd take it back home to his wife and brother for verification." His dark brown eyes shifted to the man Brad still held imprisoned in his grip. "The two of you thought of everything, didn't you?"

"Not quite," Brad supplied. "It seems they overlooked the fact that the widow's stepdaughter would inherit the plantation on her twenty-first birthday, a provision in her father's will that only the stepmother knew about. Alec," Brad went on, "I'm afraid there's more to it than that."

A chill raced across Alec's back and down his spine. Brad didn't really have to tell him the rest. He had already guessed that Daniel Heller had changed his name to Robert Gilmore and had left Williamsburg for Twin Oaks Plantation near Richmond before anyone knew he was there. What enraged him was the trick the man had played on him and how cocksure Heller was of himself that he paraded around in front of the very man who had come looking for him, a man riddled with guilt for sending his agent to his death—or so Alec had feared at the time. Alec also sensed why Heller was on the island. He wanted Rebecca.

"Alec?"

Jolted out of his thoughts, he clenched his teeth and inhaled a deep breath before he returned his attention to Brad.

"And you were right about Geoffrey Synder. He wasn't killed as a result of a robbery."

Alec quickly raised a hand to silence him. "Don't tell me. I really don't want to hear any more."

"I know," Brad sympathized. "It's hard to believe one man could be responsible for so much pain and violence. That's why I'm here . . . to stop him from getting to Rebecca. He's insane, Alec. It's more than just owning the plantation now. If he can't have her, no one will."

Suddenly realizing the danger she was in, Alec spun around, intending to hurdle the steps, go inside and find her and take her home. But the sight of Gerald Haugen standing in the middle of the crowded veranda without Rebecca at his side stopped Alec cold, and the horrified look on the young man's face revealed the distinct possibility that Robert Gilmore may have already achieved what he had come there to do. In that same instant, the explosive echo of gunfire rent the air, a sound that pierced Alec's heart.

The lead ball whizzed past Rebecca's head, but her rage blinded her fears just as the sand she had thrown in Gilmore's eyes blinded his vision. While he groped and clawed at his face, she raced for the trees. A frantic search of the ground awarded her the heavy piece of driftwood she needed, and with it held tightly in both hands, she whirled around and descended upon the unsuspecting man who continued to cough and snort sand from his mouth and nose. The first blow hit his arm and sent the pistol flying out of reach. The second landed across his ribs and knocked him to his knees as he bellowed in pain. The third struck him squarely between his shoulders, and while he screamed in agony, Rebecca relentlessly brought back her club to rain another blow.

"You killed Eli!" she howled, her face stained with wet tears and her blue eyes snapping hatred. "You killed him, and now you're going to die!"

From somewhere in the darkened recesses of her sanity, Rebecca heard her name called out. "Rebecca, no!" the voice begged, and for an instant she hesitated. "He's not worth it, Reb! Don't do it." Cold water curled around her feet, and the salty night air brushed her dampened cheeks, flooding her mind with the harsh reality of what she had planned to do. Half-crazed eyes lifted to stare at the club she held high above her head, its gnarled shape bathed in silvery moonlight, and a long moment passed before her vision cleared and the madness which had driven her so unforgivingly faded. At her feet lay Robert Gilmore, limp and motionless, the foamy waters of the sea swirling possessively about his bruised and broken body as if some cryptic being wished to sweep him up and carry him away.

"Take him!" she declared, numbly tossing the piece of driftwood aside. "Take him."

Suddenly strong arms encircled her tiny frame and pulled her close. For a second she resisted, then melted willingly within the protective embrace. She was tired of fighting . . . with her past, the present and whatever lay ahead of her. Locking her wrists behind her husband's neck, she closed her eyes and laid her head against his chest as he gently caught her up in his arms and turned with her toward the footpath.

The murmur of soft voices and bright morning sunlight spilling into her room stirred Rebecca from a restful sleep.

Opening her eyes, she stared confusedly at her surroundings until recognition wedged its way into her brain and she was able to relax. She couldn't remember with much clarity the events of last night except that when she had needed him most, Alec had come for her. It seemed now that whenever she was in trouble, he appeared just at the right moment to offer his protection and save her from a horrible fate. What puzzled her was why. His acts of gallantry spoke of caring. Yet when none were needed, he flew to another's awaiting arms. Was this all she would ever have? And how soon would he tire of it? Tears glistened in her eyes, and in a fit of stubborn pride, she left her bed to don a robe and step out onto the veranda to study the view and force herself to think about something else. But the conversation of the men in the study a few doors down from her drew her interest, and she turned her head to listen.

"You know, the one I really feel sorry for is Ivy Heller," Rebecca overheard a deep voice state. "She was better off believing her husband was dead. Now she has to live with the fact that he murdered several people, stole your money, and married another woman while he was still legally married to her. They can't hang that bastard high enough, if you ask me."

"Yes. It's tragic," she heard Alec reply. "But I think knowing the truth will help Ivy. She can forget about him now and start healing. She's a handsome woman, and I doubt she'll remain single for very long."

"What about Lenore? She was a part of wanting Rebecca dead, and even if that fool Gilmore had succeeded, the plantation would have gone to you. Didn't he realize that?"

"Apparently not. As for Lenore, I guess it's up to Reb to decide what happens to her."

A silence followed her husband's comment in which time Rebecca secretively moved in his direction. Nearing the opened doors to his study, she elected to sit down in the wicker chair beside the entrance where she could listen unobserved. She wasn't sure, but she thought she recognized Brad's voice; and from the things she'd heard him say, she guessed he'd had a hand in uncovering the mystery that had brought her and Alec together. Then she heard another speak and knew Gerald Haugen was with them.

"How's your wife holding up?" he asked.

"Better than could be expected, I suppose," Alec offered. "It was quite a shock for her to learn that her friend had died trying to get to her."

"You mean Eli?"

"Yes. And if I'd had the chance to show her that stickpin I found before Tanner stole it from me, a lot of what happened could have been avoided."

"How so?" Brad inquired.

"It belonged to her father. Tanner confessed that Gilmore had been wearing it when he killed Eli and that the boy must have torn if off his shirt during the struggle. If Reb had seen it, she would have known who murdered him."

"Alec," Gerald added a bit hesitantly. "I don't think I can say it enough times, but I'm sorry I let you down. Your wife could have been killed, and it would have been my fault."

"Gerald," Alec replied with a shake of his head, "if anyone is to blame, it's me. I shouldn't have gone to the office. My place was with her."

"Maybe," he argued. "But you entrusted her care to me, and I failed you. One minute we were talking about Meredith Stockwell, and the next minute she was gone. I didn't even have the sense to go looking for her. I thought she was in another room freshening up."

Knowing the two men could talk about the issue for a year and never agree, Brad decided it was time they laid it to rest. "Who's Meredith Stockwell?" he asked, deliberately changing the subject.

"Someone we should have introduced you to a long time ago," Gerald chuckled. "You'd have done Alec a favor."

"How so?"

"By taking her off his hands. From the first moment she laid eyes on him, she was out to get him."

"Oh, really?" Brad grinned. "And did she?"

"Never!" Alec exploded. "She wasn't my type. I've never cared for women who were as bold as she."

"Bedding them doesn't mean you have to marry them,"

444

Brad pointed out. "Except in Rebecca's case, of course." He grinned playfully at his half brother when Alec shot him a dark scowl.

"With Meredith it would. That's why I stayed clear of her. As for Rebecca," he added, leaving his chair behind the desk and strolling to the opened French doors to stare absently outside, "I married her for two reasons. I wasn't about to desert the mother of my child, but more than that, I married her because I love her."

"No fooling?" Brad mocked. "And here I thought you were just fulfilling your responsibilities." When he failed to get any response from his half brother whatsoever, Brad turned his attention on Gerald. "So when do I get to meet Miss Stockwell?" he asked.

"I think you're too late," Gerald replied with a chuckle. "Her father found out she was having an affair with one of the village boys, and he's shipping her off to some finishing school in Paris next week. Too bad he didn't learn about it sooner, huh Alec? Would have saved you a lot of—". A surprised frown wrinkled Gerald's face when he looked up and found that Alec had left the study without either he or Brad knowing it. Settling his attention on Brad, both men shrugged then quickly bolted from their chairs and hurried across the room to see where Alec had gone. To their surprise *and* approval, they stumbled to a halt in the doorway once they spotted Alec's tall frame enveloping his wife's as he held her close and kissed her hungrily.

"I don't think he loves her, do you?" Brad teased, his dark eyes sparkling devilishly and a broad grin parting his lips as he focused his gaze on the couple and draped his arm across Gerald's shoulders.

"I don't know, Brad," Gerald replied happily. "Maybe we should ask him."

Realizing that the pair would encroach upon their privacy for as long as he allowed it, Alec reluctantly ended the passionate embrace and bent to sweep his wife up in his arms. But before he turned with her to walk the distance to his bedchambers, he glanced one last time at the two men watching his every move.

445

"Yes," he replied. "I love her."

"And what about you, Rebecca?" Brad called when his half brother started down the veranda away from him. "Do you love Alec?"

Surprised by how much he wanted to hear her say the words, Alec paused once he reached the doorway, an apprehensive frown marring his brow. After all this time, he'd never once assumed it mattered one way or the other. Now it meant everything to him.

"Oh, yes," she pledged, staring deep into her husband's eyes. "I love him more than I've ever loved anything else in my life."

If either of them had ever doubted theirs could be anything more than a union of undeclared love, it vanished the instant their lips touched and the flame of passion soared high.

ZEBRA'S GOT THE ROMANCE
TO SET YOUR HEART AFIRE!

RAGING DESIRE   (2242, $3.75)
by Colleen Faulkner
A wealthy gentleman and officer in General Washington's army, Devon Marsh wasn't meant for the likes of Cassie O'Flynn, an immigrant bond servant. But from the moment their lips first met, Cassie knew she could love no other . . . even if it meant marching into the flames of war to make him hers!

TEXAS TWILIGHT   (2241, $3.75)
by Vivian Vaughan
When handsome Trace Garrett stepped onto the porch of the Santa Clara ranch, he wove a rapturous spell around Clara Ehler's heart. Though Clara planned to sell the spread and move back East, Trace was determined to keep her on the wild Western frontier where she belonged — to share with him the glory and the splendor of the passion-filled TEXAS TWILIGHT.

RENEGADE HEART   (2244, $3.75)
by Marjorie Price
Strong-willed Hannah Hatch resented her imprisonment by Captain Jake Farnsworth, even after the daring Yankee had rescued her from bloodthirsty marauders. And though Jake's rock-hard physique made Hannah tremble with desire, the spirited beauty was nevertheless resolved to exploit her femininity to the fullest and gain her independence from the virile bluecoat.

LOVING CHALLENGE   (2243, $3.75)
by Carol King
When the notorious Captain Dominic Warbrooke burst into Laurette Harker's eighteenth birthday ball, the accomplished beauty challenged the arrogant scoundrel to a duel. But when the captain named her innocence as his stakes, Laurette was terrified she'd not only lose the fight, but her heart as well!

Available wherever paperbacks are sold, or order direct from the Publisher. Send cover price plus 50¢ per copy for mailing and handling to Zebra Books, Dept. 264 8 475 Park Avenue South, New York, N.Y. 10016. Residents of New York, New Jersey and Pennsylvania must include sales tax. DO NOT SEND CASH.